Praise for Patricia Davids and her novels

"Davids' latest beautifully portrays the Amish belief that everything happens for a reason."

—*RT Book Reviews* on *The Christmas Quilt*

"Davids' deep understanding of Amish culture is evident in the compassionate characters and beautiful descriptions."

—*RT Book Reviews* on *A Home for Hannah*

"Descriptive setting and characters."

—*RT Book Reviews* on *Plain Admirer*

Praise for Jo Ann Brown and her novels

"The characters demonstrate great perseverance."

—*RT Book Reviews* on *An Amish Match*

"The story is rich with relatable…characters."

—*RT Book Reviews* on *Amish Homecoming*

"Readers will be pleased."

—*RT Book Reviews* on *Her Longed-For Family*

After thirty-five years as a nurse, **Patricia Davids** hung up her stethoscope to become a full-time writer. She enjoys spending her free time visiting her grandchildren, doing some long-overdue yard work and traveling to research her story locations. She resides in Wichita, Kansas. Pat always enjoys hearing from her readers. You can visit her online at patriciadavids.com.

Jo Ann Brown has always loved stories with happy-ever-after endings. A former military officer, she is thrilled to have the chance to write stories about people falling in love. She is also a photographer, and she travels with her husband of more than thirty years to places where she can snap pictures. They live in Nevada with three children and a spoiled cat. Drop her a note at joannbrownbooks.com.

USA TODAY Bestselling Author

PATRICIA DAVIDS

The Christmas Quilt

&

JO ANN BROWN

An Amish Match

Recycling programs for this product may not exist in your area.

ISBN-13: 978-0-373-20976-7

The Christmas Quilt and An Amish Match

This edition published by arrangement with Love Inspired Books.

www.Harlequin.com

Printed in U.S.A.

CONTENTS

THE CHRISTMAS QUILT

Patricia Davids

For my cousin Kay.
Eternal rest, grant unto her, O Lord,
and let perpetual light shine upon her.
May she rest in peace.
Amen.

For my thoughts are not your thoughts,
neither are your ways my ways, declares the Lord.
As the heavens are higher than the earth,
so are my ways higher than your ways
and my thoughts higher than your thoughts.

—*Isaiah* 55:8–9

Chapter One

"Booker, if you're gonna die, at least have the decency to go home and do it there."

Slumped over his desk, Gideon "Booker" Troyer kept his aching head pillowed on his forearms, but managed to cast a one-eyed glare at Craig Murphy, his friend and partner at Troyer Air Charter. "I'm fine."

"And pigs can fly." Craig advanced into Gideon's office.

"If they pay cash I'll fly them anywhere they want to go." Gideon sat up. His less-than-witty comeback was followed by a ragged, painful cough. A bone-deep shiver shook his body.

Craig took a step back. "You're spreading germs, man."

"So leave." Was a half hour of peace and quiet too much to ask? The drone of the television in the waiting area supplied just the right amount of white noise to let him drift off.

"You're the one leaving—for *home!*"

"I can't go anywhere until this next load of freight gets here. Then I'm taking it to Caribou." Gideon barely recognized his raspy voice. He sounded almost as bad as he felt. Almost.

"If I was sick as a dog, you wouldn't let me fly a kite, let alone your prize Cessna."

It wasn't like Gideon had a choice. Their business was finally showing a profit. A small one, but it was something to build on. He'd make today's flight. If his austere Amish upbringing had taught him anything, it was the value of hard work. "I've got a contract to fulfill."

Shaking his head, Craig said, "*We've* got a contract. I know you think you're indispensable, Booker, but you're not."

The two men had known each other for six years, since their flight school days. It had been Craig who'd given Gideon his nickname on the first day of class. Gideon—Bible—the Book. Hence, Booker. Gideon had returned the favor a few weeks later when their trainer plane experienced mechanical trouble the first two times Craig took the controls. Craig was saddled with "Law" as in Murphy's Law. If anything can go wrong, it will.

"Are you offering to take this run?" Gideon took a swig of lukewarm coffee from the black mug on the corner of his desk. It turned into razor blades sliding down his throat.

"Yes. Go home and get some rest."

Gideon looked at him in surprise. "You mean that? I thought you had plans with Melody?"

"We're sort of on the outs. Caribou in October will be warmer than the reception waiting for me the next time I see her."

A woman's voice from the other room said, "That's because you're a knucklehead."

Craig rolled his eyes and raised his voice. “Stop giving people a piece of your mind, Roseanne. It’s almost gone.”

Gideon rose to his feet. The room spun wildly for a second before settling back into his cluttered office.

Craig put out a hand to steady him. “You’re grounded, buddy. Not another word.”

Gideon hated to admit it, but he was in no shape to be in a cockpit. “Thanks, Law. I owe you one.”

Craig leaned closer. “Roseanne is making me do it.”

Gideon cracked a grin. Their secretary’s powers of persuasion were legendary. She might look like someone’s cookie-baking grandmother with her gray hair pulled back in a bun, but she didn’t have a maternal bone in her body.

“I’ll be back tomorrow,” Gideon promised.

Roseanne came around Craig with Gideon’s coat in her hands. “You will not come back for a week.”

Gideon scowled at her. “Tell me again who’s the boss here?”

Roseanne plopped her hands on her ample hips. “You two might own this business, but I run it. If I come down sick, we’re really in trouble. Who can handle the computer, the phone, the fax machine, invoices, accounts payable and the coffeepot all without leaving her chair?”

“You,” he and Craig said together.

Gideon smiled. “You’re indispensable, Roseanne.”

“And you’re sick. Get out of here and take this with you.” She held out a foam cup with a lid on it.

“What’s this?”

“Your favorite brand of blackcurrant tea. I’d send some chicken soup home with you, but I don’t have any here.”

Blackcurrant tea had been his mother's surefire remedy for sore throats when he was growing up. He'd thought about sending her a box of this gourmet blend, but he knew she wouldn't accept it. Not from the black sheep of the family. Gideon was the only one of her five children who'd left the Amish faith.

As if his thoughts of home brought up a connection, he heard the words *Amish country* on the television. Glancing toward the small screen, he saw a female reporter, bundled against the brisk October chill, gesturing to a row of Amish buggies lined up behind her.

"Roseanne, turn that up, please." His voice was failing him. The words barely squeaked out.

She sighed, but picked up the remote and raised the sound level so he could hear the reporter.

"Preparations are under way in Hope Springs, Ohio, for this quiet Amish community's largest event of the year. The Quilts of Hope charity auction is being held here this weekend."

Craig moved to stand beside Gideon. "Is that where you're from?"

"Nearby." Hope Springs was forty miles from his father's farm, but Gideon had never been there. Until he left the Amish he hadn't traveled more than twenty miles from the farm where he was born. Now he lived in Rochester, New York, and he'd been to every state and all but one Canadian province.

The camera panned away from the buggies to a group of Amish men raising an enormous red-and-white-striped tent. After a second, the camera swung back to the reporter and followed her until she stopped in front of an intricately pieced quilt hanging on a display frame. "In the past, this event has raised thousands of dollars for the special needs of Amish families throughout Ohio. This year they are helping one of their own."

Roseanne said, "Now, that's pretty. I wouldn't mind owning a quilt like that."

The reporter ran her hand down the cloth and the camera zoomed in to capture the details. "Rebecca Beachy is the Amish woman who made this incredible quilt."

"It can't be." In an instant, Gideon was transported back to his youth when he had courted the prettiest girl in Berlin, Ohio. The girl who broke his heart and turned him down flat when he'd finally found the courage to propose.

"Someone you know?" Craig asked.

"No. There are a lot of Beachys in Ohio. The girl I knew would be married to some Amish farmer or carpenter." It was the life Rebecca wanted—as long as he wasn't the farmer or the carpenter. Chances were slim that it was the same woman, but his gaze stayed glued to the screen.

The camera switched to a group of Amish women who were talking. The women didn't realize they were being filmed. They were dressed alike in dark coats and bonnets. One held a baby on her hip, but it was the woman in the center that he strained to see.

The reporter's voice cut into Gideon's thoughts. "The money from this year's auction is going to help pay for some very specialized surgery for Miss Beachy."

The camera zoomed in on the group of women and Rebecca's face filled the television screen. The sight knocked the breath from his body. After almost ten years, his heart still ached at the sight of her. She was more beautiful than ever. Her heart-shaped face with those stunning high cheekbones had matured from the soft roundness of youth into a quiet elegance.

"Why do they wear those odd white hats?" Roseanne asked.

"It's called a prayer *kapp.* Amish women believe the Bible commands them to cover their hair when they pray."

"But they don't just wear them in church?" Roseanne turned to stare at him, waiting for an explanation.

He wanted to hear what the reporter was saying. "A woman might want to pray anytime, so she keeps her head covered all day. They never cut their hair, either."

Rebecca's blond hair must be past her hips by now. He'd seen it down only once. It was the night he talked Rebecca into going to a hoedown with him and his rowdy friends.

Hoedown was a benign name for a weekend-long party with loud music, alcohol and drugs attended by some of the wilder Amish youth during their rumspringa, or running-around time. He had made the most of his rumspringa and partied hard. For Rebecca, that one party had been her only venture on the wild side.

Gideon took the remote from his secretary and turned up the volume. The TV reporter droned on. "Miss Beachy stitched this beautiful quilt entirely by hand. What's even more amazing is that she is totally blind."

"How on earth can a blind woman make a quilt?" Roseanne's skeptical comment barely registered in Gideon's brain.

Rebecca was blind?

Suddenly, he was gasping for air and coughing so

hard his head pounded. It took a minute to catch his breath. Roseanne pulled the lid off the tea and offered him some. He took a grateful sip.

Concern filled her eyes. “Do you know her?”

“I once asked her to marry me. I think if she had said yes, I would be a bearded Amish farmer now.” With a blind wife.

Rebecca was blind. He couldn’t wrap his brain around the fact. Why? When had it happened? The thought of the vibrant woman he’d known living her life in darkness left an ache in his chest that had nothing to do with the flu. Before he could gather more details, the news program moved on to the weather forecast and warnings about an artic front plowing southward delivering early ice and snow in its wake.

Craig said, “I read the Amish don’t believe in health insurance. Is that true?”

“Most don’t. The community would rally round a family that had big medical expenses, but they could only do so much.”

Gideon had to help. He pulled his phone from his pocket and prayed the news station could give him more information. It wasn’t until he tried to speak that he realized his voice was gone. He handed the phone to Roseanne and wrote a quick note on a piece of paper from her desk.

Get me all the information you can about the auction.

After a brief conversation, Roseanne hung up and handed the notepad to him. “It’s at noon the day after tomorrow.”

That gave him one day to rest up. If he headed out

early the following morning he could make the six-hour trip there and back. It would be a long day, but doable.

Craig said, "Tell me you're not going to drive to Ohio."

Roseanne studied Gideon's face. "Yes, he is."

"I know we're going to have a wonderful time today."

Rebecca Beachy didn't share her aunt Vera's optimism. She folded her white cane and tucked it under her arm. Grasping her aunt's elbow, she let Vera lead her toward the tent where the quilt auction was about to get under way. Besides Rebecca's quilt, there were thirty others being auctioned off. Rebecca kept a smile on her face as she followed her aunt even though she was anything but comfortable.

Disoriented by the noise and smells of the fairlike atmosphere, she wished she were back in her aunt's small home where everything was in its rightful place and nothing was ready to trip her up.

The thought had barely crossed her mind before something hit her legs and made her stumble.

"Sorry," a pair of childish voices called out. She heard their footsteps as the children ran away.

"Hooligans," Vera muttered.

"Excited *kinder* at play." Rebecca listened to the sound of the children's voices as they shouted to each other. A pang of longing escaped from the place in her heart where she kept her fading dreams.

Dreams she once had of being a wife and a mother, of holding a child of her own. She'd had the chance to make those dreams come true years before, but she had been too afraid to take the risk. Had she made the right choice? Only God knew.

"*Englisch* children without manners," Vera grumbled. "Come, we're almost there."

Rebecca drew a deep breath. Her life was what it was. This was God's plan for her. Impossible dreams had no place in her dark world.

But if the darkness could be lifted?

She didn't dare hope for such a miracle. This benefit auction was her aunt's doing. Rebecca had tried to convince her the surgery was too expensive. They would need more money than would be raised here today. Even if they did manage to cover the cost, there was no guarantee her sight would be restored.

She had argued long and hard to no avail. The auction was under way. It was all in God's hands, but Rebecca didn't believe He would produce a miracle for her. She was not worthy. She knew exactly why her sight had been taken from her.

She pulled the collar of her coat closed against a cold gust of wind and ugly memories. An early storm was on its way, but God had seen fit to hold it off until the auction was over. For that she was thankful. At least she and her aunt didn't need to worry about traveling home in foul weather. They had already made plans to stay in town for several days.

Suddenly, the wind was blocked, and Rebecca knew they were inside the tent. It was warmer than she expected. The smells of hot dogs, popcorn, hot chocolate and coffee told her they were near the concession stand. The sound of hundreds of voices raised to be heard over the general din assaulted her ears. When they finally reached their seats, Rebecca unbuttoned her coat and removed her heavy bonnet. Many of the people around her greeted her in her native Pennsylvania Dutch. Leaning closer to her aunt, she asked, "Is my *kapp* on straight? Do I look okay?"

"And why wouldn't you look okay?" Vera asked.

"Because I may have egg yolk from breakfast on my dress, or my backside may be covered with dust from the buggy seat. I don't know. Just tell me I look presentable." She knew everyone would be staring at her when her quilt was brought up for auction. She didn't like being the center of attention.

"You look lovely." The harsh whisper startled her.

She turned her face toward the sound coming from behind her and caught the scent of a man's spicy aftershave. The voice must belong to an *Englisch* fellow. *"Danki."*

"You're most welcome." He coughed and she realized he was sick.

"You sound as if you should be abed with that cold."

"So I've been told," he admitted.

"It is a foolish fellow who doesn't follow *goot* advice."

"Some people definitely consider me foolish." His raspy voice held a hint of amusement.

He was poking fun at himself. She liked that. There was something familiar about him but she couldn't put her finger on what it was. "Have we met?"

"I'm not from here," he said quickly.

Vera said, "I see the bishop's wife. I want to ask her how her brother is doing after his heart attack." She rose and moved away, leaving Rebecca to her own devices.

The *Englisch* fellow said, "You've been deserted."

She heard the folding chair beside her creak and his voice moved closer as if he were leaning over the seat. Although she knew it was unwise to encourage interaction with an outsider, she wanted to figure out why he seemed familiar. She wasn't sure, but she thought she heard traces of a Pennsylvania Dutch accent in his raspy speech.

She said, "I don't mind. I'm Rebecca Beachy."

There was a long hesitation, then he said, "My friends call me Booker. The quilts on display are beautiful."

"Are you a collector, Mr. Booker, or did your wife make you come today? That's often the case with the men in the audience, Amish and English alike."

"I'm not married. What about you?"

"*Nee,* I am an *alt maedel.*"

"Hardly an *old* maid. There must be something very wrong with the men in this community."

Flustered, she quickly changed the subject, but he had confirmed one suspicion. He understood at least a little of her native tongue. "Have you been to one of our auctions before?"

"No, but I know what goes into making a quilt like the ones up on stage. My mother quilts."

"They do take a lot of effort. I'm glad people such as yourself appreciate our Amish workmanship. How did you hear about our auction?"

"I caught the story on WHAM."

Puzzled, she asked, "What is WHAM?"

"A television station where I live."

"There was a story about our little auction on television?"

"Yes, and about you."

She frowned. "Me? Why would they talk about me?"

"According to the story, this auction is helping raise

money for your eye surgery." His voice was barely a whisper and fading.

Embarrassment overtook her. The heat of a blush rose up her neck and flared across her cheeks. "Perhaps Dr. White or his nurse, Amber Bradley, told them about me. I wish they had not."

"I thought it odd for an Amish person to seek publicity. The Amish normally shy away from the spotlight, don't they?"

"We do not seek to draw attention to ourselves. We seek only to live plain, humble lives. But you know that already, don't you? How is it that you are familiar with our language?"

"A long time ago I lived in a community that had Amish families." His voice cracked on the last word.

Sympathy for him overrode her curiosity about his past. "You should rest your voice."

"How long have you been blind?"

She was shocked by his abrupt personal question. Her reaction must have shown on her face because he immediately said, "I'm sorry. That was rude. It's none of my business."

She rarely spoke about the time before she'd lost her sight. It was as if that life, filled with happiness, colors and the faces of the people she loved, belonged to another woman. Remembering the way she lost her sight always left her feeling depressed. It went bit by bit over the course of three years, first details and then colors, beloved faces and finally even the light. God had given her this burden. She must bear it well.

Booker interrupted her moment of pity when he said, "I didn't mean to pry. Please forgive me."

He meant no harm. It was her pride and her inability to fully accept God's will that made remembering painful. "You are forgiven. I learned I was going blind when I was twenty. My sight left me completely seven years ago."

There was a long period of silence. What was he thinking? Did he feel sorry for her? Did he think she was helpless and useless? She rushed to dissuade him of such thoughts and repeated the words her bishop told her the day the last of her sight failed. "Do not think to pity me. My blindness has been a gift from God."

A gift meant to show her the error of her ways and lead her to repent.

"How can you call it a gift?" His scratchy voice broke. Because of his illness, or for some other reason?

She smiled sadly. "It is a struggle sometimes, but I know all that God gives us, whether hardship or happiness, is in some way a gift. We learn more about ourselves, and about how much we need God, during times of sorrow than we do in times of joy. I accept my life for what it is." At least, she tried.

"But this surgery, it can restore your sight?"

"If God wills it."

"Don't you mean if the surgeon is skilled enough?"

"God's miracles come in many forms. If my sight is restored by the skill of an *Englisch* doctor or by a flash of lightning it is all the work of God."

"Then I pray He will be merciful. I wish you the very best, Rebecca Beachy."

She heard his chair scoot back, then the sound of his footsteps until they blended into the hum of activity and voices inside the tent. A sharp sense of loss filled her but she didn't understand why.

A few moments later, her aunt returned and sat

down. Rebecca's hand found Vera's sleeve. "*Aenti,* do you know the man that was just sitting here?"

"What man?"

"He was sitting in the row behind us. He's *Englisch.*"

"There are many *Englisch* here. I didn't pay attention."

"I thought perhaps he was someone I should know, but I didn't recognize his name. He called himself Booker."

"I don't know anyone by that name. The bidding is getting ready to start. I pray your quilt does well. It's lovely."

"You picked the material. I merely stitched it together."

Her aunt's hands were twisted and gnarled with arthritis, making sewing and many daily tasks impossible for her. It was one reason why Rebecca chose to live with her aunt when her vision began to fade. She knew she could always be useful in her aunt's household.

Vera said, "I do wish you had put your Christmas Star quilt in the auction today. I'm sure it would fetch a fine price and we could use the money."

"I don't wish to sell that one, *Aenti.* It will be a gift when it is done."

There was something special about the quilt she had been working on for the past several weeks. Something in the feel of the fabrics, the way the seams lay straight and true with so little effort. Her Christmas quilt would not be for sale. It would be a gift for a wedding or for someone's birthday. She didn't know who would receive it. God would show her in His own time.

Vera patted Rebecca's hand. "Anyone that receives such a gift will be blessed. I pray it is God's will to heal you, child. I pray that one day you may see with your own eyes the beauty you have crafted."

Chapter Two

Rebecca was still the loveliest woman Gideon had ever laid eyes on, and she had lied to him.

Seeing her in person, it was as if a single day had passed—not ten years. Feelings he thought long dead and buried rushed to life, leaving him shaken. Coming here had been a bad idea.

He stood near the back of the tent where he could keep an eye on Rebecca and the auction proceedings as he pondered the stunning information she'd revealed. The noise of the crowd, the chanting voice of the auctioneer, the shouts of his helpers as they spotted raised hands in the audience, all faded into a rumbling background for Gideon's whirling mind.

She obviously had no idea who he was, and he needed to keep it that way. His missing voice was a blessing in disguise. If she knew who he was, she wouldn't have spoken to him at all.

Because he had been baptized prior to leaving the faith he had been placed under the *Meidung,* the ban, making contact with his Amish family and friends impossible unless he publicly repented and asked for the church's forgiveness. Bidding for Rebecca's quilt at this auction would be his roundabout way of giving aid she could accept.

By leaving the faith after making his vows he had cut himself off completely from everything he'd known. There were no visits from his family. No letters or phone calls telling him how they missed him. There had been many lonely nights during his first years in the non-Amish world when he'd almost gone back.

Only having the eighth-grade education the Amish allowed made it tough finding a job. It had been tougher still getting a driver's license and a social security card, worldly things the Amish rejected. If it hadn't been for his dream of learning to fly, he might have gone back.

If Rebecca had been waiting for him, he would have gone back.

He hadn't planned to speak to her today. His only intention had been to come, buy her quilt to help her raise money for her surgery and then leave town. He had the best of intentions—right up to the moment she sat down in front of him.

So close he could have reached out and touched her. So close and yet so far.

His hands ached with the need to feel her fingers entwined with his, the way they used to be when they had walked barefoot down a shady summer lane after the youth singings or a softball game. Life had been so simple then. It was so much more complicated now.

Why, after all this time, did she still have such a profound effect on him? Even from this distance he felt the pull of her presence the same way he felt the pull of the earth when he was flying above it.

He closed his eyes and shook his head. This was ridiculous. He wasn't some green farm boy enchanted by a pretty face. He was a sensible, grown man long past teenage infatuations. It had to be a combination of the flu and nostalgia brought on by being surrounded by people who shared the heritage he'd grown up with.

Everywhere he looked he saw Amish men with their beards and black felt hats. The women, wearing long dresses in muted solid colors with their white bonnets reminded him of his mother and his sisters.

Shy, solemn and subdued when among the English, the Amish were gentle, loving people, happy to quietly raise their families and continue in a life that seemed centuries out of touch with the modern world.

Would he even recognize his little brothers and sisters if they were here? Joseph, his baby brother, had been six when Gideon left. He'd be a teenager now and ready to begin his rumspringa. He would be free to explore worldly ways in order to understand what he was giving up before he took the vows of the faithful.

Did Joseph long for the outside world that had taken his older brother? If so, Gideon prayed he would go before his baptism. That way he could be free to visit his parents and see his old friends without being shunned. Gideon wondered about them often, thought of driving out to see them, but having left under such a cloud, he believed a clean break was the best way. Was it? How could he ever be sure?

Gideon adjusted his aviator sunglasses and glanced around. He doubted anyone he knew would recognize him. He wore a knit cap pulled low on his forehead. His hair was shaggy and a bit unkempt, unlike the uniformly neat haircuts of the Amish men around him.

His eyes were sunken and red from his illness and

the long road trip. Two days' worth of beard stubble shadowed his cheeks. Glances in his rearview mirror on the way down showed a man who looked like death warmed over. No, no one was likely to recognize him. That was a good thing.

He was an English stranger, not the Amish youth who once asked Rebecca Beachy for her hand in marriage. Confusion swirled through his mind when he thought again of how she had deceived him.

He'd known her since their school days. They'd grown up on neighboring farms. They had courted for two full years and he proposed to her a week before her twenty-first birthday. Yet she'd just told him she learned she was going blind when she was twenty. Why hadn't she told him back then?

She broke his heart when she said she'd been mistaken about her feelings for him. Was that the truth or had it been a lie? Her sudden change of heart hadn't made sense back then any more than it did now.

Did she think he couldn't handle the truth? Or had she known he would eventually leave the Amish and tried to protect herself from that heartache? Maybe she'd wanted to spare him a lifetime spent with a blind wife.

Shouldn't that have been his choice to make?

His fingers curled into fists. Had he known the truth he would have stood by her.

Wouldn't he? Gideon bit the corner of his lip. Would knowing her condition have changed him from a dissatisfied youth itching to leave the restrictive Amish life into one who welcomed the challenge God placed before him?

He knew Rebecca wouldn't leave the faith. They'd had plenty of discussions about it in the months they were together. She knew of his discontent. When she broke off their courtship, he left home in a fit of sullen temper and cut himself off from everything and everyone he'd known. Because of her.

No, that wasn't fair. He left because he wanted something only the outside world could offer. He wanted to fly. He'd wanted her more, but without her his choice had been clear.

Would he have married Rebecca knowing she wouldn't be able to see his face or the faces of their children? He wanted to believe he would have, but he was far from sure.

He watched as several Amish women stopped to speak to her and the woman she sat with. One of them held a baby in her arms while a fussy toddler clung to her skirt. They were the same women he'd seen with her on television. The young mother handed her baby to Rebecca and picked up her older child, a little girl with dark hair and eyes.

Seeing a babe in Rebecca's arms reminded him of all she had missed in her life. Was it her choice never to marry? How strong she must be to face her hardship alone.

What was the cause of her blindness? Was it some inherited disease she didn't want to pass on to her children?

The Amish accepted handicapped children as special blessings from God. If she chose not to marry for that reason, then she wasn't being true to her faith any more than he had been.

Gideon pulled his knit cap lower over his brow. Nothing about the past could be changed. It was pointless to wonder what would have happened if he'd stayed in their Amish community. He'd left that life long, long ago. It was closed to him now.

The past couldn't be changed but he could help shape a better future for Rebecca. He was here to raise money for her, not to reminisce about unrequited love. As the bidding began on her quilt, he raised his hand knowing it didn't matter what the quilt cost. He wasn't going home without it.

Rebecca couldn't believe her ears when a bidding war erupted over her quilt. With each jump in price shouted by the auctioneer she thought it couldn't possibly go higher, but it did. Higher and higher still.

Who could possibly want to pay so much for a quilt stitched by a blind woman? She grasped her aunt's arm. "Can you see the bidders?"

"*Ja.* It is between an *Englisch* fellow and Daniel Hershberger."

"Daniel is bidding on my quilt?"

Her aunt chuckled. "I told you the man was sweet on you."

The owner of a local mill that employed more than fifty people, Daniel was a well-respected Amish businessman. Although he was several years older than she was, he often stopped by to visit with her and her aunt. Rebecca shook her head at her aunt's assumption. "I think you're the one who caught his fancy."

"He doesn't make sheep eyes at me when he's sitting on the porch swing."

"I have only your word for that. I'm blind. What is the *Englisch* fellow like?"

"It's hard to tell. He's standing at the back. He's wearing a knit cap and a short leather jacket. He has dark glasses on."

"Is he young or old?" Rebecca wished her aunt had

paid attention to the stranger sitting behind them earlier. Was he the one offering a ridiculously high price for her handiwork?

"Not too young. He has a scruffy short beard that so many *Englisch* boys seem to like. He looks pasty, like he's been ill."

It must be Booker. Rebecca smiled in satisfaction but her delight quickly faded. Was he bidding because of the quality of her work or because he felt sorry for her? It shouldn't matter but it did. She didn't want his pity.

But if he wasn't doing it out of pity, then why?

A strange excitement settled in her midsection when she thought about his low, gravelly voice speaking quietly in her ear. There was something about him that made her want to know him better.

The auctioneer shouted, "Sold!"

As the room erupted in chatter and applause, Rebecca asked, "Who got it?"

"The *Englisch.*"

Rebecca stood up. "I must go and thank him. Can you take me to him?"

"Let the crowd thin out a little. Everyone is hurrying to get gone because the weather is getting worse. Ester Zook said it was already starting to sleet when she came in."

Once Booker left the event Rebecca knew she'd never have the chance to speak with him again. "I don't want to miss him. Please, it's important to me."

"Very well. I see him heading toward the front where people are paying for their purchases."

Rebecca walked beside her aunt against the flow of people leaving the tent and wished Vera would move faster. What if he paid for her quilt and left before she had the chance to thank him? It was foolish, really, this pressing need to speak to him. She didn't understand it, nor did she examine her feelings too closely. He was an outsider and thus forbidden to her.

Before they had gone more than a few feet, she heard Daniel Hershberger's voice at her side. "I'm right sorry I couldn't buy your quilt, Rebecca. It was uncommonly pretty."

"It was, wasn't it?" Vera replied, pausing to speak with him, to Rebecca's dismay.

"I didn't get the quilt, but rest assured I have donated what money I can to your cause. I've already given a check to Bishop Zook."

Tamping down her impatience, Rebecca recognized Dan's exceptional act of charity for the gift it was. "*Danki,* my friend. God will bless your generosity. If you will excuse us, I wish also to thank the man who outbid you for the quilt. Do you see him?"

"Ja," Daniel replied. "He is in line waiting to pay. Before you go, I wanted to ask both of you to supper this coming Sunday. Unless you have other plans? My sister is coming and she can cook a fine meal."

"We do not have other plans," Vera answered before Rebecca could come up with a workable excuse.

Daniel was a good man and a friend, but Rebecca couldn't bring herself to see him as anything else. If her aunt was right and he wished to court her, he was in for a letdown.

"Excellent. What time shall I expect you?" His delight was clear.

Rebecca waited impatiently for the two of them to work out the details. She wanted to find Booker and speak to him before he left Hope Springs for good.

She wanted to thank him, yes, but there was another reason. One she didn't understand. She felt *compelled* to speak with him again. It didn't make any sense but she had learned to follow her instincts when her sight failed her.

Vera and Daniel continued discussing his dinner invitation. Suddenly, Rebecca couldn't wait any longer. "If you'll excuse me, I must go."

She unfolded her cane and moved forward, swinging it side to side as she went. Vera caught up with her. "Rebecca, what is wrong with you? That was rude."

"I don't want to miss speaking to Mr. Booker. Do you see him? Where is he?"

"Straight ahead of you, but slow down before you trip."

The line Gideon stood in moved quickly toward a set of tables where he could collect his expensive new quilt. He hoped they'd take a personal check. The bidding had far exceeded the amount of cash in his pocket. If they wouldn't take his check, he'd have to use his credit card and hope it didn't put him over his limit. This venture was foolhardy and expensive, but he was glad he had come.

When he reached the table, he took off his glasses and hung them on his shirt pocket. "Do you accept personal checks?"

The man at the table looked up and Gideon's heart dropped when he recognized his cousin, Adam Troyer, beneath the wide-brimmed straw hat. He was ten years older and sported the beard of a married man, but there was no mistaking him. Gideon steeled his heart against the humiliation to come and prayed he wouldn't be recognized.

Adam's eyes grew round. "Gideon? Is that you?"

So much for remaining incognito.

Surging to his feet, Adam grabbed Gideon's hand and began pumping it in a hearty shake. "I can't believe my eyes. What's it been? Seven, eight years?"

"Ten," Gideon croaked.

"Too long. What's the matter with your voice? You sound terrible."

"Laryngitis. It sounds worse than it is."

"What are you doing here?" Adam finally released Gideon's hand.

"Buying a quilt."

"Which one?"

"The one made by Rebecca Beachy." Gideon handed over the yellow card with his number on it.

"So, you were the bidder! I didn't recognize you from across the room. There is a lot of speculation going on about you. This is the most any quilt has brought in the history of Hope Springs." Adam nodded toward the women folding and packing the quilts into boxes behind him. They were all glancing his way.

"If you don't mind, I'd rather not have everyone know who I am. Have you forgotten? I'm under the ban."

Adam's face grew pensive. "I had forgotten. Like you, I went out into the world for many years, but God brought me home. We would welcome you back to the church with great joy, Gideon."

"I'm not here to rejoin the faith. I'm only here to help Rebecca. She and I were…close once."

"I remember. We all thought you'd marry."

"So did I, but life doesn't often turn out the way we plan."

"Many are the plans in a man's heart, but it is the Lord's purpose that prevails."

Gideon gave his cousin a wry smile. "I should know that one."

"It's from Proverbs."

"Guess you can tell I haven't been reading my Bible."

Adam's gaze softened. "It's never too late, Gideon."

Pulling out his checkbook, Gideon ignored his cousin's comment and wrote a check for the price of the quilt. "If Rebecca learns the money came from me, from an ex-Amish, she might not accept it. I don't want to make trouble for her."

"I understand. After this meeting I will not know you, but it sure is *goot* to see you. Where are you staying?"

"I'm not staying. I'm driving back to Rochester, New York, tonight."

"Rochester? *Nee,* you aren't driving that way. The sheriff just told us the interstate has been closed south of Akron due to the ice storm."

"You're joking." This was a complication Gideon hadn't foreseen. He should have paid more attention to the weather forecast before jumping in his car and driving three hundred and fifty miles.

"It's settled," Adam declared. "You're staying with us. My wife, Emma, and I run the Wadler Inn. You can't miss it. It's on Main Street at the edge of town. We're normally booked solid during the auction, but we've had a couple of cancellations."

Gideon glanced around to make sure no one was listening. He leaned closer. "I'm under the ban, cousin.

You cannot offer me a place to stay. Just speaking to me could cause trouble for you."

"You let me worry about that. The bishop here is a good man and just. Unlike your old bishop in Berlin, he is not eager to condemn a man for his sins. He truly believes in forgiveness. Besides, it is my duty to pray for you and to give aid to those in need. You look like you're in need. Go to the inn when you leave here and tell the man at the front desk that I sent you. There is no need to mention that you are my wayward cousin."

"Thanks, Adam. I appreciate it. Is there anyone else who might recognize me?" Gideon slipped his sunglasses back on. He knew what Adam was risking by associating with him. He risked being shunned by members of his church. Gideon wouldn't stay if it meant trouble for Adam.

"Some of my family lives near here, but they did not come today. I'm not sure they would know you. You are much changed."

Relieved, Gideon signed his check and left it lying on the table knowing Adam should not accept anything from his hand.

With a slight nod, Adam acknowledged Gideon's thoughtfulness.

Gideon caught sight of Rebecca and her aunt making their way through the crowd in his direction. Turning back to Adam, he said, "As soon as the roads are open I'm out of here."

Adam's face grew serious. "Life doesn't always work out as we plan."

"If Rebecca asks for my name, tell her I wish to remain anonymous."

"I can do that. It is good to see you, cousin. I have missed you. All your family has missed you."

"I've missed you, too. How are…how are my parents?"

"I had a letter from them just last week. They are well. Your brother Levi has a new son. That makes four boys for him now."

"Levi is married? Scrawny, shy Levi?" Gideon found it hard to believe his brother had four kids. He was only a year younger than Gideon.

"Betty and Susie, too. They each have a girl and a boy."

He had eight nieces, nephews and in-laws he'd never met. How sad was that? "Grandchildren must make my mother happy."

"Not as happy as having you return."

Gideon swallowed back the lump that rose in his throat. "When you see them—"

He paused. Coming here had been a mistake. It opened up far too many painful memories. "Tell them I'm doing well."

Taking his box with the quilt packed inside, Gideon turned and made his way toward the exit. Ten feet short of the opening he heard her call his name.

"Booker, please wait!"

Keep walking. Pretend you don't hear her.

His feet slowed. He could give good advice to himself but he apparently couldn't follow it.

What would it hurt to speak to her one more time? After today he'd never see her again. Just this once more.

Turning around, he waited until she reached him. Her

aunt hung back, a faint look of displeasure on her face. It wasn't seemly for Rebecca to seek out an *Englisch* fellow.

She moved toward him until her cane touched his feet. When she opened her mouth to speak, he forestalled her. "I know what you're going to say, Miss Beachy, but there is no need."

He couldn't take his eyes off her face. He memorized the fine arch of her brows, the soft smile that curved her lips. She wore a pair of dark, wire-rimmed spectacles, but he knew her eyes were sky blue. If this was the last time he saw her face he wanted to remember it until the day he died.

"There is always a need to show our gratitude for the kindness of others, Mr. Booker."

"Consider me thanked. I've got to get going." Any second now he was going to blurt out his identity and undo all of the good he'd accomplished.

He was keenly aware of Rebecca's aunt standing a few paces back. A burly man came out of the crowd and stood with her, a look of displeasure formed on his face, too. Gideon turned his back to them. It was possible they'd met but he wasn't sure.

This was nuts. He wanted to see Rebecca again. He'd done that. He wanted to help her and he had.

Mission accomplished. Walk away.

No, what he really wanted was an answer to why she stopped loving him. But that was an answer he was never going to get.

"Good luck with your surgery, Miss Beachy. I wish you every success." He turned away and walked out into the stinging cold sleet.

Chapter Three

Rebecca held on to her aunt's arm as they entered the lobby of the Wadler Inn. The instant she stepped inside the building she was surrounded by the smells of wood smoke, baking bread and roasting meat. She felt the heat and heard the crackling of burning logs in the inn's massive fireplace to her right.

The clatter of cutlery and plates being gathered together as tables were cleared came from her left. The Shoofly Pie Café was adjacent to the inn and accessible through a set of wide pocket doors. The murmur of voices and sounds told Rebecca the doors were open. The discordant noise increased the headache growing behind her eyes.

As her aunt moved forward, Rebecca automatically counted her steps so she could navigate the room by herself in the future. Although she had stayed at the inn several times in the past, she needed to refresh the layout in her mind. She thought she knew the place well, but a chair carelessly moved by one of the guests or a new piece of furniture could present unseen obstacles for her.

The thump of feet coming down the stairs and the whisper of a hand sliding over a banister told her the inn's open staircase was just ahead. The tick-tock of a grandfather clock beside the stairway marked its location for Rebecca.

"Velkumm." Emma Troyer's cheerful voice grew closer as she left the stairs and came toward them.

"Hello, Emma." Rebecca smiled in her direction.

"I just finished readying your room. I'm so happy you decided to stay with us again."

"We're glad to be here," Vera replied.

Staying at the inn had become a ritual for the two women following the quilt auctions. It was a time Vera truly enjoyed when the work of cooking, cleaning, sewing and running the farm was put on hold for a few days so she could relax and visit her many friends in town.

Rebecca would rather be back in her aunt's small house. The openness of the inn disoriented her, but she never said as much. Rebecca loved her aunt dearly. Vera deserved her little holiday each year. If Rebecca had insisted on staying home alone, her aunt would have cancelled her plans and come home, too.

Emma said, "Rebecca, I couldn't believe it when I heard how much your quilt went for."

"God was good to us," Vera said quickly.

Rebecca shook her head. "It was not worth that much money. The *Englisch* fellow who bought it did so out of pity. He saw a story about me on his television. That's the only reason he came."

Vera patted Rebecca's arm. "It matters not what his motivation was. His being there was God's doing."

"How much more money will you need for your surgery?" Emma asked.

"Another twenty thousand dollars," Vera answered.

"So much?" Emma's voice echoed the doubt in Rebecca's heart. It was unlikely they could raise enough money in time.

She said, "Doctor White has told us the surgeon who is perfecting this operation is moving to Sweden to open a special clinic there after Christmas. If we can't raise the rest of the money before then it will be too late."

Emma laid her hand on Rebecca's shoulder. "Do not give up hope. We know not what God has planned for our lives."

Rebecca swallowed the lump in her throat and nodded. "I must accept His will in this."

"Are you hungry?" Emma asked. "We've started serving supper in the café."

Vera said, "I could eat a horse."

"*Goot.* My mother has been waiting impatiently for you. I'll tell her you're here and we can catch up on all the news. Did you hear my *Aenti* Wilma over in Sugarcreek broke her hip last week?"

Rebecca said, "You two go ahead. I think I would rather lie down for a while before I eat."

"Is your headache worse?" Vera asked.

Rebecca appreciated her aunt's concern. "*Nee.* I'm sure a few minutes of peace and quiet are all I need."

"Let me show you to your room," Emma offered.

"I can find my way," Rebecca insisted. She didn't want to be treated like an invalid.

"Very well. I've put you in number seven, the same as last year." Emma pressed an old-fashioned key into Rebecca's hand.

"*Danki.* Enjoy your visit."

She opened the white folding cane she carried and

headed toward the ticking clock she knew sat beside the staircase. The clock began to strike the hour. It was five o'clock.

When she located the first riser, she went up the steps slowly, holding tight to the banister. There were fifteen steps if she remembered correctly. When her searching toe found the top of the landing, she smiled. Fifteen it was.

She walked down the hallway, letting her cane sweep from side to side. The rooms were numbered with evens on the left and odds on the right. It took only a few moments to locate her door.

She fumbled with the key for a second and lost her grip on it. It fell, struck her toe and bounced away. The hallway was carpeted. She couldn't tell from the sound where the key landed.

Annoyed, Rebecca dropped to her knees and began searching with her hands, letting her fingers glide over the thick pile. The carpeting was a concession to the English guests that stayed at the inn. Amish homes held no such fanciness. A plain plank floor or simple linoleum was all anyone needed.

The sound of a door opening across the hall sent a rush of embarrassed heat to her cheeks. A second later the door closed.

She knew who it was. She recognized the spicy scent of his aftershave. Her heartbeat skittered and took off like a nervous colt at a wild gallop.

The silence stretched on until she thought she must have been mistaken. He didn't move, didn't speak. She cocked her head to the side. "Is someone there?"

"Can I help?" His raspy voice was a mere whisper.

It was Booker. God had given her another chance to

spend time with him. "You have already helped a great deal. The price you paid for my quilt was outrageous."

"Some works of art are priceless, but what are you doing on the floor?"

"I dropped my room key."

"Ah. I see it." A second later he grasped her hand and pressed the cool metal key into her palm, then gently closed her fingers over it.

Waves of awareness raced up her arm and sent shivers dancing across her nerve endings. She didn't trust her voice to speak as he cupped her elbows and drew her to her feet. The warmth from his hands spread through her body, making it difficult to breathe.

She'd known this dizzying sensation only once before. The first and only time Gideon Troyer had kissed her. Would this man's kiss light up her soul the way Gideon's had?

Shame rushed in on the heels of her disgraceful thought. What was the matter with her? This man was *Englisch.* He was forbidden, and she was foolish to place herself in such a situation.

She was inches away from him. Gideon's pulse pounded in his ears like a drum as he studied Rebecca's face, her lips, the curve of her cheek. Behind her tinted glasses he saw the way her full lashes lay dark and smoky against her fair skin. The long ribbons of her white *kapp* drew his attention to the faint pulse beating at the side of her neck just where he wanted to press a kiss.

She was everything he remembered and so much more. The girl he once loved had matured into a beautiful woman. He longed to pull her into his arms and kiss her. To see if those lush lips tasted as sweet as they did in his memory.

His grip tightened. Suddenly, she grew tense in his grasp and tried to pull away.

He was frightening her. This wasn't a romantic interlude from their past for her. To her he was a stranger. He released her, took a step back and tried to put her at ease. "Would you like me to open the door for you?"

"No. I can manage." She retreated until her back was against the wood.

She didn't look frightened, only flustered. A pretty blush added color to her cheeks. Adam must have known she was staying at the inn. It would have helped if his cousin had given him a heads-up.

Gideon said, "It was nice talking to you. Perhaps we'll see each other later since the ice is going to keep me here for a day. Wait, should I use the word *see,* or is that being insensitive?"

"I beg your pardon?" Her flustered look changed to confusion.

"I don't know how to address a blind person. You're the first one I've met. Can you give me a few pointers so I don't stick my foot in my mouth?"

Her charming smile twitched at the corner of her mouth. "There isn't a special way to address us, and you don't have to be concerned about using the word *see.* I use it all the time."

"Good, because I'm thinking it would be hard to have a conversation with you if I constantly had to think up a way to replace every word that relates to sight."

She nodded slowly. "I see what you mean."

"Right!"

Chuckling, she said, "I'm sure we'll run into each

other if you're staying here for a while. The inn isn't very big."

"I'd call it cozy."

"I don't find it so."

"Why not?" Was she uncomfortable because he was here?

She shrugged. "It's not important."

"Of course it is."

Following a moment of hesitation, she said, "I feel lost when I'm downstairs. The ceiling is so high that sounds echo differently. It's that way in this long hall, too. I'm used to my aunt's small farmhouse. I know where everything is. I can move about freely."

"You're comfortable there."

She smiled. "That's right. You do *see* what I mean."

"If you need help navigating your way around, just ask me."

Her smile faded. "I'm not asking for your help. I can manage quite well on my own."

"Ouch. The lady is touchy."

Her mouth dropped open in surprise. "I am not."

"Could have fooled me. That's not very Amish of you."

Her mouth snapped shut. "What is that supposed to mean?"

"The Amish are humble folks. Humble people accept help when it's offered."

Torn between scolding him and turning the other cheek, as she knew she should, Rebecca pressed her lips closed on her comment. He was baiting her. She didn't have to respond.

"I'm right. Let me hear you admit it."

She said, "The Amish strive to be humble before God."

"Gets hard to do sometimes, doesn't it?"

She blew out a long breath. "Yes, sometimes it is hard. Anything worthwhile is often hard to obtain. That is why we must depend on God to aid us."

"Sorry if I offended you."

"You did, but you are forgiven. My aunt often tells me I am too proud and I must seek humility."

"It's a foolish person who doesn't heed *goot* advice."

Hearing her own words tossed back at her made Rebecca smile. "I do need to work on that."

Downstairs she heard the grandfather clock chiming the quarter hour and realized her headache had disappeared. Conversing with Booker was interesting to say the least. No one had ever asked if talking about her blindness made her uncomfortable. Usually they stammered apologies or sought to avoid mentioning it all together.

"What kind of work do you do?" she asked.

"I own a small airplane charter service."

"You are a pilot?"

"Yes."

Sadness settled over her. "I once knew a young Amish man who wanted to fly. Is it wonderful to soar above the earth like a bird?"

"It has its moments. What happened to him?"

She grasped the key so tightly her fingers ached and she fought back tears. "The lure of the world pulled him away from our faith and he never came back."

After a long pause, he asked, "Were the two of you close?"

"*Ja,* very close." Why was she sharing this with a stranger? Perhaps, because in some odd way he reminded her of Gideon.

"Did you ever think about going with him?"

She smiled sadly. "I didn't believe he would leave. For a long time I thought it was my fault, but I know now it was not."

Booker stepped closer. "How can you be so sure?"

She raised her chin. "He vowed before God and the people of our church to live by the rules of our Amish faith. If he could turn his back on his vow to God, it was not because of me."

"I imagine you're right about that. Have you forgiven him?"

She wished she could hear him speak in his normal voice. It was hard to read his emotions in the forced whisper he had to use. "Of course."

"If he came back, what would you do?"

"If he came to ask forgiveness and repent I would be happy for him and for his family. I can have Emma Troyer make you some blackcurrant tea. It will make your throat better in no time."

"That's what my mother used to do."

Did she imagine it or did she hear sorrow in his voice? "Is something wrong?"

"I haven't seen my mother in many years."

"Why?"

"I'm estranged from my family."

"That is a very sad thing. Only God is more important than our families. You should go visit them as soon as you can. Thanksgiving is coming in a few weeks. That, surely, is reason enough to put aside your pride and go home."

"I wish that were possible, but it's not. Good day, Rebecca."

She didn't want him to leave but she couldn't think

of a way to stop him. The carpet muffled his footsteps as he walked away. She waited until she heard him descending the stairs before she entered her room.

She closed the door and leaned against it. What did he look like? Was he handsome or plain? What made him sad when he talked about his family? Why hadn't he visited them? There were many things she wanted to know about Booker.

And curiosity killed the cat.

The old adage popped into her mind like the warning it was meant to be. She knew full well it was dangerous to become involved with an outsider. Yet there was something familiar about him that nagged at the back of her mind. Something that made her believe they'd met before. If that were true, why wouldn't he simply say so?

Booker was a riddle. A riddle she wanted to solve. The thought of being cooped up at the inn suddenly took on a whole new outlook. He would be here, too.

Chapter Four

After leaving Rebecca, Gideon descended the stairs of the inn and headed for the café. For the first time in three days he had an appetite. He entered the dining area and was seated by a young Amish waitress.

He accepted an offer of coffee while he studied the menu. After the waitress filled a white mug and set it before him, he added a splash of real cream from a small pewter pitcher on the table. He took a cautious sip of the hot rich blend. Even though his voice hadn't returned, swallowing wasn't as painful. A second sip of coffee went down as smoothly as the first. Maybe he was finally on the mend.

Pulling his cell phone from his pocket he clicked the weather app and checked the local weather and road closings again. The storm that had coated the northern half of the state in ice was gearing up to add a foot or more of snow to the rest of the state.

He wasn't going home tonight, but it was unlikely the roads would be closed for long. Once the storm passed, he'd be on his way. If not first thing in the morning, at least by the afternoon. He sent a text message to Roseanne notifying her that he wouldn't be in to the office in the morning.

Her reply was succinct. *Good!*

Gideon closed his phone and turned his attention to the people around him. The café's customers were mostly Amish enjoying a special treat of eating out after the auction. He remembered many times like this with his family. Although his mother professed to be annoyed with the expense, everyone knew she secretly enjoyed not having to cook.

There were a few non-Amish present in the café, too. He was the only one dining alone. Everyone else sat with family or friends.

His gaze was drawn to an Amish father, a man about his own age, seated with four small children and his wife at the table across the aisle. When their food arrived, the man took his infant son's hands and held them between his own as he bowed his head in prayer. The baby protested only briefly before keeping still. Children were expected to behave and quickly learned the value of copying their elders.

Gideon knew the prayer the man was silently reciting. It was the *Gebet Nach Dem Essen,* the Prayer Before Meals.

O Lord God, heavenly Father, bless us and these thy gifts, which we accept from thy tender goodness. Give us food and drink also for our souls unto life eternal, that we may share at thy heavenly table, through Jesus Christ. Amen.

The Lord's Prayer, also prayed silently, would follow the prayer before meals as well as the prayer after meals. Gideon hadn't prayed much since he left home. A sense of shame crept over him. He had plenty to be grateful for and no good reason to ignore the blessings he'd received.

The Amish father lifted his head, signaling the end of the prayer for everyone at the table. He patted his son's golden curls and began cutting up the meat on the boy's plate. It was a simple act, but it moved Gideon to wonder if he would ever do the same with children of his own.

Maybe it was time he settled down and started looking around for a woman to spend his life with. He hadn't already because the business took up all of his time. He'd been so intent on making a place for himself in the English world that he'd failed to notice the place he made was hollow and empty of love.

He had few friends other than Craig. He lived in a sterile one-bedroom apartment, ate takeout in front of his flat-screen TV. He had neighbors he barely knew and rarely saw. He'd avoided going to church in spite of Roseanne's occasional urging and invitations. It wasn't much of a life when he looked at it that way. Except for the flying. When he was in the clouds he was happy.

He closed his eyes. The smell of baking bread and pot roast filled the air. He thought back to the food his mother used to make. Roast beef and pork, fried chicken, schnitzel with sauerkraut, served piping hot from her wood-burning stove with fresh bread and vegetables from her garden.

As a kid, he never gave a thought to how much work his mother did without complaint. All he'd thought about was escaping the narrow, inflexible Amish way of life. Had it really been so bad?

I must be sick if I'm longing for the good old days.

He sat up and motioned the waitress over. Before he could place his order, the outside door opened and his cousin Adam walked in. Their eyes met for a long second. Adam looked away first. He walked past Gideon without so much as a nod of recognition. Gideon didn't expect the snub to hurt as much as it did.

Adam was being true to his faith. It was his duty to shun a wayward member, to remind Gideon he had cut himself off from God as well as from his family. Gideon had known for years that he would be shunned if he returned unrepentant, but he had never experienced the treatment firsthand.

Years ago, his mother explained to him that shunning was done out of love, to show people the error of their ways, not to punish them. It didn't feel that way at the moment. Gideon's newfound appetite deserted him.

Adam stepped behind the counter and took over the cash register. The waitress beside Gideon's table asked, "Have you decided what you'd like?"

"What kind of soup do you have?"

Her eyebrows shot up in surprise at his hoarse whisper. "We've got homemade chicken noodle soup today. I'll bring you a bowl. You sound like you need it," she said with a sympathetic smile.

He folded the menu and tucked it between the sugar jar and the ketchup bottle. "That'll be fine."

His soup arrived at the same moment Rebecca walked in.

She stood poised in the doorway to the inn with her cane in hand. She tilted her head slightly, as if concentrating on the sounds of the room. A smile lit her face and she moved ahead to a booth by the window. It was then he saw her aunt seated with several older Amish women. They greeted Rebecca warmly and made room for her to sit with them.

He was impressed that she had been able to pick out her aunt's voice in the crowded room and locate her without assistance. She moved with a confidence he admired. If being at the inn made her uncomfortable it didn't show at the moment.

Gideon slowly stirred his soup and unobtrusively watched her.

Was he in the room?

Rebecca wished she could ask her aunt or her friends if Booker was in the café. She didn't, because she knew it would seem odd. The last thing she wanted was to draw attention to her preoccupation with him.

It was bad enough that she *had* this preoccupation with a total stranger. She didn't need to share her foolishness with anyone else.

"Nettie, how are Katie and Elam these days?" Vera asked.

"My boy is over the moon with his new *sohn*. Katie is a fine *mudder* and a strong woman. Little Rachel doesn't quite know what to make of her new *bruder.* She is used to being the apple of her *daed's* eye, you know."

Emma said, "I have some news that I have been dying to share."

When she didn't say anything else, Nettie prompted, "Well, what is it?"

"Adam and I are expecting." Her voice brimmed with barely contained excitement.

"Congratulations. That's *wunderbaar.*" Rebecca was truly delighted to hear that her friends were to become parents.

Vera echoed Rebecca's congratulations and said, "To think you were considered an old maid until a year ago."

Naomi, Emma's mother, chuckled. "When Adam moved to town, right away he saw my Emma for the good woman she truly is. It just goes to show God has His plans for each of us in His own time."

"That He does," Emma agreed. "Adam and I are going to visit his family and share the news tomorrow. If the weather cooperates."

Vera grasped Rebecca's arm. "We must make a quilt for this new blessing."

Rebecca agreed. "*Ja,* we will."

She toyed with her food as her companions talked about babies, the weather and the turnout for the auction. She had made quilts for all the babies of her friends and family, but there were no quilts for children of her own.

She had turned aside every romantic overture that had come her way. There had been a few over the years, but not many. In Hope Springs, the single women outnumbered the men for it was usually the young men who were lured away by the outside world. Why would a man who remained choose a blind woman for a wife when he had healthy ones to pick from?

Besides, none of the men had been Gideon. It was hard to imagine giving her heart to anyone else.

Why? What was she waiting for? Was she hoping Gideon would come back and declare his love again? She had turned down his offer of marriage because she loved him. Because she believed he deserved better than a blind millstone around his neck. Fear and the painful knowledge that she didn't deserve such happiness made her turn away from him.

If she could undo anything in her life, she would change only one thing—the night she slipped away with her sister Grace to join Gideon and his friends at a forbidden party. That one night changed everything.

She shut out the memory. Gideon wasn't coming back, and she had nothing to show for her sacrifice. One day she would be old and alone, without even her aunt to care for. What would happen to her then? She could go back to her parents, but when they were gone, which of her brothers or sisters would she go to live with? Any of them would take her in, but would they do so with joy in their hearts? It was unlikely.

Would it be so bad to marry Daniel Hershberger? If she did, she would have a house of her own and the hope of children. She might learn to love him in time. Daniel was a good man.

If only the thought of kissing him didn't leave her cold.

When their supper was finished, Rebecca went back to her room and sat alone on the bed. Her aunt had gone to her friend Naomi's home for a comfortable evening of visiting. Rebecca had been invited, but used her headache as an excuse not to go. In the silence of her room, Rebecca found herself thinking again about Booker.

How was he feeling? Was he sitting alone in his room as she was? Was he thinking about her? It warmed her to think she might be on his mind.

He was an intriguing man. Perhaps it was just his pitiful voice that made him so. When he could speak plainly, she might find him dull. Or not. She couldn't get him out of her head.

He'd said he wasn't married, and she had to wonder why.

Which was a silly thing to be thinking about!

In a fit of disgust, she got up and took out her Christmas Star quilt. She had only the binding to finish. It wouldn't take long. Perhaps if her hands were busy, her mind wouldn't wander into forbidden territory.

Early the next morning, Gideon walked out the inn's front door and entered a world frozen and cocooned in white. Snowflakes continued to fall, settling soundlessly onto the sidewalk behind a shopkeeper who had just cleared a path from his doorway to the street. Tree branches bent low beneath the weight of their white frosting. Everywhere, a hushed silence engulfed the town.

A few hardy souls had already ventured out. Directly across the street, a man worked to uncover his car with an ice scraper that was clearly too small for the job.

The quiet gave way to the jingle of harness bells. As they grew louder, Gideon looked down the street to see a horse-drawn sleigh coming his way. An Amish family with six rosy-cheeked children filling the back of the sleigh drove past him. Their eyes were bright with the excitement of the ride.

The man digging out his car met Gideon's gaze and grinned. "I've got one hundred and fifty horses under the hood for all the good they are doing me at the moment while the Amish go flying by with only one horse. I reckon the simple life has some advantages, after all."

Gideon grinned as he stood in front of the inn with no particular destination in mind. He just wanted to be out. Out in the clean fresh air of a snow-covered small Ohio town. Hope Springs was a lot like Berlin. A little bigger, but not by much. The same type of stores crowded together off the tree-lined streets.

He noticed antiques for sale and a touristy Amish

gift shop down the street. The merchandise there likely came from China and not from the local craftsmen. Across the street was a hardware store. A pharmacy sat sandwiched between the hardware store and a clothing store. A little farther on a gas station sat at the corner.

Hope Springs wasn't that different from a hundred other Ohio towns. Oddly, after ten years in the city, Gideon felt right at home on these streets. Time to explore a little. Left or right?

Before he made up his mind he heard the door of the inn open behind him. To his surprise, Rebecca came out. She was bundled up against the cold in a heavy, dark blue woolen coat. A black bonnet covered her head. In one hand she clutched her purse. In the other hand she held her white cane. With little hesitation, she turned left and began walking down the sidewalk swinging her cane lightly in front of her.

He should have spoken, but he wasn't sure how his voice would sound this morning. What if she recognized him when he spoke?

Gideon followed her and watched as she tested the height and depth of a snowdrift in her path at the corner. She wasn't really going to try and find her way around town in these conditions, was she? Where was her aunt? Why wasn't someone with her?

To his astonishment, she made her way over the snowdrift easily and continued across the icy street. It was then he saw an obstacle she couldn't detect with her cane. There was no way for her to know the snow-laden branches of the trees that lined the avenue were hanging at shoulder level. She was about to walk into a cold surprise. He tried calling out a warning but his voice failed him.

Galvanized into action, Gideon hurried after her. He raced across the slick street as fast as he dared. Rebecca would get a face full of snow in another few steps. He tried again to call out. This time he managed to croak, "Rebecca, stop."

She paused and turned her head as if searching for the source of the pitiful sound he'd made. He reached the curb but hit a patch of ice on the sidewalk. His feet flew out from under him and he landed with a painful thud at Rebecca's feet.

He moaned and rubbed the back of his smarting head. When he opened his eyes, she was standing over him, her face silhouetted against the cloudy winter sky. He knew from memory that her eyes were the blue of a bright summer's day but she held them closed now behind her dark glasses.

He wanted her to open her eyes so he could see them. He wanted to see all the memories they held of their time together.

He wanted her to see him.

Two words, his name, would be all it would take to let her know who he was. If he said those two words would she turn away? Would she shun him? He couldn't take that risk.

"Are you all right?" She located him with her cane and bent down to assist him.

He gave a groan as he managed to leverage himself to sitting position. "I think so," he whispered.

"Booker?"

"Yes."

She slipped her hand beneath his elbow. "You poor man. Let me help you."

"Thanks." He accepted her assistance as he rose to his feet and dusted the snow from his clothes.

"Are you sure you aren't hurt?"

"I've got a pretty hard head."

"You shouldn't rush on these slippery walks. What were you thinking? Where were you going in such a hurry?"

It wasn't the first time he'd been chided for his lack of common sense by this woman. He'd missed her occasional scolding as much as he'd missed her tender-hearted sweetness.

"I was hurrying to save you from walking into some snow-laden branches hanging over the walkway."

Her frown changed to the smile he adored. "Bless you for your concern, Booker. I would not enjoy getting a face full of snow."

"I didn't think you would."

"Now that I have been warned, I will be fine. Thank you for your concern."

"Where are you off to on such a cold day?"

"To the fabric shop."

"I was going that way. Do you mind if I walk along with you?"

She arched one eyebrow. "You are going to the fabric shop?"

"I didn't say I was going to the fabric shop. I said I was going that way. Two different things. If you would rather walk alone I understand."

She shook her head and started walking. "I don't mind the company, but you must promise not to continually try to help me."

"Why shouldn't I offer my help?"

She swung the cane from side to side, tapped it

briefly on the sidewalk in front of her. "Because unless I ask for it, I don't really need it."

"All right, but three steps ahead of you are those low branches."

She moved closer to the building. "Am I clear if I walk over here?"

"Yeah. Are there any other rules I should know?" For a few words his voice came out strong and normal before breaking again. He froze, wondering if she would recognize him now.

"You should not grab a blind person. It's rude. You should not shout at someone who is blind because most of us can hear quite well."

"Can I ask questions or is that rude, too?" He kept his voice to a whisper. It might be best to stay silent but he didn't want to give up this opportunity to spend time with her.

"Questions are okay."

"Is it true that your hearing becomes more acute?"

"No. A blind person's hearing does not change. We simply pay more attention to what we hear."

He glanced down the walkway ahead of them. "I guess that makes sense. How will you know when you have reached the fabric shop?"

"Because I have been here many times." She stopped in front of a store called Needles and Pins.

"You counted your steps."

"I often do, but that's hard when I'm carrying on a conversation."

"I don't understand how you did it, then."

"The answer is right under your feet." She tapped the sidewalk through the layer of snow that hadn't yet been removed.

"I still don't get it."

"Listen." She took a step back and tapped again.

He listened intently, wanting to learn all that she was willing to teach. She stepped forward and tapped twice more. This time he heard the difference in the sound. Crouching down, he swept the snow aside. "It's brick, not concrete."

Her smile was bright and genuine. "*Ja.* Very *goot.* The store has a decorative brick design on the sidewalk in front of it. It makes it easy to find. Thank you for your escort, Booker."

"My pleasure," he whispered.

She hesitated, then pulled open the door and went inside.

Warmth and the scent of new fabrics surrounded Rebecca as she entered Needles and Pins, but her thoughts stayed with the man outside. His thoughtfulness pleased her. His consideration might be motivated by pity but she didn't think so. His kindness made her feel special. Made her feel feminine, something she hadn't experienced in the company of a man for many years.

"Hello, Rebecca. I've been expecting you."

Rebecca brushed aside her thoughts about Booker and turned to smile at Sarah Wyse, an Amish widow who worked at the shop. Rebecca wished her good morning in Pennsylvania Dutch. "*Guder mariye,* Sarah. How are you?"

"I'm fine. Everyone is talking about how well your quilt did yesterday. We are so pleased God has smiled on your efforts."

"*Danki.* Has my aunt's order come in?"

"*Ja,* yesterday morning. I'll get it for you."

Rebecca heard Sarah walk away. A few minutes later she returned. A muffled thud told Rebecca she had placed a large bolt of material on the wooden countertop.

"This is the lot I was telling your aunt about. It's a soft shade of lavender and we got an excellent buy on a large quantity."

Reaching out, Rebecca fingered the fabric. It was a cotton-polyester blend that would be durable enough for everyday dresses. "You are sure it is a color the bishop will find acceptable?"

"I hope so. His wife ordered six yards of it."

"We'll take it, then. I'll also take any of the fabric remnants you have."

"I bundled some together for you last night. Tell your aunt she can send back anything that doesn't work."

"Danki."

When Sarah rang up the total, Rebecca drew out her wallet and carefully searched through the folded bills. With her aunt's help, Rebecca was able to separate the identical-feeling currency. The ones folded lengthwise were one-dollar bills, those folded in half were ten-dollar bills and the ones folded in thirds were twenty-dollar bills.

Sarah handed back Rebecca's change and asked, "Who is your friend outside? Wouldn't he like to come in out of the cold?"

"He's waiting outside?"

"He's leaning against the lamppost and beginning to look like an icicle."

"Excuse me a moment." Rebecca turned and made her way to the door. Pulling it open, she called out, "Booker, what do you think you're doing?"

Chapter Five

"Are you trying to catch pneumonia?" Rebecca demanded.

For a long moment Booker didn't answer. Then she heard the crunch of his footsteps approaching through the snow. "How did you know I was waiting?"

"I heard your teeth chattering." She stepped back to allow him inside.

"You couldn't hear that, could you? Man, it feels good in here."

"I can hear them now. You don't have the sense God gave a goose."

"I'm not sure that's true."

"Why are you waiting outside?" she demanded.

"To walk you back to the inn."

"I thought you had somewhere to go."

"Not really."

Exasperated, she said, "I'm perfectly capable of finding my way back unaided."

"I believe you."

His voice was so hoarse she wanted to wrap him up in warm flannel and poor hot tea into him. "If you know I can find my way back then why were you waiting for me?"

"I enjoy spending time with you."

And she enjoyed spending time with him. This had to stop. "Booker, you barely know me."

"That can change."

She crossed her arms and tried to look stern. "Is this concern because I'm blind?"

"No. Why would you think that?"

From behind her, Rebecca heard Sarah ask, "Is everything all right?"

"*Ja,* everything is fine," Rebecca answered.

She spoke softly to Booker. "You should go back to the inn."

"I'm not in a rush. Besides, it's toasty warm in here. This may be a dumb question, but how do you choose the fabrics for your quilts?"

Rebecca heard the outside door open. A gust of cold air carried in the sounds of several Amish women speaking in Pennsylvania Dutch. The more people who saw her with Booker the more likely it was that she would become the object of gossip. It was time to end this…whatever it was.

"I must be going." She started toward the door and hurried outside. A second later, she heard someone come out behind her. If it was Booker, it would be best to ignore him. She made her way down the sidewalk. Footsteps told her someone was walking beside her.

After a dozen steps, Booker asked, "So how do you do it? How do you know what fabrics to use?"

"Why do you want to know?"

"Because you are an interesting person, and I admire your skill."

He was as tenacious as a toothache. Other than ordering him away, she couldn't see how to rid herself of his company.

She sighed heavily. "My aunt and I work together. We decide on a pattern, she picks the fabrics. You may have noticed that her hands are crippled. The women from our church district do the cutting for us. My aunt separates the pieces by color and I stitch them together. When the piecing is done, the quilt goes into a frame and I quilt the front and back together."

"I figured it had to be something like that. Don't you prick your fingers while you're trying to sew?"

She stopped in frustration. "Very rarely. What are you doing?"

"I'm going back to the inn like you told me to do. Is there somewhere else you'd like me to go? You can tell me."

She struggled not to smile and lost the battle. "I'm not going to the inn. It's the other way."

"Then I'm lost. I'll have to stick with you until you can lead me home. Can we get moving? This cold wind is very bad for my throat."

"You should've thought of that before you left the warm, cozy inn," she countered, but started walking anyway.

"I hate being cooped up inside. I'm not used to it. I needed to get out for a while. I've been grounded for days now."

"What does that mean?"

"I haven't been able to fly."

It clearly bothered him. "Flying is important to you?"

"Very. It's my job."

Gideon had talked endlessly about wanting to fly.

Some part of her needed to understand why. They turned a corner. The building blocked the wind giving them shelter and a sense of elusive warmth. Rebecca stopped. "What's it like to fly?"

There was a long moment of silence, then he said, "How can I describe it? It's freedom. I've been inside the clouds. I've looked down on mountaintops. Fields and farms below look like one of your quilts. I've seen the backs of birds flying beneath me, and I understand what makes them sing. To be suspended between heaven and earth is like no other feeling. It's…freedom."

"Walking upon the earth God has made is not joy enough?"

"It never has been for me."

She shook her head. "I don't think I understand."

He stepped closer. "I think you do. Because even though you can hear the birds sing you would give anything to see them winging their way across an expanse of bright blue sky. We can't control what we feel. Some things make us happy. Other things make us sad. You're sad right now."

How could this stranger see so deeply into her heart? "Maybe I am."

"You said you learned you were going blind when you were twenty. What caused it?"

"A simple, innocent thing."

"Tell me about it."

"Someone threw a snowball that had a sliver of a pine needle in it. It struck me in the eye."

She heard Booker suck in his breath and rushed to reassure him it was an accident. "My friend had no intention of hurting me. We were having fun. He took me straight to the doctor as soon as he realized what had happened. The doctor removed the sliver from my eye and we thought everything was fine."

"But you weren't fine."

"No. A few months later, I noticed the color of things starting to fade away. I went back to the doctor. His nurse drove me to see a specialist. There, I learned that I had a rare form of a disease called uveitis. There was little that could be done for me. I was told I would go completely blind within a year or two."

After a long pause of silence, Booker said, "Your friend, he must have felt terrible."

"I never told him."

"Why not?"

"My blindness is God's will, Booker. Why should I burden the heart of a friend with the knowledge that he was the instrument God chose?"

"Maybe because he had thc right to know."

She struggled against the lump forming at the back of her throat. "He gave up that right."

"Why do you say that?

"He left the Amish. If his faith had been stronger, I might have told him, but he was gone before I could gather my courage."

"If you'd told him the truth, perhaps his faith would have been strong enough."

Didn't she wonder that very thing? No, Gideon had made his choice of his own free will.

"It's in the past. It can't be changed." She started walking again. She didn't care if Booker followed or not.

Gideon remembered the day it happened. It had been a snowy day much like today. Their friends, a dozen teenagers, had all gathered together for a skating party on his family's farm pond. He wasn't sure who threw the first snowball, but everyone joined in the free-for-all.

He could still see Rebecca, laughing as she scooped up a handful to chuck his way. He ducked around a little pine tree, the only available cover. He knew she had a good aim. When her shot splattered against the tree trunk, he grabbed a handful of snow, packed it tight and hurled one back at her. His aim had been dead-on. It hit her square in the face. He'd laughed like crazy until he saw she was hurt.

His foolish act had caused her blindness. No wonder she had turned down his offer of marriage.

But it had been an accident. He never meant to hurt her. Never meant to hurt anyone. In the buggy on the way to the doctor he begged her forgiveness. She gave it freely. He clung to that thought. She forgave him for the injury, but she clearly hadn't forgiven him for leaving the faith.

He followed and caught up with her as she crossed the next street. It was time to tell her who he was.

And then what?

Would she insist on returning his money? If he wouldn't take it she might give it away. She was stubborn to a fault. Would his confession jeopardize her only chance at regaining her sight?

"I know you are following me, Booker."

He couldn't risk telling her the truth. "I can't leave while you're giving me such a wonderful tour of the town."

"I believe your voice is sounding stronger."

He whispered, "It comes and goes. Where to next?"

"The harness shop."

"It's got to be more interesting than the fabric store."

She chuckled. "*Ja,* for you, maybe."

Turning aside without warning, Rebecca entered a narrow alley. Overhead, large icicles had formed along the roof edges of the buildings. In the center of the alley the snow was deep. She stumbled, and Gideon took her arm. "Careful. If I lose you I'll never find my way back to the inn. I can see the headlines now. Frozen Tourist Turned into Tall Popsicle."

"Are you *ever* serious?"

"If you could see my face you'd know I'm dead serious."

She flashed a smile that warmed him down to his toes. "I doubt that."

They came out of the alley into a clearing where several buggies sat waiting for repairs. They made their way between the vehicles and up to the back door of a wooden building. She didn't bother knocking. Instead, she opened the door and went inside.

Gideon followed her into the cavernous interior where every type of harness and tack were hanging from the walls, the ceiling and display racks. A large propane-powered sewing machine sat in the center of the room by an enormous cutting table. Along one wall, an ancient workbench held dozens of awls and leather-working tools, all arranged neatly in holders. Near the front of the store, a coal-burning stove added warmth to the large space.

Rebecca called out, "*Daadi,* are you here?"

"What is this? Has my favorite grandchild come to visit at last?" A small bandy-legged Amish elder came from the front of the store.

His snow-white hair held a permanent crease from the hat he normally wore. His beard, as white as his hair, reached the center of the dark vest buttoned over his pale blue shirt. His sharp eyes looked Gideon up and down in an assessing manner that made Gideon wish he'd stayed outside. He'd met her grandfather only once and years ago. Would the old man remember him? Hopefully not.

Rebecca held out her hands. Her grandfather grasped them both and planted a kiss on each of her cheeks. He looked straight at Gideon. "And who is this?"

"This is Booker. He purchased my quilt at the auction yesterday."

"And paid a fine price for it, too, I hear."

"It was a fair price for a good cause." Gideon answered in his hoarse whisper.

The old man's bushy eyebrows shot upward. "You are ill?"

"I've lost my voice, that's all."

Nodding wisely, Reuben said, "I will keep a lookout for it."

Gideon cracked a smile. Rebecca giggled and said, "Booker, this is my grandfather, Reuben Beachy."

"God will bless your generosity, Booker. I pray with my whole heart that my granddaughter's vision may be restored."

"As do I," Gideon replied, gazing intently at the woman beside him.

She said, "*Aenti* Vera has sent me to tell you she needs a new set of driving lines for Boppli."

"Did your mare break another pair?"

"*Ja,* she can be headstrong at times," Rebecca admitted.

"Like her owners. Does Vera want leather or nylon reins this time?" Reuben placed her hand on his arm and led her toward the front of the store. Gideon tagged after them.

"*Aenti* says the nylon lines are lighter and easier for her to hold."

While Rebecca and Reuben chatted, Gideon walked among the harnesses displayed on curved wooden racks that simulated a horse's back. The quality of the workmanship was easy to see. As he stood admiring a leather horse collar, the front door opened and a man about Gideon's age walked in. He was dressed plain with a dark hat and dark clothing, but he was clean-shaven. Only married men wore beards. Gideon scratched the stubble on his cheeks.

"*Guder mariye,* Reuben," the stranger called out.

Gideon took a closer look at the man. His greeting in Pennsylvanian Dutch was right, but his accent was all wrong.

Reuben said, "Hello, Jonathan. What can I do for you today?"

"I got a new horse in yesterday and I need a collar and harness for him. He's a little fellow and none of mine will fit him. I have him outside. Is it all right if I try a couple on him?"

"Sure. A poor-fitting collar has damaged many a good horse. Make sure it isn't too big on him. Four fingers should fit snugly between his neck and the collar."

"I know. *Danki.* Hello, Rebecca." The stranger smiled warmly at her.

"Jonathan, how are you?"

"Cold. And you?"

"The same."

Gideon could tell by the tone of her voice that she was friends with this man. Close friends? How close?

He turned his back to the group. He was an intruder in their circle. An outsider. He had no reason to be jealous of Rebecca's friendship with this man, but annoyance pricked at him anyway.

When Reuben and Jonathan took their collars outside, Gideon moved to stand by Rebecca. "Your friend looks Amish but he doesn't sound Amish."

"He was *Englisch,* but he has chosen to live among us and become one of us."

"That is a rare thing."

"*Ja,* it is. He has lived here for a year now and his Pennsylvania Dutch is pretty good. I think he will ask to be baptized soon."

"And then what?"

She leaned toward Gideon and whispered, "Hopefully, there will be a wedding in the fall."

"Yours?"

She straightened abruptly. "*Nee.* Jonathan is not courting me. He has his eye on my friend, Karen Imhoff."

Gideon was hard put to explain the rush of relief that filled him. "And does she have her eye on Jonathan?"

"Most definitely. Are you ready to go?"

"Where to next?"

"I am done with my errands, so it is back to the inn."

He didn't want their morning to end. "Do we really have to go back?"

He watched the uncertainty flit across her face. An instant later, her uncertainty vanished. "There is no rush. Do you have any shopping you would like to do?"

"I'll think of something."

Suddenly, a loud scraping noise reverberated through the building. Rebecca took a step closer to him and grasped his jacket sleeve. "What was that?"

"My guess? Snow and ice sliding off the roof." He covered her hand with his.

She relaxed and pulled her hand away slowly. "Of course, how silly of me to be frightened."

"Don't apologize."

Clearly flustered, she said, "I really should get back. My aunt will be waiting for me. We…we have plans for today."

It took all his willpower to step away from her. "I understand."

They crossed through the store to the back door, but when she tried to open it the door barely moved. "There's something blocking it."

He put his shoulder against it and pushed. It budged a few inches, enough for him to see it was snow blocking the door. The pile was at least four feet deep. "Looks like this is where the snow from the roof landed."

"We can go out the other way."

They returned to the front of the store. Jonathan had gone. Reuben was placing a number of bills in his cash register.

Rebecca said, "*Daadi,* the back door is blocked."

"I heard the avalanche. I will take care of it." Reuben sighed and moved to pick up a snow shovel by the front door.

Gideon stepped forward and took hold of the tool. "Let me do that for you."

Reuben frowned at him. "I can shovel a little snow."

"I can, too." Gideon grinned. The man must be close to eighty years old.

Reuben relinquished his hold. "*Danki,* Booker."

Gideon turned to Rebecca. "You should go back to the inn. I can find my way. I was only teasing you about being lost."

Her lips curved slightly. "I know. I don't mind waiting."

After Gideon left the building, Rebecca's grandfather spoke to her in Pennsylvania Dutch. "How well do you know this *Englisch* fellow?"

"We only met at the auction, but he has been most kind."

"Do I need to put a word of caution in your ear?" Reuben asked in a firm tone he rarely used with her.

Her pleasure dimmed. "No, *Daadi,* I know what is proper."

"I'm happy to hear that. Do not be fooled by his interest."

"I don't know what you mean." She did, but she didn't want to hear it put into words.

"You are a lovely woman. He is an outsider, stuck in our little town until the roads are clear. Do not be flattered by his attention. It will vanish when the roads are open."

Was she so pathetic? Tears pricked at the back of her eyes. "Is it wrong to show him kindness after all he has done for me? We took a walk through town. Nothing else."

Pressing her lips together, she waited for her grandfather to respond. How could it be wrong to enjoy a stroll with Booker? She knew nothing could come of the relationship. He made her feel special. He made her smile. Didn't she deserve a few hours of enjoyment?

"You are a grown woman with a *goot* head on your shoulders. I don't wish to see you hurt."

"When Jonathan came among us you were not suspicious of his motives."

"Jonathan was a man with no memory. He didn't know his own name. It was clear God brought him to us so that he might be healed in body and soul."

"Perhaps God has such a reason for bringing Booker here."

"That may be true, but Booker looks more like a man with something to hide than a man looking to find God's will."

"Why do you say that?"

"There is something about the way he doesn't look a man in the eye."

"Perhaps he's shy. Maybe he feels uncomfortable because we look at him with suspicion." She felt compelled to defend Booker.

"Perhaps you are right and I am wrong to judge him harshly. 'It is better to suffer wrong than to do it.'"

"'And happier to be sometimes cheated than to never trust.'" She finished the proverb for him.

"All I'm trying to say is be careful, child."

"I will be, Grandfather. Don't worry."

Harness bells chimed as the front door opened. When the new arrival called a greeting in Pennsylvania Dutch Rebecca knew it wasn't Booker returning.

The customer was shopping for a new halter. Rebecca waited by the counter as her grandfather went to help him.

She had always heeded her grandfather's counsel, so why was she unwilling to do so now? He thought it unwise of her to spend time with Booker. One day spent in the company of a man who found her companionship pleasant. Where was the harm in that?

She knew. She didn't want to admit it, but she knew. The harm was in wanting more than one day with such a man.

She had been foolish. It was time to go back to the life she was meant to lead. Skating on thin ice would only lead to a cold bath.

"Tell Booker that I changed my mind. I've decided to return to the inn after all."

"That is a wise decision, child. Give Vera my love and tell her you are both invited to supper come Sunday."

"I'm afraid we have other plans."

"Oh?"

"Daniel Hershburger has already invited us to eat with him and his sister."

"Has he, now? Well, well. He is a fine man, a devout man. I'm glad to hear this. You and Vera must come by some evening when you are free. Why don't you invite Daniel, too? I haven't had a good game of checkers in a long while. What do you think of that idea?"

She forced herself to smile. "I think it sounds fine, *Daadi.*"

Chapter Six

When Gideon finished his labor, he opened the back door of the harness shop and carried the snow shovel through the building. Rebecca's grandfather sat behind the counter on a tall stool tooling a length of harness. He looked up when he heard Gideon and nodded. "*Danki,* your help is appreciated."

"I'm happy to do it." Gideon's voice was barely audible and the sensation of swallowing razor blades was back. He looked around but didn't see Rebecca.

"My granddaughter decided to go back to the inn," Reuben said before Gideon could ask.

Gideon tried to hide his disappointment. Reuben returned to his work without another word. Recognizing a dismissal when he saw it, Gideon walked out the front door. Had he made trouble for Rebecca? He knew a few Amish elders who would see her casual friendship with him as brazen behavior.

Standing on the sidewalk, he pushed his hands deeper into his coat pockets. The day seemed colder without Rebecca's company. He had worked up a sweat shoveling. Now a chill was setting in.

Traffic had picked up on the streets. Chances were good that the interstate would be open soon, if it wasn't already. The narrow rural highway between Hope Springs and the interstate might be another story, but Gideon found he wasn't eager to leave the quiet village.

Okay, he wasn't eager to leave Rebecca. The connection was still there between them. He felt it. The question was—what should he do about it?

He shook his head at his foolishness. What was the point of resurrecting his emotions from their old relationship when Rebecca had no idea who he was? He wasn't being fair to her or to himself. Suddenly he realized how tired he was. His illness had seriously sapped his energy. His good deed of shoveling aside four feet of packed snow had burned through what little he had left.

Or maybe it was his guilty conscience making him tired. Pretending to be someone he wasn't was harder than he thought. With heavy steps, he started walking toward the inn.

By the time he reached the building he was ready to crawl under the covers and hide. He wasn't in any shape to attempt the six-hour drive home. When he entered the lobby, he was relieved to see his cousin wasn't on duty. The elderly man behind the desk was the same fellow that checked Gideon in. He wasn't Amish.

"Did you enjoy your stay with us, Mr. Troyer?"

Gideon glanced around to see who might have overheard his name. There was no one about. He managed a smile and said, "Call me Booker. It's a very comfortable place. I know I'm due to check out today, but is there any way I can stay another night?"

"Certainly. I can keep you in the same room for two more days if you like."

"One more will be fine." Relieved, Gideon climbed the stairs and walked slowly down the hall. At the door to Rebecca's room he paused. He considered knocking to see if she had made it back okay but decided against it. It would be better all around if he let their budding relationship die a natural death. As far as she knew they were two strangers staying at the same inn. They had enjoyed a walk together and nothing more. He should let it go at that.

He needed to let go of her.

Unlocking his own door, he entered the cozy room where an old-fashioned four-poster bed with a blue-and-white quilted coverlet was calling his name. He tossed his coat over a chair, kicked off his shoes and lay down fully dressed on the bed. After a minute, he rolled to his side and dragged the corner of the bedspread across his shoulders.

The next time he opened his eyes the room was completely dark. Squinting at the clock on the bedside table, he saw it was nearly eleven-thirty at night and he was starving. Had he really slept for twelve hours?

It was too late to call Roseanne or Craig now. He'd have to try to catch them early in the morning to let them know he wouldn't be back until the day after tomorrow. Although the company had three flights booked for the next two days, Craig would just have to pick up the slack.

Gideon sat up and rubbed his gritty eyes. His chin itched. He ran a hand over his bristly cheeks and scratched his face. He needed a shave. A few more days and he could pass for an Amish newlywed. He'd be glad when his halfhearted disguise wasn't needed anymore.

Rising, he moved to the window and looked out. At

least it wasn't snowing. From his vantage point he could see the outline of the shops across the street highlighted by a red glow behind them. It took his sleep-stupid brain a full ten seconds to process what he was seeing.

There was a building on fire.

Dashing back to the bed, he grabbed the phone on the nightstand and dialed 911, praying this sleepy little town had an emergency dispatch. To his relief, a woman's voice said, "911 operator. What is your emergency?"

He tried to speak, but his voice failed him. Apparently, getting chilled had set back his recovery.

"What is your emergency?" the woman asked, louder this time.

He tried harder, straining his vocal cords. "I can see a building on fire from my window."

"I'm sorry, I can't understand you. Would you repeat that, please?"

He dropped the receiver beside the phone and headed out the door. He had to find someone with a voice. In the dark hallway, he saw a sliver of light coming from beneath Rebecca's door. He pounded on the wooden panel.

When there was no response, he knocked again. This time, he heard her uncertain voice. "Who is it?"

"It's Booker." Great, he couldn't identify himself beyond a harsh whisper he doubted she could hear through the thick door. He knocked again.

The door opened a crack. "Booker? Is that you?"

He drew his hand across his throat hoping she would understand he couldn't talk and then realized she couldn't see him, either. He swallowed hard and struggled to speak. "Rebecca, I need your help."

The door opened wide. She stood with a soft blue robe pulled over her floor-length white nightgown. Her hair was in a long braid hanging over her shoulder. He had been right. It was past her waist now. She stared sightlessly past him.

He leaned forward, close to her ear and whispered, "I see a building on fire from my window."

From inside the room, he heard her aunt call out. "Rebecca, what's going on? It's nearly midnight."

"Booker says he sees a building on fire."

"Where?"

They were wasting valuable time. Gideon took Rebecca's hand and pulled her across the hall to his room. Picking up the phone, he placed it to her ear and said, "Tell them."

Clearly, the 911 operator was still on the line. Rebecca said, "Hello, this is Rebecca Beachy. I want to report a fire."

Gideon placed his ear on the outside of the receiver to hear the woman's response.

"Can you give me your address?"

"I'm staying at the Wadler Inn in Hope Springs."

"Is the fire at the inn?"

Gideon said no and Rebecca repeated the information.

"Can you give me the location of the fire?"

By this time Rebecca's aunt had followed them into the room. Gideon led her to his window. Now that the women would be able to stay on the line with the dispatcher, he could go get more help. He pulled on his shoes and grabbed his coat.

Rebecca said, "They're putting a call into the Hope Springs volunteer fire department. They will be on their way soon, but they need an address."

Gideon pointed to himself then to the fire and retrieved his cell phone. Vera nodded in understanding.

She said, "Rebecca, tell them Mr. Booker is heading toward the fire now. He'll have someone call them on his cell phone. I'll rouse the house."

Gideon grabbed his coat and sprinted out the door. At the foot of the stairs, he looked back once and saw Vera coming down, too. She would raise the alarm and get help from the staff at the inn.

Outside, he raced across the street and followed the same path he and Rebecca had walked that morning. As he ran down the sidewalk a sick feeling settled in the pit of his stomach. He wasn't sure until he passed the fabric shop and reached the alley they had taken to her grandfather's shop. Through the narrow walkway he saw the flames licking up the back wall of the harness shop. The snow-covered ground reflected the dancing orange glow. The stench of smoke fouled the night air.

Gideon hurried down the alley. Already the heat had broken out several windows at the rear of the building. No one was about yet. The windows of the homes on either side of the building were dark. It wasn't going to take much for the fire to spread across the narrow spaces between the wooden structures. He had to wake people.

Looking around he spotted a metal trash can at the side of the alley. He picked up the lid and started banging it against the can for all he was worth. It seemed like an eternity before the back door of one house finally opened and an irate voice shouted, "Knock off that racket!"

From above, he heard a window open. This time a woman screeched, "Fire!"

Now that he was sure the alarm would be spread, Gideon dropped his noisemaker and raced around to the front of the building. The shop was adjacent to Reuben's home. He had to make sure the elderly couple was safe.

Reuben's home was dark, but Gideon saw someone standing in the street in front of it. It wasn't Reuben. The bystander was a boy of about sixteen. He already had his cell phone to his ear. Trusting that the boy was calling 911, Gideon sprinted up the steps of Reuben's house and began pounding on the door. The flames were clearly visible over the roof of the shop now.

He was ready to break down the door when Reuben finally appeared. He held a battery-powered lantern in his hand. Raising it high, he squinted at Gideon. "What is the meaning of this?"

The boy from the street ran up. "Mr. Beachy, your shop is on fire."

Reuben's eyes widened. "*Gott,* have mercy."

He turned back into the house and Gideon heard him shouting for his wife. In the distance, he heard the faint wail of sirens. Help was on its way at last.

A moment later, Reuben came out of his house pulling his coat over his nightclothes. He hurried past Gideon to the front door of his shop, opened it and disappeared inside.

"Is the old man crazy?" the boy standing beside Gideon asked in astonishment.

The Amish didn't believe in insurance. Reuben had to save as much of his merchandise as he could. Knowing that it was the stupidest thing he had ever done, Gideon followed Rebecca's grandfather into the harness shop.

Rebecca learned it was her grandfather's shop nearly thirty minutes after Booker left her. Having returned to their room and dressed, she and Vera were in the lobby of the inn when word reached them by way of Naomi Wadler.

Now, an hour later, the three women were in the kitchen preparing thermoses of coffee and sandwiches that would be taken to the volunteers working to contain the blaze.

The back door of the kitchen banged open. Naomi asked, "What news is there, Kyle?"

A young boy's voice answered, "The roof just fell in. You should've seen the sparks fly."

Rebecca didn't share young Kyle's sense of excitement. She wished the news had been better. "Are you sure my *daadi* is all right?"

"He's fine, but Adrian says the shop can't be saved. They're still trying to keep it from spreading to Reuben's house and some others."

Adrian Lapp, Kyle's stepfather, was one of the volunteer firefighters. Word had spread slowly since most Amish families lived without telephones, but within an hour men from miles around were pouring in to help. The street in front of the inn was lined with buggies and hastily saddled horses.

Vera said, "It's a blessing there is so much snow on the roofs. It may help stop the fire from spreading."

"Has anyone been hurt?" Naomi asked.

Kyle said, "I seen Dr. White and his nurse taking care of somebody. Don't know who it was."

Rebecca screwed the lid on the thermos she had just filled and handed it to Kyle. "Have you seen an *Englisch* fellow named Booker?"

"Maybe. There's lots of *Englisch* there, too. I got to

go." The slamming of the back door told Rebecca he was gone.

"I'm sure Booker is fine." Vera patted Rebecca's hand.

A few moments later, the back door opened again. "Naomi, have you any more cups?" This time it was Faith Lapp, Kyle's mother. Although she and her adopted son were new to the area, they had quickly become well-loved members of the Hope Springs community. Perhaps she had more information.

Naomi said, "*Ja,* I have stacks of foam cups in the pantry. I'll get them."

Rebecca asked, "Faith, could you check on a man named Booker for us? He has been staying at the inn. He's the one who spotted the fire and we haven't heard from him since."

"Of course. I'll send Kylc with news when I have it. Is he the fellow that bought your quilt?"

"Ja." Rebecca prayed he was safe. Why hadn't he come back?

She heard Naomi return. "Faith, I have extra blankets and quilts if you need them. I have empty rooms, too, if someone needs a place to stay."

"*Danki,* at least four families have had to evacuate their homes. I will see if they want to bring the children here. The men are busy trying to save what furnishing they can."

"Has anyone been hurt?" Vera asked. Rebecca held her breath waiting for an answer.

"A few minor burns. Your father breathed in too much smoke, but the doctor says he will be fine. Someone pulled him out of the building in the nick of time."

"Praise the Lord." Vera's voice broke and she started

to cry. Rebecca slipped her arms around Vera's shoulders to offer what comfort she could.

Faith's voice softened. "His wife was busy scolding him for his foolishness when I left."

Vera sniffed once and chuckled. "My stepmother is a wise woman. Better than Papa deserves. God is *goot*."

"*Ja*. He has been merciful tonight," Faith added.

The sound of the back door closing told Rebecca Faith was gone.

"I should gather those blankets together in case they are needed," Naomi announced.

"Let me get them," Rebecca offered. She needed to keep busy.

"The linen room is the last door on the left at the end of the hall upstairs. Any of them will do."

"I'll find them." Rebecca made her way upstairs and located the room without difficulty. The linens were stored on open shelves, making it easy for her to find blankets by feel. Gathering a large armload, she started back down the hall. Suddenly, she caught the sharp smell of smoke and soot.

She stopped in her tracks. A second later, she heard muffled footsteps. "Is someone there?"

"Just me."

His harsh whisper sent joy leaping through her chest. "Booker, are you all right?"

"I'm fine."

"You smell terrible."

"Like charred barbecue?" His laugh turned into a cough.

"Are you truly okay?" She tried to tell herself she was worried about everyone who was battling the fire, but the truth was she cared about Booker more than she should.

"I'm fine. Don't worry about me."

She was thankful for the load of blankets in her arms. They kept her from reaching out and "seeing" for herself with her hands that he was unharmed. Gripping the stack tighter, she asked, "Is the blaze out?"

"Not out but under control. A second fire company arrived from Sugarcreek. They sent a lot of us home."

"My grandfather?"

"He's one tough old bird. His house was damaged, but it won't take much to repair. He and his wife are downstairs. I think they plan to stay here tonight."

"I heard his shop is completely gone."

"Ja."

She smiled. "*Ja?* You've been hanging around us Amish too long."

"Maybe so."

An awkward silence stretched between them. She shifted the load in her arms. "Are you leaving tomorrow?"

"That's the plan."

"Back to soaring with the birds?"

"Something like that."

She nodded. He had to leave sooner or later. She had to stay. Drawing a deep breath, she said, "I need to get these downstairs. Come down when you've cleaned up and I'll fix you a sandwich and some tea."

"I'm not hungry. I just want to turn in."

"Of course. We owe you a debt of gratitude, Booker. Had you not seen the fire when you did, lives may have been lost."

"It was nothing."

"God brought you here for a reason. I think this was it."

She heard him sigh. Quietly, he whispered, "Good night, Rebecca."

"*Guten nacht,* Booker. Sleep well."

She heard the door to his room open and close. She stood in the hall for another minute to compose herself, then she went downstairs to join her family.

"I owe you much, Booker." Reuben Beachy stroked his beard and then pushed the brim of his dark hat up with one finger.

"Next time run out of a burning building instead of into it." Gideon's voice was making a comeback. He sounded almost like himself this afternoon. He would have to be careful if he spoke to Rebecca again.

He could see her working along the women who were helping sort and clean the merchandise he and Reuben had carried out before the roof fell in. The memory of the smoke burning his lungs and eyes as he dragged out tools and materials was one he'd rather forget. He glanced down at the bandage on his left arm. He would always have a scar to remind him of his visit to Hope Springs.

All morning long teams of horses and wagons had hauled away loads of charred debris. By noon the old foundation stones of the building had been washed down and made ready to bear a new structure. After that, wagonloads of lumber and building materials began to arrive along with several truckloads donated by the local lumberyard. The sounds of hammers and saws echoed off the surrounding buildings. Everyone,

Amish and English townspeople alike, were pitching in to help one of their own recover from a disaster.

Well over fifty men continued working in the cold afternoon air while the women supplied them with hot drinks and food of every sort from roast pork sandwiches to chocolate chip cookies and whoopie pies. The army of denim-clad Amish farmers and carpenters in black hats and tool belts swarmed over the site like bees over a honeycomb. By four o'clock the skeleton of a new building was rising against the blue sky.

As Gideon stood beside Reuben, two dozen of Reuben's Amish neighbors prepared to lift a twenty-five-foot beam into the building they were raising where only ashes lay the night before.

When the beam settled safely into place, Reuben turned to Gideon. He cleared his throat. "I misjudged you, English. I warned my granddaughter against you. I would do so again, but I would not mistrust your motives in being kind to her. I owe you my life."

Reuben's unconscious body was the last thing Gideon had carried out of the burning shop. It had been a close call. "You are concerned about Rebecca. I understand and respect that. I'm just sorry you lost your business."

"*So ist das Leben.* Such is life!" Reuben declared. "I am a man blessed."

"How can you say that when all you worked for is gone?"

"Look about you. Why should I feel sorrow? My children and grandchildren, my friends and my neighbors are here to help. I could not survive without them or without my faith in God. The things I lost are merely… things. I do not worry about tomorrow—too much. That is in God's hands."

Someone called Reuben away. Gideon knew that within a week Reuben would be open for business again. It might take him a while to replace his large inventory and machinery, but he wasn't the kind of man to quit because things were hard.

Gideon took his time getting back to the inn. When he stepped inside, he saw Adam carrying a pair of suitcases. Approaching his cousin, Gideon said, "Adam, I need you to do something for me."

"I go out of town for two days and look what happens. I understand we have you to thank for spotting the fire before it had a chance to spread. God was with you. How is Reuben?"

"He's tough. He'll get through this."

"What can I do for you?"

"I want to give Rebecca's quilt to you. I want you to sell it again and give the money to Reuben to help him rebuild."

"That is a generous thing, Gideon."

"It's the least I can do."

"My wife and I are leaving this evening to visit your folks for a few days and share our good news."

"What news?"

"We are expecting our first child."

"Wow. Congratulations. That's wonderful."

"I would be happy to take a letter to your mother, if you'd like to write one."

Gideon met Adam's gaze. Maybe it was time he tried making amends. A letter to his family would be a good place to start. "I would appreciate that."

Adam's eyes brightened. "You mean it? You will write?"

"I'm not sure what I will say."

"Say what is in your heart, cousin."

"I'll try."

Thirty minutes later, Gideon met Adam in the lobby again. He laid an envelope on the front desk and shoved his hands in his pockets. "It's a long overdue apology. I expect my mother will cry."

"This is a good thing, Gideon."

"If I went for a visit, do you think I could meet my nephews and nieces?"

"I will ask. Those that have not been baptized are free to speak with you."

"Only if their parents let them."

"As I said, I will ask. And I will tell them the good you have done here."

The letter wasn't much, but it was a start. Gideon tried not to get his hopes up, but the thought of seeing his family again suddenly made him as homesick as he'd been the first week after he left.

Rebecca was right. He'd been hanging around the Amish too long. Their focus on God, family and community had him realizing how shallow his life was. He heard the front door of the inn open. He looked over as Rebecca walked in. The sight of her lifted his spirits.

She carried a large woven hamper with one arm. Gideon rushed toward her. "Let me give you a hand with that."

"*Danki,* Booker." She smiled at him as if she could see him.

His heart turned over in his chest. If he told her the truth, confessed his sins and begged her forgiveness, could he have the life he once turned his back on? Could he find happiness living among the Amish? Was this what God wanted for him?

To return to the Amish would mean giving up flying. How could he do that? If Rebecca knew the truth could he convince her to leave this life behind? What did she have? A close family, yes, but not children, not a husband. She deserved more.

Tell her. Tell her who you are.

Before he could open his mouth, his cell phone rang. Annoyed at the interruption, he pulled it out intending to silence it. When he saw the number was Roseanne's home phone, he frowned. He snapped open the phone. "What's going on, Roseanne?"

"Gideon, how soon can you get back here?"

"I was thinking about staying a few more days."

"No. You have to come back now."

A pit of fear formed in his midsection. "You're scaring me, Roseanne. What's wrong?"

"It's Craig. His plane is missing. He left here five hours ago and never reached his destination. He hasn't been heard from since he took off."

Chapter Seven

Rebecca listened to Booker rattling off instructions to the person on the phone. She wasn't sure what was wrong but she heard the distress in his voice. When he ended the call, she asked, "What has happened?"

"My partner has been making flights that I was supposed to make so I could stay here. Now the plane is missing. If anything has happened to him…" His voice trailed off.

"I pray he is safe, but he is in God's hands. You must not despair."

"I've forgotten what that is like."

"I don't understand."

"Accepting that everything is God's will. I've forgotten what that's like. I have to get back to Rochester."

"The Lord is our strength and our salvation, Booker. Lean on Him, for He loves all His children. Though we may not understand His plan for us, never doubt that He has one."

"I want to thank you, Rebecca."

"For what?"

"Let's just say for helping me realize some important

truths. I wanted to say more, but to explain would take more time than I have now. I guess it wasn't meant to be. I've got to get going."

His voice was stronger today and more familiar. How was it that he seemed to grow more important to her with each passing minute? She listened to his footsteps bounding up the stairs. He would be gone as soon as he could pack and she would never spend time with him again.

"Is something wrong?" Adam asked. She hadn't heard him approach.

"Booker has to leave. His friend is in trouble."

"Is there anything we can do?"

"No, he is going home."

A car horn honked outside. Adam called out, "Emma, our driver is here."

"Coming." The rapid tapping of sturdy heels on the plank floor signaled Emma's approach. Breathlessly, she asked, "Did you tell Rebecca?"

"Tell me what?"

"The fellow who bought your quilt had donated it to help raise money for your grandfather. What a nice man he is. He reminds me of you, Adam."

"Come," Adam cut her short. "We mustn't keep the car waiting."

"All right. Goodbye, Rebecca. It was wonderful having you and your aunt here. I only wish we could have spent more time together."

"Goodbye. Have a safe trip," Rebecca called after them as they left.

Quiet filled the lobby. Rebecca listened for the sound of Booker coming down, but heard only the quiet ticking of the grandfather clock.

Would Booker think of her sometimes when he was

gone from this place? He would have nothing to remember her by. He had given her quilt away.

She would have liked to think of him wrapped up in the comfort of her creation. She was sorry he decided to part with it, but she was thankful for his kindness toward her grandfather.

The clock began to strike the hour.

What was she thinking? Booker might not have the quilt from the auction, but he could still have one of hers. She'd finished her Christmas Star quilt late last night, placing her signature in Braille with French knots in the last square as she did with all her quilts. She knew God would direct her gift where it was needed the most.

She crossed the lobby quickly and found the stairs with her cane. Tucking her stick under her arm, she hurried up the steps.

The quilt was where she had left it, folded neatly in a box beside her bed. She lifted the lid of the box and ran her hand across the folded fabric.

She tried to imagine how it must look. Her aunt told her it was made up of green, red and gold colors that formed a many-pointed star on a cream background. She tried to imagine it but her memory of colors was fading. Was the green the color of spring grass or the color of the summer woods?

It didn't matter. All that mattered was that her work brought joy or comfort to someone. To Booker. Gathering it in her arms, she started toward the door but paused with her hand on the cool metal knob.

Would he accept it? It was a valuable item in his eyes. He'd paid dearly for her previous work.

Perhaps he would think she was too forward in giving him such a gift. It was forward and unlike her.

She heard the sound of a door opening across the hall. It was now or never. Either she could let Booker walk away or she could open the door. The choice was hers. She took a deep breath and turned the handle. "Booker, is that you?"

She stood waiting for an answer. She knew he was in the hall with her. She could smell his cologne, she could hear his breathing. Why didn't he speak?

Gathering her courage, she took a step closer. "I have something for you."

"Why are you doing this?" His raspy voice held a note of pain.

"Doing what?" Hurting him was the last thing she wanted to do.

"Why are you making it so hard for me to leave?"

"I didn't realize I was."

"If only this had been another place, another time."

He stepped closer. She knew if she stretched out her hand she could touch him. She locked her fingers together beneath the quilt she held. "I don't know what you mean."

"Yes, you do. You are woman enough to know exactly what I mean. You feel it, too, this bond we have."

She did feel it, but she could never admit it. She smiled sadly. "Another time and another place would not have mattered, Booker. You come from a world I could not inhabit. I live where everyone's feet are planted firmly on the earth."

"I would stay, but my friend needs me."

"Go to him. I belong here."

"There's nothing for you here. No husband, no children, no ties that can't be broken. You could step into the world I come from. You could know freedom. I could find you the best medical care. You wouldn't have to work your fingers to the bone stitching quilts year after year."

Rebecca shook her head and clutched her quilt tightly. "There are ties you cannot see, Booker. My soul is tied to God and to my people through my faith. I could no more break those cords than I could fly."

"I could take you flying. You could see the tops of the clouds and..." His voice trailed away, as if he'd forgotten her blindness for a moment and suddenly realized how foolish his words sounded.

She took pity on him. "I have no wish to fly, Booker. That is for the birds of the air."

He sighed deeply. "I hope you're not offended by my offer."

She bowed her head hoping he would not notice the heat rushing to her cheeks. "*Nee,* I shall cherish it as the wish of one friend to aid another."

To her surprise, he slipped his fingers under her chin and raised her face. Her heart pounded so hard she thought he must hear it. If only she could see his face.

He said, "I could have been more than a friend to you...in another time and in another place."

Swallowing hard, she struggled to keep her voice steady. "I know you gave away the quilt you bought."

He took his hand away from her face. She missed the warmth and gentleness of his touch. He said, "I wish now that I hadn't. You're a very remarkable woman, Rebecca."

She struggled to maintain her composure. "It is not my goal to be remarkable. It is my goal to be a humble servant of God."

"And that is the goal of all Amish. Am I right?"

"Ja." She extended the quilt toward him. "This is

my gift to you. Please take it and remember me with kindness whenever you see it."

To her relief, he took the quilt from her. She stepped back a pace. "May God go with you, Booker, whether your feet be on the ground or skipping across the clouds above."

She turned away, found the doorknob of her room with trembling hands and entered with tears stinging her eyes. She leaned against the door and wondered if God would forgive her for wanting to go with him.

Hours later, Gideon learned Craig and the plane had been found following a crash landing. His friend was alive, but their plane wasn't in one piece. After hearing the details from Roseanne, Gideon knew exactly how lucky his friend had been.

Gideon pushed open the door of the hospital room and stepped inside. The lights had been turned down low and the shades were drawn. Craig lay with his eyes closed on the crisp white sheets. A thick bandage covered the right side of his head.

Gideon might have thought he was sleeping except that his hands were clenching into tight fists. Stepping closer, Gideon said, "I thought the idea was to keep our planes in one piece."

Craig opened his eyes. "Look what the cat dragged in."

"How you doing?"

Craig grimaced. "I've been better."

"You can have pain medication. You don't have to tough it out."

"They just gave me something. I don't like whatever it is. It makes me go to sleep and then I get these awful nightmares. How bad is the plane?"

Gideon saw no reason to sugarcoat it. "A total loss. How bad are you?"

"I'm not as pretty as I was before. I think they put twenty stitches in my forehead. My ribs are bruised. My ankle is sprained, not broken. That's the good news. They want to keep me overnight for observation. I'm sorry. This is gonna set us back."

"Don't worry about it. We have one plane left and our insurance will go a long way toward getting us a replacement for the one you ditched in the lake."

"I put her down on the shore. It if hadn't been for the boulders that jumped into my path, I would have made a fine landing."

"You were lucky to get out in one piece. Just mend and get back in the air. Unless this has put you off flying."

"Are you kidding? You think one little crash is gonna ground me for good? Not hardly. I'll be back up there before you know it."

"It wasn't a little crash, Craig."

His gaze grew pensive. "Yeah, I know. I saw the ground coming up and… I wasn't ready."

"You weren't ready for what?"

"I wasn't ready to die. In that second, man, I knew my time was up, and I hadn't done the one thing I needed to do. I didn't want to die without telling a certain person how much she means to me, how much I love her."

"I can pass that sentiment on to Roseanne if you like."

Craig laughed then grimaced as he clutched his sides. "Don't do that. Don't make me laugh. It hurts."

"Then I will tell you that Melody is outside with Roseanne. She got here a couple minutes after I did."

"She's here?" Craig's pain-filled expression lightened for an instant then darkened again.

Gideon studied Craig's face. Softly, he asked, "What happened? I thought you and Melody were doing great."

"I thought we were, too. She has a kid, Gideon."

"And you just found this out?"

"Yeah. Apparently, my reaction to the news wasn't all she hoped it would be. It got a little ugly. I said some things, she said some things. The whole argument was totally stupid."

"I'm sorry, Craig."

"Me, too. Don't get me wrong. I've thought about having kids, but I thought…someday, not right now. Then yesterday, all my somedays came real close to being never. I got a second chance. Do you know how rare that is, Gideon? God gave me a second chance to try and make things right."

Gideon did understand. God had given him a second chance to know Rebecca. She wasn't the girl he left behind. She had become a strong woman, steadfast in her faith in spite of her trials. He admired her with a newfound respect and longed to see her again, but Craig's chances of a happy reunion were much better.

Gideon said, "I know how rare second chances are. I also know that Melody would like to see you. Shall I have her come in?"

"What if I mess this up? What if she can't forgive me? What if she thinks I'll make a lousy father? Will I?"

His friend's dilemma wasn't something Gideon could answer. Having a family and kids had fallen off his radar years ago. "I think if you love each other you'll find a way to make it work."

Craig fixed his gaze on the door. "Booker, if it had

been you going down in the plane, would you have had regrets?"

Rebecca's face came back to haunt Gideon. "I would have my share."

"Was the Amish woman on television one of them?"

"It's complicated, Craig." Complicated and hopeless.

Craig put his head back and closed his eyes. "Want some advice from a guy who saw his life flash before his eyes? Don't wait until your plane is going down to think about making things right."

"I'll let Melody come in now." Gideon opened the door and stepped outside. Melody stood in the hallway with Roseanne. The fear and worry etched on her young face told Gideon everything he needed to know about her feelings for Craig.

He said, "He'd like to see you now. His pain medication is making him a little groggy. In case he falls asleep before he has a chance to tell you he was a jerk, I'm telling you now he knows he was."

A smile trembled briefly on her lips. "I can put up with a man who's a jerk once in a while as long as he's alive."

After she went in and closed the door, Gideon slipped his hands in the front pockets of his jeans and faced Roseanne. "It should've been me. I should've made that flight."

Roseanne shook her head. "Everything happens for a reason, Gideon. There was a reason Craig was in the plane. There was a reason you were stranded in a little town in Ohio. We just don't always get to know what those reasons are."

"With only one plane we aren't going to have much business."

"Maybe now I can get caught up on my paperwork.

Our insurance will take care of another plane. Isn't that why we pay those outlandish premiums?"

"Yes, but that will take time."

A couple came down the hall toward them and Gideon realized they were Craig's parents. There was a strong family resemblance between father and son. Funny, he had known Craig for five years and had never met his family. Such a thing would have been inconceivable in the close-knit Amish community where Gideon grew up.

Everyone knew everyone. Members took turns hosting church services in each other's homes. One family's troubles belonged to all. He had only to think about Reuben's fire to know the truth of that. The waiting room would have been filled to overflowing with concerned and prayerful parents, siblings, aunts, uncles and cousins if an Amish man had been as seriously injured as Craig had been.

If it had been Gideon in that room, would his family have come had they known? Would they be there to pray for him and to urge him to come back to God and his faith?

Craig's father, a distinguished-looking man with wings of silver at his temples, stopped beside them. Craig's mother, a dainty woman barely five feet tall, clutched her husband's arm.

Gideon extended his hand to Craig's father. "Hello, sir. I'm Gideon Troyer, Craig's partner."

Craig's mother asked, "Where is he? How badly is he hurt? We couldn't get any information."

Gideon smiled to reassure her. "He's pretty banged up. He has a mild concussion, some bruised ribs and a sprained ankle, but he's going to be fine."

Craig's father looked relieved but his mother's worried expression didn't change. "Can I see him?"

"Sure, go on in."

As the couple stepped past them and entered the room, Roseanne asked, "Should I have warned them about Melody?"

"No, Craig's a big boy."

Don't wait until your plane is going down to make things right.

Craig's words repeated in Gideon's mind, then he thought, *I knew before I left Hope Springs what I wanted to do. I reckon now is the time to do it. Craig will do okay without me. He has a good head for business. Roseanne will help him every step of the way.*

"What's the matter, Gideon? You've been different since you came back from Ohio." Roseanne was studying him intently.

"I know."

"This wasn't your fault, if that's what's troubling you."

"No, it's not Craig. He's going to be fine."

A sudden rush of excitement mushroomed in Gideon's body. Was it possible? Could he go back and make a life for himself within the Amish community? Could he humble himself before the church and admit he'd made a bad decision? Would he be forgiven and welcomed by his family after so long?

He'd gone into the outside world determined to leave his Amish past behind. Until he'd gone to Hope Springs, he didn't realize what a hole leaving his faith made inside of him. Yes, he missed Rebecca, but he missed his family, too. He missed his father's stern teachings and his mother's warm-hearted kindness. He loved them, and he'd cut himself off out of false pride.

He missed feeling at one with God and his community. Yes, he'd become a successful man, but at what cost to his soul? He could go back. He could make amends for everything he'd done. If he didn't go now, it might be too late.

It was a huge step. There would be no turning back if he took it. He had broken his vow once before. He wouldn't do it again, but was he considering this only because of Rebecca? What if she wasn't interested in sharing his life?

But what if she was?

He made up his mind and a weight lifted from his soul. He smiled at his secretary. "Roseanne, you've been a good friend as well as a good employee. When the insurance check comes in I want you to make sure Craig gets a good deal on a sound plane."

"Sure, but where will you be?"

"I'm going back to Ohio."

"For how long?"

"I'm going back for good."

Her eyes widened in disbelief. "To the Amish? Why?"

"Because I made a mistake a long time ago. I feel I've been given a chance to make that right. When Craig is up and around, I'll talk to him about buying out my half of the company. I know he can handle it. I've got to sell my car and get rid of the stuff at my apartment. You can have anything you like from the place."

"Gideon, you can't just leave us."

He leaned forward and kissed her cheek. "Keep the knucklehead in line."

"Thank you for coming in today, Rebecca." Dr. Harold White pulled his chair closer to her.

"I was surprised to get your message." Rebecca, perched on an exam table in the Hope Springs medical clinic, couldn't help wondering why she was here.

"I received a surprising call from my grandson yesterday evening."

Dr. Philip White was completing his internship in genetic studies at the University of Cleveland. It had been Philip who mentioned Rebecca's case to a visiting eye surgeon at the clinic. He had been instrumental in convincing the surgeon, Dr. Tuva Eriksson, to see Rebecca.

She said, "I hope Dr. Philip is well?"

"He's fine. The reason he called has to do with you. It seems Dr. Eriksson's clinic in New York has received a substantial donation of money toward your upcoming surgery. In fact, your procedure is now tentatively scheduled for the week before Christmas."

"My surgery has been approved?" Rebecca couldn't believe what she was hearing.

"Yes."

Joy followed by abject terror poured through her body. "It's all paid for?"

"The donation, along with the money that has been raised here, will cover the cost of your surgery and hospital stay. Dr. Eriksson has offered to waive her fee. You are all set."

"Who has done this? Who sent them so much money?"

"Someone who wished to remain anonymous."

"I don't know what to say." Her head was in a whirl.

"That's why you're here today. Are you ready to start the preparations and treatment we talked about?"

"Am I ready to begin chemotherapy?" Dr. White had already explained the powerful drugs were needed to decrease the inflammation the disease produced inside her eyes. Like a cancer, her cells had gone haywire making her blind.

"Dr. Eriksson feels unless we begin soon, we won't be able to reduce the inflammation in your eyes enough to have the surgery. A lot hinges on your response to these two drugs. I must tell you, I'm no expert on this type of thing."

"I understand. Dr. Eriksson explained there is no assurance of success. It is an experimental surgery and has only been tried a few times before."

The doctor took her hand. "There is less than a fifty percent chance that this will work, Rebecca. I don't know how to tell you not to get your hopes up."

She managed a lopsided grin. "Are you telling me that this surgery could leave me blind? Doctor, I'm already blind."

"I know you're trying to make light of the situation, but the truth is, this procedure could prevent any hope of a cure in the future. New research on uveitis could uncover a better procedure or better medication in the near future. Research is ongoing in the field."

"I pray a cure is discovered, for I am not the only person with this disease. When do we start?"

"Today. I'm going to read you this consent. You must sign it before we can start the medications. I want you to stop me if you have any questions. I'm going to have your aunt step in now, if that's all right? She should hear this, too."

With her aunt at her side, Rebecca listened as the doctor described the side effects she was likely to have on the chemotherapy. Although the dosages of the drugs were much smaller than when they were used to treat cancer, she might still be affected with nausea, vomiting, headaches, body aches and more. The list went on and on. He made it clear she might endure all the side effects and still not be able to have her surgery.

Was it worth it? She was accustomed to being in the dark. For a moment she was tempted to back out, to return to her aunt's home and live there quietly until the end of her days. Then she recalled Booker's voice as he talked about looking down from the clouds. She would never look down from the clouds, but she would give anything to look up and see them in the sky overhead once more.

After the doctor finished, Rebecca signed her name where he indicated and tried to still her racing heart. It was finally going to happen thanks to an anonymous donor. In her heart, she knew the money had come from Booker. She would be forever in his debt.

That afternoon and forty miles away, Gideon sat in the front seat of Roseanne's car as she turned onto a farm lane outside Berlin, Ohio. His hands grew cold as ice as his heart pounded like a runaway train. He was here. This was the exact place where his Amish life had ended. It seemed fitting that this was where his English life would end, as well.

He said, "Stop here."

Roseanne shot him a funny look. "Don't you want me to drive up to the house?"

"No. I want to walk."

"It's freezing outside."

"I'll be fine."

She stopped the car and put it in Park. "Are you sure about this, Gideon?"

He knew she wasn't asking about his hike up the lane. Laying a hand on her shoulder, he said, "I'll be fine, Roseanne. This is what I want."

She sniffed and wiped her eyes. "If you ever need anything, *anything,* you just give me a shout."

Leaning over, he kissed her cheek. "I never would've made it without you. Craig is going to need all the help he can get. Don't let him do anything I wouldn't do."

"Melody and I'll take good care of him."

"I know you will." Tears stung the back of his eyes, but he blinked them away. Pushing open the door, he stepped out. From the backseat of the car he pulled a small satchel and then stepped aside. Roseanne backed the car onto the main road. She waved once then drove back the way they had come.

Gideon faced the lane leading toward a large, rambling white house. Smoke rose from two of the home's three chimneys. Over the years, his family had added on to the original home with a second smaller house for his mother's parents.

The addition of a *Dawdi Haus,* or grandfather house, was a common practice among the Amish. Grandparents and elderly relatives were able to maintain their own households when they retired and yet were surrounded and included by their extended families. It was a good way to grow old.

A large well-tended barn and outbuildings stood a few dozen yards back from house. There were horses in the corral and cattle in the pasture. This was the home Gideon hadn't seen in ten years. From this spot nothing much had changed. Only everything had changed. He had changed.

Hefting his bag, he started walking up the road. The

cold wind slipped under the collar of his coat, making him hunch his shoulders to block the breeze. The snow on the ground crunched beneath his feet, making him think of his walk with Rebecca through the snow-covered streets of Hope Springs.

She wasn't the only reason he'd come back. Rebecca had merely been the needle on the compass pointing him to his way home. He hadn't realized how lost he truly was until he saw her again. Perhaps someday he would tell her she had been the instrument of his return.

In Gideon's mind, Booker no longer existed. His life in the English world was at an end. It was Booker who soared above the clouds and looked down on the backs of birds flying beneath him. It was plain Gideon Troyer walking this rural road with his feet planted firmly on the good earth God had made.

Even as Gideon faced the fact that he would never fly again, he wondered if he could do it. Could he gaze at the sky and not long to be up there? Giving up flying hurt as much as giving up an arm or a leg.

It wouldn't be easy to come back, but it was the right thing to do.

Plain Gideon had many tasks before him. The first was to gain his family's forgiveness. Facing his father and mother was shaping up to be a difficult thing as he approached the farmhouse. His heart started hammering. His palms grew sweaty. Admitting his mistake, making amends for the way he'd left, he had a lot to atone for. He prayed God would grant him the courage he needed this day.

When plain Gideon took his rightful place among the faithful, only then would he be free to discover if

Rebecca Beachy still cared for him. If she did not, he would accept that it was God's will.

Please, Lord, give me the wisdom to convince her we belong together.

He arrived at the front door of his childhood home with a growing sense that he had finally made the right decision. This was where he was meant to be.

When the front door opened and his father walked out, Gideon's courage failed him. He couldn't speak.

His father's eyes widened in shock. "Gideon?"

Abraham Troyer had aged in the ten years that had passed. He seemed frail now. His shoulders bowed forward, as if the weight of his life was hard to carry. How much of the gray hair, how many of the worry lines on his face were due to Gideon's selfishness?

His father took a step toward. It broke the spell holding Gideon rooted to the spot. Dropping to one knee, Gideon bowed his head, closed his eyes and spoke the words that burned in his heart. "Father, forgive me, for I have sinned."

He heard a muffled gasp, but he was afraid to look up. What if too much time had passed? What if merely asking for forgiveness wasn't enough? What could he do to convince his father that he was sincere?

Suddenly, he felt his father's hands drawing him to his feet. He opened his eyes and met his father's gaze. Tears rolled down his father's lean, leathery cheeks.

In a voice that shook, Abraham Troyer said, "*Mie, sohn,* you were forgiven the very day that you left. There is only rejoicing now that you have returned. *Gott* has answered my prayers. Praise be to Him."

Chapter Eight

Rebecca sat at her quilting frame stitching while Vera read to her from her siblings' letter that had arrived in the mail that morning. Each one of Rebecca's brothers and sisters added their pages to the letter and sent it on to the next in line so everyone could stay caught up on the family news. Rebecca, with Vera's help, would add her updates and send it on to her oldest sister to start the process all over again. Everyone except Grace. There were never any letters from her.

"Your brother William says his family is traveling to see your brother Leroy in Indiana after Christmas. He wants to know if you'd like to go along."

It had been four weeks since the auction and two weeks since Dr. White had started Rebecca on chemotherapy. Her surgery, scheduled for December twenty-first, was only three weeks away. By Christmas Eve she would know if her sight had been restored or not. Either way, it would be good to visit her brother. They hadn't seen each other for over a year.

"I look forward to going."

"Do you mean that?"

Vera's astonishment didn't surprise Rebecca. Vera knew Rebecca didn't like to travel. While her parents and siblings went often went to visit each other for extended stays, especially over Christmas, Rebecca rarely went along. She didn't like finding her way in new places.

"William says they'll leave the day after old Christmas."

Old Christmas was the Feast of the Epiphany, January sixth. "I will see if Samson Carter can drive me to William's home on that day. If he can't, I'll try to find another driver."

"I heard there is a new woman in town who drives Amish folks. Her name is Miriam Kauffman. She might be able to give you a ride if Samson is booked," Vera suggested.

"I will keep her name in mind. I can't believe how quickly Christmas is coming. We need to start baking. What else does William say?"

"He says the community is in turmoil because Gideon Troyer has come home."

Rebecca stabbed her finger with a needle. "Ouch!"

Her aunt asked, "What's wrong?"

Sucking her finger to ease the sting, Rebecca used the moment to cover her shock. When she had her turbulent emotions under control, she said, "Gideon Troyer has come back? To stay?"

"That's what William says."

"Gideon's family must be overjoyed."

"I daresay they are, especially his mother. Imagine, returning to our faith after ten years in the outside world. It cannot be an easy thing. I wonder what brought him back."

Rebecca wondered the same thing. "Why is the community in turmoil?"

"According to your brother, there are some that don't believe he has truly repented."

"One of those would be Bishop Stoltzfus, I reckon." The bishop from her old community was distrustful of outsiders and ruled his flock with an iron hand, as she knew from unhappy personal experience.

"Weren't you sweet on the boy at one time?" her aunt asked.

Rebecca bent over her sewing again. "That was years ago."

"I remember your mother telling me the two of you were quite serious. That you might even marry."

"She was mistaken," Rebecca mumbled.

Gideon had come home. After all this time, it was hard to believe. What was he like now? Was he as handsome as she remembered? Was he still a bold, outspoken fellow who never took anything at face value? Unless he had changed a lot he would have a hard time reentering the Amish world.

In their youth, Gideon had often talked about leaving and about learning to fly. But after they were both baptized on the same September morning, she believed he had given up his outlandish plans.

If she had accepted his offer, would he have stayed among the faithful? For years she blamed herself for his leaving. Knowing how his parents suffered only made her feel worse.

"Then it was God's blessing that you didn't marry the boy. I wonder if he'll stay this time. I reckon all we can do is pray for him."

Gideon had been in Rebecca's prayers since the day

of his departure. Why had he returned? "What else does my brother say?"

"Will says his boy David has come down with the mumps."

"He doesn't say anything else about Gideon?" Rebecca heard the rustle of paper as her aunt turned the page.

"No, he doesn't mention him again."

Rebecca had a hard time sorting out her feelings. Gideon had come back. On one hand she was happy for him and for his family, but on the other hand she worried for them. What if he couldn't adjust to living Amish after so many years away?

Vera finished the letter but Rebecca barely heard a word. When she went home to visit her family it was possible she might run into Gideon. What would she say? Did she want to meet him again?

A flutter of nervousness caused her hand to shake as she tried to set her next stitch. Why were men always at the center of her distress? First it had been Gideon all those years ago, then Booker, and now Gideon again.

The sound of a horse and buggy pulling up outside caused Rebecca to set her stitching aside. "Are we expecting someone?"

"When Emma came by the other day, I asked if her husband could look at our washing machine. It's been making that funny noise again."

Adam Troyer was a handyman in the village as well as owner of the Wadler Inn with his wife. His prices were reasonable, and there were very few things he couldn't fix.

Rebecca asked, "Should I put on some *kaffi?*"

"That would be just the thing on such a cold day. Put

out the peanut-butter cookies we made yesterday, too. I know for a fact that Adam likes them."

Rising from her chair, Rebecca made her way into the kitchen. At the sink, she filled their coffeepot with water until it touched her finger inside the rim. She opened the cupboard and pulled out the coffee can. After carefully filling the percolator basket with grounds, she carried the pot to the stove and put it on the back burner. After that, she opened a second cupboard and withdrew a plate.

The sound of the front door opening and a blast of cold air announced Adam's arrival. She said, "*Wilkumm,* have a seat, Adam, and the *kaffi* will be ready in no time. Do you take it black or with cream? I can't remember. *Aenti* Vera tells me you like peanut-butter cookies. You're in luck. I made some yesterday."

"*Danki,* Rebecca."

She moved along the counter, located the cookie jar and began piling cookies on the plate. She heard Adam clear his throat.

"I brought a helper today."

"Did you?" She added another handful of cookies and turned around.

Adam said, "You remember my cousin Gideon, don't you?"

"Hello, Rebecca."

The deep-timbered voice robbed her of coherent thought and made her knees go weak. The plate slipped from her numb fingers and crashed to the floor.

The stricken look on Rebecca's face cut Gideon to the quick. He knew this wouldn't be easy, but he wasn't expecting her to cringe at the sound of his voice.

She muttered, "I'm so sorry. That was careless of me."

Vera rushed to help her. "Don't worry, dear, it was an old dish, and I'm sure we have more cookies. Let me get it. I don't want you to cut your hands on the broken glass. Stay where you are and I'll get a broom."

Adam grabbed Gideon's sleeve. "Let's take a look at that washing machine. We may not deserve cookies if we can't get it fixed."

Gideon hated to leave Rebecca standing in the kitchen looking mortified, but Adam gave him no choice. He led the way to a small back porch where an ancient wringer washer stood on rusting legs.

Looking from the wreck to his cousin, Gideon asked, "Are you sure you can fix this thing? It looks older than the hills."

Adam chuckled. "They made things to last back in the day."

"By back in the day I take it you mean 1925?"

"You've got a thing or two to learn if you're going to work with me. This is a Maytag model E2L from 1969. It's one of the best wringer washers ever made."

Adam turned on the water and began filling the machine. Gideon blew on his bare hands. Even with the afternoon sun streaming in through the windows the room was frigid. "This is a cold place to do laundry. Why don't they put the thing inside?"

"It was good enough for our mothers and grandmothers. We see no need to move the chore indoors."

"Is that your way of telling me I'm soft, cousin?"

"That's my way of reminding you that you must be careful how you speak."

Gideon adjusted the flat-topped black hat he wasn't yet accustomed to wearing. "How long did it take you?"

"To stop reaching for the nonexistent light switch every time I went into a dark room? About six months. I try to remind myself that it's not about electricity or cars or using buggies to get around. It's about living apart from a world that is filled with temptation and evil. Living a Plain life makes it easier to keep my mind on God and on His will. Not just every single day, but every hour of every single day."

"Not all of the outside world is evil."

"*Nee,* there is much *goot* in the hearts of men everywhere, but here, I find it is easier to be close to God."

"Do you ever regret coming back?"

"Every man faces temptations, Gideon. But when I see my wife's face each morning, I know this is where God wants me to be. If it is His will, I'll raise my children here and pray that they find the strength to stay among the people."

"I wish I had the strength of conviction you have."

"If you seek it with your whole heart it will be given to you."

When the washer tub was half full Adam turned off the water and turned on the machine. Instantly, they heard the strange noise Vera had reported.

Adam crossed his arms over his chest. "What are you thinking?"

"If this was a plane I wouldn't even taxi down the runway in it. The gears are slipping."

"I agree. Let's drain her, tip her over and get this motor apart."

Gideon flipped the switch that began to pump the water out a hose that drained to the backyard.

"When do you plan to tell her?" Adam asked as he unscrewed the cover.

"Tell who what?"

Adam shot Gideon a stern look. "When do you plan to tell Rebecca that you are Booker?"

Gideon couldn't meet his cousin's gaze. "Booker doesn't exist anymore."

"I doubt that will be the way Rebecca sees it. She believes Booker is responsible for making her surgery possible. Hand me that crescent wrench."

"It was one of the few good things he did with his life." Gideon laid the tool in Adam's outstretched hand.

Adam pointed to the wrench at Gideon's face. "You have no idea how grateful Rebecca and our entire community is for your gift."

"And that is exactly why I don't wish anyone to know it was me. I don't want the community's gratitude. I don't want Rebecca's gratitude. Can you understand that?" Gideon glanced toward the back door. This wasn't about money or status or acceptance. This was about helping Rebecca.

Adam shook his head. "I thought the point of you moving to Hope Springs was to pick up where you left off with Rebecca."

"The point of my coming here was to pick up where Gideon left off with Rebecca, not where Booker and Rebecca left off."

"I still think you're wrong. Secrets will come out."

"Hopefully, by the time that happens people will have formed their own opinions about me. I think they will understand that I didn't want to use my generosity to gain favor and I believe they will respect that."

"You mean you hope Rebecca will respect that."

"I'm not a fool, Adam. There's no guarantee that Rebecca will return my affections. I came back to my

Amish heritage because I believe this is the life God wishes me to live. You, of all people, must understand that?"

"I do, for that is why I gave up the English world and returned to my family and my faith. I pray God will bless your decision. Ah, I believe I see what's wrong with this washer. Hand me my half-inch socket drive."

"Adam, have I thanked you for giving me a job and a place to stay?"

"About a hundred times. Let's see if I made the right decision. Hand me the crosshead screwdriver."

Twenty minutes later, Adam and Gideon were elbow-deep in motor parts when the back door opened. Vera stood there with her head cocked to the side. "Have you found the trouble?"

Rebecca came up behind Vera. "What's the verdict?"

Adam rose to his feet and held out a gear. "Your washer has a broken tooth, Vera. It's not something we can fix today. I'm going to have to take this piece to the shop and see if I can find a replacement for it. If I can't, perhaps Eli Imhoff can make a new one."

"Who is Eli?" Gideon asked. He forced himself to stay calm. So far Vera hadn't recognized him, but she could put two and two together at any minute. During the auction he'd been wearing his sunglasses and knit cap, but the night of the fire she would have seen his face clearly when she came to his room. That night he'd been hollow-eyed with several days' growth of beard on his cheeks and shaggy hair. He was clean-shaven now, and his mother had cut his hair in the traditional Amish style. Was there enough of a difference?

"Eli Imhoff is the local blacksmith," Adam replied.

Vera took the part from Adam's hand. "I've seen a

gear like this hanging in the barn. There are dozens of similar pieces out there. My *Onkel* Atlee, God rest his soul, never threw anything away."

Adam smiled at her. "If you have one that would be great. I could get your machine together today."

"Let me get my coat, and I will show you where he kept his things." Vera turned and went inside with Adam following close behind her. Gideon relaxed. It seemed Vera hadn't paid much attention to Booker during his time at the inn.

After Vera and Adam left, Gideon found himself alone with Rebecca. This was exactly where he had hoped to be. So why was he suddenly tongue-tied?

He gathered his courage. "Could we wait inside where it's warm?"

"Of course." Rebecca held the door open wider in invitation.

"Thanks. I mean, *danki*."

"Your Pennsylvania Dutch is rusty." She went ahead of him down the hall keeping one hand lightly in contact with the wall.

"I'm sure it will come back to me." Did she recognize his voice now that his illness had healed? Did she suspect he was the man she knew as Booker? He longed to tell her, but he wasn't Booker anymore. He'd left that life behind. He wanted her to know the man he was intent on becoming.

When they reached the kitchen she moved to the far side of the table and faced him. "Are you ready for coffee and cookies now?"

"Have you picked all the glass shards out of them?"

"All that I could see." A smile twitched at the corner of her mouth.

"Blind humor. Are you trying to put me at ease?"

"Why would you be ill at ease?"

Because I left you. Because I spent ten years excommunicated from the church and nobody believes I intend to stay now.

Instead of baring his soul, he took a seat at the table. "I have not spent much time with the sight-impaired. Feel free to correct me if I say something stupid."

She pulled a pair of mugs from the cabinet beside the sink and carried them to the stove. He watched her fill them just to the brim and wondered how she managed a task he couldn't do with his eyes closed.

Finally, his curiosity won out. "How can you do that without spilling any?"

She stiffened. "Practice."

"This is where you tell me that was a stupid question."

"Your question is not stupid. I've had years to learn how to do almost everything a sighted person can do. I simply do things differently."

"I'm impressed by your skills."

She carried the mugs to the table. "My skill at dropping plates?"

"Something tells me you don't do that often. I'm sorry if my unannounced arrival was a shock."

"I learned of your return to Berlin in a letter that arrived from my brother this morning, but I didn't expect you to show up in my kitchen a few minutes later."

"Did your brother pass on the juicy details of my trouble with Bishop Stoltzfus?" It was hard to keep that bitterness out of his voice. It had taken more courage than he thought he possessed to beg forgiveness from his bishop. When the man announced he didn't believe

Gideon was sincere, it caused quite a stir and a division in the church.

"William didn't mention any details. Your family must have been overjoyed when you came back."

He nodded his head and then realized she couldn't see that. "My mother kept hugging me. She cried all day. When I told her to stop being sad, she said they were tears of joy and could not be stemmed."

"I'm sure she meant it."

"My youngest brother wasn't quite so demonstrative."

"He wasn't happy at your return?"

"Let's just say Joseph has reservations about whether or not I will stay." Along with the bishop and half of his family's congregation.

She rolled her cup between her palms. "I'm sorry, but can you blame him?"

"Not really." It was hard to read her expression. Did she doubt his resolve in returning, too? How could she not? *He* wasn't sure if he could stay.

Propping her elbows on the table, she said, "Time will give him the answer. Is that why you aren't staying with them?"

"My mother thought it best if I spend some time with Adam, being as he spent a long time in the English world and came back to stay."

She folded her arms across her chest. She had yet to take a sip of her coffee. It was clear she was struggling to be cordial.

He said, "I know it was a shock to you when I left the way I did."

"You were never content with our slow Amish ways. I remember you as a wild, defiant boy."

"And I remember you as a sweet-natured girl who forgave all my indiscretions. We had some fine times together during our rumspringa."

Her face grew pale. She folded her arms tightly across her chest. "*Ja,* fine times."

"I was sorry to learn about your affliction. Adam told me the community has raised enough money for you to have surgery."

"I don't think of it as an affliction. It's just the way my life is. The surgery's chances of success are only fifty-fifty. I'm trying not to get my hopes up. I am happy here with my *aenti.* I have nieces and nephews who come to visit, so I am not lonely. I still have my quilting, and I enjoy that immensely."

"That's good."

She finally took a sip of her coffee and he took a drink of his. The silence stretched out between them.

"I hope Adam can fix our washer. I know Vera doesn't want to have to buy a new one."

"I hear he's a pretty good handyman."

"*Ja,* people say so." She nervously raised the cup to her lips again.

This small talk wasn't what he wanted. He wanted to start over with her. Earn her trust. Win her love. And he had absolutely no idea how to do that.

Rebecca wasn't sure how much longer she could sit and pretend that Gideon Troyer was a normal visitor. Her heart was hammering. Her hands were shaking. She wanted him to leave. Even though she was the one who turned down his offer of marriage, she never gave up loving him. When he left it was as if he took a piece of her heart with him.

Now that scar on her heart was open and bleeding again.

She rose from her chair, knocking against the table in her haste. She heard the cups rattle but she didn't care if they spilled. "Vera and Adam have been gone a long time. Perhaps you should see if you can help."

"Rebecca, can you forgive me?"

She had sent him away. When the darkness descended over her life it wasn't his fault he wasn't there to hold her and comfort her. And yet it was his fault. If his faith had been strong, he would have been there for her.

She spoke the words her Amish teaching required her to say. "Of course I forgive you. I forgave you a long time ago."

"Thank you, Rebecca. It means the world to me."

The sound of the outside door opening saved her from having to reply. When Vera and Adam returned, Rebecca excused herself and rushed up the stairs to her bedroom.

She closed the door and leaned against it. Angry tears stung her eyes. Wiping at them with fierce swipes, she vowed they would be the last tears she shed over Gideon Troyer.

Up until a month ago, her life had a simple rhythm. Gardening in the spring and summer, canning in the fall and quilting over the long winter days. It didn't matter that she couldn't see the fresh greenness of the spring. She could smell it in the air and feel the warmth of the sun on her face. It didn't matter that she couldn't watch the snow fall. She knew when it fell by the silence that blanketed the land. It was enough for her to work and feel the seasons passing by, for they defined her life.

Then, a few short weeks ago, she met a man who touched her soul the way only one man had before. That he was forbidden to her was as painful as holding someone else's child and knowing she would never hold her own babe. The day she gave him her quilt was the first time in her life she questioned her decision to stay among the Amish.

The morning after he left, she woke knowing he had been the test—and she passed. If she never regained her vision, her faith was strong enough to sustain that disappointment. Contentment had entered her soul.

Now Gideon was back and her heart was being torn once more. All her old feelings for him came rushing back to life at the sound of his voice.

Why now? Why, after so many years of darkness and bitterness overcome, was she being tested again?

"Haven't I suffered enough, Lord? Haven't I paid long enough for my sin?"

Chapter Nine

Gideon arrived at Rebecca's home the following afternoon with the needed part in his pocket. In spite of all the parts in Vera's barn, Adam couldn't find the right one. Yesterday hadn't gone as well as Gideon hoped. Instead of being thrilled to see him, Rebecca had looked terrified. Hopefully, once the shock of his arrival wore off she would remember how close they had been.

As he climbed out of Adam's buggy, he noticed the sounds of several wind chimes around the property. He'd been too nervous to notice them yesterday. He wondered if it was Vera or Rebecca who enjoyed the musical notes.

To his relief, Rebecca answered the door when he knocked. He'd been half afraid she would be hiding in her room or gone. "Good afternoon, Rebecca. It's Gideon. I have come to finish the work on your washing machine."

"I've been expecting you. My aunt will be back shortly. She took a kettle of soup to a neighbor who has been ill." She stepped back to let him enter.

He stomped his feet to rid his boots of the clinging

snow and entered the kitchen with his toolbox in hand. The smell of cooking apples filled the air.

She said, "I'm sure you remember where the washer is. I will let you find your own way." Her nonchalant tone took him aback. She went to the stove, picked up a ladle and began stirring the contents of a large pan.

Again, not the reaction he had hoped for. He said, "Something sure smells good."

"Pie filling."

When she didn't elaborate he searched his mind for something to breech the growing chasm he sensed between them. "As I recall, you were a pretty good cook."

She laid the ladle down. "I don't recollect that you were interested in my housewifely skills."

"True. I was more about finding ways to sneak a kiss from you than trying out your cooking." He waited for her response.

Turning around, she crossed her arms over her chest. "*Ja,* that is the way I remember you—as a shallow fellow often up to no good."

Definitely not the reaction he was hoping for. "That about sums up my misspent youth. Fortunately, I grew up."

"Better late than never." She turned back to the stove, but he noticed her hand wasn't quite steady as she put the lid on the kettle.

Accepting his dismissal with a heavy heart, Gideon went out to the rear porch and began reassembling her washing machine. He took his time, making sure the new piece fit perfectly, then he fired up the gas motor and began filling the machine.

When it looked as if everything was going to work, he stuck his head inside the back door. "Rebecca, do you have some clothes to be washed? I want to run a cycle and make sure the drum empties as it should and I don't want to waste all the water."

She came to the hallway, but didn't come toward him. "I have baking to do. The laundry can wait."

"I know it can, but why should it? Let me get one load out of your way."

"Laundry is woman's work."

"Unless a man is unmarried, then he must learn to do his own."

She hesitated, but finally nodded once. "We have several loads, but they aren't sorted."

"I promise not to mix whites and colors."

"I doubt you used a wringer washer where you lived before."

"No, but I remember helping my mother with her laundry chores. I think I can manage."

"Very well. I will get the hamper."

She entered a room partway down the hall and came out a few seconds later with a tall, woven wood clothes basket. "My aunt will be grateful to have her work cut in half before wash day. Don't add too much soap."

"No problem." He took the burden from her and returned to the machine. She stood for a moment as if she wanted to say something more, but in the end, she went inside without another comment.

He found the laundry detergent inside a cabinet hanging on the wall. After adding the recommended amount to the tub, he followed with a dozen dresses and aprons in assorted colors of blue. The old washer chugged along without missing a beat. Glancing up, he happened to notice a reflection in the porch window. Rebecca stood just inside the door listening to him.

He started to hum while he worked, a German hymn, a song he knew Rebecca liked when they were young. She had a sweet voice and often led the girls during the youth singings they had attended. Memories of the tame gatherings he'd found boring as a teenager now ranked among the highlights of his time with Rebecca.

When the wash cycle was done, he fed the clothes through the wringer and into the rinse tub. After letting them soak a few minutes, he stirred them with a wooden stick he found propped in the corner, and then fed them back through the wringer again. He piled the wet clothes on a Formica-topped table beside the back door.

He stopped humming and said as if to himself, "If I were Vera's clothespins, where would I be hiding?" He started opening cabinets.

After a second, Rebecca stepped through the doorway. Her expression had softened. "They are out on the clothesline post in a clothespin bag."

"I would have found them." He tried to sound defensive, but he was smiling.

"Maybe you would. Maybe not."

He didn't want to break the thin thread of friendliness he saw forming between them. "The machine seems to be working fine. Eli Imhoff made a perfect replacement for the gear."

"You must thank him for us."

"I will. I'll see him at church services on Sunday." He hoped his statement made it clear he was returning to his Amish faith, not just paying it lip service.

He walked out the porch door to the clothesline reel hanging off the side of the house. Over the doorway, he noticed another small set of brass wind chimes clinking in the breeze. After pulling the retractable line from the side of the house, he stretched it to a T-post in the center of the yard and fastened it.

Setting the basket of clothes carefully in the snow, he began to hang them up, humming again as he did. This time he chose an English hymn with a familiar tune although he couldn't recall the exact words of the song.

He had five dresses pinned to the line before she ventured out the door. She stopped a few feet away from him with her arms crossed against the cold. "'Amazing Grace' has always been one of my favorites."

"I'm a bit rusty on the words. How does it go?"

She sang the opening lines. "'Amazing Grace, how sweet the sound, that saved a wretch like me. I once was lost but now am found, was blind, but now I see.'"

He could have kicked himself. He stammered, "I didn't mean to… That was thoughtless of me. Forgive me."

She arched one eyebrow. "Gideon, I don't need the lyrics of a song to remind me that I'm blind."

"No, I guess not." From friend to fool in three seconds flat. Maybe he didn't deserve to win her heart.

He might be able to accept that if he didn't care for her so deeply.

"It's still one of my favorite hymns," she insisted.

He relaxed when he realized she wasn't upset. "You should go back in the house before you catch your death. You don't even have a coat on."

"Don't forget to empty the water from the washer tub. I don't want to find a giant ice cube in it the next time I need to use it."

"I'll take care of it. Don't worry," he assured her.

She cocked her head to the side slightly, as if listening, then she turned around and headed straight toward the back door. He realized the wind chimes were a means to help her find her way.

She opened the porch door, but paused. "You weren't shallow and always up to no good when we were young. I shouldn't have said that."

Before he could reply, she went inside. Gideon watched her disappear into the house and seeds of happiness sprouted in his heart. Things might be looking up for him, after all.

Inside the house, Rebecca moved her pie filling off the stove and set it to cooling on the counter. Nervous butterflies churned in her stomach. She felt like a teenager waiting to sneak out of her first date. Gideon Troyer was back.

She had spent a sleepless night building up her defenses against the charm he possessed. A lot of good it had done.

Hearing him stutter an apology for reminding her that she was blind made her remember the little boy she used to know. The boy who had gotten in trouble in the third grade for cutting the ribbons off her *kapp.* The boy who dared her to ride standing up on the back of her papa's plow horse and bore the brunt of her father's displeasure when she fell off and sprained her ankle.

Gideon had charmed her from the age of eight. Why did she think it would be different now?

She heard the back door open and close and then his footsteps coming up the hallway. If he would be living in Hope Springs she would have to accustom herself to meeting him now and again. They had been friends long before they became starry-eyed teenagers in love with the idea of being in love.

"Have you anything else that needs fixing?" he asked.

Could he fix an old broken heart? Where would he find the parts for that?

"*Nee,* I don't believe we do. Would you like some coffee before you go?"

"I would. Will you be making one of your pies soon?" She heard the smile in his voice and smiled back.

"I'll be making apple strudel soon."

"Sounds great. What can I do to help?"

"Stay out of my way and enjoy your coffee."

"Bossy as ever, aren't you?"

She rose to his bait. "I was never bossy."

"Yes, you were."

"Do you want strudel or not?" she demanded with mock severity.

"You've always had a wonderful personality, a giving nature, a sweet temper."

"That's better."

"Was that good enough for hot strudel with maybe a touch of cream?"

She chuckled. *"Ja."*

"Wunderbaar!"

"See, it is always better to tell the truth, Gideon. The truth earns its own reward."

A warm glow of satisfaction settled in the middle of her chest. She would hold fast to their friendship. Perhaps in time, she would even learn to let go of the love that was never meant to be.

The sound of the front door opening signaled her aunt's return. Vera came into the kitchen along with a gust of cold winter wind. "I believe we are going to get more snow. Hello, Gideon. I see by the clothes on the line that my washer has been repaired. Rebecca, I told you not to worry about getting the wash done."

"It was not me. It was Gideon who did your laundry."

"I only did one load to make sure the machine was working correctly," he said.

"Perhaps I should take out a piece of the motor before every wash day and call you to come out and fix it."

"Then the price of my service call will go up sharply," he said with a chuckle.

"How is Mr. Pater?" Rebecca asked. When Vera learned their English neighbor was suffering from a bad chest cold, she started taking soup to him each day.

"He is much better today. Gideon, how is your family?" Vera asked.

"As far as I know they are all well."

Vera pulled out a chair and took a seat at the table. "What a wonderful time you must have had getting to know them and their spouses."

He said, "I still have trouble telling Levi's *kinders* apart. They all look like their father did when he was a child."

Rebecca listened with delight to his account of meeting his newest family members. She could hear the happiness beneath his words as clearly as she heard the wind chimes that hung from the rear of the house. She put her pan of strudel in the oven and set the windup timer for twenty minutes.

Gideon said, "Catch me up on your family, Rebecca. I know you said you have nieces and nephews. Which of your brothers and sisters have children of their own?"

"They all have children," Rebecca replied. A tang of regret touched her but she brushed it aside. She was happy for every one of her siblings.

"Who did Grace marry?" Gideon asked. "I remember the way she tormented my brother Levi. She liked him—she didn't like him—she liked him again. It drove him crazy."

Rebecca froze. He didn't know. No one had told him.

He must have seen her distress because he asked, "Did I say something wrong?"

She folded her arms across her middle. "Grace isn't with us anymore."

"She died? How?" he asked, shock clear in his voice.

Vera said quietly, "She isn't dead, but we no longer mention her name."

Rebecca bit her lip and remained silent. The disgrace should have been hers, not her sister's.

On Sunday, Rebecca rode in silence beside her aunt in their buggy as they traveled the ten miles to an outlying farm for the preaching service. Even with the curtains tied down and quilts on their laps it was chilly inside the buggy. The bricks they had heated to keep their feet warm on the journey were growing cool by the time they reached their destination.

During the long ride she had plenty of time to think about Gideon's visit the day before. Far from being as awkward as she imagined it would be, Gideon's company had felt comfortable.

"We must be among the last to arrive judging by the number of buggies here," Vera commented as she drew their horse to a stop.

The door opened and a young man's voice greeted them. It was one of the farmer's sons. "I will take care of your horse."

"Danki," Vera replied. "There is grain for her in the back."

Leaving the buggy, Rebecca wondered if Gideon was there before them. She wanted to ask, but she didn't. Knowing her aunt, she would soon have the details on everyone in attendance. Vera's love of gossip was well known.

"Now that is odd," Vera said with a lowered voice.

"What?" Rebecca prompted, waiting for more of an explanation.

"There is an English woman here. That must be Ada Kauffman's English daughter. I see the resemblance. She's the one I told you who offers taxi service."

Rebecca was more interested in finding out if Gideon had arrived. She knew he was staying with Adam and Emma so she asked, "Do you see Emma? I hope her pregnancy is going well."

"Yes, she is chatting with Katie Sutter, Faith Lapp and Karen Imhoff. Emma has that glow about her. Pregnancy certainly agrees with her."

"I wonder if Adam feels the same way. Do you see him?"

"*Ja,* he's looking more like a proud papa now that he has some chin hair. His cousin is with him."

"His cousin? Oh, you mean Gideon." She tried to sound barely interested, but she could feel her aunt's gaze boring into her.

"He's looking this way."

Rebecca perked up. "Is he?"

"He is indeed, and so is Daniel Hershberger. He's coming our way. The man is interested in you, mark my words."

"Gideon? That's ridiculous."

"No, silly. Daniel."

"*Guder mariye,* Rebecca." Daniel's booming voice filled the farmyard.

"*Guder mariye,* Daniel," Rebecca replied in a soft tone, hoping he would take the hint and lower his voice. It was a foolish hope.

"I thought what a beautiful day this is, but it is much brighter now that you are here."

Rebecca lowered her voice further. "You should not say such a thing."

"A modest woman is a man's true treasure." He wasn't shouting, but he might as well have been. The hum of conversations around them died away.

Rebecca pasted a smile on her face and pinched her aunt's arm. "Isn't it time we went inside?"

"If you wish. Daniel, we will see you later."

"I look forward to speaking with you and your niece again. I must go tell Reuben I'm waiting for a rematch on our checkers game."

Rebecca had endured one long, tedious evening with Daniel at her grandfather's home a week after the fire. She would avoid a repeat if it were possible. How could she have entertained the idea of marriage to the man?

As she took her place beside her aunt on the women's side of the wooden benches lined up inside the farmhouse, she wondered if Gideon had overheard Daniel's compliments to her. Although it was vain, some small part of her hoped that he had.

Gideon joined Adam and his friends in the airy barn following the three-hour-long service. Bishop Zook was a gifted preacher, clearly inspired by God to bring the Lord's words to his flock. Up at the house, the benches were being rearranged to make seating for the congregation to share a midday meal. Because the elders would eat first, the younger members amused themselves with games or visiting while they waited their turns.

Gideon stood among the men and saw a few faces from the night of the fire around him. He wondered if any of them recognized him from his time in Hope Springs as Booker. If they did, no one mentioned it. Perhaps they were willing to accept him for who he was now and not for who he'd been. He prayed it was so.

"How are you adjusting to Amish life again?" Jonathan Dressler asked. Beside him, fifteen-year-old Jacob Imhoff was trying to look as if he belonged in this group of men twice his age.

Gideon folded his arms over his chest. "I will admit it's tough sometimes. How are you doing? English to Amish, that's a rare move. Not many can accept our ways. At least I knew what I was getting into when I came back."

"I miss my computer," Jonathan answered with a grin.

"I think I miss having my pickup the most," Adam said, a tinge of wistfulness in his voice.

"Is it true you were a pilot?" Jacob focused his awe-filled gaze on Gideon. "I can't believe you don't miss flying."

"I do, but I try not to dwell on it." That didn't always work. He missed the freedom of the air, but he was striving to find contentment on the ground.

"What he needs is an Amish wife to take his mind off his English ways," Adam suggested with a chuckle. "It worked for me."

Jonathan nudged Gideon and tipped his head toward

the young women grouped together across the way. "See one you like?"

Gideon accepted their good-natured ribbing and pretended to look over the women. "Jacob, your sister is single, isn't she?"

"*Nee,* she will soon be taken." Jonathan's sharp reply set Adam, Gideon and Jacob to laughing.

Adam stroked his beard. "The bishop's oldest daughter is of age."

The men looked toward the bishop's hawk-faced wife, then looked at each other. They all shook their heads. "Not a chance," Gideon said.

His new friends continued to suggest possible mates, but no one brought up Rebecca's name. Finally, he couldn't keep silent any longer. "Rebecca Beachy is still single. She's not a youngster, but she's not too old. We're the same age."

Jacob frowned. "She's pretty enough, but she is blind."

"That doesn't mean she can't be a wife and mother. Adam, do you know what became of her sister Grace?"

Adam shrugged. "She left the Amish, that's all I know."

"Rebecca said her family doesn't speak of her anymore. I wondered why." It was the change in Rebecca's expression at the mention of her sister that had piqued his interest. He'd never seen such sadness on her face.

Eli Imhoff joined their group. "Gideon, how did my washer part work out?"

"It fit like a glove," Gideon assured him.

Jacob spoke up. "Papa, we were trying to find a woman for Gideon. Any suggestions?"

"Find a woman who can cook," Eli stated firmly. "Looks fade, cooking doesn't."

"Rebecca is a good cook." Gideon was happy to list her accomplishments. He didn't like that she had been overlooked in her own community.

"There are plenty of healthy women to choose from around here. A man needs a strong wife to stand by his side," Jacob insisted with all the assurance of a teenager who had yet to go on his first date.

Gideon glanced toward the house and saw Rebecca come out with her aunt. He said, "What a man needs most is a woman who loves him."

The problem he faced was how to convince Rebecca that they were meant for each other. When he looked her way again, he saw her grandfather standing at her side. Reuben was staring straight at Gideon.

Chapter Ten

"Emma, Gideon is desperately in need of your help."

Gideon caught Adam's cheeky grin and wanted nothing more than to stuff a sock in his cousin's big mouth. Muttering under his breath, Gideon said, "See if I confide in you again."

The two men were stacking chairs on tables in the café in preparation for cleaning the floors after closing. Outside the windows, the street of the town blinked with Christmas cheer as the townspeople and businessmen turned on their holiday lights.

"What help can I give, Gideon?" Emma asked. She was sweeping beneath the tables and booths.

"Never mind," he said quickly.

"My cousin wants to court a woman and he has forgotten how we Amish do it." Adam chuckled with glee as he ducked Gideon's halfhearted punch.

"Adam, stop teasing Gideon." Her stern tone made both men look in her direction. She leveled a no-nonsense glare at her spouse.

Adam wasn't the least bit intimidated. He grinned at her and said, "I'll go fill the sugar dispensers."

He took the tray of glass containers and carried them into the kitchen. When he was out of sight, Emma turned to Gideon. "Pay no attention to your cousin. He loves to tease. Who is this special woman?"

"I'd rather not say. Courting was much easier when I was young."

"You are not so very old."

"Maybe not, but I'm too old to attend the singings and such. I can't ask her to a movie. I'm at a loss."

"There are many ways for you to get together. You can take her to visit her family. You can take her on a buggy or sleigh ride, just the two of you some evening. You can bring her here for a meal. Every woman likes a break from cooking."

"I've already thought of those things, but I'm not sure they set the right tone."

Emma tilted her head to the side. "Isn't showing her you want to spend time together the right tone?"

"The thing is, I'm afraid she'll say no if I come straight out and ask her to dinner or to go for a sleigh ride. I want her to get to know me better, but in a friendly way. I want her to feel comfortable in my company."

"You are new to our church. Well, perhaps we could get up an ice-skating party and make sure she is invited."

"I'm pretty sure she won't skate."

Emma laid her broom aside and planted her hands on her hips. "I could make more useful suggestions if I knew who I was talking about."

Gideon knew Emma and Rebecca were friends. He took a second to wonder what Emma would think about him courting her friend. After all, how could Emma be certain he would remain Amish? He knew a lot of people had their doubts. Unless he found a few dozen things to repair in Rebecca's house he didn't have an excuse to spend much time in her company.

If he could convince Rebecca of his feelings before she had her surgery, he could be by her side no matter what her results were. He needed her to understand his affection had nothing to do with her sight or lack of it. He decided to take this chance.

Drawing a deep breath, he said, "It's Rebecca Beachy."

Emma's brows arched in surprise. "You wish to court Rebecca? You don't mind that she is blind?"

"Why should I mind? She is funny, she is devout, she is hard-working and she has a wonderful smile. I loved her when we were young. I never thought I'd have a chance to love her again, but God has been good to me. After all these years she is not married and beyond my reach. Rebecca is the woman of my heart."

Smiling broadly, Emma said, "Rebecca enjoys ice-skating."

It was his turn to be stunned. "She does?"

"Have you solved my cousin's woes?" Adam asked as he brought the filled sugar containers back from the kitchen.

Emma winked at Gideon. "*Nee,* but we have decided to have a skating party this coming weekend. Do you think Elam Sutter will let us use his pond?"

Adam plunked down his tray on the table beside her. "No harm in asking. It sounds like right *goot* fun."

Laying a finger on her lips, Emma tapped them slowly. "I will make up a picnic basket and bake some pies. We may even close the café so the girls who work for us can come."

Adam grinned. "She will let our English guests starve. It does not matter that they pay the bills."

"Nonsense. I will make sure there is plenty of bread and meat for sandwiches on the sideboard."

She started sweeping again. "This is a *goot* idea if I do say so myself."

Gideon didn't care whose idea it was as long as Rebecca was there.

Emma stopped what she was doing. "Gideon, I almost forgot. Reuben Beachy came in today. He wanted me to tell you he has a used leather-cutting machine being delivered next week and he wants you to make some repairs on it."

A shiver of unease slipped down Gideon's spine. "He asked for me, not for Adam?"

Smiling brightly, Emma nodded. "*Ja.* He said giving you the job was his way of helping you get started in the business community. He is a fine man."

Adam glanced at Gideon and his smile disappeared. "He's a fine man and very sharp for his age. Do not assume otherwise."

"A skating party. What a wonderful idea. I'm so excited." Katie Sutter clapped her hands together. Her two-year-old daughter, Rachel, playing on the floor at her feet, clapped, too, making all the women smile.

"What do you think, Rebecca?" Emma asked as they sat together around the kitchen table in the home of Faith and Adrian Lapp.

"I think it sounds like fun." Rebecca held a skein of yarn open on her hands as Faith unwound it. Katie, Emma and Sarah were cutting pieces of fabric remnants and sorting them in preparation for Rebecca's next quilting project. Since Rebecca didn't feel comfortable attacking pieces of cloth with scissors, she was helping Faith with her knitting.

"We can have a bonfire and roast hot dogs. I love doing that. Elam is going to make sure we have plenty of benches to sit on, too. I can't wait until Saturday." Katie's enthusiasm was catching and her friends were happy to indulge her.

Katie's childhood, under the thumb of her cruel older brother, had been bereft of childish fun. Elam, her doting husband, was happy to help her make wonderful new memories for her and their children.

Faith said, "I don't skate, but I can't wait to see Kyle learn. He'll enjoy it for sure."

Rebecca heard the door bang open and suspected the culprit was Faith's nephew. When she heard his voice she knew she had guessed correctly. "*Mamm,* Myrtle spit on *Daed* and me again."

A sour smell permeated the room as heavy footsteps followed Kyle's into the kitchen. Adrian's deep voice said, "Faith, I know you love that alpaca, but she is going to find her long scrawny neck tied in a bow one of these days."

Everyone giggled for there wasn't an ounce of malice in his words. Faith sighed, rose to her feet and handed her half-wound ball of yarn to Rebecca. "I'll be the one tying the knot because I'm the one doing the extra laundry. There are clean shirts in the bedroom. Take those off and let me soak them."

As they trooped out of the room, Sarah whispered, "Did you notice Kyle is calling them *Mamm* and *Daed,* now? I knew he would be happy here, but I never expected to see my cousin Adrian so happy again after his first wife and child perished. God was good to bring Faith and Kyle into his life."

Katie said, "Kyle has adjusted well to our Amish ways. To look at him you would never know he was raised in an English home."

"I know someone else who is adjusting well to our Amish ways," Emma added.

"Are you talking about Jonathan?" Katie asked. "It's hard to believe he has been with us for a year now. Elam tells me he plans to be baptized soon."

Emma said, "I was talking about Gideon Troyer."

Rebecca kept her voice level. "He has not been with us long. He may fall back into his old ways. If a man breaks his vow once, he may do it again."

"Do you really think so?" It was Katie's voice this time.

Emma was quick to speak up for Gideon. "I believe he is sincere."

"What did I miss?" Faith asked as she came back into the room. She went to the sink and began filling it with water. The smell of lemon-scented laundry detergent quickly overpowered the stink of alpaca spit.

Emma said, "We were talking about Gideon Troyer. I said I think he is sincere in his desire to live Amish."

"That's because you love Adam and he returned from the outside world," Rebecca pointed out.

Faith began swishing the shirts in the water. "I agree with Emma. I see a man who wants to live Plain. If I didn't, I wouldn't have rented my old house to him."

Rebecca perked up. "Gideon has rented a house?" That did sound as if he intended to stay a while.

"*Ja.* Adrian and I didn't want it to sit vacant, but we didn't want to sell it. We would like Kyle to live there when he is grown, but the place needs many repairs. Gideon said he would do them in exchange for a lower rent. It was an excellent solution so we agreed. I believe Gideon's mind is made up. I think he is here to stay."

Rebecca wished she could be as certain. "Time will give us the answer."

"It's no easy thing to give up the English life," Katie said quietly.

"You did it," Sarah pointed out. Everyone knew Katie had followed her English boyfriend into the outside world and only returned to Hope Springs after he left her pregnant and destitute. With no place to go, she had returned to her brother's house to beg his forgiveness only to find he and his wife had moved away.

"If it had not been for the kindness of Elam and his mother I would have gone back. We must all show Gideon that he has made the right choice."

"How do we do that?" Rebecca asked.

"Do what Elam and Nettie did for me. Treat Gideon with kindness and forgiveness. Treat him like he has always been, and will always be, one of us. If we doubt him we show him our own lack of faith."

Rebecca nodded. They were wise words and she held them in her heart. She wanted to believe Gideon would stay more than she cared to admit, but did she dare?

Gideon was stunned to see a passenger van pull up and stop in front of his new home Friday afternoon. He was even more shocked to see the doors open and members of his family begin climbing out.

He moved toward them. "What is this? Why didn't you tell me you were coming?"

"Then it wouldn't have been a surprise," his mother

announced as Abraham helped her out of the van. Behind his parents came Levi and his young wife, Mary, carrying a baby in her arms and followed by three stair-step blond boys in identical black hats like the one their father wore.

From the far side of the vehicle came his sisters, Betty and Susie. Each of them had toddlers in tow. They both greeted Gideon with a quick peck on the cheek. Joseph was the last one out of the vehicle. He hung back from the others.

Gideon's father looked the house over. "Is the roof sound?"

His father, although primarily a farmer, had worked odd jobs in construction for as long as Gideon could remember. "As near as I can tell it is, but I would value a second opinion."

"I will take a look. Have you a ladder?" Abraham asked.

Gideon nodded. "*Ja,* it's leaning against the back porch."

Waneta motioned to Joseph who was watching Levi unload boxes and baskets from the back of the van. "Joseph, go with your father and make sure the he doesn't fall off the roof."

"Have Gideon go. He isn't afraid of heights," Joseph countered.

Waneta gave him a stern look. "Neither are you and I want to speak to Gideon."

She and the women bustled up the steps and into the house. Levi brought a large box and pushed it into Gideon's hands. "I will go help *Daed.* You can unload the van."

Levi glanced after their mother and said, "I hope

you have a ready list of eligible women in the area for *Mamm.* I think you're about to get the, 'It takes a good woman to make a good home' speech. If you don't, I'll bake you a pie."

Gideon inclined his head closer to Levi. "I don't have a long list. I have one name. Is the speech true?"

Levi smiled fondly at his boys. "*Ja.* It's true. But as happy as you will be with a wife, just wait till the babies arrive."

Talk of marriage and babies could wait. For now, Gideon was overjoyed to have his family around him. After ten long years of solitude, he was part of something bigger, something wonderful once again. He was part of the Troyer family.

He looked down at Levi's boys, standing quiet and patient beside their papa. He said, "How would you boys like to see some very strange animals?"

The youngsters looked at Levi. He nodded. "You may go with your *Onkel* Gideon."

Gideon gave Levi back the box and said, "Put it in the kitchen and tell the women I'll be back in a few minutes."

"What kind of animals?" the oldest one asked. He reached up to take Gideon's hand.

A thrill of happiness shot through Gideon as he grasped the small fingers. Smiling, he said, "The woman who owns this place raises alpacas. They are out in the orchard."

"What's an almapa?" the second youngest asked.

Joseph answered, "An alpaca is like a camel. Are they mean?"

Gideon looked at Joseph and saw the light of interest in his eyes. Pleased, Gideon said, "Some of them spit."

Joseph came toward Gideon and picked up the youngest child. Holding the two-year-old, Joseph spoke to him. "We can spit back, right, Melvin?"

The toddler nodded. "Me 'pit." He proceeded to demonstrate his skill.

Gideon laughed. "Maybe I should warn the herd that Melvin is on the way."

Joseph adjusted the child's hat. "The barn cats at home give him a wide berth."

Walking toward the orchard, Gideon was filled with a deep sense of contentment. In the future his children would play with these cousins. They would gather together at his parents' farm for holidays, weddings and birthdays. He would never be excluded again.

The skating party was well under way on Saturday when Gideon, along with Adam and Emma, arrived at the Sutter farm. After helping Emma down from the buggy, Gideon unhitched their horse and led him to the corral where several dozen horses were tied up along the fence. Still in their harnesses, the animals munched contentedly on the hay spread out at their feet and waited for their owners to claim them when they were ready to go home.

Gideon met up with Adam and Emma again. Taking one of the baskets Emma had packed with goodies from her arm, Gideon walked behind them as they followed a trampled path to a large pond at the base of the hill. A bonfire burned in a flattened area two dozen feet from the edge of the pond. There were at least twenty adults and twice that many children already skating.

"Emma, I'm so glad you could make it." Katie Sutter waved at them from a makeshift table loaded down with food.

Gideon handed over his basket and looked around for Rebecca. She wasn't among the women around the table, nor was she sitting on the wooden benches Elam Sutter had supplied for spectators and tired skaters. The party had seemed like a good idea when Emma suggested it, but if Rebecca didn't come he was back to square one.

Emma moved to stand beside him. "She's already out on the ice. Get your skates on."

He looked at the crowd of people circling the pond and spotted her skating beside a young woman. Rebecca held on to her partner's hand but she skated with ease, occasionally turning to glide backward. He gazed at her in amazement.

"Get your skates on," Emma prompted again. "I'm sure Sally would like a chance to skate with some of the young fellows here. I know several who are eager to offer."

Gideon didn't need to be told twice. He took a seat on one of the nearby benches and traded his boots for a pair of skates he had borrowed from Adam. After lacing them up, he took a few uncertain steps out onto the ice.

He didn't fall, but he came close. It had been a few years since he last ventured onto a frozen pond. His confidence grew quickly as his skills returned. When he was sure he wouldn't make a fool of himself, he skated toward Rebecca.

Reaching her side, he said, "You continue to amaze me, Rebecca."

"Do I?" Her smile was bright and her cheeks flushed pink from the cold and her exertion.

"Would you mind if I made a round or two with you?" He held his breath as he waited for her reply.

The young woman with her said, "I could use a cup of hot cocoa."

"Of course, Sally. Run along and thank you for your company."

As Sally skated away Gideon offered Rebecca his arm. "Ready?"

"When you are."

He pushed off and wobbled badly. She grasped his arm tightly to hold him up. "Careful."

He was glad she couldn't see embarrassment written all over his face. "Sorry. Guess I'm out of practice."

"It will come back to you," she assured him.

Gideon pushed off again and stayed upright. After a few moments they fell into an easy rhythm as they glided side by side.

They passed several older couples including her grandfather and his wife taking a slow, stately journey around the perimeter. Three boys shot past them racing each other and weaving in and out of their fellow skaters with juvenile recklessness.

Rebecca let go of Gideon and extended her arms out from her sides. "I love skating. It almost feels like flying."

Grasping her fingers lightly, he said, "Almost."

She lowered her arms. "Do you miss it terribly?"

"Yes."

She didn't say anything else. They continued to glide over the ice in a comfortable silence. He was deeply aware of the woman by his side. The need to hold her in his arms and kiss her was overwhelming. The need to protect her and make her his own grew stronger every day. This wasn't the kind of love he'd known in the past.

Oh, he had loved Rebecca when he was young, but it was a pale thing compared to the emotion she awoke in him now. The intensity of his feelings frightened him. What if she couldn't love him back?

She let go of his hand again, this time to spin in a tight circle. Then, with a spray of ice, she stopped abruptly. She was breathing hard and smiling. She said, "Let me see you do that."

"Okay." He turned around once slowly. "How was that?"

"Your technique needs work."

"Are you blind? That was perfect."

She skated toward him. "Perfectly awful."

He stood still until her outstretched hands touched his chest. He captured them beneath his own, wishing neither of them were wearing gloves. He wanted to feel her touch on his bare skin. He wanted to cup her face between his hands and kiss her until they were both breathless.

She moved back and he let her. This wasn't the time or the place to reveal the depth of his emotions. He would be patient and wait for her no matter how long it took.

Reaching out with one hand she said, "I believe I'm ready for some hot chocolate now."

"As you wish." He led her across the ice and warned her when she reached the edge. She followed his instructions and found the bench with one hand.

Sitting down, she said, "Goodness, I didn't realize how tired I was."

"Does your chemotherapy make you tired?"

"A little."

"Is your treatment going well? Adam told me you won't be able to have the surgery unless you respond to the drugs they are giving you."

"Dr. White assures me all is going as hoped. I'm afraid to believe that."

He left her and returned a few minutes later with two steaming cups in his hands. He gave her one and sat beside her. Gideon sipped his hot drink but it was Rebecca's nearness that kept the afternoon chill at bay.

The trio of speed skaters went flying past again. A group of the girls on the sidelines began egging them on. Elam's booming voice called for an official race. The pleasure skaters happily moved aside. Start and finish lines were set up and a track outlined by spectators. A dozen boys took their places.

Bishop Zook raised his hand. "Three times around. Go!"

Cheers broke out as families urged on their favorites. With nearly everyone out on the ice, he and Rebecca were alone on the bench.

Rebecca set her empty cup aside. "I remember some wonderful skating parties when we were young. Grace could fly like lightning on the ice. She beat every boy who raced her."

A cloud of unhappiness settled over Rebecca's face. It broke Gideon's heart to see her joy turned to sadness. He took her hand to offer his comfort. "Rebecca, what happened? I know the two of you were very close."

Gideon's touch startled her. She wanted to pull away, but the kindness in his voice held her fast. She could feel the warmth of his touch even through her mittens. As Booker once told her, she was woman enough to sense the bond forming between her and Gideon. She thought she knew where he wanted this relationship to go but everything was happening too fast.

Was she ready to start down the path he offered? A long time ago she turned aside from the love Gideon offered because of Grace. She lost her sight and her one true love. Was it possible that God would restore both to her? Had she truly been forgiven?

"Rebecca, I can see you are troubled. Sometimes it helps to talk."

His gentle encouragement brought tears to her eyes. "Grace has been on my mind a lot lately. Do you remember the time she and I went to a hoedown with you?"

"It was the only time you came to one of those wild parties."

"I wish I hadn't gone even that once."

"You were with me most of that night. Did something happen to you?"

"Not to me. To Grace. She said you thought I was hopelessly uncool, a scaredy cat. That's why I went. I wanted to impress you with how modern I could be. Maybe I wanted to impress my sister a little, too."

"I never thought you were uncool. I thought you were everything an Amish woman should be."

"You were wrong."

"I know it was the first hoedown you both went to, but I saw Grace plenty of times after that. Your sister liked to party."

"Do you remember her boyfriend?"

"Not really. I remember that my brother wanted to court her but she wasn't interested in him."

"That was because she had started going out with an English boy. He was trouble, but she couldn't see it."

"What kind of trouble?"

"Drugs. Grace became an addict."

"I'm sorry. I didn't know."

"No one knew for a long time, but I suspected something was wrong after that night."

"It is truly sad that the plague of drugs has reached into our Amish communities. Has your sister sought help for her addiction?"

"Several times that I know of, but each time she has fallen back into the pit. It has such a powerful hold on her mind."

"Is that why your parents no longer speak of her?"

"They poured their hearts and their money into trying to help her. She used their love to feed her habit for years, begging for money, stealing things from our home to sell for drugs. When she was arrested for selling drugs to other Amish girls Bishop Stoltzfus told my parents that she was lost to them. He forbade us to have any contact with her. If we did, we would be placed under the ban, too. It was a terrible time for them. I could have prevented it all."

"You can't blame yourself for her choices."

"You don't understand. The night of the party, I saw her boyfriend buying drugs. I overheard him telling his friends that he and Grace were going to get high, but I didn't warn her. She knew I didn't like him. I didn't think she would believe me, but I should have told her. I should have made her listen me."

"Rebecca, taking drugs was still her decision."

"No, it wasn't. She told me later that he put them in her drink. She didn't know what she was taking. It wasn't just at that party although that was the start. She sneaked out to see him almost every night that summer. She was hooked on the drugs before she knew what was happening to her."

"Rebecca, you don't know that Grace would have listened to you even if you had warned her."

"She blames me. She told me so. I was older. It was my responsibility to watch out for her. I turned a blind eye to her when she was in danger and God punished me because of that. How right she was."

"And you think that is why you lost your sight?"

"It was a just punishment. Grace lost her soul because of me. I don't want to go into surgery until I know for certain if she has forgiven me."

He was silent for a long moment. Rebecca could hear the cheers of the crowd spike then die down. Someone had won. Others had lost.

Gideon asked, "Do you know where she lives? Can you reach out to her?"

He didn't tell her she was being foolish. She could have kissed him for that. His understanding gave her the courage to make her next request. If he refused, she didn't know where else to turn. She squeezed his hand. "I don't know where she is. Will you help me find her?"

Chapter Eleven

Gideon hadn't expected this. Rebecca was asking him to help her find her runaway sister, a sister she was forbidden to contact. What if her family or Bishop Stoltzfus found out about it?

The bishop would jump at the chance to excommunicate Gideon again. He had accepted Gideon's confession, but he made it clear he wouldn't tolerate any transgressions against the *Ordnung.* His attitude was the reason Gideon's family had arranged for him to stay with Adam. While Gideon had been attending church services in Hope Springs, he wasn't an official member of Bishop Zook's congregation. He belonged to Bishop Stoltzfus's church, as did Rebecca's parents.

Gideon knew his actions could have serious repercussions. If it were discovered that he helped Rebecca against the bishop's express wishes, he would forfeit his ability to see his family. It was a lot to risk after all he'd given up to return to the fold.

He looked down at the woman holding his hand. That she trusted him enough to ask such a favor was heady knowledge. He was only beginning to understand the extent of the suffering she endured in silence during the years he was gone. He had sought her forgiveness to make a fresh start in his life. How could he deny her the same blessing?

Many of the skaters were leaving the ice and coming their way. Rebecca tugged her hand from his. He let go reluctantly. Part of the reason he'd given up his career and everything he'd worked for was simply for the right to reenter her life. How could he refuse her request?

He asked, "What if you can't find her before your surgery date? It's only ten days away."

"I will go to New York because so many people have worked to make it possible. I am not ungrateful, but I know the chances of recovering my vision are slim."

"Slim because the surgery is difficult, or because you feel you don't deserve to see?"

"You are as astute as an English fellow I met recently. Or perhaps my face is easier to read than I think."

"Rebecca, forgiveness begins in our own hearts."

"I know that."

"So you profess, but you have not forgiven yourself for the mistakes of your past. Your guilt is a useless burden."

She turned her face away from him. "I expected you to understand. You sought the forgiveness of your family, my forgiveness. How is what I seek any different?"

He pressed his lips into a tight line. She was right about that. He carried his own share of guilt. "I do understand. I will see what I can find out."

Her head came up. "You will?"

"Where was she the last you knew?"

"Millersburg."

"I'll make a few calls. If she was arrested, the sheriff

should have a last known address for her. I can use the computer at the public library to search for her online."

"Thank you, Gideon. You know the English ways and how they live. If anyone can find her, I'm sure it is you. Each day I find new reasons to be grateful God has returned you to us."

Daniel Hershberger walked up to them. "Rebecca, would you take a turn around the pond with me?"

She nodded. "Of course."

Gideon watched her skate away with Daniel. Under his breath Gideon said, "It's not your gratitude that I want, Rebecca. It's your love."

Three days after the skating party, Vera dropped Rebecca in front of the doctor's office for her treatment. As Rebecca unfolded her cane, she said, "Don't wait on me today. I have some errands I'd like to run and then I'm meeting a friend for supper so I will be late coming home."

"A date for supper? Can I hope this friend is Daniel Hershberger?"

Rebecca forced herself to smile, but she couldn't lie. "I would rather not say."

Gideon had stopped by their farm that morning. Luckily, Vera had been outside feeding the chickens and gathering eggs. Gideon had an address and he was willing to go with her today.

"Oh, a secret, is it?" Vera chuckled. "That is the way courtships should be. I will not wait up." With a slap of the reins, she set her buggy in motion.

Inside the clinic building, Rebecca waited her turn to see the doctor. When his nurse, Amber, called Rebecca's name, Rebecca followed her to the exam room. When the door was closed behind them, Rebecca said, "I have heard there is a new woman in town that offers rides to the Amish. I think her name is Miriam Kauffman?"

"Yes, I met her at church last Sunday. She was raised Amish but didn't join the Amish faith and moved away. She came back to help her mother when her father became ill. He passed away not long ago."

"Would you call her and see if she is free today? I have a trip I'd like to make."

"Of course. I'll have our receptionist give her a call. Mrs. Nolan keeps a list of everyone who can help with transportation. Do you want me to check if Samson Carter is free, too?"

"Nee." Samson was a gossip. Rebecca didn't want news of her visit getting back to her family.

After her lab tests and the infusion of her chemo, Rebecca returned to the waiting room. Wilma Nolan, the doctor's elderly receptionist, said, "I called Miss Kauffman. She is free today and can provide you with taxi services. Shall I call her back and tell her you're ready to go?"

"That will be fine. *Danki.*"

"Just have a seat, and I'll let you know when she arrives."

Rebecca sat and waited with growing dread. Was this the right thing to do? Would Miriam be discreet, or would she spread gossip about who and where she drove folks?

Rebecca didn't have long to fret. A few minutes later, she heard the door to the clinic open. A woman's voice asked quietly, "Are you Rebecca Beachy?"

Rebecca rose to her feet. "I am."

"Where can I take you?"

Unaware of who might be listening, Rebecca decided against giving out the address. Instead, she said, "I have directions in my purse. I'll find them for you when we are in the car."

"Okay, fine. How do we do this?"

Rebecca held out her hand. "If I take your arm, it's easy for me to follow you."

Outside, Miriam asked, "Do you want to sit in the front seat or the back?"

"The back. Someone will be joining me." Once she was seated, Rebecca waited until Miriam got in on the driver's side. When she heard the door close, she held out a slip of paper. "We need to pick up another passenger at the Wadler Inn, then I'd like you to take us to this address."

"375 North Broadway in New Philadelphia, is that right?"

"Ja." If Grace lived there, Rebecca wasn't sure what she would say to her sister. No, she knew what she would say. What she was afraid of was her sister's answer. What if Grace couldn't forgive? What then?

The drive to the Wadler Inn took only a few minutes. When the car stopped, the door beside Rebecca opened and she heard Gideon get in.

Miriam asked, "Are we waiting on anyone else?"

"No," Gideon answered.

"Okay, then, we're off."

The first few miles of the trip were spent in silence. Rebecca was too nervous to engage in chitchat. Finally, it was Gideon who spoke. "I understand you are ex-Amish, Miss Kauffman?"

"I chose not to be baptized. It wasn't the life for me.

I grew up near Millersburg. My family was Swartzentruber Amish."

The Swartzentruber Amish were a strict Old Order sect. They lived austere lives even by Amish standards. They had no indoor plumbing. They didn't allow cushions on their furniture. Nor did they allow lights or the reflective orange triangles on their buggies that warned they were slow-moving vehicles in spite of the dangers. Their teenagers did not enjoy a rumspringa, but were expected to join the faith without question.

Gideon said, "I've heard Swartzentruber young people who don't choose baptism are shunned by their families."

"They are. My family had a falling-out with the bishop in their church district after I left. They moved to Hope Springs a few years ago and joined a more liberal church. When my father became ill, my mother asked me to return."

"Not all bishops are created equal. I can vouch for that." Gideon's voice held a hint of bitterness.

Rebecca thought of all he had gone through to make the transition back the Amish life and still the bishop of his former congregation did not welcome him.

Gideon leaned close to Rebecca. "You look nervous."

"I shouldn't be. I'm only going to visit my sister. Are you sure we will find her in New Philadelphia?"

"This is the only address the sheriff had for her. It's more than a year old. She might not be there, but at least she hasn't been in trouble with the law in the last thirteen months."

"Gideon, I appreciate your help with this. I would not have known where to start."

"I guess my time in the outside world wasn't a complete waste. I was able to use the computer at the public library. I'm glad I could help, Rebecca. I'm glad you asked me."

His last words, spoken so softly against her ear, sent shivers down her spine and filled her with excitement. If she turned her face a little their lips would meet. He wanted to kiss her. She knew it. What surprised her was how much she wanted to be kissed by him.

She faced straight ahead. After a moment, he moved away but she wasn't able to relax. The ride seemed to take forever. Gideon tried to put her at ease by relating things he saw along the roadside. Any other time, she would have appreciated his kindness. Today, she was too keyed up.

At long last, Miriam said, "This is New Philadelphia."

Rebecca sat up straight. "Is it a big city? How will we find her address?"

"GPS," Miriam and Gideon said at the same time. Then they both laughed.

Rebecca had no idea what they were talking about or why it was funny. Gideon had much more in common with their English driver than she did.

He said, "This is a nice midsize. How's the gas mileage?"

"Thirty-two highway. Not bad."

"That's better than my Audi SS got."

"You drove an SS? I've always wanted one. Do they handle as well as people say?"

"Better. It's a sweet machine. Zero to sixty in nothing flat. I was sorry to sell it."

"I can imagine. Still, it would have looked funny being pulled by a horse, even in Amish country."

"I might have gotten by with it. It was black." He was joking, but Rebecca sensed how much he missed the vehicle he once owned. How could he be content with a horse and buggy after driving fast cars and flying planes?

Miriam made several turns and finally came to a stop. She said, "I believe this is it."

Rebecca reached for Gideon's hand and squeezed his fingers tightly. "What do you see? What kind of house is it?"

"It's a nice neighborhood. The house is an older home with a porch that wraps around it on two sides. It's two stories tall and painted blue with white trim. There are white shutters on the windows. And…"

"And what?" she insisted.

"It doesn't look like the kind of place a drug addict would hang out."

"That is *goot,* isn't it?"

"Maybe. Or maybe we have the wrong address. I guess there is only one way to find out." He pushed open the car door.

Rebecca wanted to follow him but her body wouldn't move.

Please Lord, give me the courage I need.

Gideon said, "You didn't come this far to sit in a car."

"*Nee.* I did not." Forcing her trembling muscles to move, Rebecca scooted out of the car and stood.

"I will be right beside you," he said quietly. Taking her hand, he tucked it in the crook of his elbow and started forward. Rebecca had no choice but to follow him.

He said, "We're at the front steps. There are five of them. There is a handrail on your left side."

Grasping the rail, she walked up the steps. The boards of the porch creaked as Gideon led her across them. "We are at the front door. Do you want me to ring the bell?"

Her body was shaking, but she managed to nod. "I did not come all this way just to stand on the porch."

"That's my girl."

She wasn't his girl, but she liked the sound of that.

Gideon rang the bell. Inside the house, the chime played a brief tune.

When the door opened, Rebecca braced herself. Only it wasn't her sister's voice she heard. A man asked, "Can I help you?"

Rebecca spoke up. "We are looking for Grace Beachy. Does she live here?"

"Beachy was my wife's maiden name. May I ask who you are?"

"I am her sister."

"Really? My wife never mentioned she had a sister. Are you sure you have the right house?" His voice grew suspicious.

Grace was married. Perhaps she had found happiness far from her past. Rebecca prayed it was so.

"Who is it, dear?" It was Grace's voice. Rebecca heard footsteps approaching and then a sudden, harsh intake of breath.

She said, "Hello, Grace."

"Rebecca? Is it really you?"

"*Ja*. I'm so glad I found you."

"Why did you come here? Why?" There was such pain in her sister's voice. She wanted to reach out and gather Grace into her arms.

Grace's husband said, "Honey, what's going on?"

"Clearly, a blast from my past. It's all right, Randy. I'll explain everything later."

He lowered his voice, but confusion colored his tone. "You told me your family was dead."

"I'm dead to them. They are dead to me."

Gideon spoke up. "We'll only take a few minutes of your time. May we come in?"

Rebecca said, "This is my friend Gideon Troyer."

"It's been a long time, Grace. You may not remember me."

"You're Levi Troyer's older brother."

"That's right."

"I never thought you'd return to the Plain folk."

Grace sounded so bitter. Rebecca saw her chances of making amends with her sister slipping away.

"Life has a way of changing what we see as important. May we come in?" Gideon asked again.

"I guess." The door creaked slightly as Grace opened it wider.

Rebecca was grateful for Gideon's solid presence beside her as she entered the house. They took a seat on a sofa. The room simmered with tension. Rebecca prayed for wisdom. She wanted her sister's forgiveness. She needed it.

Grace's husband asked, "Can I get you anything? Something to drink?"

Rebecca shook her head. "No, *danki*…thank you."

Grace said, "Randy, why don't you take Mr. Troyer outside and show him your greenhouse? I'd like to speak to Rebecca alone."

"Are you sure, hon?"

"Yes."

After the two men left the room, Grace said, "Randy

has ten green thumbs. He would have made a good farmer. Fortunately for me, he's a banker."

Rebecca took a deep breath. "The reason I have come is to beg your forgiveness, sister, for the way I failed you when we were young."

"You're asking for my forgiveness? Wow. That's not the way I thought this conversation would go if it ever happened."

Rebecca sensed that she was entering an emotional quagmire. One false step and all would be lost. "I, too, have thought about this day. Many times. I have missed you."

"You miss a naive sixteen-year-old Amish girl. I haven't been that person in a long time."

"I miss my sister."

"But not enough to look for me in last eight years."

"You know the reason I could not seek you out."

"Sure. So what has changed? Are Mom and Dad okay?"

Rebecca realized the tension in her sister's voice wasn't anger. It was fear. She thought Rebecca had come to deliver bad news. "*Mamm* and *Daed* are the same as always. She complains that he spends too much time gossiping with neighbors. He complains that she enjoys bossing him around."

With a nervous laugh, Grace said, "She does enjoy bossing him around."

"Very much so. Grace, how did you think this conversation would go?"

"I never really thought it would happen. I was always afraid I'd run into someone from the family on the street or in the new superstore that opened two years ago. In my mind, I could see the stunned looks and then the inevitable question. Have I repented my evil ways? It never occurred to me that you would seek me out. Not once did I think you would be here begging *my* forgiveness."

"I am begging it now. As you told me so long ago, I failed to protect you when you needed your big sister the most."

"I said that?"

"You did, and you were right. The night we went to the hoedown together I saw your boyfriend buying drugs. I tried to find you to tell you his intentions, but I didn't find you until it was too late."

"Too late for what?"

"He'd already put the drugs in your drink. My failure led to your downfall. Months later you told me what happened. If I had warned you…you never would have become addicted to that terrible stuff. I could have saved you."

"What else did I say?"

"That God had punished me by taking away my sight. I knew you were right."

"That's cold. Was I high when I said it?"

Puzzled, Rebecca frowned. "We were at home. Don't you remember the day I found the drugs you'd hidden in your room?"

"I can't have hidden them very well if a half-blind woman found them. No, Rebecca, I don't remember saying those things, but I'm sure I did."

It had been the most painful day of Rebecca's life. It was the day she learned she would soon be completely blind and there was nothing that could be done for her.

Depressed and suffering in a world growing darker by the day, she cried out asking God why? Grace gave her the answer and she accepted it. That evening she refused Gideon's offer of marriage and shut away all her hopes for the future.

She shook her head as she tried to comprehend what Grace was telling her. "How could you forget saying such a thing to me?"

"I was an addict. I would say or do anything to gain more dope or protect my stash. The night of the hoedown wasn't my first experience with drugs. I sent… wow… I can't even remember his name. I sent him to buy the drugs. I'd been using for months before that."

"What?" Rebecca couldn't believe what she was hearing.

"I started using marijuana when I was fifteen. By the time that hoedown rolled around I had graduated to meth."

"You lied? You lied to me? Why? Why make me believe I was to blame?"

"Because I was an addict. Don't you get it? Addicts don't take responsibility for their actions. They lie, they cheat, they steal, they manipulate and they blame everyone but themselves. It's easier than facing the truth."

Rebecca leaned back into the sofa. It had all been a lie, but Grace's words had changed everything. Because of her, Rebecca told Gideon she couldn't marry him, believing she didn't deserve happiness with him when Grace had suffered so much because of her. She believed God had taken her sight as a way to punish her.

How poor was her faith to believe such a thing of her Father in heaven?

Rebecca jumped when Grace touched her hands. "I'm sorry I lied to you, Rebecca. I'm sorry for the way I treated our parents and for the pain I caused more people than you will ever know. I've been clean for three years now. Although I don't deserve it, I ask your forgiveness."

"I forgive you." Rebecca muttered the words even as she was reeling with grief. She'd lost so much.

"Randy knows I was an addict. He knows I have a record. He has been my second greatest supporter. God has been my first. It seems odd to say an Amish girl found God in rehab, but that is exactly what happened. Faith is a tricky thing. You can be raised with it all around you, but if you don't open your heart to God, you will never truly know Him."

"I'm happy for you, Grace." Rebecca rose to her feet. She heard the sound of a door open and the murmur of male voices.

"Tell the family that I did manage to turn my life around. Do you think there is any chance that Mom and Dad would come for a visit?"

The quiver in Grace's voice touched Rebecca deeply. She had hoped to find forgiveness here. Instead, she was the one who needed to forgive. She had already uttered the words, but in this moment, she knew the truth of them in her soul.

"I will do my best to convince them." Rebecca held open her arms and the baby sister she prayed would forgive her rushed into them.

Chapter Twelve

Gideon stopped in the doorway to Grace's living room and smiled at the sight of Rebecca with Grace in her arms. The two women looked so much alike that they could have been twins. One English, one Amish.

From the expression on their faces, he decided that at least one of his prayers had been answered. Rebecca had gained the forgiveness she sought.

Grace's husband said to him, "Maybe we should go back to the greenhouse."

Grace pulled away from Rebecca and wiped the tears from her cheeks. "Don't be silly. We were just saying goodbye."

Rebecca managed to smile. "I will write and share all the family news with you."

Grace nodded. "That will be a good start. It's going to take me a while to explain to Randy how many in-laws he actually has."

"I can't promise he will ever get to meet them," Rebecca said quietly.

Grace took her hand. "I know, but it means the world to me that you came."

"I will come again when I can stay longer. I must get back now."

Grace extended her hand to Gideon. "Thank you for bringing her here."

"You're welcome. Did she tell you about her surgery?"

Grace glanced from his face to Rebecca's. "No. What surgery?"

"There is a doctor in New York who thinks she can restore Rebecca's sight."

"There's no guarantee," Rebecca added quickly.

Grace cupped Rebecca's face in her hands. "Nothing is beyond His powers. I will pray for your healing."

The sisters embraced once more and then Gideon led Rebecca out to the car where Miriam sat reading a book. She closed it when she saw them and got out to open the door.

"Did you have a nice visit?"

"*Ja,* it was *goot,*" was all Rebecca said.

She was quiet all the way back to Hope Springs. He had little to do but watch the snow-covered countryside slide past. He wanted to press her about her conversation with her sister but he didn't want to do it in front of Miriam.

At the inn, Rebecca got out with him. When the car pulled away, she said, "My thanks for arranging this, Gideon."

"Let me get my horse and buggy, and I'll drop you off on my way home. You can wait inside the inn for me."

She raised her face to the cold evening air. "I don't feel like going inside. Where do you keep your horse?"

"Naomi Wadler lives behind the inn. She lets me keep Homer in her little stable when I'm working in town. She says her mare likes the company."

"What does the sky look like tonight, Gideon?"

He took her hand and placed it in the crook of his arm. "The sun is going down. There are high clouds above us."

They began walking. "What kind of clouds?" she asked.

"Cirrus clouds." She looked puzzled so he said, "Mares' tails."

"I remember them. They're curly wisps high in the air. They mean the weather is going to change in a day or so. Have you flown through them?"

"Cirrus clouds normally form above twenty thousand feet. That's higher than my type of plane would typically fly." He wasn't sure what to make of the mood she was in. She seemed pensive. Had he been mistaken about her visit with Grace?

"When I hear the sound of a plane engine in the sky I wonder where they are going in such a hurry. Where did you fly to?"

"Many places. I often took passengers on sightseeing flights over the Great Lakes. I carried supplies up to remote areas in Canada or fishermen on a wilderness holiday. I took fresh fruit to markets in the Midwest. I took a grandmother to see her new grandson on Drummond Island. Every day was different."

"It must have been exciting."

"That it was."

"There isn't much excitement in Hope Springs when an ice-skating party is the biggest thing to happen all week."

"It can get quiet here. I'm still not used to the businesses closing up at five. No all-night grocery stores, no fast-food places open at one in the morning, no traffic on the roads. I'd give almost anything for a pizza place that stays open until midnight."

When she didn't speak, he wondered what she was thinking. Finally, she asked, "Are the clouds tinted red and gold by the sunset?"

"The sun is below the horizon so they're barely pink now. It won't be long before it's full dark."

"Then everyone will see what I see." She fell silent. He didn't know what to say.

They reached the stable a few minutes later. Sliding open the door, Gideon was greeted by a whinny from Homer. Rebecca said, "He sounds happy to see you."

"Homer thinks he's going to get a treat." A second whinny followed from Naomi's little mare.

Rebecca smiled. "She is hoping for one, too. If Homer has to go out on a cold night, he should have a treat. Where do you keep them?"

"Hold out your hands." She did, and he poured a cup of alfalfa nuggets into her palms from a pail hanging on a hook. He led her forward until she was standing at the stall door. Homer stretched his neck out and began to nibble them up.

When her hands were empty, she dusted them together. Reaching out, she located Homer's face and scratched him under his chin. "What color is he?"

"He's a dark dapple gray. His sire was a Percheron. He's not a fast horse, but he gets the job done."

"I imagine he's pretty."

"Not so much. He's got a Roman nose and sloping shoulders."

"You have to look past his physical defects. On the inside he is pretty."

"So are you. Inside and out." Gideon held his breath

waiting for her reply. He wanted her to know he still cared for her, but he wasn't sure she was ready to hear that.

"That is kind of you to say." It was too dark in the barn to tell if she was blushing, but he suspected she was. She moved down the aisle to where Naomi's mare stood with her head over the stall door watching the activity.

Gideon harnessed Homer and led him outside. It took him a few minutes to hitch up. When he went back inside the barn, he saw Rebecca sitting on the floor. She was crying. He rushed forward. "What's wrong?"

"Nothing. I'm being foolish, that's all." She drew her knees up to her chin and wrapped her arms around them.

He sat beside her on the dirt floor. "It isn't foolish to cry. You've had an emotional day."

"It wasn't at all what I expected."

"Are you sorry you went?"

"*Nee,* I'm not, but I'm sorry for many other things."

"Like what?"

She drew a deep breath. "It doesn't matter. I can't put spilled milk back in the glass. Forgive my bout of self-pity. We should be getting home. I don't want Vera to start worrying."

Reluctantly, Gideon rose and helped her to her feet. As he held her hand a moment longer, he fought the urge to wrap his arms around her and draw her close. He needed to hold her as much as he needed his next breath.

Rebecca wanted nothing more than to throw herself into Gideon's embrace and erase the years they had wasted. He had offered his friendship. Did she have the right to ask for more after sending him away all those years ago?

Would he welcome her advances or would he rebuff her? Or would he pity her, a blind old maid looking for love where there was none.

She wasn't brave enough to find out. If only she could read the truth in his eyes.

After her surgery, God willing, she might be able to see for herself. If the surgery healed her. If Gideon was still here when she came home.

She'd felt how at ease he was with Miriam in the car. It was familiar for him. She'd heard the longing in his voice when he spoke about his car, about flying and the parts of the English world that he missed. Would his faith hold him here against the freedoms he'd known and given up?

Only time would tell. She had to fight this attraction she had for him. She couldn't stand loving and losing him all over again.

Stepping away from him, she withdrew her cane from the pocket of her coat and extended it. "Please take me home. I have one of my headaches coming on."

She found her way to the stable door and to the buggy outside. Gideon helped her in and then went around to the other side. The buggy dipped on its springs as he climbed in. The motion tipped her toward him. Her shoulder came in contact with his.

She didn't move away. If this were the only closeness she could share with him, she would accept that. For now. If the surgery made her whole, things might be different. For the first time, she allowed herself to hope for her own recovery.

Gideon clicked his tongue and set Homer in motion.

The plodding clop of his hooves, the jingle of the harness and the drone of the tires on the pavement were the only sounds as they drove out of town.

The following morning, Gideon entered the office at the Wadler Inn to meet with Adam about what service calls were scheduled for the day. Adam's high-quality repair work brought back repeat customers both in and outside of Hope Springs. When he married Emma and became part owner of the inn, he had trouble keeping up with the demands on his time. Gideon was thrilled to work for Adam. It gave him a chance to use the skills he had acquired during his time in the English world. Adam was easygoing and a good boss to work for.

Adam looked up from his desk and the pile of paperwork in front of him. "Good, you're here. Reuben Beachy stopped by looking for you."

Gideon's heart skipped a beat. Had Rebecca's grandfather found out about their visit to Grace? Was he angry that Gideon had helped Rebecca arrange it? Gideon tried to keep his trepidation hidden. "Did he say what he wanted?"

"His used cutting machine has arrived."

Gideon relaxed only slightly. "I'll drop over and see if I can get it running for him."

After leaving the inn, Gideon walked through Hope Springs and down the back alley leading to Reuben's store. A new store stood where only ashes had been a few weeks ago, but the style of the shop was the same. Gideon entered through the back door.

The faint smell of smoke still lingered in the air triggering a rush of memories. Gideon felt the heat of the flames on his face. He felt the smoke burning his lungs. His brain screamed at him to get out.

"*Goot* day, Gideon Troyer." Reuben's jovial voice pulled Gideon out of the darkness. He was in a bright new workroom. There were fewer tack pieces on display, but a new workbench had replaced the old one at the side of the room and new tools hung from their slots.

Gideon nodded to Reuben. "I understand you have some new equipment you'd like me to look at."

"*Ja.* I will show you."

Reuben led the way to a machine in the corner. Gideon set down his toolbox and squatted beside it to examine the motor first. "Have you tried turning it on?"

"What do you think of my new shop, Booker? The place looks much different than the last time you were here."

Gideon looked up and met Reuben's sharp eyes. His hope that the old man wouldn't recognize him died a quick death. "How long have you known?"

"From the first moment I saw you. Rebecca is the only blind one in my family."

Gideon rose to his feet. "I'm sorry for the deception. I felt I had to keep my identity a secret when I came for the auction. I was under the ban, but I wanted to help Rebecca. I thought if she knew who I was she would refuse the money I paid for her quilt."

"I expect she would have done so, but dishonesty, no matter how noble the cause, is still dishonesty, Booker."

Gideon folded his arms. "I wanted to help. I had no intention of staying in Hope Springs, but the weather kept me in town and I maintained my disguise."

"Why?"

"So that I could spend time with Rebecca. We were

close once. I wanted to know why she suddenly turned her back on me when I asked her to marry me."

"And did you discover the reason?"

"I discovered that I still cared deeply for Rebecca."

"This is why you came back here?"

"It was more than my feeling for Rebecca that made me return. I saw things when I was Booker that I missed more than I knew. I missed the closeness to God that the Amish have. I missed the sense of family and community. I wanted to become a part of that again."

"And?"

"I didn't realize how empty my life was until I saw Rebecca again. I wanted a chance to win her heart."

"A woman is a poor reason to take up the yoke of our faith."

"I'd like to think Rebecca is the instrument God used to bring me back to my senses and back to our faith. I did not make my confession lightly. I meant every word."

Reuben stroked his beard as he pondered Gideon's words. "Many an Amish lad might have left the faith but for the Amish lass who caught his eye. Myself included. What do you intend to do?"

"Live Amish. I already have a job. I'm renting a house. One day I will build a home of my own. I plan to court Rebecca, and I pray daily that she finds it in her heart to become my wife."

"Have you told her you are the one she calls Booker?"

"No."

Reuben's shaggy eyebrows rose on his forehead. "You have not? Why?"

"Because Booker is gone. All that Booker was ended when I knelt before my father and begged his forgiveness. Rebecca is grateful to the man who paid for her surgery. I don't want her gratitude. I wanted Rebecca to know and love me, Gideon Troyer."

"For such a smart man, you've been pretty stupid."

Gideon swallowed hard. "Are you going to tell her?"

"I will not. That is between the two of you. I understand your motives even if I don't agree with them. You know her surgery may not give her back her sight."

"That makes no difference to the way I feel about her."

"Then I have something to ask of you. Soon, Rebecca and Vera will travel to New York City. Do you know this place?"

"I've been there many times."

"I have read much about the city. I do not think it is a place I want my daughter and my granddaughter to travel alone."

"Are you saying you don't want Rebecca to have the surgery?"

"*Nee,* I'm asking you to travel with them. To see that they make it safely there and back. Will you do this for me?"

"I will."

"Goot."

"How will they travel there?"

"We have not decided. Perhaps by train from Akron, perhaps we will hire a driver for the entire trip."

"The train will take a full day. The drive is nine hours at least. It would be better to fly from Akron."

"Our ways are not about convenience, Booker. Gideon should know this."

"You're right. A day's worth of travel is not a hardship. I will find a driver for Rebecca and Vera."

"*Goot.* Now let us see if we can get this machine running. I have many orders to fill."

Gideon hooked the motor to a car battery and turned the switch to start the propane-powered engine. The machine roared to life. He looked over his shoulder at Reuben leaning over him. "I don't see anything wrong with this."

"*Wunderbaar!* You are a fine mechanic, Gideon Troyer."

Standing, Gideon gathered his unopened tool chest. "And you are a sneaky fellow, Reuben Beachy."

Two days later, Gideon rounded a curve in the road on his way to town. The bright sunshine of the early morning had given way to encroaching clouds pushed by a sharp north wind. As was his habit when he passed Vera's farm, he glanced toward the two-story frame house set back from the road in hopes of spotting Rebecca. The yard and lane were empty. Not that he really expected her to be standing out in the snow.

He slapped the lines against Homer's rump. The gelding picked up the pace and put his head down as he started up the steep hill past Vera's lane. As they reached the top, Gideon passed an Amish woman walking along the highway. To his surprise, it was Rebecca. She was heading toward Hope Springs.

He pulled to a stop and got out. "Would you be needing a ride? I have room."

She stopped. Indecision flitted across her face but the next gust of cold wind settled matters. "*Ja,* a ride would be most welcome. It wasn't this cold when I started out."

Gideon took her arm and guided her to the buggy. "What are you doing walking to town?"

"Vera's arthritis is giving her a great deal of pain today. I can do a lot of things, but I can't drive a horse. So I must walk to town to see Dr. White."

He climbed in beside her and closed the door. It was warmer out of the wind. "Is it the day for your chemo?"

She nodded. "Three days a week I must go and be poked and prodded to make sure the drugs are helping and not hurting me."

"Do the treatments make you sick?"

"Nee." She didn't seem inclined to elaborate.

He set the horse in motion. He'd been hoping to spend time alone with Rebecca ever since he arrived in Hope Springs. Now that he had her to himself, he didn't know what to say. He could see the outskirts of the town ahead. He didn't have much time left. Homer wasn't speedy by any stretch of the imagination, but it wouldn't take him long to cover the last half mile.

Feeling the pressure, Gideon decided it was best to take the bull by the horns. "Your grandfather has asked that I go with you and Vera to New York when you travel there for your surgery."

"Why on earth would Grandfather suggest such a thing?"

"He feels I will have a better understanding of the English city. He thinks my presence will make things easier and safer for the two of you."

"Aren't you worried that going out into the English world will provide a great temptation for you?"

"No." Did she still doubt he would remain Amish? The thought was a sobering one. He wanted her to believe in him.

They rode in silence for the next several minutes.

Finally, she asked, "Are you so sure your old life will not call you back?"

"Everything I want…no, everything I need in my life is here. Except for one thing."

He glanced at her from the corner of his eye. He could see the curiosity simmering in her expression. Finally, she asked, "What one thing are you missing?"

"My *mamm* and my friends tell me it's time I looked about for a wife. What do you think?"

Her brow furrowed. "What do you mean, what do I think? It is none of my business if you wish to take a wife."

The subject made her uncomfortable. That was promising. He pressed harder. "You know the women in this community. I haven't been here for very long. Is it too soon for me to be thinking about finding a mate?"

"How should I know?" She was miffed. It meant she cared.

He said, "Women talk. Have any of the women in our church expressed an interest in me?"

"If you are fishing for a compliment, Gideon Troyer, I must tell you your hook is bare."

"I'm not fishing for compliments. I'm just trying to gauge my chances. I'm not all that handsome. I don't have much to offer. I'm a handyman. I'm renting a home. What do people think about me?"

She shrugged then said, "I heard Sally thinks you're handsome. If I remember right, you were a nice-looking fellow."

"*Danki.* Which Sally?"

"Sally Yoder."

"What? She can't be older than seventeen."

"She is nineteen. Old enough to be courting."

"I am not robbing the cradle. I need someone closer to my own age."

"Well, there is Sarah."

He pretended to consider her. "Sarah. Hmm. Has she ever mentioned me?"

"Not within my hearing."

"I'm afraid a widow would always be comparing me to her dead husband. I don't think I would like that. Who else would you suggest?"

She folded her arms. "There is the schoolteacher, Leah Belier. She is in her early twenties."

"No. She's too smart."

"Too smart for you?"

"Too smart to fall for a fellow like me."

"Very true. It would be a foolish woman who set her heart on the likes of you."

"You liked me once," he reminded her to gauge her reaction.

Her chin came up a notch. "I outgrew it. What about Susan Lapp?"

"I am not so desperate as to ask out Susan Lapp."

"'A plump wife and the big barn never did any man harm.'" She recited the old adage with a smirk.

"She's also at least fifteen years older than I am and she likes garlic. I don't think you are taking this seriously."

Crossing her arms, Rebecca blew out a sharp breath. "Very well. What about Helen Bender?"

"Too old."

"Mary Beth Zook?"

"The Bishop's daughter? Would you want Ester Zook as your mother-in-law?"

"You have a point."

She went through a half dozen more suggestions. He found an objection to each and every one and enjoyed watching the play of emotions across her face. She did care for him.

When they reached the medical clinic, Gideon turned the horse into the parking lot in front of the building. He said, "We're here."

He couldn't wait any longer. He had to know if he stood any sort of chance with her. He took her hand in his.

Flustered, she said, "I'm sorry I could not think of a wife to suit you. I fear I have listed everyone in Hope Springs who is single."

He leaned closer, keeping hold of her hand. "Not everyone, Rebecca. You left out the one I have wanted to court all along."

Her fingers twitched nervously in his grasp. "And who might that be?"

He leaned forward and whispered in her ear. "You."

Chapter Thirteen

"What did you say?" Rebecca held her breath. Had she heard Gideon correctly?

"I want to court you, Rebecca Beachy."

"Is this some kind of joke?" she demanded. She could pretend to play along with his wish list of brides, but hearing her heart's most secret wish tossed into the game wasn't funny.

"No. Why would you think that?"

"I'm blind, Gideon. I'm not stupid. I can't be a wife to you or anyone else."

"Why? Because you can't see? Blind people can do almost anything a sighted person can do, just in a different way. You told me that. It takes a heart to love someone, not a pair of eyes."

She turned her face away from him. "Don't do this to me. I sent you away, and you have a right to be angry, but don't punish me for something I did ten years ago."

He cupped his fingers beneath her chin and lifted her face. If only she could read what was in his eyes.

"Rebecca, I'm not trying to punish you. In my own awkward way, I'm trying to tell you that my feelings for you have grown into something deep and wonderful. I love you, Rebecca."

"You don't mean that. You feel sorry for me, that's all."

"Darling, I pray you may one day see the love I have for you written on my face. If it is God's will that you never look upon me, then I will whisper my love to you every day and every night so that you never doubt it."

Slowly, her disbelief was pushed aside by the sincerity in his voice. *Please, Lord, don't let this be a joke at my expense.*

"Gideon, we've only known each other these few short weeks. The feelings we had for each other as children no longer count. We aren't the same people we were back then. Do you expect me to believe this brief time has been long enough for you to grow to love me? I'm not sure it can be."

He sighed heavily. "You would have to be sensible. My timing isn't great. I know that. You have a lot on your mind. I understand this must feel rushed to you. Only, say you will think about what I have said. Trust me when I say I have loved you for a long time. I don't think I ever stopped loving you."

"But you went away. You left without a word."

"Yes, I did. I was a fool. No amount of anger or blame is going to bring back those lost years."

"I shouldn't have brought that up. I'm not angry with you anymore."

"If you can forgive me, you must forgive yourself, too."

She had the chance now to erase the pain she had caused. If she was brave enough to take it. "I will think on all you have said."

She'd spent a decade believing she didn't deserve

to be loved. To hear Gideon say that he still loved her was almost more than she could bear. She wasn't ready to share her feelings with him. She wasn't certain how she felt. Her emotions were all jumbled.

"What are your plans, Gideon?"

"To stay."

"Here in Hope Springs?"

"Yes. This is my home now."

It was the right answer, the one she wanted to hear.

He asked, "Would you like me to wait and take you home after you're finished with the doctor?"

"*Nee,* I will enjoy the walk back. It will give me time to think."

"Are you sure? I don't mind waiting."

"I am not a child that must be guarded. You have work you must do. Do not let me keep you from it."

"Spoken like the sensible woman you are. Very well. May I stop by to see you tomorrow evening?"

She smiled. "I would like that."

Rebecca left his buggy and entered the medical clinic with her mind in a whirl. What should she do? What answer should she give him? Her sensible side said wait and see if Gideon could live true to their faith. Her heart cried out to grasp this chance at happiness before it was too late.

When it was her turn to see the doctor, she sat through the battery of tests with barely a thought for them. Finally, Dr. White entered the room and pulled his chair up beside her. "I've just spoken with Dr. Eriksson. We both feel the inflammation in your eyes has improved enough to go ahead with the surgery."

"I thought it would be several more weeks yet."

"Happily, you've responded to this treatment much better than we expected."

"How soon does she wish to do the surgery?" Rebecca could barely breathe.

"The day after tomorrow. You're to check into the hospital at seven in the morning. The surgery will take place at ten. If all goes well, you'll find out twenty-four hours later if the surgery was a success."

"I can't believe it's going to happen." She would be home before Christmas. The thought of seeing her family's faces after so many years brought tears to her eyes.

Please, God, let it be possible.

Dr. White said, "Rebecca, I caution you not to get your hopes up. It's possible you won't recover your sight."

"I understand. I have faith, Dr. White. Faith that this surgery and the outcome is God's will."

He laid his hand over hers. "Everyone here will be praying for you."

A whirlwind of packing and preparations followed that afternoon as Emma and Sarah came to help Rebecca and Vera get ready for their trip. With each article of clothing Rebecca put in her suitcase the situation became more real. She was going to New York. If all went well, she would be able to see again. Her hands started shaking at the thought.

Please, please, please, Lord, let me see.

After a sleepless night, Rebecca came down to the kitchen the following morning. Vera was already up ahead of her. She said, "Do I hear a buggy?"

"I don't hear anything."

Vera opened the front door. "Well, bless my soul."

"What is it?" Rebecca moved to stand beside her aunt.

"There are a dozen buggies in the yard and more coming."

Overwhelmed, the two women greeted the people who came to wish them Godspeed and offer prayers for their safe return. By the time Samson Carter pulled his van into the yard at eight o'clock, most of Rebecca's church was waiting to see her off.

On the steps of the house, Bishop Zook pronounced a blessing over Rebecca as her grandfather and her aunt stood beside her gripping her hands. Her heart expanded with love for the gift of her family and friends and she gave thanks for all the people who loved her.

Getting into the van, she found Gideon already seated inside. He asked, "Are you ready for this?"

"I'm not sure."

"Too late now. I've already paid for the van and booked the motel rooms. We're off to the Big Apple."

"I thought we were going to New York," Vera said as she climbed in the front seat beside Samson.

Samson and Gideon chuckled. "So we are," Samson declared.

The first half hour was exciting, but before long the car trip became exhausting for Rebecca. She soon had a headache and a queasy stomach brought on by the motion of the car. At their first stop, a roadside diner in eastern Ohio, Gideon ordered peppermint tea for her and an ice pack which he placed on the back of her neck. It helped, but she knew she was in for a rough day.

Gideon tried to distract her by painting word pictures of the countryside they traveled through. It was easy to imagine the rolling hills, the frozen lakes and rivers and the towns they passed as they traveled east. The occasional snore she heard from her aunt made her envious.

Sometime in the afternoon, she must have dozed off because she awoke with a start to find her head resting on Gideon's shoulder. She started to sit up, but he held her still. "You're fine where you are."

If only he knew how much she wanted to stay exactly where she was.

He asked, "How's the headache?"

"Some better."

"Do you get them often?"

"Once or twice a month. Sometimes they're just headaches, sometime they get very bad. Dr. White calls them migraine headaches. They started after I went blind."

"Are you worried about this surgery?"

"I try not to be, but I can't help it. My faith is not always strong enough."

"You don't have to be strong. You have friends who will be strong for you."

"Friends like you?"

"I'm honored you count me a friend. I will always be that, no matter what decision you make about us."

She didn't want to think about their relationship. She only wanted to stay where she was at the moment. Safe in his arms, her head resting against his chest, listening to his heartbeat. She could hear the strong steady sound beneath her ear. It soothed her fears and gave her strength.

She said, "Tell me what you see outside the windows."

"It's dark now. We're passing a small town. I see Christmas lights outlining the rooftops. Some are twinkling like the stars in the sky, some burn a steady red or blue. There are plastic reindeer in the front yard of the house we just passed. The one beside it has two blow-up plastic snowmen in their yard. I see a tall toy soldier down the block."

"The English chose a funny way to celebrate the birth of our savior. He came among us in a lowly stable. There were no lights or toys to announce his coming."

"Many English know the true meaning of Christmas. We can only pray those who don't will find it in their hearts to believe."

"How did you celebrate the day when you lived out in the world?"

"Sometimes I went to church with the woman who worked for me. Usually, I spent it alone. Christmas was a sad time for me after I left home. I missed my family. I missed going to the schoolhouse to watch the children give their program. Remember the year you and I had a poem to recite together?"

"I do. I messed up my lines and I cried. You were so kind to me later."

"I had to make up for cutting the ties off your *kapp* somehow."

She chuckled at the memory. "What will you do this year?"

"My parents and most of my family are coming to spend it with me. I'm not sure where I'll put everyone in my house, but I sure will enjoy my mother's cooking. I told her I'd like a big pan of her peach cobbler and pot roast with biscuits. She makes the best biscuits."

"You say that, but you haven't had one of mine."

"Are you a good cook?"

"I have a certain talent with biscuits."

"Are they light?"

"So light you have to hold a pot over the oven door to catch them when they float out."

"But are they flaky?"

"So flaky that they have been mistaken for the pages of a book."

"I *lieb* flaky biscuits with butter and honey. How is your shoo-fly pie?"

"Passable."

"Eli Imhoff says I should marry a good cook because good looks fade but good cooking doesn't."

Rebecca giggled. "I don't doubt that Nettie keeps him well fed."

"What will you do for Christmas?"

"Vera and I will be at home for Christmas Day with my grandfather and his wife. We plan to travel to my parents' home for old Christmas. After that, we will go to see my brother in Indiana."

"Perhaps all of you could come and spend Christmas Day with my family," he suggested.

"I would like that. I know my grandfather would, too. We haven't spoken to your parents in many years."

"I know my mother will be delighted to visit with you, but be prepared."

"For what?"

"Many hints and suggestions about me. She wishes to see me married."

"Is that why you're on the lookout for a wife?"

"I'm not on the lookout for a wife. I've found the woman I want. I'm content to wait and see if she wants me."

"For how long?"

"As long as it takes her to make up her mind. Enough about that. Try and go back to sleep." He settled lower, adjusting his body to make her more comfortable.

She nestled against him and pretended to sleep but she never drifted off again. She didn't want to miss a minute of being held in his arms. Suspended between the past and the future, she cherished the long miles and wished, just for a little while, that their journey never had to end.

After a while, Samson pulled off the highway and said, "This is our motel."

She sat up reluctantly, missing Gideon's warmth and the tenderness of his touch. As she stepped out of the car, the smells and sounds of a strange city surrounded her. She was far from everything she'd ever known.

Tomorrow could start a new phase of her life or leave her forever in darkness. Either way, she realized that she wanted one person beside her as she moved into the uncertain future. She wanted Gideon Troyer in her life.

Rebecca's frayed nerves kept her from enjoying even Gideon's company as they rode in a taxi toward the clinic the morning of her surgery. Samson preferred not to drive into the crowded streets of the city. He remained at the motel outside of the city to take them home the day after tomorrow.

This is it. It's going to happen today.

Gideon and Vera kept up a lighthearted conversation about the sights they were passing, but Rebecca remained silent. What if the surgery succeeded? What if it failed? The possibilities ran around and around in her head like a kitten chasing its own tail.

At the clinic, she went inside holding on to her aunt's arm with a hand that trembled. For a second, she wondered if her knees would support her.

"Relax," Gideon said quietly. "It's going to be all right."

Vera said, "I pray God hears your words."

When they stopped, Rebecca asked, "Is this it?"

"It's the elevator," Gideon replied.

A ding sounded. Rebecca felt the rush of people moving past them. Gideon spoke from behind her. "Dr. Tuva Eriksson is on the fourteenth floor."

When the crowd departed, her aunt led her forward and then turned around.

"I have heard of these contraptions but I've never been in one." Vera's voice sounded as shaky as Rebecca felt.

Rebecca noted a faint sensation of movement as the elevator rose. Twice it stopped with a slight jerk and more people got on. Finally, Gideon said, "This is our floor."

Vera moved forward, forcing Rebecca to follow. A few steps later, they entered what she assumed was the doctor's waiting room. A cheerful woman's voice greeted them and presented them with forms to fill out.

Vera said, "Why don't you sit down, child?"

Gideon took hold of her hand. "This way."

He led her to a chair and took a seat beside her across the room. Quietly, he asked, "Are you nervous? Don't be. It is in God's hands." He covered her clenched fingers with his large warm hand.

"I know that whatever happens is His will. I must accept this."

"I've been wearing out my knees praying for you."

She grinned at that. "Your knees will recover. Prayer is *goot* for you."

"You are *goot* for me, too. You make me want to be a better man."

"Can Vera hear us?"

"No, she's talking to the nurse. Why?"

"About what you said the other day."

"I've said a lot of things."

"The thing you asked me to think about." Was he going to make this difficult?

"Oh, that I want to marry you."

The teasing tone of his words made her relax. "Have you changed your mind?"

"Not in the least. I want it with all my heart."

She had to be sure. "You wish to marry me even if this surgery fails?"

"Even then. I love you, Rebecca Beachy. I can't imagine my life without you in it."

What was she waiting for? She'd been alone for ten years because she had been afraid he wouldn't want her with her handicap, afraid she didn't deserve happiness with him. Now, he was offering her the love she had turned down and regretted for all these years.

She drew a deep breath. "I want you to know that I love you, too, Gideon Troyer."

"You do?" His shocked surprise made her smile.

From across the room a woman's voice called out, "Rebecca Beachy, we're ready for you."

She loved him!

Gideon was forced to wait quietly as Rebecca was led away when what he wanted to do was throw his arms around her and kiss her breathless.

He'd never been happier. He'd never been more terrified.

Vera sat down beside him. "Your presence has been a great comfort to me, Gideon. I'm glad my father suggested that you come."

"I'm happy to help. Rebecca has always been dear to me."

"So I gathered," she said with a sympathetic smile.

He wanted to share his good news but he knew that would be up to Rebecca. "I want only what is best for her."

"As do I, but her fate is up to God." Vera clasped her hands together, closed her eyes and bowed her head.

Gideon knew she was praying. He closed his eyes and did the same.

Fifteen minutes later, the same nurse came to the doorway and spoke to them. "You can come back for a few minutes. The doctor would like to talk to all of you."

Gideon jumped to his feet to follow her down a short hallway. They entered a darkened room. Rebecca lay on a bed with the sheets drawn up to her chin and a pale blue surgical bonnet covering her hair.

Vera took her hand. "How are you doing?"

"*Goot.* Is Gideon here?"

"*Ja,* I'm right here." He wanted to hold her in his arms but had to settle for touching her cheek.

As he stood beside Rebecca, the doctor came into the room. "Good morning, Miss Beachy. I'm Dr. Tuva Eriksson. I'll be doing your surgery today. The surgery itself will take approximately two hours. During that time, I'll separate your iris, the colored part of your eye, from the lens behind it. Because of your uveitus, your lens is opaque and hardened. I'll use an ultrasound probe to liquefy the damaged lens and extract it. Then I'll replace your lens with an acrylic prosthetic lens. Are you with me so far?"

Rebecca nodded. "I understand."

"Once the surgery is finished, your eyes will be covered with gauze and special hard eye patches to prevent you from accidentally injuring them. Tomorrow morning, I'll have you come to my office and we'll remove the bandages there. Any questions?"

She shook her head. "No. I wanted to thank you for waiving your fee. That was very kind of you."

"When Dr. Philip White explained that the Amish live without medical insurance and how they collectively pay for the cost of such care when it is needed, I had to help. You must understand this may not be successful, that the damage inside your eye may be too severe to allow vision even with a new lens."

"I do."

"All right. I've got to go scrub in. You may say goodbye to your family, and the nurse will take you back to the O.R."

Gideon thanked the doctor and waited as Vera kissed Rebecca's cheek and left the room. When they were alone, he bent and kissed her lips. "Be brave, my love."

"I'm so scared."

"I know. I am, too. But courage is simply fear that has said its prayers." The nurse came back into the room and he was forced to leave. Out in the waiting room, he prayed as he had never prayed before.

Three hours later, Dr. Eriksson came in with a smile on her face. "It went well, and she is in recovery."

"Can she see?" Gideon asked.

"We won't know that until we take her dressings off tomorrow, but I'm hopeful. There was less scarring than I feared. She should be ready to be released in half an hour. Make sure she gets lots of rest. Tomorrow will be a big day for all of us."

Chapter Fourteen

The following morning, Gideon called for a cab and waited impatiently outside Rebecca and Vera's motel room. When the car pulled up, Gideon knocked on Rebecca's door. It opened almost instantly. He saw Rebecca's pale face and he wanted to pull her into his arms and kiss her.

Instead, he said, "The taxi is waiting."

She merely nodded. Her bottom lip was clenched between her teeth but he saw the tremor she was trying to hide. She was scared. He would be, too, if he were in her shoes. When he helped her into the backseat of the cab, he asked, "Bad night?"

"I didn't sleep much. My eyes feel as if they are full of sand."

"The doctor said to expect that."

"I know, but it doesn't make it easy to endure."

Vera came out of the room. "I miss my own bed. I will be glad to get home."

Gideon moved aside as Vera climbed in, then took a seat beside her. No one said what he knew they were all thinking. In a few minutes, they would know if Rebecca could see.

He thought of all he'd given up to have her reach this point. He'd given up his business and friends. He'd given up the very thing he loved most besides Rebecca. Flying. If it wasn't enough, he'd give up his arms and his legs if the Lord asked it of him, if only she could be made whole.

They made the ride to the eye clinic in silence. Looking over at his companions, Gideon saw Vera had her eyes closed, but her lips were moving in silent prayer. He added his own silent pleas for Rebecca's recovery.

At the clinic they took the elevator to the fourteenth floor but today they didn't have to wait to see the doctor. As soon as they arrived they were ushered into an exam room. The cheerful nursing staff expressed their well wishes and then Dr. Eriksson walked in.

"Dim the lights, please."

The nurse by the door lowered the lights. Gideon's pulse shot up. *Please, God, let her see.*

Dr. Eriksson said, "Rebecca, I'm going to take the eye patches off first."

After the cupped protectors were removed, there were only two small gauze pads taped to Rebecca's face.

"All right, I'm taking the gauze off now." The doctor peeled back the strips of tape that held them in place and the dressings fell away.

Rebecca sat with her eyes closed and her hands clenched together in her lap. Her knuckles stood out white against the blue of her dress.

"Open your eyes when you're ready," the doctor coaxed.

"I can't."

"Yes, you can." Gideon dropped to one knee in front of her and took her hand.

She squeezed his fingers. "I'm afraid."

"We can bear all things by the grace of God."

"By the grace of God," she whispered. Taking a deep breath, she opened her eyes.

Light stabbed into Rebecca's eyes. She pressed them closed against the foreign sensation. She squinted through one eye. Colors and shapes began to form. Elation made her draw a quick breath.

A woman in a white coat stood in front of her. This must be the doctor through whose hands God had worked a miracle. Her Aunt Vera, looking so much older than she remembered, stood at her side. Her hands were clasped together in front of her mouth. A man dressed in plain clothes knelt before her. Her long-lost love. Gideon Troyer had matured from a boy into a ruggedly handsome man. His face was filled with hope and worry and love.

Everything blurred as tears filled her eyes and ran down her cheeks. She began to sob.

Gideon pressed her hands in a tight grip. "It's all right, love. It's all right. I'm so sorry. We can bear this together."

Rebecca blinked to clear her vision. There were tears on Gideon's cheek, too. Gently, she stretched out her fingers and brushed them away. "Don't cry."

Wonder filled his voice. "How do you know I'm crying?"

"I see your tears."

"You see them? You can see?" Joy bloomed in his eyes. His wonderful, beautiful eyes.

"Yes, I can."

Overcome, he bowed his head and covered his face

with his hands. She looked down in wonder at her dress. "I'm wearing blue. I always thought this dress was dark blue, but it's not. It's indigo blue." She looked at her fingers and down at her shoes as she wiggled them.

She looked up at the nurses standing near the door. They all wore colorful uniforms. "I see red flowers and a rainbow and an eye chart. I see the big *E*. I can see all of the letters, even the small ones. I can see everything."

Rebecca grasped the hand of Dr. Eriksson. "Thank you. Thank you so much."

Smiling, Dr. Eriksson said, "I am happy we have succeeded."

Vera rushed forward and engulfed Rebecca in a bear hug as the nurses clapped and cheered. Gideon rose and stepped back but he was smiling, too. Finally, Dr. Eriksson called for quiet. "There is someone waiting to hear your news, Rebecca. Let me get him on the phone."

Rebecca pulled back from her aunt's embrace to gaze at the face of the woman who'd given her a home for so many years. "*Aenti* Vera, your *kapp* is on crooked."

"So is yours," Gideon said, reaching to pull it straight by the ties that hung beside her cheeks. The knuckles of his hands brushed her face in a sweet, soft caress. Quietly he said, "Your *kapp* is on straight. There's no egg yolk from breakfast on your dress, no dust from the buggy seat on your behind. You look lovely."

She tipped her head to the side. "Have you said that to me before?"

An odd look flitted across his face and was gone. "I don't think I have."

"Funny, I seem to remember someone saying it."

Dr. Eriksson interrupted her. "Rebecca, I'm putting this caller on speaker phone so everyone can hear."

"Rebecca? Is that you?" It was her grandfather. In the background she heard the sound of Amish voices singing hymns.

"*Ja, Daadi,* it's me."

She waited but he didn't speak again. Instead, she heard Dr. White. "Quiet, everyone. Quiet, please. Rebecca, many of your family and friends have gathered here in the medical clinic to await your news this morning."

Her heart turned over with happiness when she realized how much everyone cared. "Then I won't keep them in suspense any longer. God has been merciful. I can see."

The sounds of happy chatter, laughter and praises to God's goodness filled the air. Rebecca closed her eyes to listen to each voice. She heard Emma's happy squeal and Sarah's voice. Even Faith was there along with so many others who called out their well wishes.

Vera moved closer to the phone. "We will be home late tonight, but on Sunday we will see all of you at the preaching at Adrian Lapp's farm. Bless you for your thoughts and prayers."

"I will be there," her grandfather said with a catch in his voice.

Rebecca squeezed her aunt's hand. "I can't wait to see each and every one of you. Goodbye for now."

"God speed you safely home," her grandfather called out. Dr. Eriksson pushed a button and the phone when silent.

Rebecca rose and turned to Gideon, wobbling slightly as she struggled to keep her balance in her newly sighted world. "I want to go outside. I want to see the sky."

"Before you go, I want you to take this card." Dr. Eriksson handed one to Vera and to Rebecca. "I am leaving for Sweden on Christmas Day. Until then, anything that you need, don't hesitate to call me. If you have any trouble with your vision, I want to know about it. This surgery is in the early experimental stages. There may be side effects we haven't encountered yet. After I leave, you can contact Dr. Barbara Kennedy. Her number is also on the card. She is familiar with my work, and she will be happy to follow you. The nurse is going to give you some eye drops. I want you to use them exactly as I have prescribed."

Rebecca accepted the small bottles and listened to the instructions from the nurse. When the woman was finished, Rebecca spoke to the doctor again. "I will take good care of my eyes, I promise. I don't have the words to thank you for all you have done."

"It was my pleasure, Rebecca. I wish you the best of luck in the future."

Eager to be outside, Rebecca headed for the door with Vera and Gideon right behind her. The second she stepped into the hallway she stopped. The walls and the floor seemed to be rushing at her. She closed her eyes to regain her balance.

Gideon said, "What's wrong?"

She blew out a hollow breath. "I reckon I need to go slower."

"Take my arm." He offered his elbow.

Grateful, she held on to him and they started forward. The rushing sensation became too much; she closed her eyes and followed him trustingly.

When the cold air hit her face she knew they were outside. She opened her eyes and looked up. Steel, glass and concrete towers leaned over her. The tall buildings blocked much of the sky. It was like being at the bottom of a deep well.

Gideon must have sensed her disappointment. "You will see the sky soon enough when we leave the city."

She glanced at his face, taking in each of his features in turn, his broad forehead and strong brows, his wide blue eyes and handsome lips that she wanted to kiss. Reaching out, she touched a scar in his eyebrow. "I remember when you got this."

"I fell sliding into home plate at school."

She touched his chin. "This one I don't remember."

He rubbed it. "I got this one from a propeller before I learned to watch where I was walking around planes."

"You've changed so much from what I remember."

"Have I? You haven't changed at all."

"I doubt that. I'm almost afraid to look in a mirror."

"I still see the prettiest girl in Berlin, Ohio."

He started walking toward the taxi stand. She closed her eyes and shook her head. "This is hard to get used to."

"Then keep your eyes closed for a while. I'll take care of you."

She squeezed his arm. "I know you will."

The car ride home was like a trip through a magical wonderland. Rebecca couldn't get enough of the sights flying past her window. She wanted to see everything, but it wasn't long before her eyes began to ache and burn. At Gideon's insistence, she put on her dark glasses and tried to rest.

Like a reluctant toddler, she fought the weariness dragging at her mind and body. Each time she closed her eyes she was afraid her vision would be gone when she opened them again. Finally, she fell asleep as the car headed westward. She dreamed she was flying. She woke in complete darkness and cried out in fear.

"It's okay." Gideon spoke softly to her.

She clutched his hand. "Everything has gone black."

"That's because it is nighttime." Gradually, his face came into focus.

"How long have I been asleep?"

"Hours. We're almost home. You've been worn out with worry and lack of sleep. I almost didn't have the heart to wake you, but it's time for your eye drops."

She accepted the small vials from his hands, put her head back and blinked at the sting of the liquid hitting her eyes. After wiping away the excess, she glanced at the front seat where Vera dozed, too. "You have taken good care of us, Gideon."

"I will always take good care of you, Rebecca." He kissed her forehead.

It wasn't enough for her. She raised her face to his and drew him close. His kiss, tender and tentative at first, quickly deepened with passion. His firm lips sparked an ardent answering need in her that left her breathless. When he pulled away she sensed his reluctance to let her go.

"I love you, Rebecca Beachy," he whispered in her ear.

"And I you."

He kissed her once more and she settled against his side, more content than she'd been for ten years. God had been good to her.

Chapter Fifteen

The first week Rebecca was home, a constant stream of visitors kept her busy. She made a game of trying to guess who her visitors were before they spoke. Emma she guessed because she was with Adam. Sarah, she didn't know until she heard her voice. Faith she guessed because she walked with a slight limp.

Rebecca wrote the first of several lengthy letters to Grace and was delighted when a reply arrived a few days later. She left the letter lying on the kitchen table when her parents and her grandfather were visiting. It disappeared a short time later and she knew her mother had taken it to read.

Perhaps in time, God would show them a way to heal the breach in the family. Until then, she was happy to serve as a bridge between Grace and the rest of the family.

What Rebecca missed was seeing Gideon every day, but she understood that he had work to do, both for Adam and at his new home. As Christmas drew closer, she grew used to her restored vision. The only time she found she had to keep her eyes closed was when she tried to quilt. Her fingers knew what to do. Her eyes only served to mess her up.

When Sunday finally arrived, Rebecca traveled to Adrian Lapp's farm with a happy heart. She had so much to be thankful for. She looked forward to lifting her voice in song praising God's mercy and love.

As her aunt drove the buggy down the highway, Rebecca paid careful attention to the route. Soon, she would try driving again. Gideon's new home was on the farm adjacent to the Lapps' property. When his house came into view, she craned her neck to see it. It was small by Amish standards but it had a pretty front porch. The barn was in need of some repairs. He had spoken about love but not about marriage; still she found it exciting to imagine living there with Gideon if they were wed one day.

What was the inside of the house like? She owned a few pieces of furniture. Was there room for her special things, or had Gideon brought a houseful of furniture with him? What she wouldn't give to turn down the lane this minute and see his home. She didn't bother suggesting it for Vera was in a hurry. She would have to wait until Christmas for Gideon to show her around the place.

The minute they reached the Lapp farm, Gideon sought them out and Rebecca's heart skipped with happiness at the sight of his face. He offered to unhitch their horse and to help carry their baskets of food to the house. Vera smiled at him and walked off to speak with her friends leaving the two of them alone for a few minutes. Bless Aunt Vera for her understanding of young hearts.

"I've missed you," he said as he set to work on the harness.

A sweet thrill raced through her. "I've missed you, too."

"Are things getting back to normal?"

Pulling her coat tight against the cold, she raised her face to the heavens. "I can see the sky, Gideon. I see the birds in the air. I see the snow-blanketed fields waiting for the warm sun of spring to awaken them. My life will never be normal. It can only be miraculous."

He smiled at her. "I'm happy for you."

She giggled. "I'm happy for me, too."

He sobered and said, "There are some things we need to discuss, Rebecca."

"What things?"

"There are things about my past you need to hear."

Another buggy drove in and stopped beside them. As the family climbed out, Rebecca heard Katie Sutter calling her name. She waved and turned back to Gideon. "What did you wish to tell me?"

"It can wait. Go and visit with your friends."

She lingered knowing Katie would wait. "Tomorrow is Christmas Eve. Is your family coming?"

"Not until Christmas Day, thank goodness. My house is a wreck. I've got to get some cleaning done before my mother arrives. Do you know of a girl who might want to earn some extra wages?"

This was her chance to do Gideon a favor after all he had done for her. "I know just the person."

"Really? Do you think she could come tomorrow?"

"I'm sure of it."

"Great. I've got a job tomorrow morning in Sugarcreek, but I should be home by ten o'clock."

"Write out a list of things you want done and leave

it on the table. You can settle up her wages when you get back."

"That's one less thing I have to worry about."

"I'm glad I could help." She patted the horse as he led the mare away. Joining Katie who was waiting for her, Rebecca went into the house to get ready for worship.

Early the next morning, she took her aunt's horse and buggy and drove for the first time since recovering her sight. It was scary, but when Gideon's house came into view, her spirits soared.

True to her suggestion, he'd made a list of things to be cleaned. Rolling up her sleeves, she set to work in the kitchen and thought about the meals she might one day make here. The morning passed quickly as she cleaned and dusted the furniture in the living room, aired out the sheets in the guest rooms and put a shine on the linoleum floor of the bathroom. It was past ten before she was done with Gideon's list and the extra things she found on her own.

After taking a short break to have a cup of coffee, she couldn't resist a peek into the one room Gideon didn't have on his cleaning list. His bedroom.

She eased open the door and smiled. Gideon wasn't a slob. The room and its contents were neat enough. His clothes hung from pegs on the wall. A straw hat for summer sat on top of the bureau along with a comb and brush. The plank floor was bare except for a rag rug at the side of the bed. A beautiful star-patterned quilt covered the bed itself in shades of gold, greens and muted reds.

She blushed at the thought of lying beneath the quilt in Gideon's arms. If their love was real and they took the next step in their relationship, this was where she would spend her wedding night, where her children, if they were so blessed, would be born. She ran her hand over the workmanship of the quilt and admired the fine stitching.

As her fingers traced the pattern of the squares and triangles they seemed familiar. She closed her eyes. Her heart started pounding. It wasn't possible. How could Gideon own one of her quilts?

She kept her eyes closed and with trembling fingers, she searched for the corner block, the last block sewn. Relief made her knees weak when she found nothing in the first corner. There was no earthly reason for this quilt to be the one she had given to Booker, yet it felt so familiar. She had worked for weeks on one just like this.

She moved to the foot of the bed and untucked the second corner and then the third. Still nothing.

It was just a quilt. Most likely his mother had made it for him. At the top of the bed, she folded back the last corner. When she did, her fingers brushed crossed the tiny rows of dots. Dots of Braille that spelled her name and the date she had finished her work. November 2.

How was this possible? Booker had said he would treasure it forever. Could he have sold it or given it to Gideon? Did they know each other?

Another possibility took the strength from her legs. Rebecca sank onto the bed. From the moment she met Booker there had been something familiar about him. It was as if she had known him forever. Booker was a pilot as Gideon had been. Gideon returned home only weeks after she said goodbye to Booker.

If only we'd met in another time and another place.

She recalled Booker's whisper and the touch of his fingers on her cheek.

Please, God, I don't want to believe that he lied to me, that he played some kind of game at my expense.

From outside, she heard Gideon calling hello. She couldn't answer. She remained on the bed, hands folded, praying there was a logical explanation.

The door opened and Gideon poked his head in. "I saw your buggy outside. What are you doing here? The house looks great, by the way. Where is your cleaning girl?"

"I'm the cleaning girl. I've been admiring your quilt, Gideon. The craftsmanship is very good. Where did you get it?"

He didn't say anything, but she saw the change come over his face and she knew. Her heart sank. "All this time, I thought I'd given it to a friend."

"You did." He crossed the room and sank to his knees beside her.

She shook her head. "How you must have laughed at the blind woman stumbling around. It must have seemed so funny that I didn't recognize the man I once planned to marry. Did you really have a cold or was that an act? You did a great job. I never suspected it was you."

"I wasn't laughing at you, Rebecca. I was getting to know a remarkable woman who was forbidden to me. Please, let me explain."

"You've had weeks to explain yourself. You deceived me. You lied." She stood and tried to walk past him but he grabbed her arm.

"I didn't tell you I was Booker because he no longer exists. I gave up that life. I knew I could never have you unless I did."

"And the money for my surgery, that came from you, too?" A headache began pandering behind her eyes.

"Yes."

"I should be grateful for that. I am grateful, but I can't love a man who has deceived me to such a degree."

"I was under the ban when I bid on your quilt. I was afraid you wouldn't use the money if you knew it was from me. I didn't tell you about the money because I didn't want your gratitude. I wanted you to love me, to love Gideon Troyer, an Amish handyman, not Booker, the man who gave you back your sight."

She stared at his hand until he let go of her arm. "I did love Gideon Troyer, Amish handyman. Sadly, he isn't what he claims to be."

Gideon raked his fingers through his hair. "That's not true. This is who I am now. I promise you, this is the truth. I believe God brought me to my senses and brought me home so that I could devote my life to loving you. I know I was wrong to keep it a secret. I should have had the courage to tell you the truth, but I was afraid. Forgive me, Rebecca. I'll do anything to make this up to you."

"You are forgiven, Gideon. But I never want to see you again."

She fled from the room and rushed down the steps of his home toward the buggy waiting in the yard. She heard him calling her name, heard his footsteps pounding after her. Tears blurred her vision and streamed down her face. She never saw the rock she stumbled over. She fell, striking her head with sickening pain against the buggy wheel.

"Rebecca? Rebecca, darling, are you all right?"

She felt his hands on her shoulders as he gently lifted her. Pain sent flashes of light lancing through her skull.

"You're bleeding. Hold still."

She raised a hand to her forehead and felt it come away sticky. The smell of blood filled her nostrils. She opened her eyes and a scream ripped from her throat.

Gideon pulled a kerchief from his pocket and pressed it against the gash on Rebecca's head. "It's all right. You're going to be all right."

"No, no, no." She began sobbing uncontrollably.

Sitting in the snow beside her, he tried to soothe her. "Head wounds bleed a lot, but it's not as bad as you think."

"I'm sorry. I'm so sorry," she muttered as she grabbed the front of his coat.

"It's all right. Do you think you can stand?"

He helped her to her feet but she kept her death grip on his jacket. Her eyes were wide with shock. Tears flowed down her face unchecked.

He gathered her close. This was his fault. He should have found the courage to confess his deception weeks ago. He never should have asked for her love until everything was out in the open.

He disengaged her fingers and put his kerchief in her hand. "Keep this pressed against the cut. I think the bleeding has slowed."

She took his kerchief with trembling fingers and pressed it to her forehead. All the color was gone from her face. He wasn't sure she could stand unaided. Her prayer *kapp* had come off. He bent down to pick it up and held out her. "Here is your *kapp*."

She stretched out her free hand—six inches to the side of his. Her eyes were unfocused and staring.

Icy fear poured through his body. "Rebecca, what's wrong?"

"I can't see, Gideon. I'm blind."

No, please God, not after all she had endured.

He scooped her up and placed her in the buggy. "I'm taking you to the doctor."

She trembled on the bench. "It won't matter."

Gideon raced around the other side and climbed in. He gathered the reins and wrapped one arm around Rebecca. He slapped the reins against the horse's rump, setting the animal in motion. Once they reached the highway, he urged the animal to a faster pace.

It was reckless driving at such a speed with only one hand holding the lines, but he didn't dare let go of Rebecca as she slumped against him. She was so pale. There didn't seem to be any strength in her body.

Please God, why are You doing this? Don't leave her blind. She doesn't deserve this. Take my sight instead, I beg You.

The trip into Hope Springs seemed to take forever. Finally, they hit Main Street. Heads turned as people stared at his breakneck speed through town.

One more corner. If he didn't overturn them here the medical clinic was on the next block. His wheels skidded on the snow-covered street as Vera's mare made the turn. The buggy stayed upright. Gideon hauled her to a sliding stop when they reached the front of the building.

"We're here, Rebecca. Dr. White is going to fix you up. Don't worry about a thing." He was babbling, but he didn't care. He helped her out of the buggy and gently led her to the clinic door.

Please, God, let her be okay.

Inside, he gave a hurried explanation to the receptionist. Moments later, Amber and Dr. White came out and took Rebecca with them to the exam room. Gideon sank down on the waiting-room chair and stared at his hands. They were stained with blood. Folding them tightly together, he began to pray.

Twenty minutes later, Dr. White came to the doorway and motioned for Gideon to come with him. Gideon followed the doctor to his office. Impatiently, he asked, "How is she?"

Dr. White opened his door. "Please sit down."

When Gideon entered, he saw Rebecca already seated in a chair in front of the doctor's desk. Gideon took the empty seat beside her.

He wanted to take her hand, reassure himself that she was okay, but he could tell from the frozen look on her face that she wouldn't welcome the gesture. The doctor took a seat behind the desk and faced them.

Gideon braced himself to hear what he feared most.

The doctor steepled his fingers together. "The blow to Rebecca's head doesn't seem to be serious. I can't find a physical reason for her blindness. I see no signs of hemorrhage in her eyes, no evidence of detached retina. Frankly, I'm stumped."

Rebecca said, "I have a bad migraine right now."

The weight of worry made it hard for Gideon to draw a breath. "Is this permanent?"

Dr. White met Gideon's gaze. "I can't say for sure. In light of her recent surgery, I put a call in to Dr. Eriksson. She's concerned there may be a complication from the surgery that is unrelated to this bump on the head. She feels it's imperative that she see Rebecca as soon as possible."

Puzzled, Gideon said, "I thought she was leaving the country?"

"She is. Tomorrow morning. She wants to see Rebecca today. She suggested she be flown via an air ambulance to New York this afternoon."

Gideon glanced from Rebecca's stoic face to Dr. White's concerned one. "Why do I hear a 'but' coming?"

"Rebecca's condition doesn't meet the urgent care criteria for an air ambulance."

Gideon couldn't believe what he was hearing. "You've got to be kidding! She struck her head and went blind. That's not urgent?"

"We're not sending her to a hospital for intensive care. We're sending her to an eye surgeon for an examination. It's a big difference to the air transport companies."

Gideon nodded. "What are our other options?"

"We can contact a private air ambulance company, but it will be very costly, and they may not be available on such short notice."

"Can we get a commercial flight from Akron or Cleveland?" Gideon wasn't going to sit still and do nothing.

"I may have a better option. I've contacted a friend of mine who owns a small plane. He's in L.A. on business, but his wife has agreed to let us use the plane. I understand you're a pilot, Mr. Troyer. Can you fly a Piper Cub?"

Finally, a solution. "Yes."

"No," Rebecca said just as quickly.

Gideon glanced at her face and felt his blood turning to sludge that barely moved through his veins. "You don't mean that."

"You told me that Booker is gone. You promised me. You are an Amish handyman, Gideon Troyer. You cannot fly a plane. I cannot ride in a plane. It is against the *Ordnung* of our church."

Dr. White said gently, "Rebecca, you can fly if Bishop Zook gives you permission. It will only take a few minutes for Amber to fetch him from his farm."

"But he cannot give Gideon permission to pilot the plane."

The doctor said, "This may be a case where it is better to ask forgiveness than permission."

Gideon swallowed hard. He had the knowledge and the power that might save Rebecca's sight. If he used that knowledge and went against the teachings of their church, he would lose her love.

He slipped from his chair to kneel beside her and took her hand between his own. "I love you with all my heart, Rebecca. If it is God's will that you never see again, it changes nothing. But, I beg you, don't make me stand by helplessly when I can save you."

She stared straight ahead as a single tear rolled down her cheek. "A vow cannot be discarded because it is inconvenient, my love."

"Please, Rebecca." His voice broke as his heart shattered into tiny bits.

"You promised. Did you mean it?" she whispered.

That he held true to his vow meant more to her than her sight. He would never disappoint her again. "I did."

He laid his head in her lap. A sob broke free from him and then another. He barely felt the comfort of her hand stroking his hair.

Chapter Sixteen

After a few minutes, Gideon stood and wiped the tears from his face with the back of his sleeve. "I will not break my vows again, but I can't stand by and do nothing."

Rebecca said, "We must leave this in God's hands."

"If I can be the instrument of your blindness, I can be the instrument He uses to heal you—within the rules of the *Ordnung*. I'm not the only one who can fly a plane. Dr. White, may I use your phone?"

"Certainly." The doctor handed him the receiver.

Gideon dialed the number of his old business. He felt his spirits rise when Roseanne answered the phone. He said, "Roseanne, it's Gideon."

"It's about time you called. We've been feeling neglected."

"I'm sorry. I'd love to chat but I need to speak to Craig. It's important."

"He's on the runway with the young couple who are about to take a sightseeing tour of the lakes for their honeymoon. I can patch him through to you if you would like."

"That would be great." Gideon waited impatiently until Craig came on the line.

"Booker, is that you? How's the Amish life treating you?"

"Let's just say it has its challenges as well as its rewards." Gideon squeezed Rebecca's hand. She gripped his fingers tightly in return.

"What can I do for you?"

"I need you to fly someone from Hope Springs to New York today."

"Seriously?"

"I've never been more serious in my life. She's very important to me, and she needs to see an eye specialist as soon as possible. I need your help, buddy."

"Okay. Hang on just a second. Mr. and Mrs. Weaver, I'm sorry but I'm going to have to cancel your tour today. I'm having some technical difficulties. Don't worry, you'll get a full refund and we can reschedule any time that is convenient for you at a ten-percent discount."

The sound of the plane powering down was followed by a rapid exchange of words Gideon couldn't understand. He heard the plane doors open and slam shut again. After a few minutes, Craig came back on the phone. "Okay, where's the closest airport?"

Gideon said, "Craig, you didn't have to lie for me."

His friend chuckled. "Booker, I didn't lie. It would be technically difficult to come get your friend with these people on board. Think of the fuel consumption."

"I'll never be able to repay you for this."

"Just tell me where to land."

Gideon gave the phone to Dr. White. He, in turn, gave Craig the location of the private airstrip. When he was done relaying the information, Dr. White handed the phone back to Gideon.

"Thanks, Craig. You're the best." Gideon knew words could not convey his gratitude.

"I know it. See you in a little over an hour."

After hanging up the phone, Gideon looked to Dr. White. "We should get Bishop Zook here. Rebecca won't go, I won't take her, unless he gives his permission."

"I understand." The doctor left the room.

Gideon took a seat beside Rebecca again. He grasped her cold hands. "Don't worry. Everything will be fine."

She didn't speak. Not when the bishop arrived and gave his blessing for the trip. Not when Amber drove them to the airfield, not even when Gideon helped her into the plane and snapped her seat belt closed.

She had retreated to somewhere he couldn't follow. He wasn't sure she would ever come back to him.

Rebecca blinked as the drops hit her eyes. She hated this part. The drops always burned. Her headache was unbearable. Her stomach churned with nausea.

"Try to relax," the nurse said. "Dr. Eriksson will be in soon. Call if you need anything." She pressed a buzzer into Rebecca's hand. The sound of the door closing signaled that she had left the room.

"How are you feeling?" Gideon asked, his voice thick with emotion.

She couldn't believe she hadn't realized who Booker really was. She had been blind in more ways than one. "My head is splitting."

"I wish I could help."

"I know you do. I have only myself to blame. Pride sent me running away from you."

He took her hand and she squeezed his fingers. He said, "We are a well-matched pair, then. It was pride that sent me running away years ago. It was stubbornness and pride that kept me away."

"Bishop Zook says all men must battle false pride. He says none of us are truly humble before God, but that we must strive always for that humility. It is only by being humble that we can hear God's voice."

"I need you to help keep me on the right path."

"As I need you. Don't think this is your fault."

"How can I not?"

"You don't have the power to take away my sight any more than you have the power to restore it. There is a lesson for us in this. We must seek God's help to understand what He wishes us to learn."

"I've learned I will never keep a secret from you again."

"If we can't trust each other, we have nothing together."

"God has shown me the error of my ways. From this day forward I will never keep anything from you."

The door opened and Dr. Eriksson said, "Tell me what's going on. Rebecca, what kind of pain are you having?"

"I have a bad headache. I can't see anything."

"Is it like a migraine?"

"Ja."

"I want you to sit still. Mr. Troyer, help move her chair up to the table." Gideon did as the doctor asked.

"Good. Now, Rebecca, there is a chin rest in front of you. Can you feel it?"

"I do."

"Good. Put your chin on the rest and hold still. Try not to move your eyes. Stare straight ahead. I'm going to look into them and take some pictures."

Rebecca heard the sound of the shutter clicking. She

followed the doctor's instructions. Once, she thought she caught a flicker of light, but it was gone so quickly she thought she had imagined it.

"You may sit back now," the doctor said.

"Can you tell us what's wrong?" Gideon asked.

"The surgical site looks fine. I'm happy to say there's no sign of infection or other serious medical complications."

"But she's blind."

"I saw several cases like this when I was in Australia. Rebecca, are you prone to car sickness or motion sickness?"

"I have been all my life."

"There is a rare syndrome called Footballer's Migraine. It's a severe migraine headache and visual impairment triggered by a blow to the head such as soccer players get when they head the ball. It's thought that dilation of the blood vessels in the brain puts pressure on the optic nerves."

"Is there a treatment?" Hope began to uncurl inside Rebecca.

"There is. I'm going to have the nurse give you an injection of sumatriptan. It should take care of the headache and visual impairment in an hour or two."

"Will it happen again?" Gideon asked.

"Avoiding blows to the head should keep it from reoccurring, but if it does, Dr. White will be able to administer the drug at his office."

A huge weight lifted from Gideon's chest. He squeezed Rebecca's hand. "That's wonderful news."

"If it doesn't work, I suggest Rebecca enter the hospital and undergo a CT and MRI of the head to rule out other causes as soon as possible."

"I'll see that she does," Gideon promised.

"I know this has given you both a fright, but I'm thankful that I'm not seeing any complications from the surgery. The nurse will be in a few minutes. Try to relax, Rebecca. It's going to be fine. I'm going to cover your eyes with gauze pads just to keep the light out of them. Leave them on until your headache is completely gone."

"Thank you, Doctor," she muttered.

Once Dr. Eriksson was out of the room, Gideon cupped Rebecca's face in his hands and kissed her cheeks. "Did you hear? You're going to be fine."

"Maybe." Her voice was weak.

He knew better than to ask if she loved him. She was in pain. All he wanted was for her to feel better. The future would take care of itself.

The nurse came in and gave Rebecca a shot in her arm. After that, they were free to go. He led her out of the eye clinic and onto the crowded sidewalk. Christmas shoppers were out in droves this final day before the holiday.

Rebecca pressed close to his side. She didn't like crowds, didn't like to be jostled. He managed to flag down a taxi and gave the address of the airport where Craig was waiting for them. Christmas music blared from the car's radio.

Gideon spoke to the driver. "Could you turn the music down, please?"

Annoyed, the fellow said, "What? You Amish don't celebrate Christmas?"

"We do, but this young woman has a bad headache and loud sounds make it worse."

"Oh, sure. Sorry." The driver snapped the radio off.

"Danki," Rebecca murmured.

"What's that?" the cabbie asked as he pulled away.

"It means 'thank you,'" Gideon replied.

"You folks speak Dutch, don't you? My grandmother came from Holland."

"People call it Pennsylvania Dutch, but it's really Pennsylvania *Deitsch,* a German dialect," Gideon explained.

"Huh. I learn something new every day."

Thankfully, the man fell silent and Gideon was able to concentrate on Rebecca. Quietly, he asked, "Is the medicine helping?"

"*Nee.* Not yet."

"It will." It had to. It broke his heart to see her suffering.

When they reached the small airport at the outskirts of the city, Gideon paid the taxi driver and helped Rebecca to the plane where Craig was waiting for them.

"What's the verdict?" he asked.

Gideon said, "The doctor thinks it's temporary."

"Hey, that's great news."

It was great news if it were true. Gideon clung to his faith and prayed God would grant her a complete recovery as he helped her into the plane.

They had been in the air for nearly an hour when Rebecca's headache lessened and she noticed a faint crescent of light at the edge of the bandages over her eyes. Was her sight coming back?

Joy skipped across the surface of her heart the way a stone skips over the surface of a still pond and then settles into the depths. Carefully, she pushed the edge of the gauze pad upward.

The light increased. She closed her eyes tight and

pulled the dressings off. If she opened her eyes would everything go dark again?

Have faith. Have faith, for God has chosen you to be one of His own.

Drawing a calming breath, she slowly opened her eyes. The tan leather grain of the seat in front of her came into focus. Above the seat, she saw the back of a man's head. His hair was short and blond. She was tempted to reach out and touch it just to assure herself that he was real.

She looked down at her hands clenched tightly together. Her vision suddenly blurred and fear shot through her until she realized it was her own tears making the world watery. Blinking them away, she glanced to the left.

Gideon sat beside her. His gaze was focused out the window beside him. He looked so tired. There were lines on his forehead and around his eyes that hadn't been there this morning. Had it only been this morning when she found the quilt? A lifetime had passed.

As she gazed at Gideon she wondered why she didn't recognize that Booker and he were the same person. His kindness, his sense of humor, the way his touch made her heart race, only one man could make her feel this way—as happy as thistledown on the wind.

They had faced a great test of their love and their faith and passed it. She had no idea what God had in store for her life, but each moment she had with Gideon would be a moment to treasure.

As though he sensed her eyes upon him, he looked in her direction. She smiled and said, "You look tired."

The range of emotions that crossed his face was priceless. It went from shock to hope to utter joy in the blink of an eye.

"You can see?" he whispered.

She could barely hear him over the drone of the airplane engine. "I can see how much you love me."

The relief on his face changed to deep thankfulness. "You don't need eyes for that. I promise you will always know how much I love you whether you can see me or not."

He leaned toward her until his lips brushed hers. Heady excitement rushed through her blood, leaving her dizzy. Her hands cupped his face as she deepened the kiss. How was it possible to love someone so much?

"You two are steaming up the windows!" Craig's voice penetrated Rebecca's haze of happiness.

"Mind your own business and keep your eyes toward the front, Law." Gideon smiled at Rebecca tenderly.

"You have such a beautiful smile." She would never grow tired of seeing it.

"I'm glad you like what you see."

How could she not? "I like the color of your eyes. I like the way your hair wants to curl over your ears. I love the way you look so Plain in those clothes. I could go on looking at you forever, Gideon Troyer."

Gideon gazed into her eyes. "That's what I had in mind. I love you, Rebecca, with all my heart and soul."

Craig said, "He's not much of a prize, Rebecca. You could do better."

Rebecca liked this English friend of Gideon's. She raised her voice so he could hear her. "I'm not so sure I could. He is a fine Amish man."

He glanced back at them and grinned. "I hope you know what you're getting into."

Gideon leaned over and kissed her. "Pay no attention to him."

She squeezed Gideon's hand, thankful and content to be near him, to see his face and read the love in his eyes. "So this is flying. I can see why you love it." Peering past him, she gasped at the sight. "The earth is so far away. Surely it would take us a day to fall so far."

Craig and Gideon laughed out loud. She blushed, knowing how foolish she must sound to these men of the air.

Gideon kissed her hand. "Let's hope we don't find out how long it takes, but with Murphy's Law at the controls, odds are anything can happen."

"Hey, I've only crashed one plane," Craig shot back.

Gideon brushed a wisp of hair back from Rebecca's face. "If I died today I would still be the happiest man on God's earth."

She gripped his hand. "I would rather be *down* on God's earth, but it is beautiful up here. You gave up so much to return to me. I'm sorry I doubted you. I will never doubt you again."

"I will never give you a reason to doubt my faith or my love. Flying is only one kind of freedom. The love we share is another, more potent kind. I've made the better trade."

"You say that now, but how will you feel in a year or ten years?"

"Rebecca, flying has always been my substitute for you. I don't need a substitute any longer. Not if I have the real thing."

"I think I need to pinch myself and see if this is real."

"Go ahead. You'll find I'm real and really in love with you."

"God has truly blessed us, hasn't He?" She smiled at her beloved and read the answer in his eyes.

Chapter Seventeen

Gideon opened his eyes and stared at the ceiling of his bedroom. It was Christmas morning. The day the whole world celebrated the birth of the Christ Child. Rather than leave mankind to live in the darkness of sin, God sent His only son to bring light and forgiveness to all who would accept His gift.

Gideon rose from bed and dropped to his knees beside it. Bowing his head, he welcomed God's gift into his heart and gave thanks for the blessings in his life.

God willing, he and Rebecca would spend many Christmas mornings together with their children and grandchildren gathered around them. He prayed for her well-being as he wondered how she was doing after the adventures of yesterday.

Rising, he dressed quickly in the cold room and looked out the window. Fresh snow had fallen during the night, but the sun was shining on the horizon. It promised to be a beautiful day.

Down in the kitchen, he stoked the stove and brewed coffee. His family would be arriving in the early afternoon and there was much to be done.

He was finishing up his chores in the barn when he heard the bells of a sleigh coming up the lane. He looked out to see Rebecca guiding her horse toward the barn. Stepping out to meet her, he smiled as happiness poured through his veins. She was bundled up against the cold, but he'd never seen her look more beautiful.

"Merry Christmas. You must be frozen." He held out his arms to help her down.

"I am, but I'm sure you can find a way to warm me up." With a bright grin, she planted her hands on his shoulders as he grasped her slender waist.

He wasn't a man to turn from a challenge. He lifted her from her perch, but didn't set her feet on the snow. Instead, he held her against his chest, her face mere inches from his.

"Merry Christmas," she whispered before she slipped her arms around his neck and kissed him.

After a long moment, he lowered her to the ground but he didn't let her go. "How are you?"

She blew out a deep breath. "I'm a bit dizzy, but I don't think it has anything to do with my bump on the head."

He loved this lightness between them. "Are you saying I make your head spin?"

"And my heart, too."

"I don't have words to describe the way you make me feel, but I will spend a lifetime trying to make you understand how much I love you."

She pushed away slightly. "I look forward to that, but don't we have things to do?"

"*Ja,* we have much work to finish before my family arrives. Let me put your horse up and we can get started."

It took him only a few minutes to stable her mare. When he was finished, she asked, "What's first?"

"I thought we could gather some greenery for my mantel."

"Sounds like fun. Do you have a hatchet?"

He picked one up from his workbench near the barn door. "What self-respecting Amish handyman doesn't have a hatchet?"

"'Self-respecting.' That makes you sound so serious." She giggled and darted out the door.

Laughing, he chased after her. She was waiting with a snowball in hand. She let it fly and it smashed against his coat. He stumbled to a halt and held up his hand. "No. I refuse to throw snowballs at you."

She scooped up another handful and casually packed it together. "You don't have to throw any."

"Good. After what happened last time, I'm not taking that chance again."

"Fine. I'll do all the throwing." She let loose and knocked his hat from his head.

"Rebecca Marie Beachy, stop that." He bent to pick up his hat and felt a snowball hit his rear end. He straightened with as much dignity as he could muster, dusted off his hat and settled it on his head. He bent to scoop up a handful of snow and turned to face her.

Rebecca took a few steps back. "You said you weren't going to throw any at me."

"I can put snow down your collar without throwing it." He shifted his weapon from one hand to the other.

"Only if you can catch me." She took off toward the house at a run.

He caught up with her before she'd gone a dozen feet and swung her into his arms. She shrieked and squirmed, but he held on and turned her to face him. He gazed into her sparkling eyes and knew the joy that had been missing in his heart for a decade. "I love you."

"Not as much as I love you." She rose on tiptoe and planted a quick kiss on his lips.

Dropping back on her heels, she patted his chest. "Go cut the greenery. I've got to start baking the ham. Vera, Grandpa Reuben and his wife will be here soon. Adam and Emma are on their way, too."

Within the next two hours, Gideon's simple home came alive with the spirit of an Amish Christmas. The smell of pine boughs and food scented the air. Cookies, candy and snacks appeared on the countertops. His family arrived an hour after Rebecca's. The sounds of happy chatter and conversations filled the rooms as everyone became acquainted. Emma and Adam arrived shortly before three o'clock.

Gideon, his brothers and his nephews spent the afternoon trekking through the orchard to find the alpacas. Snow clung to the animals' thick coats and long eyelashes as they munched on hay bales Gideon had set out for them that morning. Afterward, the boys occupied themselves with games and coloring books on the living-room floor, enjoying the presents they had received from their parents that morning.

When everyone was settled, Gideon called his mother, his sisters and Rebecca in from the kitchen where they were putting the finishing touches on the dinner they were about to share. Gideon crossed the room and handed his Bible to Reuben. "Would you read to us the story?"

Everyone grew quiet. Reuben opened the Bible and

began in a strong, steady voice to read the Christmas story.

Even the children remained quiet until Reuben finished reading from the second chapter of Luke. Gideon glanced at Rebecca. She smiled softly at him and he knew it was time. He thanked Reuben and said, "Before we eat, I have a gift for Rebecca." He withdrew a large bundle from inside the closet and carried it across the room to her.

She blushed as everyone looked at her with curiosity. The package was wrapped with plain brown paper and string. Rebecca began to carefully work the string off.

"Me do it." Little Melvin rushed to help. Grabbing the paper, he yanked it apart, smiling at the ripping sound. His mother quickly snagged him and held him in her lap. He protested until his father spoke sternly in his ear.

Rebecca pushed the rest of the paper aside to reveal the quilt she had made. She looked up at Gideon. "You're giving it back to me?"

"I took it under false pretenses. It is your gift to give, and I understand if you wish to give it to someone else."

Everyone laughed. As the families filed into the kitchen, Gideon hung back to speak with Rebecca. "I hope you like your gift."

"I like it, but it belongs to you."

"*Danki.* One day I pray we will share it as husband and wife. Will you marry me, Rebecca?"

"Ja," she answered without hesitation. Her eyes sparkled with her love as she drew his face down for a tender kiss.

"Marry me soon," he whispered. "I can't wait long to make you mine."

"Only a little longer," she promised.

"When?"

"Amish weddings take place in the fall. You know that."

"I can't wait that long."

She drew back and shook her head. "We could have a spring wedding, but you know what folks will think."

"That we've got a babe on the way and need to rush things along."

"Exactly."

"All right, a fall wedding it is, but early fall," he insisted.

"October?"

"September," he countered.

"September," she agreed. He kissed her once more and she settled against his side, more content than she'd been for ten years. God had been good to her.

Gideon laid his forehead against hers. "Do we really have to wait until September?"

"Ja!" a chorus of women's voices answered from the kitchen.

Smiling, Gideon gave Rebecca a quick kiss and together they went in to join the Christmas feast and begin a new life.

* * * * *

AN AMISH MATCH

Jo Ann Brown

For Linda Parisi
A dear friend who always makes me smile
just thinking of her

Have not I commanded thee?
Be strong and of a good courage; be not afraid,
neither be thou dismayed: for the Lord thy God
is with thee whithersoever thou goest.
—*Joshua* 1:9

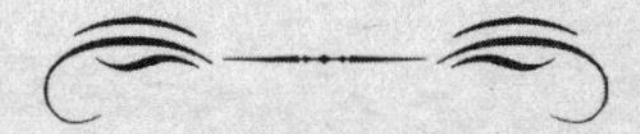

Chapter One

Paradise Springs
Lancaster County, Pennsylvania

The rainy summer afternoon was as dismal as the hearts of those who had gathered at the cemetery. Most of the mourners were walking back to their buggies, umbrellas over their heads like a parade of black mushrooms. The cemetery with its identical stones set in almost straight lines on the neatly trimmed grass was edged by a worn wooden rail fence. The branches on a single ancient tree on the far side of the cemetery rocked with the wind that lashed rain on the few people remaining by the newly covered grave.

Rebekah Burkholder knew she should leave the Stoltzfus family in private to mourn their loss, but she remained to say a silent prayer over the fresh earth. Rose Mast Stoltzfus had been her first cousin, and as *kinder* they'd spent hours together every week doing their chores and exploring the fields, hills and creeks near their families' farms. Now Rose, two years younger than Rebekah, was dead from a horrific asthma attack at twenty-four.

The whole Stoltzfus family encircled the grave where a stone would be placed in a few weeks. Taking a step back, Rebekah tightened her hold on both her son's hand and her umbrella that danced in the fickle wind. Sammy, who would be three in a few months, watched everything with two fingers stuck in his mouth. She knew that over the next few days she would be bombarded with questions—as she had been when his *daed* died. She hoped she'd be better prepared to answer this time. At least she could tell him the truth rather than skirt it because she didn't want him ever to know what sort of man his *daed* had been.

"It's time to go, Sammy," she said in little more than a whisper when he didn't move.

"Say bye-bye?" He looked up at her with his large blue eyes that were his sole legacy from her. He had Lloyd's black hair and apple-round cheeks instead of the red curls she kept restrained beneath her *kapp* and the freckles scattered across her nose and cheeks.

"Ja." She bent to hug him, shifting so her expanding belly didn't bump her son. Lloyd hadn't known about his second *kind* because he'd died before she was certain she was pregnant again. "We have said bye-bye."

"Go bye-bye?"

Her indulgent smile felt out of place at the graveside. Yet, as he had throughout his young life, her son gave her courage and a reason to go on.

"Ja."

Standing slowly because her center of balance changed every day, she held out her hand to him again.

He put his fingers back in his mouth, glanced once more at the grave, then stepped away from it along with her.

Suddenly the wind yanked on Rebekah's umbrella, turning it inside out. As the rain struck them, Sammy pressed his face against her skirt. She fought to hold on to the umbrella. Even the smallest things scared him; no wonder after what he had seen and witnessed in those horrible final months of his *daed*'s life.

No! She would not think of that time again. She didn't want to remember any of it. Lloyd had died last December, almost five months ago, and he couldn't hurt her or their *kinder* again.

"Mamm," Sammy groaned as he clung to her.

"It's all right," she cooed as she tried to fix her umbrella.

She didn't look at any of the other mourners as she forced her umbrella down to her side where the wind couldn't grab it again. Too many people had told her that she mollycoddled her son, and he needed to leave his babyish ways behind now that he was almost three. They thought she was spoiling him because he had lost his *daed*, but none of those people knew Sammy had experienced more fear and despair in his short life than they had in their far longer ones.

"Here. Let me help," said a deep voice from her left.

She tilted her head to look past the brim of her black bonnet. Her gaze rose and rose until it met Joshua Stoltzfus's earth-brown eyes through the pouring rain. He was almost six feet tall, almost ten inches taller than she was. His dark brown hair was damp beneath his black hat that dripped water off its edge. His beard was plastered to the front of the coat he wore to church Sundays, and soaked patches were even more ebony on the wide shoulders of his coat. He'd gotten drenched while helping to fill in the grave.

"Take this," he said, holding his umbrella over her head. "I'll see if I can repair yours."

"Danki." She held the umbrella higher so it was over his head, as well. She hoped Joshua hadn't seen how she flinched away when he moved his hand toward her. Recoiling away from a man's hand was a habit she couldn't break.

"Mamm!" Sammy cried. "I wet now!"

Before she could pull her son back under the umbrella's protection, Joshua looked to a young girl beside him, "Deborah, can you take Samuel under your umbrella while I fix Rebekah's?"

Deborah, who must have been around nine or ten, had the same dark eyes and hair as Joshua. Her face was red from where she'd rubbed away tears, but she smiled as she took Sammy's hand. "*Komm.* It's dry with me."

He didn't hesitate, surprising Rebekah. He usually waited for permission before he accepted any invitation. Perhaps, at last, he realized he didn't have to ask now that Lloyd was dead.

Joshua turned her umbrella right side out, but half of it hung limply. The ribs must have been broken by the gust.

"Danki," she said. "It's *gut* enough to get me to our buggy."

"Don't be silly." He tucked the ruined umbrella under his left arm and put his hand above hers on the handle of his umbrella.

Again she flinched, and he gave her a puzzled look. Before she could let go, his fingers slid down to cover hers, holding them to the handle.

"We'll go with you back to your buggy," he said.

She didn't look at him because she didn't want to see his confusion. How could she explain to Lloyd's best friend about her reaction that had become instinctive? "I don't want to intrude on..." She gulped, unable to go on as she glanced at the other members of the Stoltzfus family by the grave.

"It's no intrusion. I told *Mamm* we'd go back to the house to make sure everything was ready for those gathering there."

She suspected he wasn't being completely honest. The *Leit*, the members of their church district, would oversee everything so the family need not worry about any detail of the day. However, she was grateful for his kindness. She'd always admired that about him, especially when she saw him with one of his three *kinder.*

Glancing at the grave, she realized neither of his boys remained. Timothy, who must have been around sixteen, had already left with his younger brother, Levi, who was a year older than Deborah.

"Ready to go?" Joshua asked as he tugged gently on the umbrella handle and her hand.

"Ja." Instantly she changed her mind. "No."

Stepping away, she was surprised when he followed to keep the umbrella over her head. She appreciated staying out of the rain as she walked to Isaiah, her cousin's widower. The young man who couldn't yet be thirty looked as haggard as a man twice his age as he stared at the overturned earth. Some sound must have alerted him, because he turned to see her and his older brother coming toward him.

Rebekah didn't speak as she put her hand on Isaiah's black sleeve. So many things she longed to say, because from everything she had heard the newlyweds had been deeply in love. They would have celebrated their first anniversary in November.

All she could manage to say was, "I'm sorry, Isaiah. Rose will be missed."

"*Danki,* Rebekah." He looked past her to his oldest brother. "Joshua?"

"Rebekah's umbrella broke," Joshua said simply. "I'm walking her to her buggy. We'll see you back at the house."

Isaiah nodded but said nothing more as he turned to look at the grave.

Joshua gripped his brother's shoulder in silent commiseration, then motioned for Rebekah to come with him. As soon as they were out of earshot of the remaining mourners, he said, "It was very kind. What you said to Isaiah."

"I don't know if he really heard me or not. At Lloyd's funeral, people talked to me but I didn't hear much other than a buzz like a swarm of bees."

"I remember feeling that way, too, when my Matilda died." He steered her around a puddle in the grass. "Even though we had warning as she sickened, nothing could ease my heart when she breathed her last."

"She was blessed to have you with her until the end." She once had believed she and Lloyd could have such a love. Would she have been as caring if Lloyd had been ill instead of dying because he'd fallen from the hayloft in a drunken stupor?

No! She wasn't going to think about that awful moment again, a moment when only her faith had kept her from giving in to panic. The certainty that God would hold her up through the horrible days ahead had allowed her to move like a sleepwalker through the following month. Her son and the discovery she was pregnant again had pulled her back into life. Her *kinder* needed her, and she wouldn't let them down any longer. It was important that nobody know the truth about Lloyd, because she didn't want people watching Sammy, looking for signs that he was like his *daed.*

"I know Rose's death must be extra hard for you," Joshua murmured beneath the steady thump of rain on his umbrella, "because it's been barely half a year since you buried Lloyd. My Matilda has been gone for more than four years, and the grief hasn't lessened. I've simply become accustomed to it, but the grief is still new for you."

She didn't answer.

He glanced down at her, his brown eyes shadowed, but his voice filled with compassion. "I know how much I miss Lloyd. He was my best friend from our first day of school. But nothing compares with losing a spouse, especially a *gut* man like Lloyd Burkholder."

"That's true." But, for her, mourning was not sad in the way Joshua described his own.

Lloyd Burkholder had been a *gut* man…when he'd been sober. As he had never been drunk beyond their home, nobody knew about how a *gut* man became a cruel man as alcohol claimed him. The teasing about how she was clumsy, the excuse she gave for the bruises and her broken finger, hurt almost as much as his fist had.

She put her hand over her distended belly. Lloyd would never be able to endanger their second *kind* as he had his first. Now she wouldn't have to worry about doing everything she could to avoid inciting his rage, which he'd, more than once, aimed at their unborn *kind* the last time she was pregnant. Before Sammy was born, she'd been fearful Lloyd's blows might have damaged their *boppli.* God had heard her desperate prayers because Sammy was perfect when he was born, and he was growing quickly and talking nonstop.

Joshua started to say more, then closed his mouth. She understood. Too many sad memories stood between them, but there were *gut* ones, as well. She couldn't deny that. On the days when Lloyd hadn't been drunk, he had often taken her to visit Joshua and Matilda. Those summery Sunday afternoons spent on the porch of Joshua and Matilda's comfortable white house while they'd enjoyed iced tea had been *wunderbaar.* They had ended when Matilda became ill and was diagnosed with brain cancer.

A handful of gray buggies remained by the cemetery's gate. The horses had their heads down as rain pelted them, and Rebekah guessed they were as eager to return to their dry stalls and a *gut* rubdown as Dolly, her black buggy horse, was.

"Mamm!" Sammy's squeal of delight sounded out of place in the cemetery.

She whirled to see him running toward them. Every possible inch of him was wet, and his clothes were covered with mud. Laughter bubbled up from deep inside her. She struggled to keep it from bursting out.

When she felt Joshua shake beside her, she discovered he was trying to restrain his own amusement. She looked quickly away. If their gazes met, even for a second, she might not be able to control her laughter.

"Whoa!" Joshua said, stretching out a long arm to keep Sammy from throwing himself against Rebekah. "You don't want to get your *mamm* dirty, do you?"

"Dirty?" the toddler asked, puzzled.

Deborah came to a stop right behind Sammy. "I tried to stop him." Her eyes filled with tears again. "But he jumped into the puddle before I could."

Rebekah pulled a cloth out from beneath her cape. She'd pinned it there for an emergency like this. Wiping her son's face, she gave the little girl a consoling smile. "Don't worry. He does this sort of thing a lot. I hope he didn't splash mud on you."

"He missed me." The girl's smile returned. "I learned how to move fast from being around *Aenti* Ruth's *kinder.* I wish I could have been fast enough to keep him from jumping in the puddle in the first place."

"No one is faster than a boy who wants to play in the water." Joshua surprised her by winking at Sammy. "Isn't that right?"

Her son's smile vanished, and he edged closer to Rebekah. He kept her between Joshua and himself. Her yearning to laugh disappeared. Her son didn't trust any man, and he had *gut* reason not to. His *daed*, the man he should have been able to trust most, could change from a jovial man to a brutal beast for no reason a toddler could comprehend.

"Let's get you in the buggy." Joshua's voice was strained, and his dark brown eyes narrowed as he clearly tried to understand why Sammy would shy away from him in such obvious fear.

She wished she could explain, but she didn't want to add to Joshua's grief by telling him the truth about the man her husband truly had been.

"Hold this," he said as he ducked from under the umbrella. Motioning for his daughter to take Sammy's hand again, he led them around the buggy. Rain struck him, but he paid no attention. He opened the door on the passenger side. "You probably want to put something on the seat to protect the fabric."

"*Danki*, Joshua. That's a *gut* idea." She stretched forward to spread the dirty cloth on the seat. She shouldn't be surprised that he was concerned about the buggy, because he worked repairing and making buggies not far from his home in Paradise Springs. She stepped back while Joshua swung her son up into the carriage. If he noticed how Sammy stiffened, he didn't say anything.

Once Sammy was perched on the seat with his two fingers firmly in his mouth, Joshua drew the passenger side door closed and made sure it was latched so her son couldn't open it and tumble out. He took his daughter's hand before they came back to stand beside her.

Rebekah raised the umbrella to keep the rain off them. When he grasped the handle, she relinquished it to him, proud that she had managed not to shrink away. He smiled tautly, then offered his hand to assist her into the buggy.

"Be careful," he warned as if she were no older than her son. "The step up is slick, and you don't want to end up as muddy as Samuel."

"You're right." She appreciated his attempt to lighten her spirits as much as she did his offer.

Placing her hand on his palm, she bit her lower lip as his broad fingers closed over it. She'd expected his hands to be as chilled as hers, but they weren't. Warmth seeped past the thick wall she'd raised to keep others from discovering what a fool she'd been to marry Lloyd Burkholder.

Quickly she climbed into the buggy. Joshua didn't hold her hand longer than was proper. Yet the gentle heat of his touch remained, a reminder of how much she'd distanced herself from everyone else in their community.

"*Danki*, Joshua." She lowered her eyes, which were oddly almost even with his as she sat on the buggy seat. "I keep saying that, but I'm truly grateful for your help." She smiled at Deborah. "*Danki* to you, too. You made Sammy giggle, and I appreciate that."

"He's fun," she said, waving to him before running to another buggy farther along the fence.

"We'll see you back at *Mamm*'s house," Joshua said as he unlashed the reins and handed them to her.

She didn't say anything one way or the other. She could use her muddy son as an excuse not to spend the afternoon with the other mourners, but she didn't want to be false with Joshua, who had always treated her with respect and goodness. Letting him think she'd be there wasn't right, either. She stayed silent.

"Drive carefully," he added before he took a step back.

Unexpected tears swelled in her eyes, and she closed the door on her side. When they were first married, Lloyd had said that to her whenever she left the farm. He'd stopped before the end of their second month as man and wife. Like so much else about him, she hadn't known why he'd halted, even when he was sober.

It felt *wunderbaar* to hear a man use those commonplace words again.

"Go?" asked her son, cutting through her thoughts.

"Ja." She steered the horse onto the road after looking back to make sure Joshua or someone else wasn't driving past. With the battery operated lights and windshield wiper working, she edged the buggy's wheels onto the wet asphalt. She didn't want to chance them

getting stuck in the mud along the shoulder. In this weather it would take them almost an hour to reach their farm beyond Bird-in-Hand.

Sammy put his dirty hand on her cape. "That man was mad at me."

"Why do you think so?" she asked, surprised. From what she'd seen, Joshua had been nothing but friendly with her son.

"His eyes were funny. One went down while the other stayed up."

It took her a full minute to realize her son was describing Joshua's wink. Pain pierced her heart, which, no matter how she'd tried, refused to harden completely. Her darling *kind* didn't understand what a wink was because there had been too few cheerful times in his short life.

She had to find a way to change that. No matter what. Her *kinder* were the most important parts of her world, and she would do whatever she must to make sure they had a *gut* life from this day forward.

Joshua walked into the farmhouse's large but cozy kitchen and closed the back door behind him, glad to be inside where the unseasonable humidity didn't make everything stick to him. He'd waved goodbye to the last of the mourners who'd came to the house for a meal after the funeral. Their buggy was already vanishing into the night by the time he reached the house.

He was surprised to see only his younger sister Esther and *Mamm* there. Earlier, their neighbors, Leah Beiler and her *mamm*, had helped serve food and collected dishes, which they'd piled on the long table in the middle of the simple kitchen. They had insisted on helping because his older sister Ruth was having a difficult pregnancy, and her family had gone home hours ago.

The thought of his pregnant sister brought Rebekah to mind. Even though she was going to have a *boppli*, too, she had no one to help her on the farm Lloyd had left her. He wondered again why she hadn't joined the mourners at his *mamm*'s house. Being alone in the aftermath of a funeral was wrong, especially when she'd suffered such a loss herself.

Take care of her, Lord, he prayed silently. *Her need is great at this time.*

A pulse of guilt rushed through him. Why hadn't he considered that before? Though it was difficult to see her because she brought forth memories of her late husband and Matilda, that was no excuse to turn his back on her.

Tomorrow, he promised himself. Tomorrow he would go to her farm and see exactly what help she needed. The trip would take him a long way from his buggy shop in Paradise Springs, but he'd neglected his obligations to Lloyd's wife too long. Maybe she would explain why she'd pulled away, her face growing pale each time he came near. He couldn't remember her acting like that before Lloyd died.

"Everyone's gone." Joshua hung his black hat on the peg by the door and went to the refrigerator. He poured himself a glass of lemonade. He'd forgotten what dusty work feeding, milking and cleaning up after cows could be.

And hungry work. He picked up a piece of ham from the plate on the counter. It was the first thing he'd eaten all day, in spite of half the women in the *Leit* insisting he take a bite of this casserole or that cake. They didn't hide the fact they believed a widower with three *kinder* must never eat a *gut* meal.

"*Mamm*, will you please sit and let me clear the table?" Esther frowned and put her hands on the waist of her black dress.

"I want to help." Their *mamm*'s voice was raspy because she'd talked so much in the past few days greeting mourners, consoling her family and Rose's, and talking with friends. She glowered at the cast on her left arm.

The day before Rose died, *Mamm* had slipped on her freshly mopped floor and stumbled against the table. Hard. Both bones in her lower left arm had broken, requiring a trip to the medical clinic in Paradise Springs. She'd come home with a heavy cast from the base of her fingers to above her elbow, as well as a jar of calcium tablets to strengthen her bones.

"I know, but…" Esther squared her shoulders. "*Mamm*, it's taking me exactly twice as long to do a task because I have to keep my eye on you to make sure you *don't* do it."

"There must be something I can do."

Joshua gave his younger sister a sympathetic smile as he poured a second glass of lemonade. *Mamm* wasn't accustomed to sitting, but she needed to rest her broken arm. Balancing the second glass in the crook of one arm, he gently put his hand on *Mamm*'s right shoulder and guided her to the front room that some of the mourners had put back in order before they'd left. The biggest space in the house, it was where church Sunday services were held once a year when it was *Mamm*'s turn to host them. Fortunately that had happened in the spring, because she was in no state now to invite in the whole congregation.

He felt his *mamm* tremble beneath his fingers, so he reached to open the front door. He didn't want to pause in this big room. It held too many sad memories because it was where his *daed* had been waked years ago.

Not wanting to linger, he steered his *mamm* out on the porch. He assisted her to one of the rocking chairs before he sat on the porch swing. It squeaked as it moved beneath him. He'd try to remember to oil it before he headed home in the morning to his place about a mile down the road.

"Is Isaiah asleep already?" he asked. "When I was coming in, I saw the light go out in the room where he used to sleep upstairs."

"I doubt he's asleep, though it would be the best thing for him. You remember how difficult it is to sleep after..." She glanced toward the barn.

His other brothers should be returning to the house soon, but he guessed *Mamm* was thinking of the many times she'd watched *Daed* cross the grass between the barn and the house. Exactly as he'd looked out the window as if Matilda would come in with a basket of laundry or fresh carrots and peas from her garden. Now he struggled to keep up with the wash and the garden had more weeds than vegetables.

Mamm sighed. "What are you going to do, Joshua?"

"Do?"

"You need to find someone to watch Levi and Deborah during the day while you're at the shop."

It was his turn to sigh into his sweaty glass. "I'm not sure. The *kinder* loved spending time with Rose, and it's going to be hard for them to realize she won't be watching them again."

"Those who have gone before us keep an eye on us always." She gave him a tremulous smile. "But as far as the *kinder*, I can—"

He shook his head. "No, you can't have them come here. Not while you've got a broken arm. And don't suggest Esther. She'll be doubly busy taking care of the house while you're healing. The doctor said it would take at least six weeks for your bones to knit, and I can't have the *kinder* at the shop for that long."

Levi and Deborah would want to help. As Esther had said to *Mamm*, such assistance made every job take twice as long as necessary. In addition, he couldn't work beneath a buggy, making a repair or putting it together, and keep an eye on them. Many of the tools at the buggy shop were dangerous if mishandled.

"There is an easy solution, Joshua."

"What?"

"Get yourself a wife."

His eyes were caught by the flash of lightning from beyond the tree line along the creek. The stars were vanishing, one after another, as clouds rose high in the night sky. Thunder was muted by the distance, but it rolled across the hills like buggy wheels on a rough road. A stronger storm than the one that morning would break the humidity and bring in fresher air.

Looking back at his *mamm*, he forced a smile. "Get a wife like that?" He snapped his fingers. "And my problems are solved?"

"Matilda died four years ago." Her voice was gentle, and he guessed the subject was as hard for her to speak about as it was for him to listen to. "Your *kinder* have been without a *mamm*, and you've been without a wife. Don't you want more *kinder* and the company of a woman in your home?"

Again he was saved from having to answer right

away by another bolt of lightning cutting through the sky. "Looks like the storm is coming fast."

"Not as fast as you're changing the subject to avoid answering me."

He never could fool *Mamm*, and he usually didn't try. On the other hand, she hadn't been trying to match him with some woman before now.

"All right, *Mamm*. I'll answer your question. When the time is right, I may remarry again. The time hasn't been right, because I haven't found the right woman." He drained his lemonade and set the glass beside him. "From your expression, however, I assume you have someone specific in mind."

"*Ja*. I have been thinking about one special person, and seeing you with Rebekah Burkholder today confirmed it for me. She needs a husband."

"Rebekah?" He couldn't hide his shock as *Mamm* spoke of the woman who had remained on his mind since he'd left the cemetery.

"*Ja*, Rebekah. With a young son and a *boppli* coming soon, she can't handle Lloyd's farm on her own. She needs to marry before she has to sell out and has no place to go." *Mamm* shifted, then winced as she readjusted her broken arm. "You know her well, Joshua. She is the widow of your best friend."

That was true. Lloyd Burkholder had been his best friend. When Joshua had married Matilda, Lloyd had served as one of his *Newehockers*, the two male and two female attendants who sat beside the bride and groom throughout their wedding day. It was an honor to be asked, and Lloyd had been thrilled to accept.

"Rebekah is almost ten years younger than I am, *Mamm*."

"Lloyd was your age."

"And she is barely ten years older than Timothy."

"True. That might have made a difference years ago, but now you are adults with *kinder*. And you need a wife."

"I don't need a wife right now. I need someone to watch the *kinder*." He held up his hand. "And Rebekah lives too far away for me to ask her to do that."

"What about the housework? The laundry? The cooking? Rose did much of those chores for you, and you eat your other meals here. Deborah can do some of the work, but not all of it. With Esther having to do my chores as well as her own around the house and preparations for the end of the school year, she would appreciate having fewer people at the table each night."

"*Mamm*, I doubt that," he replied with a laugh, though he knew his sister worked hard at their local school.

His *mamm* wagged a finger at him. "True, true. Esther would gladly feed anyone who showed up every night." As quickly as she'd smiled, she became serious again. "But it's also true Rebekah Burkholder needs a husband. That poor woman can't manage on her own."

He didn't want to admit his own thoughts had gone in that direction, too, and how guilty he felt that he'd turned his back on her.

His face must have betrayed his thoughts because *Mamm* asked, "Will you at least think of it?"

"*Ja*."

What else could he say? Rebekah likely had no interest in remarrying so quickly after Lloyd's death, but if she didn't take another husband, she could lose Lloyd's legacy to her and his *kinder*. The idea twisted in Joshua's gut.

It was time for him to decide exactly what he was willing to do to help his best friend's widow.

Chapter Two

Even as Joshua was turning his buggy onto the lane leading to the Burkholders' farm the next morning, he fought his own yearning to turn around and leave at the buggy's top speed. He hadn't slept last night, tossing and turning and seeking God's guidance while the loud thunderstorm had banished the humidity. A cool breeze had rushed into the rooms where his three *kinder* had been lost in their dreams, but he had been awake until dawn trying to decide what he should do.

Or, to be more accurate, to accept what he should do. *God never promised life would be simple.* That thought echoed through his head during breakfast and as he prepared for the day.

Into his mind came the verse from Psalm 118 that he had prayed so many times since his wife died. *This is the day which the Lord hath made; we will rejoice and be glad in it.*

At sunrise on this crisp morning, he'd arranged for the younger two *kinder* to go to the Beilers' house, but he couldn't take advantage of their generosity often. Abram Beiler suffered from Parkinson's disease, and Leah and her *mamm* had to keep an eye on him as he went about his chores. Even though Leah had told Joshua to depend on her help for as long as he needed because Leah's niece Mandy and Deborah were close in age and enjoyed playing together, he must find a more permanent solution.

His next stop had been to drop off Timothy at his buggy shop at the Stoltzfus Family Shops in the village. The other shops as well as the smithy behind the long building were run by his brothers. He asked the sixteen-year-old to wait on any customers who came in and to let them know Joshua would be there by midday. Even a year ago, he could have trusted Timothy to sort out parts or paint sections of wood that were ready to be assembled, but his older son had grown less reliable in recent months. Joshua tried to give him space and privacy to sort out the answers every teenager wrestled with, which was why he hadn't said anything when he'd noticed Timothy had a portable music device and earphones hidden beneath his shirt.

Until he decided to be baptized and join the church, Timothy could have such items, though many members of the *Leit* frowned on their use at any age. Most *kinder* chose to be baptized, though a few like Leah's twin brother turned their backs on the community and left to seek a different life among the *Englischers*.

He stopped the family buggy, which was almost twice the size of the one Rebekah had driven away from the cemetery yesterday. Looking out the front, he appraised the small white house. He hadn't been here since at least three years before Matilda died. Only now did he realize how odd it was that they had seldom visited the Burkholders' house.

The house was in poor shape. Though the yard was

neat and flowers had been planted by the front door, paint was chipped on the clapboards and the roof resembled a swaybacked horse. He frowned when he noticed several bricks had fallen off the chimney and tumbled partway down the shingles. Even from where he sat, he could see broken and missing shingles.

What had happened? This damage couldn't have happened in the five months since Lloyd's death. It must have taken years of neglect to bring the house to such a miserable state.

He stroked his beard thoughtfully as he looked at the barn and the outbuildings. They were in a little bit better shape, but not much. One silo was leaning at a precarious angle away from the barn, and a strong wind could topple it. A tree had fallen on a section of the fence. Its branches were bare and the trunk was silvery-gray, which told him it had been lying in the sunshine for several seasons.

Why had Lloyd let his house and buildings deteriorate like this?

Joshua reminded himself he wasn't going to learn any answers sitting in his buggy. After getting out, he lashed the reins around a nearby tree and left his buggy horse Benny to graze on the longer grass at the edge of the driveway. He walked up the sloping yard to the back door. As he looked beyond the barn, he saw two cows in the pasture. Not enough to keep the farm going unless Rebekah was making money in other ways, like selling eggs or vegetables at one of the farmers' markets near the tourist areas.

He knocked on the back door and waited for an answer. The door didn't have a window like his kitchen door, but he could hear soft footsteps coming toward him.

Rebekah opened the door and stared at him, clearly

astonished at his unannounced visit in the middle of a workday morning.

He couldn't help staring back. Yesterday her face had been half hidden beneath her bonnet, and he'd somehow pushed out of his mind how beautiful she was. Her deep auburn hair was hidden beneath a scarf she'd tied at her nape. A splotch of soap suds clung to her right cheek and sparkled as brightly as her blue eyes. Her freckles looked as if someone had blown cinnamon across her nose and high cheekbones. There was something ethereal about her when she looked up at him, her eyes wide and her lips parted in surprise. Her hand was protectively on her belly. Damp spots littered the apron she wore over her black dress. He wasn't surprised her feet were bare. *Mamm* and his sisters preferred to go without shoes when cleaning floors.

Then he noticed the gray arcs beneath her eyes and how drawn her face was. Exhaustion. It was the first description that came to mind.

She put her hand to the scarf. "I didn't expect company."

"I know, but it's long past time I paid you and the boy a visit."

For a moment he thought she'd argue, then she edged back and opened the door wider. "Joshua, *komm* in. How is Isaiah?"

"He was still asleep when I went over there this morning." Guilt twinged in him. He'd been so focused on his own problems that he hadn't been praying for his brother's grieving heart. *God, forgive me for being selfish. I need to be there to hold my brother up at this sad time. I know, too well, the emptiness he is feeling today.*

"How's your *mamm*? I have been praying for her to heal quickly."

He stepped into a kitchen that was as neat as the

outside of the house was a mess. The tempting scents of freshly made bread and whatever chicken she was cooking on top of the stove for the midday meal teased him to ask her for a sample. When Lloyd and she had come over to his house, she'd always brought cookies or cake, which rivaled the very best he'd ever tasted.

You wouldn't have to eat your own cooking or Deborah's burned meals any longer if Rebekah agrees to marry you, so ask her.

He wished that voice in his head would be quiet. This was tough enough without being nagged by his own thoughts.

Taking off his straw hat and holding it by the brim, Joshua slowly turned it around and around. "*Danki* for asking. *Mamm* is doing as well as can be expected. You know she's not one for sitting around. She's already figuring out what she can do with one hand."

"I'm not surprised." She gave him a kind smile. "Will you sit down? I've got coffee and hot water for tea. Would you like a cup?"

"*Danki*, Rebekah. Tea sounds *gut*," he said as he set his hat on a peg by the door. He pulled out one of the chairs by the well-polished oak table.

"Coming up." She crossed the room to the large propane stove next to the refrigerator that operated on the same fuel.

"Mamm?" came her son's voice from the front room. It was followed by the little boy rushing into the kitchen. He skidded to a halt and gawped at Joshua before running to grab Rebekah's skirt.

She put a loving hand on Sammy's dark curls. "You remember Joshua, right?"

He heard a peculiar tension underlying her question and couldn't keep from recalling how Sammy had been skittish around him at the cemetery. Some *kinder* were shy with adults. He'd need to be patient while he gave the boy a chance to get to know him better.

Joshua smiled at the toddler. It seemed as if only yesterday his sons, Timothy and Levi, were no bigger than little Samuel. How sweet those days had been when his sons had shadowed him and listened to what he could share with them! As soon as Deborah was able to toddle, she'd joined them. They'd had fun together while he'd let them help with small chores around the buggy shop and on the two acres where he kept a cow and some chickens.

But that had ended when Timothy had changed from a *gut* and devoted son to someone Joshua didn't know. He argued about everything when he was talking, which wasn't often because he had days when he was sullen and did little more than grunt in response to anything Joshua or his siblings said.

"Go?" asked Samuel.

Joshua wasn't sure if the boy wanted to leave or wanted Joshua to leave, but Rebekah shook her head and took a cup out of a cupboard. The hinges screamed like a bobcat, and he saw her face flush.

"It needs some oil," he said quietly.

"I keep planning on doing that, but I get busy with other things, and it doesn't get done." She reached for the kettle and looked over her shoulder at him. "You know how it is."

"I know you must be overwhelmed here, but I'm concerned more about the shape of your roof than a squeaky hinge. If Lloyd hadn't been able to maintain the farm on his own, he should have asked for help. We would have come right away."

"I know, but..."

When her eyes shifted, he let his sigh slip silently past his lips. She didn't want to talk about Lloyd, and he shouldn't push the issue. They couldn't change the past. He was well aware of how painful even thinking of his past with Matilda could be.

He thanked her when she set a cup of steeping tea in front of him. She went to the refrigerator, with her son holding her skirt, and came back with a small pitcher of cream. He hadn't expected her to remember he liked it in his tea.

"*Danki*, Rebekah." He gave her the best smile he could. "Now I'm the one saying it over and over."

"You don't need to say it for this." She set a piece of fresh apple pie in front of him. "I appreciate you having some of the pie. Otherwise I will eat most of it myself." She put her hand on her stomach, which strained the front of her dress. "It looks as if I've had enough."

"You are eating for two."

"As much as I've been eating, you'd think I was eating for a whole litter." She made a face as she pressed her hand to her side. "The way this *boppli* kicks, it feels like I'm carrying around a large crowd that is playing an enthusiastic game of volleyball."

He laughed and was rewarded with a brilliant smile from her. When was the last time he'd seen her genuine smile? He was sad to realize it'd been so long he didn't know.

After bringing a small cup of milk to the table, she sat as he took one bite, then another of her delicious pie. Her son climbed onto her lap, and she offered him a drink. He drank but squirmed. Excusing herself, she stood and went into the other room with Samuel on her hip. She came back and sat. She put crayons and paper in front of her son, who began scribbling intently.

"This way he's occupied while we talk," she said.

"Gut." If he'd had any doubts about her love of *kinder*, they were gone now. She was a gentle and caring *mamm*.

"It's nice of you to come to visit, Joshua, but I know you, and you always have a reason for anything you do. Why are you here today?"

He should be thanking God for Rebekah giving him such a perfect opening to say for what he'd come to say. Yet words refused to form on his lips. Once he asked her to be his wife, there would be no turning back. He risked ruining their friendship, no matter how she replied. He hated the idea of jeopardizing that.

Samuel pushed a piece of paper toward him with a tentative smile.

"He wants you to have the picture he drew," Rebekah said.

Jacob looked at the crayon lines zigzagging across the page in every direction. "It's very colorful."

The little boy whispered in Rebekah's ear.

She nodded, then said, "He tells me it's a picture of your horse and buggy."

"I see," he replied, though he didn't. The collection of darting lines bore no resemblance he could discern to either Benny or his buggy. "*Gut* job, Samuel."

The *kind* started to smile, then hid his face in Rebekah's shoulder. She murmured something to him and picked up a green crayon. When she handed it to him along with another piece of paper, he began drawing again.

"You never answered my question, Joshua," she said. "Why did you come here today?"

"In part to apologize for not coming sooner. I should have been here to help you during the past few months."

Her smile wavered. "I know I've let the house and buildings go."

He started to ask another question, but when he met her steady gaze and saw how her chin trembled as she tried to hide her dismay, he nodded. "It doesn't take long once wind and rain get through one spot to start wrecking a whole building."

"That's true. I know I eventually will need to sell the farm. I've already had several offers to buy it."

"Amish or *Englisch*?"

"Both, though I wouldn't want to see the acres broken up and a bunch of *Englisch* houses built here."

"Some *Englischers* like to live on a small farm, as we do." He used the last piece of crust to collect the remaining apple filling on the plate. "My neighbors are like that."

"I didn't realize you had *Englisch* neighbors."

"Ja." He picked up his cup of tea. "Their Alexis and my Timothy have played together from the time they could walk."

"Will Alexis babysit for you?"

Joshua shook his head, lowering his untasted tea to the table. "She's involved in many activities at the high school and her part-time job, so she's seldom around. I hear her driving into their yard late every evening."

"Who's going to take care of Levi and Deborah while you're at work?"

God, You guided our conversation to this point. Be with me now if it's Your will for this marriage to go forward.

He took a deep breath, then said, "I'm hoping you'll help me, Rebekah."

"Me? I'd be glad to once school is out, but come fall

we live too far away for the *kinder* to walk here after school."

"I was hoping you might consider a move." He chided himself for what sounded like a stupid answer.

"I'd like to live in Paradise Springs, but I can't think of moving until I sell the farm. A lot needs to be repaired before I do, or I'll get next to nothing for it."

"I'd be glad to help."

"In exchange for babysitting?" She shook her head with a sad smile. "It's a *wunderbaar* idea, but it doesn't solve the distance problem."

He looked down at the table and the picture Samuel had drawn. Right now his life felt as jumbled as those lines. He couldn't meet Rebekah's eyes as he asked, "What if distance wasn't a problem?"

"I don't understand."

Talking in circles wasn't getting him anywhere and putting off asking the question any longer was *dumm*. He caught her puzzled gaze and held it, trying not to lose himself in her soft blue eyes. "Rebekah Burkholder, will you marry me?"

Rebekah choked on her gasp. She'd been puzzled about the reason for Joshua Stoltzfus's visit, but if she'd guessed every minute for the rest of her life, she couldn't have imagined it would be for him to propose.

Her son let out a protest, and she realized she'd tightened her hold around his waist until he couldn't breathe. Loosening her arm, she set Sammy on the floor. She urged him to go and play with his wooden blocks stacked near the arch into the front room.

"He doesn't need to be a part of this conversation." She watched the little boy toddle to the blocks. She needed time to get her features back under control before she answered Joshua's astonishing question.

"I agree," Joshua said in a tense voice.

She clasped her hands in her lap and looked at him. His brown hair glistened in the sunlight coming through the kitchen windows, but his eyes, which were even darker, had become bottomless, shadowed pools. He was even more handsome than he'd been when she'd first met him years ago, because his sharply sculpted nose now fit with his other strong features. His black suspenders drew her eyes to his powerful shoulders and arms, which had been honed by years of building buggies. His broad hands, which now gripped the edge of the table, had been compassionate when they'd touched hers yesterday.

Had he planned to ask her to be his wife even then? Was that why he'd been solicitous of her and Sammy? She was confused because Joshua Stoltzfus didn't seem to have a duplicitous bone in his body. But if he hadn't been thinking about proposing yesterday, why had he today?

The only way to know was to ask. She forced out the words she must. "Why would you propose to me?"

"You need a husband, and I need a wife." His voice was as emotionless as if they spoke about last week's weather. "We've known each other for a very long time, and it's common for Amish widows and widowers to remarry. But even more important, you're Lloyd's widow."

"Why is that more important?"

"Lloyd and I once told each other that if something happened to one of us, we would take care of the other's family."

"It isn't our way to make vows."

"I know, but Lloyd was insistent that I agree to make sure his wife and family were cared for if something happened to him. I saw the *gut* sense and asked if he would do the same for me." He folded his arms on the table. "He was my friend, and I can't imagine anyone I would have trusted more with my family."

Rebekah quickly lowered her eyes from his sincere gaze. He truly believed Lloyd was the man she once had believed he was, too. She couldn't tell him the truth. Not about Lloyd, but she could tell him the truth about how foolish he was to ask her to be his wife.

"There's a big difference between taking care of your friend's family and..." She couldn't even say the word *marry.*

"But I haven't even taken care of you as I promised him."

"We've managed, and we will until I can sell the farm. *Danki* for your concern, Joshua. I appreciate what you are doing, but it's not necessary."

"I disagree. The fact remains I need a wife and you need a husband."

"You need a babysitter and I need a carpenter."

His lips twitched and she wanted to ask what he found amusing about this absurd conversation. Was it a jest he'd devised to make her smile? She pushed aside that thought as quickly as it'd formed. Joshua was a *gut* man. That was what everyone said, and she agreed. He wouldn't play such a prank on her. He must be sincere.

A dozen different emotions spiraled through her. She didn't know what to feel. Flattered that he'd considered her as a prospect to be his wife? Fear she might be as foolish as she had been the last time a man had proposed? Not that she believed Joshua would raise his hand and strike her, but then she hadn't guessed Lloyd would, either. And, to be honest, she never could have envisioned Joshua asking her to marry him.

"Rebekah," he said as his gaze captured hers again. "I know this is sudden, and I know you must think I'm *ab in kopp*—"

"The thought *you're crazy* has crossed my mind. More than once."

He chuckled, the sound soothing because it reminded her of the many other times she'd heard him laugh. He never laughed at another's expense.

"I'm sure it has, but I assure you that I haven't lost my mind." He paused, toyed with his cup, then asked, "Will you give me an answer, Rebekah? Will you marry me?"

"But why? I don't love you." Her cheeks turned to fire as she hurried to add, "That sounded awful. I'm sorry. The truth is you've always been a *gut* friend, Joshua, which is why I feel I can be blunt."

"If we can't speak honestly now, I can't imagine when we could."

"Then I will honestly say I don't understand why you'd ask me to m-m-marry you." She hated how she stumbled over the simple word.

No, it wasn't simple. There was nothing simple about Joshua Stoltzfus appearing at her door to ask her to become his wife. As he'd assured her, he wasn't *ab in kopp*. In fact, Joshua—up until today—had been the sanest man she'd ever met.

"Because we could help each other. Isn't that what a husband and wife are? Helpmeets?" He cleared his throat. "I would rather marry a woman I know and respect as a friend. We've both married once for love, and we've both lost the ones we love. Is it wrong to be more practical this time?"

Every inch of her wanted to shout, *"Ja!"* But his words made sense.

She had married Lloyd because she'd been infatuated with him and the idea of being his wife, so much so that she had convinced herself while they were courting to ignore how rough and demanding he had been with her when she'd caught the odor of beer on his breath. She'd accepted his excuses and his reassurances it wouldn't happen again…even when it had. She'd been blinded by love. How much better would it be to marry with her eyes wide open? No surprises and a husband whom she counted among her friends.

A pulse of excitement rushed up through her. She could escape, at last, from this farm, which had become a prison of pain and grief and second-guessing herself while she spun lies to protect the very person who had hurt her. She'd be a fool not to agree immediately.

Once she would have asked for time to pray about her decision, but she'd stopped reaching out to God when He hadn't delivered her from Lloyd's abuse. She believed in Him, and she trusted God to take care of the great issues of the world. Those kept Him so busy He didn't have time for small problems like hers.

"All right," she said. "I will marry you."

"Really?" He appeared shocked, as if he hadn't thought she'd agree quickly.

"Ja." She didn't add anything more, because there wasn't anything more to say. They would be wed, for better and for worse. And she was sure the worse couldn't be as bad as her marriage to Lloyd.

Chapter Three

Rebekah straightened her son's shirt. Even though Sammy was almost three, she continued to make his shirts with snaps at the bottom like a *boppli's* gown. They kept his shirt from popping out the back of his pants and flapping behind him.

"It's time to go downstairs," she said to him as she glanced at her *mamm*, who sat on the bed in the room that once had been Rebekah and Lloyd's. "*Grossmammi* can't wait to have you sit with her."

"Sit with *Mamm*." His lower lip stuck out in a pout.

"But I have cookies." Almina Mast smiled at her grandson. She was a tiny woman, and her hair was the same white as her *kapp*. With a kind heart and a generous spirit, she and her husband Uriah had hoped for more *kinder*, but Rebekah had been their only one. The love they had heaped on her now was offered to Sammy.

"Cookies? *Ja, ja!*" He danced about to his tuneless song.

Mamm put a finger to her lips. "Quiet boys get cookies."

Sammy stilled, and Rebekah almost smiled at his

antics. If she'd smiled, it would have been the first time since Joshua had asked her to marry three weeks ago. Since then the time had sped past like the landscape outside the window when she rode in an *Englischer's* van last week while they'd gone to Lancaster to get their marriage license. Otherwise she hadn't seen him. She understood he was busy repairing equipment damaged during last year's harvest.

"Blessings on you, Rebekah." *Mamm* kissed her cheek. "May God bless you and bring you even more happiness with your second husband than he did with your first."

Rebekah stiffened. Did *Mamm* know the truth of how Lloyd had treated her? No, *Mamm* simply was wishing her a happy marriage.

A shiver ached along her stiff shoulders. Nobody knew what had happened in the house she'd shared with Lloyd. And she had no idea what life was like in Joshua Stoltzfus's home. His wife had always been cheerful when they'd been together, but so had Rebekah. Joshua showed affection for his wife and his *kinder*...as Lloyd had when he was sober.

She'd chosen the wrong man to marry once. What if she was making the same mistake? How well did she know Joshua Stoltzfus? At least she and Lloyd had courted for a while. She was walking into this marriage blind. Actually she was entering into it with her eyes wide open. She was familiar with the dark side of what Lloyd had called love. His true love had been for beer. She would watch closely and be prepared if Joshua began to drink. She would leave and return to her farm.

When *Mamm* left with Sammy, Rebekah kneaded her hands together. She was getting remarried. If tongues wagged because Lloyd hadn't been dead for a year, she hadn't heard it. She guessed most of the *Leit* here and in Paradise Springs thought she'd been smart to accept the proposal from a man willing to raise her two *kinder* along with his own.

The door opened again, and Leah Beiler and Joshua's sister Esther came in. They were serving as her attendants.

"What a lovely bride!" Leah gushed, and Rebekah wondered if Leah was thinking about when the day would come for her marriage to Joshua's younger brother Ezra. Leah was preparing to become a church member, and that was an important step toward marriage. Even though nothing had been announced and wouldn't be until the engagement was published two weeks before the marriage, it was generally suspected that the couple, who'd been separated for ten years, planned to wed in the fall.

Esther brushed invisible dust off the royal blue sleeve of Rebekah's dress. For this one day, Rebekah would be forgiven for not wearing black as she should for a year of mourning.

"Ja," Esther said as she moved to stand behind Rebekah. "It makes your eyes look an even prettier blue. Let us help you with your apron."

Every bride wore a white apron to match her *kapp* on her wedding day. She shouldn't have worn it again until she was buried with it, but Rebekah was putting it on for a second time today. Pulling it over her head, she slipped her arms through and let the sheer fabric settle on her dress.

"Oh." Esther chuckled. "There may be a problem."

Rebekah looked down and realized her wedding

apron was stretched tightly across her belly. Looking over her shoulder at the other two women who were focused on the tabs that closed it with straight pins at the back, she asked, "Are they long enough?"

"I think so." Leah muttered something under her breath, then said, "There. They're pinned."

"Will it hold? It will be humiliating if one of the pins popped when I kneel."

"We'll pray they will stay in place." Esther chuckled. "If one goes flying, it'll make for a memorable wedding service."

Leah laughed, too. "I'm going to make my apron tabs extra long on my aprons from now on."

Rebekah couldn't manage more than a weak smile. "That's a *gut* idea."

The door opened and Joshua's daughter, Deborah, peeked in. "The ministers and the bishop have come in. Are you ready to go down?"

"Ja," Rebekah replied, though she wanted to climb out the window and run as far away as she could. What had she been thinking when she'd told Joshua yes? She was marrying a man whom she didn't love, a man who needed someone to watch his *kinder* and keep his house. She should have stopped this before it started. Now it was too late for second thoughts, but she was having second thoughts and third and fourth ones.

As she followed the others down the stairs to the room where the service was to be held, she tried not to think of the girl she'd been the last time she'd made this journey. It was impossible. She'd been optimistic and naive and in love as she'd walked on air to marry Lloyd Burkholder.

A longing to pray filled her, but she hadn't reached

out to God in more than a year. She didn't know how to start now.

As she entered the room where more than two hundred guests stood, her gaze riveted on Joshua who waited among the men on the far side of the room. The sight of him dressed in his very best clothing and flanked by his two sons made the whole of this irrevocably real.

It has to be better than being married to Lloyd, she reminded herself. She and Sammy and her *boppli* wouldn't have to hide in an outbuilding as they had on nights when Lloyd had gone on a drunken rampage. She'd seen Joshua with his late wife, and he'd been an attentive husband. When Lloyd had teased him about doing a woman's work after Joshua brought extra lemonade out to the porch for them to enjoy, Joshua had laughed away his words.

But he doesn't love you. This is little more than a business arrangement.

She hoped none of her thoughts were visible as she affixed a smile in place and went with Leah and Esther to the bench facing the men's. As they sat so the service could begin, Sammy waved to her from where he perched next to *Mamm*. She smiled at him, a sincere smile this time. She was doing this for him. There was no price too high to give him a safe home.

Squaring her shoulders, she prepared herself to speak the words that would tie her life to Joshua Stoltzfus's for the rest of their lives.

Joshua put a hand on his younger son's shoulder. Levi always had a tough time sitting still, but the boy wiggled more every second as the long service went on. Usually Levi sat with the unmarried men and boys, where his squirming wasn't a problem. Maybe Joshua shouldn't have asked him to be one of his *Newehockers*, but Levi would have been hurt if Timothy had been asked and he hadn't.

He smiled his approval at Levi when the boy stopped shifting around on the bench. He meant to look at Reuben Lapp, their bishop who was preaching about the usual wedding service verses from the seventh chapter of the Book of Corinthians. His gaze went to Rebekah, who sat with her head slightly bowed.

Her red hair seemed to catch fire in the sunshine. A faint smile tipped the corners of her mouth, and he thought of how her eyes sparkled when she laughed. Were they bright with silver sparks now?

He'd almost forgotten how to breathe when he'd seen her walk into the room. This beautiful woman would be his wife. Even though tomorrow she would return to wearing black for the rest of her year of mourning for Lloyd, the rich blue of her dress beneath her white apron banished the darkness of her grief from her face. He felt blessed that she'd agreed to become his wife.

Joshua shook that thought out of his head. He was no lovesick young man who had won the heart of the girl he'd dreamed of marrying. Instead of letting his mind wander away on such thoughts, he should be listening to Reuben.

At the end of the sermon, the bishop said, "As we are gathered here to witness this marriage, it would seem there can't be any objections to it."

Beside Joshua, his oldest mumbled, "As if that would do any *gut*."

Joshua glanced at Timothy. His son hadn't voiced

any protests about the marriage plans in the weeks since Joshua had told his *kinder* Rebekah was to be his wife. Why now?

"Let the two who wish to marry come forward," Reuben said, saving Joshua from having to point out that Timothy could have raised his concerns earlier.

Or was his son taking the opportunity to be unpleasant, as he'd often been since he'd turned sixteen? Now was not the time to try to figure that out. Now was the time to do what was right for his *kinder* and Rebekah's while he fulfilled his promise to his best friend.

Joshua stood and watched as Rebekah did the same a bit more slowly. When he held out his hand to her, she took it. Relief rushed through him because he'd been unsure if she would. He should say something to her, but what? *Danki?* That wasn't what a bridegroom said to his future wife as they prepared to exchange vows.

He led her to Reuben, who smiled warmly at them. Joshua released Rebekah's hand and felt strangely alone. Of the more than two hundred people in the room, she was the only one who knew the truth of why they were getting married. He was glad they'd been honest with each other when he'd asked her to marry. Now there would be no misunderstandings between them, and they should be able to have a comfortable life.

Is that what you want? A comfortable life?

His conscience had been nagging him more as their wedding day drew closer. Every way he examined their arrangement, it seemed to be the best choice for them.

As long as you don't add love into the equation, or do you think you don't deserve love?

Ridiculous question. He'd had the love of his life

with his first wife. No man should expect to have such a gift a second time.

"Is everything all right?" Reuben asked quietly.

Realizing the battle within him must have altered his expression, Joshua nodded. "Better than all right." He didn't look at Rebekah. If her face showed she was having second thoughts, too, he wasn't sure he could go through with the marriage. No matter how much they needed each other's help.

"Gut." Raising his voice to be heard throughout the room, the bishop asked, "My brother, do you take our sister to be your wife until such hour as when death parts you? Do you believe this is the Lord's will, and your prayers and faith have brought you to each other?"

"Ja."

Reuben looked at Rebekah and asked her the same, and Joshua felt her quiver. Or was he the one shaking? When she replied *ja*, he released the breath he'd been holding.

The bishop led them through their vows, and they promised to be loyal and stand beside each other no matter what challenges they faced. Rebekah's voice became steadier with each response. After Reuben placed her right hand in Joshua's right hand and blessed them, he declared them man and wife.

The simple words struck Joshua as hard as if a half-finished buggy had collapsed on him. Wife. Rebekah Burkholder was his wife. He was no longer a widower. He was a married man with four *kinder* and another on the way. The bonds that connected him to Matilda had been supplanted by the ones he had just made with Rebekah.

But I will love you always, Tildie.

He glanced guiltily at his new wife and saw her own face had grown so pale that her freckles stood out like chocolate chips in a cookie. Was she thinking the same thing about Lloyd?

It might not be an auspicious beginning for their marriage that their first thoughts after saying their vows were focused on the loves they had lost.

Rebekah stifled a yawn as the family buggy slowed to a stop in front of a simple house that was larger than the one she'd shared with Lloyd. The trip from Bird-in-Hand had taken almost a half hour, and Sammy had fallen asleep on her lap. He'd spent the day running around with the other youngsters. She had planned to have him sleep in his own bed tonight until Joshua asked her to return with him to his house. She'd hesitated, because a thunderstorm was brewing to the west. Even when he'd told her, with a wink, that it was his way of getting her away from the cleanup work at the end of their wedding day, she had hesitated. She'd agreed after *Mamm* had reminded her that a *gut* wife heeded her husband's wishes.

Joshua's three *kinder* sat behind them, and when she looked back she saw the two younger ones had fallen asleep, too. Timothy sat with his arms folded over his chest, and he was scowling. That seemed to be his favorite expression.

A flash caught her eye. Through the trees to the left glowed the bright lights she knew came from the house where the *Englischers* lived. She'd always had plain neighbors, and she hadn't thought about how the darkness at day's end would be disturbed by the glare of electric lights.

"The Grangers are *gut* neighbors," Joshua said as if she'd spoken her thoughts aloud. "That's their back porch light. They don't turn it on unless they're going to be out after dark, and they're considerate enough to turn it off when they get home. Brad put up a motion-detector light, but it kept lighting when an animal triggered it. Because it woke us, he went back to a regular light."

"They sound like nice people."

"Very. We have been blessed to have them as neighbors. Our *kinder* played together years ago, but now their older ones are off to college and only Alexis is at home."

"Are we going to sit here yakking all night?" asked Timothy. "It's stifling back here!"

Rebekah stiffened at his disrespectful tone, then she reminded herself they were tired.

Joshua jumped down before coming around to her side. "I'll carry him in." He held out his arms for Sammy.

She placed her precious *kind* in his arms, grateful for Joshua's thoughtfulness. She'd been on her feet too long today, and she'd become accustomed to taking a nap when Sammy did. As she stepped down, she didn't try to stifle her yawn.

"Let's get you inside," he said. "Then I'll take care of the horse."

"I'll put Benny away, *Daed*." Timothy bounced out and climbed on to the front seat after his brother and sister got out.

"*Danki*, but I expect you to come directly into the house when you're done."

"But, *Daed*, my friends—"

"Will see you on Saturday night as they always do."

Muttering something, Timothy drove the buggy toward the barn.

Joshua watched until the vehicle was swallowed by the building's shadow. Rebekah stood beside him, unsure if she should follow Deborah and Levi, who carried the bag she'd brought with a change of clothing for her and Sammy, into the house or remain by the man who was now her husband.

Husband! How long would it take her to get accustomed to the fact that she'd married Joshua? She was now Rebekah Mast Burkholder… Stoltzfus. Even connecting herself to him in her thoughts seemed impossible. She could have called a halt to the wedding plans right up until they'd exchanged vows. Reuben had given her that chance when he'd asked if everything was all right. Joshua had replied swiftly. Had he thought she might jilt him at the last minute?

"I'm sorry," Joshua said, jerking her away from her unsettling thoughts.

"For what?"

"I'd hoped Timothy would want to spend time with his family this one day at least." He looked down at Sammy. "He used to be as sweet as this little one."

Rebekah didn't know what to say. She started to put her hand on his arm to offer silent consolation. After pulling it back before she touched him, she locked her fingers in front of her. The easy camaraderie she'd felt for him was gone. Everything, even ordinary contact between friends, had changed with a few words. Nothing was casual any longer. Any word, any motion, any glance had taken on a deeper meaning.

Feeling as if she'd already disappointed him because she had said nothing, she followed him into the light green kitchen. Joshua turned on the propane floor lamp while Levi lit a kerosene lantern in the center of the table.

Again Rebekah was speechless, but this time with shock. Every flat surface, including the stove and the top of the refrigerator, was covered with stacks of dirty dishes. What looked to be a laundry basket was so full that the clothes had fallen into jumbled heaps around it. She couldn't tell if the clothes were clean or dirty.

"*Daedi* cooked our breakfast," Deborah said in a loud whisper beneath the hiss of the propane.

Joshua had the decency to look embarrassed as he set Sammy on the floor. Her son had woken as they'd stepped inside. "I meant to clean the house before you arrived, Rebekah, but I had a rush job yesterday, and then we had to get over to your house early today and..." He leaned one hand on the table, then yanked it away with a grimace.

Going to the sink beneath a large window, Rebekah dampened a dishrag. She took it to Joshua and as he wiped his hand off said, "You asked me to come back here tonight because you didn't want me to have to straighten up at my house after such a long day. And then you brought me *here* to *this*?" She burst into laughter. Maybe it was fueled by exhaustion and the stress of pretending to be a happy bride. The whole situation was so ludicrous that if she didn't laugh, she'd start weeping.

"I can see where you'd find that confusing," he said as he glanced around the kitchen.

"Confusing?" More laughter erupted from her, and she pressed her hands over her belly. "Is that what you call this chaos?"

Deborah giggled. "*Daedi* always uses twice as many

dishes and pans because he starts making one thing and ends up cooking something else entirely."

"It's usually because I don't have one of the ingredients," Joshua said, his lips twitching.

"Or you don't remember the recipe," Levi crowed.

"*Ja*, that's true." Joshua dropped the dishrag on the table and took off his best hat. "I can put a buggy together with my eyes closed—or near to that—but baking a casserole trips me up every time."

Laughter filled the kitchen as everyone joined in.

Picking up the cloth, Rebekah put it on the sink. "I'll face this in the morning."

"A *gut* idea." To his *kinder*, he said, "Off to bed with you."

"Will you come up for our prayers?" Levi asked.

"Ja."

Deborah took Sammy's hand. "*Komm* upstairs with me."

"No," Rebekah and Joshua said at the same time.

The little girl halted, clearly wondering what she'd done wrong.

"I'll put him to bed," Rebekah added. "Everything is new to him. Sammy, why don't you give Deborah and Levi hugs?"

The little boy, who was half asleep on his feet, nodded and complied.

"You're my brother now." Deborah's smile brightened her whole face. "When we found out *Daedi* was going to marry you, Rebekah, I was happy. I'm not the *boppli* of the family any longer."

"Sammy will be glad to have a big sister and big brothers." She looked at Levi, who gave her a shy smile. Should she offer to hug the *kinder*, too?

Before she could decide, the back door opened. Timothy came in, bringing a puff of humid air with him. He glared at them, especially Joshua, before striding through the kitchen. His footsteps resounded on the stairs as he went up.

Rebekah saw Joshua's eyes narrow. Timothy hadn't spoken to her once. At sixteen he didn't need a *mamm*, but perhaps he would come to see her as someone he could trust. Maybe even eventually as a friend.

Subdued, Deborah and Levi went out of the kitchen. Their footfalls were much softer on the stairs.

"I'm sorry," Joshua said into the silence.

She scooped up Sammy and cradled him. "He's a teenager. It's not easy."

"I realize that, but I hope you realize his rudeness isn't aimed at you. It's aimed at me." He rubbed his hand along his jaw, then down his beard. "I don't know how to handle him because I wasn't a rebellious kid myself."

"I wasn't, either."

"Too bad." The twinkle returned to his eyes. "If you'd been, you might be able to give me some hints on dealing with him."

She smiled at his teasing. He'd been someone she'd deemed a friend for years. She must—they must—make sure they didn't lose that friendship as they navigated this strange path they'd promised to walk together.

Joshua pointed at her and put a finger to his lips. She looked down to see Sammy was once more asleep. Joshua motioned for her to come with him.

Rebekah followed him through the living room. It looked as it had the last time she had been there before Matilda died. The same furniture, the same paint, the same sewing machine in a corner. She glanced toward the front door. The same wooden clock that didn't work.

With a start she realized that under the piles of dishes and scattered clothing the kitchen was identical to when Matilda had been alive. It was as if time had stopped in this house with Matilda's last breath.

Opening a door on the other side of the stairs, Joshua lit a lamp. The double bed was topped by a wild-goose-chase-patterned quilt done in cheerful shades of red and yellow and blue. He walked past it to a small bed his *kinder* must have used when they were Sammy's age. Another pretty quilt, this one in the sunshine-and-shadow pattern done in blacks and grays and white, was spread across it. Drawing it back along with the sheet beneath it, he stepped aside so she could slip the little boy in without waking him.

She straightened and looked around. The bedroom was large. A tall bureau was set against the wall opposite the room's two windows, and the bare floors shone with years of care. A quartet of pegs held a *kapp*, a dusty black bonnet and a straw hat. She wasn't surprised when Joshua placed his *gut* hat on the empty peg.

This must have been Joshua and Matilda's room. Suddenly the room seemed way too small. Aware of Joshua going to the bureau and opening the drawers, she lowered the dark green shades on the windows. She doubted Sammy would sleep late in the morning. Usually he was up with the sun.

She faced Joshua and saw he had gathered his work clothes. He picked them up from the blanket chest at the foot of the bed. His gaze slowly moved along her, and so many emotions flooded his eyes she wasn't sure if he felt one or all at the same time. Realizing she was wringing her hands, she forced her arms to her sides.

It was the first time they'd been alone as man and wife.

They stood in the room he'd shared with his first wife. She didn't trust her voice to speak, even if she had the slightest idea what to say as she looked at the man who was now her husband. The weight on the first word she spoke was enormous. There were a lot of things she wanted to ask about the life they'd be sharing. She didn't know how.

"Gut nacht," he said into the strained silence. "I'll be upstairs. Second door to the left. Don't hesitate to knock if you or Samuel need anything. I know it'll take you a while to get used to living in a new place."

"Danki."

He waited, but she couldn't force her lips to form another word. Finally, with a nod, he began to edge past her. When she jumped back, fearful he was angry with her, he stared at her in astonishment.

"Are you okay?" he asked.

She nodded, though she was as far from okay as she could be. It was beginning again. The ever-present anxiety of saying or doing the wrong thing and being punished by her husband's heavy hand.

"Are you sure?" His eyes searched her face, so she struggled to keep her expression calm as she nodded again.

He started to say something else, then seemed to think better of it. He bid her *gut nacht* again before he went out of the room.

She pressed her hands to her mouth to silence her soft sob as the tears she'd kept dammed for the whole day cascaded down her cheeks. She should be grateful Joshua had given her and Sammy this lovely room. And she was. But she also felt utterly alone and scared.

"What have I done?" she whispered to the silence.

She'd made, she feared, another huge mistake by doing the wrong thing for the right reasons.

Chapter Four

Joshua's first thought when he opened his eyes the next morning was, *Where am I?* The angle of the ceiling was wrong. There was a single window, and the walls were too close to the bed.

Memory rushed through his mind like a tempest, wild and flowing in every direction. Yesterday he'd married Rebekah, his best friend's widow.

Throwing back the covers, he put his feet on the rug by the bed. His beloved Tildie had started making rugs for the bedrooms shortly after they were wed, and she'd replaced each one when it became too worn. As he looked down through the thick twilight before dawn, he saw rough edges on the one under his feet. Sorrow clutched his heart. His sweet wife would never make another rug for the *kinder*.

Rebekah was his wife now. For better or for worse, and for as long as they lived.

He drew in a deep breath, then let it sift past his taut lips. He'd honored Lloyd's request, and he shouldn't have any regrets. He didn't. Just a question.

Where did he and Rebekah go from here?

Unable to answer that, because he was not ready to consider the question too closely, he pushed himself to his feet. He dressed and did his best to shave his upper lip without a mirror. As he pulled his black suspenders over his shoulders, he walked out of the bedroom.

Light trickled from beneath one door on the other side of the hall. He heard heavy footfalls beyond it. Timothy must already have gotten up, which was a surprise because most mornings Joshua had to wake his older son. Not hearing any voices, he guessed Levi was still asleep. Not even the cacophony of a thunderstorm could wake the boy. The other doorway was dark. He considered making sure Deborah was up so she wouldn't be late for school, but decided to let her sleep. It had been late by the time the *kinder* had gone to bed last night.

As he went down the stairs, Joshua heard the rumble of a car engine and the crunch of tires on gravel. His neighbor must be heading into Philadelphia this morning. Brad always left before sunup when he wanted to catch the train into the city, because he had to drive a half hour east to reach the station.

It was the only normal thing today, because as he reached the bottom of the stairs, he smelled the enticing aromas of breakfast cooking. He glanced at the bedroom where he usually slept. The door was closed.

The propane lamp hissed in the kitchen as he walked in to see Rebekah at the stove. She wore a dark bandana over her glistening hair. Beneath her simple black dress and apron, her feet were bare.

"Sit down," she said as if she'd made breakfast for him dozens of times. "Do you want milk in your *kaffi*?"

"No, I drink it black in the morning."

"Are the others awake?"

"Only Timothy." He was astounded how they spoke about such ordinary matters. There was nothing ordinary about Rebekah being in his kitchen before dawn.

"*Gut*. I assumed he'd get up early, too, so I made plenty of eggs and bacon." Turning from the stove, she picked up a plate topped by biscuits. She took a single step toward the table, then halted as her gaze locked with his.

A whirlwind of emotions crisscrossed her face, and he knew he should say something to put her at ease. But what? Her fingers trembled on the plate. Before she could drop it, he reached for it. His knuckle brushed hers so lightly he wouldn't have noticed the contact with anyone else. A heated shiver rippled across his hand and up his arm. He tightened his hold on the plate before *he* let it fall to the floor.

He put the biscuits on the table as she went back to the stove. Searching for something to say, he had no chance before Timothy entered the kitchen. His son walked to the table, his head down, not looking either right or left as he took his seat to the left of Joshua's chair at the head of the table.

Rebekah came back. Setting the coffeepot on a trivet in the center of the table, she hesitated.

"Why don't you sit here?" Joshua asked when he realized she was unsure which chair to use. He pointed to the one separated from his by the high chair he'd brought down from the attic before the wedding yesterday. He'd guessed she would want it for her son, but now discovered it created a no-man's-land between them.

She nodded as she sat. Was that relief he saw on her face? Relief they were no longer alone in the kitchen?

Relief the high chair erased any chance their elbows might inadvertently bump while they ate?

He pushed those thoughts aside as he bent his head to signal it was time for the silent grace before they ate. His prayers were more focused on his new marriage than food, and he hoped God wouldn't mind. After all, God knew the truth about why he'd asked Rebekah to be his wife.

As soon as Joshua cleared his throat to end the prayer, Timothy reached for the bowl containing fluffy eggs. He served himself, then passed the bowl to Joshua. That was followed by biscuits and apple butter as well as bacon and sausage.

Each bite he took was more delicious. The biscuits were so light he wondered why they hadn't floated up from the plate while they'd prayed. The *kaffi* had exactly the right bite for breakfast. He could not recall the last time he'd enjoyed a second cup at breakfast, because his own brew resembled sludge.

For the first time in months, Timothy was talkative. He had seconds and then thirds while chattering about a baseball game he'd heard about yesterday at the wedding, a game won by his beloved Phillies. It was as if the younger version of his son had returned, banishing the sulky teen he'd become. Even after they finished their breakfast with another silent prayer, Timothy was smiling as he left to do the barn chores he usually complained should be Levi's now that he worked every day at the buggy shop.

Joshua waited until the back door closed behind his oldest, then said, "Tell me how you did that."

"Did what?" Rebekah asked as she rose and picked up the used plates. After setting them on top of others stacked on the counter, she began running water to begin the massive task of washing the dirty dishes that had gathered since the last time he'd helped Deborah with them.

"Make my oldest act like a human being rather than a grumpy mule," he replied.

"Don't let him—or any of the other *kinder*—hear you say that. He wouldn't appreciate it."

"Or having his sister and brother repeat it."

"And Sammy, too. *Kinder* his age grab on to a word and use it over and over." She smiled as she put soap into the water and reached for a dishrag. Not finding one, she glanced around.

"Second drawer," he said, hoping there was a clean dishcloth. Like the dishes, laundry had piled up, ignored during the past week.

"Danki." She opened the drawer and pulled out a cloth. "I'll get accustomed to where everything is eventually."

He knew she didn't mean to, but her words were like a pail of icy water splashing in his face. A reminder that no matter how much they might pretend, everything had changed.

No, not everything. He still held on to his love for Tildie.

That will never change, he silently promised his late wife.

Never, because he wasn't going to chance putting his heart through such pain ever again.

Everything seemed unfamiliar in the Stoltzfus kitchen, yet familiar at the same time.

Rebekah was cooking breakfast as she did each

morning while she waited for the bread dough to rise a second time. She prepared enough for Levi and Deborah. Or she thought she had until she saw Levi could tuck away as much as his older brother. She fried the last two eggs for the boy, who ate them with enthusiasm.

"You cook *gut*! Real *gut*!" Levi said as he took his straw hat off the peg by the back door. With a grin at his sister, he added, "You should learn from her."

"She will," Rebekah replied gently when she saw the dismay on the little girl's face. "After school, Levi, while you are doing your chores, Deborah and I will be preparing your supper."

She was rewarded by a broad smile from Joshua's daughter, who said, "Levi is going to *Onkel* Daniel's shop after school." Deborah picked up the blue plastic lunch box and stepped aside so her brother could take the green one. "I'll be walking home with Mandy Beiler. Mandy lives down the road from *Grossmammi* Stoltzfus. She used to live in Philadelphia, but she lives here now. She is almost the same age I am. We—"

"We need to go." Levi frowned at his sister. "We don't want to arrive after the school bell rings. We won't have time to play baseball if we're late."

Deborah rolled her eyes as if ancient and world-weary. "All he thinks about is baseball."

"Like Timothy," Rebekah said as she wiped Sammy's hands before giving him another half biscuit.

"Timothy thinks about girls, too, especially Alexis next door. He talks to her every chance he can get." Levi put his hand over his mouth and gave a guilty glance toward his sister.

"I'm sure he does," Rebekah said quietly. "They've been friends their whole lives, haven't they?"

"*Ja*, friends." Deborah scowled at her brother. "Saying otherwise is silly. She is *Englisch*."

Levi nodded and opened the door. His smile returned when he added, "At the wedding he was talking to some girls from Bird-in-Hand. I think he really liked—"

"Whom he likes is Timothy's business." Rebekah smiled. "You know we don't talk about such things, so it can be a surprise when a couple is published to marry."

"Like you and *Daedi*?" asked Deborah. "Lots of folks were surprised. I heard them say so."

Nobody more than I, she was tempted to reply, but she made a shooing motion toward the door. The two scholars skipped across the yard to where their scooters were waiting. They hooked their lunch boxes over the handles before pushing them along the driveway toward the road.

She prayed the Lord would keep them safe. There were fewer cars along this road than in Bird-in-Hand, where carloads of tourists visited shops and restaurants.

She remained in the doorway and looked at the gray clouds thickening overhead. She hadn't expected to watch *kinder* leave for school for another couple of years. When Deborah looked over her shoulder and waved, the tension that had kept Rebekah tossing and turning last night diminished.

Help me make this marriage work, Lord, she prayed. *For the* kinder'*s sakes. They have known too much sorrow, and it's time for them to be happy as* kinder *should be.*

Seeing Sammy had found the box of crayons she'd packed to bring to Joshua's house, Rebekah turned to the sink. She had to refill the sink with the water heated by solar panels on the roof. When she'd met Joshua's second-youngest brother, Micah, at the wedding, he'd mentioned how he had recently finished the installation.

She hummed a tuneless song as she washed dishes, dried them and put them in the cupboards. Outside, it began to rain steadily. Maybe she should have told the *kinder* to take umbrellas to school.

By the time she had baked the bread as well as a batch of snickerdoodles, it was time for the midday meal. Lloyd always wanted his big meal at noon, but Joshua worked off the farm, so she would prepare their dinner for the evening. She had no idea what Joshua and his *kinder* liked to eat.

Rebekah pushed aside that thought as she put Sammy in the high chair and gave him his sandwich and a glass of milk. Sitting beside him, she ate quickly, then returned to work. She was scooping up an armful of dirty laundry from the floor when she heard Sammy call her.

Turning, she asked over her shoulder, "What is it, *liebling*?"

"Go home?" Thick tears rolled down his full cheeks.

She dropped the clothes to the floor. Sitting, she lifted Sammy out of the high chair and set him beside her. There wasn't enough room on her lap for him any longer. Putting her arm around his shoulders, she nestled him close. Her heart ached to hear his grief.

"I thought we would stay here and see Deborah and Levi when they get home from school," she said and kissed the top of his head.

"When that?"

"After Sammy has his nap."

He wiggled away and got down. "Nap now?"

"Not until you finish your sandwich." As she set him back in the high chair, she smiled at how eager he was to see Joshua's younger *kinder* again.

In Bird-in-Hand, Sammy had encountered other

kinder only on church Sundays. Their neighbors didn't have youngsters, and even if they had, Sammy was too young to cross the fields on his own. She'd become accustomed to remaining home in the months before Lloyd's death because he had flown into rages when he didn't know where she was. After his death, she'd had an excuse to stay behind her closed door.

But it hadn't been fair to Sammy.

Guilt clamped around her heart. Now *that* was familiar. Each time Lloyd had lashed out at her, she'd tried to figure out what she'd done to make him strike her again.

She was Joshua Stoltzfus's wife now. Her past was gone, buried with Lloyd.

Repeating it over and over to convince herself, she cleaned Sammy up after his lunch. She took him into the bedroom for his nap, but he was too excited. Each time she settled him on the small bed with his beloved stuffed dog, he was up afterward and sneaking out of the bedroom to explore the house.

Rebekah gave up after a half hour. Skipping his nap one day wouldn't hurt him, and she was curious, too, about the rest of the house. She glanced around the kitchen. The dishes were cleaned and put away, though she suspected she hadn't put them in their proper places. She would check with Deborah so everything was as it should be when Joshua arrived home. The dirty clothes were piled on the floor in the laundry room. In the morning before breakfast, if the rain stopped, she would start the first load. She hadn't mopped the floor. That made no sense when Joshua and the *kinder* would be tracking in water and mud.

There wasn't any reason for her *not* to explore the house.

Sammy grinned and chattered like an excited squirrel as they walked into the large front room where church could be held when it was their turn to host it. She wondered when that would be. Surely no one would expect the newlyweds to hold church at their house right away. Most newlyweds spent the first month of their marriage visiting family and friends nearby and far away. Joshua hadn't mentioned making calls, and she guessed his business wouldn't allow him time away. Just as well, because she didn't want to upset Sammy by uprooting him day after day.

When her son scrambled up the stairs, dragging the stuffed dog with him, she followed slowly, not wanting to slip on the smooth, wooden steps. But there was another reason she hesitated. She hoped Joshua wouldn't care if she went upstairs while he was at the buggy shop. Last night he'd told her to come and get him if she or Sammy needed anything, so her exploring shouldn't make him angry.

She wrapped her arms around herself. She hated how every thought, every action, had to be considered with care. After Lloyd's death, she'd been gloriously free from a husband's expectations. Now she was subjected to them once more. But would Joshua be as heavy-handed as Lloyd had been? She must make sure she never found out.

Lord, is this Your will? If so, guide my steps and my words on a path where we will remain safe.

Rebekah opened the first door on the second floor. A pair of dresses hung from pegs on the wall, along with a white apron Deborah would wear to church. A black bonnet waited beside them. By the window, the bed was covered with a beautiful quilt. The diamond-in-a-square pattern was done in cheerful shades of blue, purple and green. A rag rug beside the bed would keep little feet from the chill of a wintry floor.

The room beside it clearly belonged to Timothy because a man-size pair of shoes were set beneath the window, but a second mattress had been dragged into the room. She realized Levi must have given up his room to Joshua and was sleeping with his brother. She appreciated the boys' kindness, especially when they had no idea how long Levi would be sharing with Timothy.

Sammy ran to the door across the hall. She hurried after him, not wanting him to disturb Joshua's things. Grabbing her son's arm, she remained in the doorway.

Nothing about the room gave her a clue to the man she'd married. It was the same as the other rooms, except the ceiling slanted sharply on either side of a single dormer. Like his *kinder*'s rooms, the bed was neatly made and a rag rug brightened the wooden floor. She hadn't realized how she'd hoped to find something to reassure her that he was truly as gentle as he appeared. If he proved to be a chameleon like Lloyd…

"Cold, *Mammi*?" asked Sammy.

She smiled at him, even as she curbed another shiver. If a *kind* as young as her son could sense her disquiet, she must hide her feelings more deeply. She could not allow Joshua to suspect the secrets of her first marriage. If the truth of Lloyd's weaknesses became known, it could ruin her son's life.

She wouldn't let that happen.

Ever.

Chapter Five

As he drove toward his house, Joshua couldn't recall another day at the buggy shop that had seemed so long. Usually the hours sped past as he kept himself occupied with the work and trying to teach Timothy the skills his son would need to take over the shop after him.

He *had* been busy today, but his thoughts hadn't stayed on the antique carriage he was restoring for Mr. Carpenter, an *Englischer* who lived in a fancy community north of Philadelphia. Too often instead of the red velvet he was using to reupholster the interior of the vehicle that dwarfed his family buggy, Joshua had seen Rebekah's face.

Her uncertainty when she'd stood beside him in front of their bishop to take their wedding vows. Her laughter when they'd come into the messy kitchen. Her glowing eyes filled with questions as he bid her *gut nacht*. Her kind smile for his teenage son this morning.

"Watch out!" Timothy shouted as Levi yelped a wordless warning from behind him.

Joshua yanked on the reins, though the horse had already started to turn away from the oncoming milk truck. The driver gave a friendly wave as the vehicle rumbled past before turning into the lane leading to a neighboring farm.

Lowering his hands to his lap, Joshua took a steadying breath. He couldn't get so lost in his thoughts that he missed what was going on around him. He'd lost Tildie. He couldn't bear the idea of losing his two sons.

Help me focus, Lord, on what is important in my life.

"Want me to drive, *Daed*?" asked Timothy with a grin.

"I'll drive!" Levi wasn't going to be left out, especially after assisting his *onkel* at Daniel's carpentry shop.

"*Danki*, but I think I can manage to get us home from here in one piece." Joshua kept his eyes on the road as he guided the horse onto the driveway. He sent up a prayer of gratitude that he and his two sons hadn't been hurt.

What was wrong with him? He was showing less sense than his teenage son. If Timothy had been driving, Joshua would have reprimanded him for not paying attention. Even after he'd brought the buggy to a stop between the house and the barn, his hands shook. He nodded when Levi offered to help Timothy unhook Benny and get the horse settled for the night.

"Dinner will be on the table soon," he said as he did every evening after work. "So don't dawdle."

"Are you sure your bride will have it ready?" Timothy asked.

He glanced at his grinning teenage son. Tempted to remind his son that Timothy didn't know anything about Rebekah, he refrained. Joshua would have to admit he didn't know much about her, either. He wasn't going to confess that to his *kinder*.

"We'll see, won't we?" Joshua strode toward the kitchen door.

He paused to check the garden. It needed weeding again. He glanced at the chicken coop. The patch he'd put on the roof last month was still in *gut* shape. Reaching up, he gave the clothesline that ran from the back stoop to the barn a gentle tug. The tension remained *gut*, so he didn't need to tighten it yet to keep clean clothes from dragging in the grass.

Joshua sighed. He'd told the boys not to dawdle, and he was doing it himself. *Coward!* When he'd asked Rebekah to wed him, he'd known there would be changes. There had to be, because the marriage was bringing her and a toddler and soon a *boppli* into the family. He'd convinced himself he understood that.

But he hadn't.

Not really.

Knowing he could not loiter in his own yard any longer, he climbed the two steps to the small porch at the back door. He wasn't sure what he'd find, but when he opened the back door, he stared. Every inch of the kitchen shone like a pond in the bright sunlight. Even the stain he'd assumed would never come out of the counter was gone. Dishes were stacked neatly in the cupboards, and each breath he drew in contained the luscious aromas of freshly baked bread as well as the casserole Rebekah was removing from the oven.

The last time the kitchen had smelled so enticing was before Tildie became ill. Supper at his *mamm*'s house was accompanied by great scents, but his own kitchen had been filled with odors of smoke and scorched pans and foods that didn't go together.

His gaze riveted on her. Strands of red hair had escaped her *kapp* and floated around her face like wisps of cloud. Her face glowed with the heat from the oven, and she smiled as she drew in a deep breath of the steam coming from the casserole.

He had never seen her look so beautiful or so at ease. The thought shocked him. He'd always considered her pretty, but he'd never thought about how taut her shoulders usually were. Not just since he'd asked her to marry. Every time he'd seen her.

"Daedi!"

Deborah rushed over and threw her arms around his waist. He embraced her, turning his attention from Rebekah and the kitchen's transformation to his daughter. Her smile was wider than he'd seen in a long time. She must have enjoyed her time with Rebekah and Sammy after school.

A pulse of an unexpected envy tugged at him. He dismissed it, not wanting to examine too closely how he wished he could have shared that time with them.

"Perfect timing," Rebekah said as she carried the casserole of scalloped potatoes to the table. Platters of sliced roast beef were set beside bowls holding corn and green beans. Sliced bread was flanked by butter and apple butter. Chowchow and pickled beets completed the feast. She looked past him, and he realized Timothy and Levi stood behind him when she asked, "Do you boys need to wash up?"

His mouth watered. His sons' expressions were bright with anticipation, and he wondered if his own face looked the same. Even so, he motioned for the boys to go into the laundry room to wash their hands. They went with a speed he hadn't seen them show before dinner…ever.

As he went to the kitchen sink, he almost bumped into Sammy, who was racing to his *mamm*. The *kind* glanced at him fearfully. He hoped the little boy would get used to him soon. Maybe in his own young way Sammy mourned for Lloyd and wasn't ready to replace his *daed* with another man.

Joshua doubted he could ever be the man Lloyd Burkholder had been. When people spoke of Lloyd, they always mentioned his dedication to his neighbors and his family. More than once, he'd heard someone say Lloyd always accompanied Rebekah wherever she went. A truly devoted husband. With his work taking him to the shop each day, Joshua couldn't be the doting husband his friend had been. He hoped Rebekah understood.

As soon as everyone was seated at the table, he signaled for them to bow their heads for silent grace. He was pleased to see Sammy do so, too. Rebekah had taught her son well.

He didn't linger over his prayers, which again had more to do with making his new marriage work and less to do with the food in front of him. Clearing his throat, he raised his head. The *kinder* didn't need prompting to start passing the food along the table.

His worry about what to discuss during the meal vanished when Levi monopolized the conversation. His younger son was excited that he'd learned how to use one of the specialty saws Daniel had for his construction projects. As he described the tool in detail, Rebekah helped Sammy eat with as little mess as possible. Deborah and Timothy were busy enjoying the meal.

Joshua realized he was, too. He'd been dependent on his own cooking or Deborah's struggling attempts for too long. There had been plenty of meals at his *mamm*'s house, but even she wasn't the cook Rebekah was. Each dish he tried was more flavorful than the one before. Like his sons, he had seconds.

"Don't fill up completely," Rebekah said as she smiled at his daughter. "There's peach pie for dessert."

"You're spoiling us with your *wunderbaar* food," he replied.

She flushed prettily when the boys hurried to add their approval. She deflected it by saying quietly, "God gave each of us a unique talent, and the praise should go to Him."

Deborah jumped up, announcing she would serve dessert. She cut the pie and brought the first plate to the table and set it in front of Joshua with a hopeful smile. "Try it, *Daedi*." Her voice dropped almost to a whisper. "I made it."

"You made the pie, Deborah?" He hoped his disappointment didn't come through in his voice. As *gut* as the rest of the meal had been, he'd been looking forward to sampling Rebekah's peach pie. She'd brought one to the house years ago, and he still recalled how delicious it had been.

Her brothers regarded the pieces their sister handed them with suspicion. As one they glanced at him. Neither reached for a fork, even when Deborah sat again at the table. When dismay lengthened his daughter's face, he couldn't delay any longer.

Picking up his fork, he broke off a corner from the pie. Flakes fell on to the plate. That was a surprise because Deborah's last attempt at making a pie had resulted in a crust as crisp as a cracker. Aware how everyone was watching, he raised the fork to his mouth.

Flavors came to life on his tongue. Peaches, cinnamon and even a hint of nutmeg.

"This is…" He had to search for the best word. Not *surprising* or *astounding* and most especially not *impossible*, though he couldn't believe Deborah had made the flaky crust that was as light as the biscuits at breakfast.

When his daughter regarded him with anticipation, he finished, "Beyond *wunderbaar*."

"Danki," his daughter said as she turned toward the other end of the table to watch her brothers dig in now that Joshua had announced the pie was *gut*. "Rebekah taught me a really easy way to make the crust. It's important not to handle it too much. Mix it, roll it out and get it in the pan."

"She did a *gut* job." He broadened his smile as he took another bite.

"It wasn't hard when I have such an eager student," Rebekah replied,

When they finished the meal with a silent prayer, Joshua asked Timothy to help Levi with the dishes while Deborah played with Sammy. Before they could answer, he stood and invited Rebekah to come out on the front porch with him. He wasn't sure who looked the most surprised at his requests.

But one thing he knew for certain. He and Rebekah needed some time to talk and come to terms with the life they had chosen together. He had put off the discussion since he asked her to be his wife.

Rebekah lifted Sammy down from the high chair and told him to show Deborah the pictures he'd colored earlier. As the toddler rushed to the little girl, he shot an uneasy glance in Joshua's direction. His *mamm* looked dismayed, and she bit her lower lip.

Joshua said nothing as he motioned for her to lead the way to the front door. When he reached over her head to hold the screen door, she recoiled sharply. Had he surprised her? She must have known he was right behind her, and she should have guessed he'd hold the door for her.

A grim realization rushed through him. She must be worried that if she lowered the walls between them, even enough to thank him for a common courtesy, he would insist on his rights as her husband. He wanted to reassure her that he understood her anxiety, but anything he could think to say might make the situation even more tense.

If that were even possible.

Scolding herself for showing her reaction to Joshua's hand moving past her face, Rebekah knew she needed to take care. He hadn't been about to slap her, and acting as if he was could betray the secret she kept in the darkest corners of her heart. She hurried to the closer of the two rocking chairs on the front porch. She'd always loved the rockers Joshua and Matilda had received as wedding gifts. Whenever she and Lloyd had visited, she had happily sat in one and watched the traffic on the narrow road in front of the house.

Now…

She pushed aside thoughts of being a trespasser. Upon marrying Joshua, this had become her home. She had to stop considering it another woman's.

"I thought you might appreciate a bit of rest," Joshua said as he leaned against the railing so he could face her. "I never expected you to toil so hard in the kitchen."

"You know how it is. You do one thing and that leads to another and then to another, and before you know it, the whole task is done."

He smiled and something spun with joy within her. He was a handsome man, even more so when he grinned because his dark brown eyes glistened. He was past due for a haircut, and strands fell forward into his eyes. She folded her hands on her lap to keep from reaching up to discover if it was as silken as it looked.

"And I had lots of help," she added so silence didn't

fall between them. "Deborah is like a sponge, soaking up everything I tell her."

"Especially about making pie." He patted his stomach. "I may have to take up jogging like the *Englischers* if you keep feeding us such amazing food."

"If you do, I will sew an under-the-chin strap for your hat like I do for Sammy's so it won't bounce off."

He roared a laugh, slapping his hand against the roof pole beside him. She smiled, glad she'd been able to ease the strain on his face…if only for a short time.

When he waved at a buggy driving past, he said, "Daniel is late returning home tonight. I wonder if he is courting someone again."

"Sometimes it takes time to find the right person to marry."

"Oh, that doesn't seem to be his problem." He stared after the buggy until it vanished over a hill. "I hope this time he doesn't get cold feet and put an end to it. He's courted two different girls we thought he might wed. The girls joined the church in anticipation of a proposal, but he hasn't been baptized. They married other men."

"Maybe he isn't ready."

"I was baptized, married and had a *kind* by the time I was his age."

She slowed her rocking to stop. "Each of us is different, Joshua. Daniel will make the right decision when it's God's will for him to do so."

"*Ja*. Daniel is a *gut* man." With a sigh he looked back at her. "I meant to ask you. Daniel was glad to have Levi help him this afternoon. He'd like Levi to come back a day or two each week if you can spare him."

"It would be *gut* for Levi to learn more about what his *onkel* does." She smiled as she began rocking again slowly and watched the lights from a car ripple through the trees along the road. "With only a few years of school left for him, he can learn about a craft he might want to pursue."

"My thoughts exactly, but I don't want him neglecting his chores here. The garden needs—"

"Deborah, Sammy and I will take care of the garden. You don't need to worry about it."

"I wasn't." He paused and looked everywhere but at her. "How did Sammy do today?"

"He spent the day exploring the house. Fortunately I was able to block the cellar door with a chair before he took it into his head to investigate down there."

Again he drew in a deep breath. "I know it may take time, but I wish he felt more comfortable around me."

"It *will* take time."

"I know that, but I wish he wouldn't cringe away in fear. Every time that happens, I feel like a horrible beast."

Was he still talking about Sammy, or was he referring to her reaction by the door? She must not ask.

"Sammy has had a lot of changes in his life over the past couple of days. He was too wound up today to take a nap, so he's overly tired, too."

"At least he's happy to spend time with Deborah."

"And she with him." She started to add more, but put her hand to the side of her belly when the *boppli* kicked. "Ouch!"

"A strong one?" he asked.

She smiled. "It kicks like a horse. Maybe it's warning me that I won't get much chance to sit once it's born. When I'm busy, it's quiet. As soon as I take a moment's rest, it begins its footrace."

"Do you have names chosen?"

She shook her head, not wanting to hear his next words. The ones everyone said. If it was a boy, surely she would name it for its late *daed*. How could she explain Lloyd was the last name she would select? Without being honest about the man he'd been, she would sound petty and coldhearted.

"Don't let the *kinder* know," he said, startling her with his smile. "You'll be bombarded with more name suggestions than you could use for a dozen litters of kittens. I doubt the names Mittens and Spot would be of much use to you."

She laughed honestly and freely. The sound burst out of a place within her she'd kept silent for so long she'd almost forgotten it existed. Tears teased the corners of her eyes. Not tears of pain or fear but tears of joy.

"That's a nice sound," he said, his smile growing wider. "It gives me hope that we're going to make this marriage work better than either of us can guess right now."

"I hope so."

"And to that end..." He moved to the other rocking chair. When he began to ask about her daily schedule and if she wanted him to pick up the few groceries they'd need from his brother's store or if she preferred to do the shopping herself, his questions showed he had many of the same anxieties she did, along with the determination to overcome them.

She answered each question the best she could. She had some of her own, which he replied to with a smile. More than once he mentioned he was glad she had thought of some matter he hadn't. His words made her feel part of the family, not an outsider who'd come to cook and clean and watch over the youngsters.

By the time they rose to go inside and spend time

with the *kinder*, her shoulders felt lighter. She brought Sammy to sit beside her on a bench not far from the stove that would warm the room next winter. With her arm around him, she watched Joshua don a pair of dark-rimmed glasses. She'd had no idea he needed glasses.

Joshua read from Psalm 146, and she was comforted by the words of praise. "Happy is he that hath the God of Jacob for his help, whose hope is in the Lord his God… The Lord preserveth the strangers, He relieveth the fatherless and widow…"

She stroked her son's hair while he fell asleep. Holding him, she listened as Joshua continued. His warm voice rose and fell with the joyous words, and she found her own eyes growing heavy as she let the sound soothe her.

This was the future she'd imagined when she had accepted Lloyd's proposal. Evenings with the family gathered together, savoring the words inspired by God's love. The perfect end to the day as the gas lamp hissed and the last light of the day faded into night. An affirmation of faith and love with the people who were in her heart.

It wasn't perfect. Her marriage to Joshua wasn't a true one. However, there was no reason they couldn't work together to make a *gut* and happy home. He had treated her with kindness, and she prayed she'd seen the real man and that he had no secret life as Lloyd had.

After Joshua finished reading and the family prayed together, Rebekah took Sammy into the downstairs bedroom while Joshua and his *kinder* went upstairs. Their footfalls sounded along with the occasional creaking board while she settled her son into bed. He roused enough to ask for Spot, the stuffed dog he slept with each night. Telling him to stay where he was, she went into the dark kitchen. She used the flashlight she'd found in a drawer earlier, but had no luck finding Spot.

Sammy had had the stuffed toy with him when they'd gone upstairs that afternoon. Maybe he'd left it up there somewhere. If she hurried she could retrieve it before the other *kinder* were asleep.

After pausing to tell Sammy she would bring Spot to him in a few minutes, she went up the stairs far more slowly than Deborah and Levi had a few minutes ago. Gas lamps were on in the two bedrooms on the right side of the hallway. From beyond the first door to the left, she heard water splashing and guessed someone was brushing his or her teeth.

She glanced into Deborah's room. It was empty, and a quick scan told her Sammy's precious toy wasn't there. Maybe in the room the boys shared…

As she went to look there, a voice came from the half open door on the other side of the hall. Low, deep and fraught with pain. She froze when she realized it belonged to Joshua.

She should back away, but she couldn't move. She saw Joshua sitting on the bed with his back to her. His head was bowed, and, at first, she thought he was praying. Then she realized he held something in his hands.

A rag rug that was frayed with wear around the edges.

He held it as if the worn fabric was a treasured lifeline. His gaze was so focused on the rug he was oblivious to everything else, even the fact his door had come ajar.

Go! she told herself, but her legs refused to work.

"Tildie, I hope you understand why I've done what I have," Joshua said. "I know you'd want our *kinder* to have the best care, and Rebekah is already giving them that. You told Lloyd often that he was blessed to have her as his wife. He was, and I am blessed to have her help and to be able to help her. But I miss having you here, Tildie. Nobody will ever take your place. Even if I can't show it any longer in public now that I'm married again, I'll never stop loving you."

The pain in his words matched what twisted through her heart. Her hope Joshua would be open and honest with her was dashed. So easily he spoke of keeping his love for his late wife a secret.

Secrets! They had dominated her first marriage. Now they dashed her hopes for her second one.

She edged away and pressed back against the wall so not even her shadow would betray her presence. Eavesdropping was wrong, especially during such a private conversation.

She walked away as quietly as she had come up the stairs. She knew it would be silly to run away as she longed to. She could fall and hurt herself on the stairs.

When she looked in the bedroom to check on Sammy, she saw him curled up in bed, his toy in his arms. He must have remembered where he'd left it and gotten it on his own. She blinked back abrupt tears. The way Sammy cuddled with his precious Spot reminded her of how Joshua had held the torn rag rug with such love and sadness. A peculiar sensation surged through her.

Envy.

Envy that Joshua's love for his wife had survived even after her death, while Lloyd's had vanished as soon as he had had that first drink after their wedding. She wondered what it would be like to be loved like Joshua loved his Tildie and if she'd ever find out for herself.

Chapter Six

"Gute mariye!"

Joshua's *mamm* called out the greeting. Deborah rushed to hug her *grossmammi.* Wiping her hand on a towel, Rebekah smiled at Wanda Stoltzfus. The older woman's casted arm was wrapped in a black sling, but her eyes twinkled as she handed a basket topped with a blue cloth to her granddaughter.

During the two weeks since the wedding, the *kinder* had often visited the house down the road where Wanda lived with her six unmarried sons and younger daughter. Rebekah and Joshua and Sammy had been invited along with the rest of the family to dinner one night last week, but a bad storm had kept them at home. At church services on Sunday, Rebekah had appreciated her mother-in-law introducing her again to people she'd met at the wedding. She hoped she'd match names and faces better when the next church Sunday came around.

The past fourteen days had been a whirlwind. The lives of Joshua's family and her own had fallen into a pattern with meals and work and family time in the evening, but Rebekah avoided spending time on the porch—or anywhere else—alone with her husband. If he'd noticed, he hadn't said anything. Perhaps he was relieved she expected no more from him.

"Wanda, why are you waiting for an invitation?" Rebekah asked, glad a visitor gave her the excuse to think of something other than her peculiar marriage. "Come in, come in."

Putting her arm around her granddaughter, Wanda walked in. Her expression softened when her gaze alighted on Sammy.

"How is our big boy?" she asked.

Sammy clutched Rebekah's skirt. She scooped him up and settled him on her hip. He pressed his face against her shoulder.

Wanda winked at Rebekah before she said, "I hope you don't hide too long, my boy. Chocolate chip cookies are best when they're warm."

He didn't look up, but shifted so he could watch what the others did. The cookies smelled *wunderbaar*, and she guessed he was wavering between his shyness and his yearning for a treat.

"Deborah, will you unpack the basket?" Rebekah asked, earning a wide grin from the little girl. "Wanda, would you like to sit down?"

"*Ja*. This cast feels like it weighs more every day." She sat at the table and grimaced as she readjusted her arm. "I thank God I broke my left arm, though I had no idea how much I did with that hand until I couldn't use it."

"I discovered that when I broke my finger." She fought to keep her smile from wavering as the brutality of her past poked out to darken the day. "I appreciate you coming for a visit."

"I wanted to give you time to become accustomed to your new home." She looked around. "I'd say you are settling in well and making this a home again."

Deborah piped up, "She's teaching me to make lots of yummy things, *Grossmammi*."

"So I hear from your brothers." She winked at Rebekah. "Maybe I'll even share the recipe for my chocolate chip cookies with her."

"And me?" asked the little girl.

"Of course." She wagged a finger at the *kind*. "As long as you listen to me and don't try to make up your own recipes as you used to."

"*Daed* always did that."

"And how did it turn out?"

When Deborah burst into giggles, Rebekah laughed, too. "Let me heat some water, and we'll have tea. Deborah, would you mind getting the tea down?"

The little girl pulled a chair beside the cupboard and climbed up to take out a box of teabags.

As she turned to put on the kettle, Rebekah almost stumbled. She tightened her hold on Sammy.

"Give him to me," Wanda urged.

She doubted he would go to Wanda. "I don't want him to bump your injured arm."

"He won't."

"He's shy."

"So I see, but, Sammy, I know you want one of my chocolate chip cookies."

Her son astonished her when, after a quick glance at Wanda, he stretched out his arms to her. Hoping her face didn't reveal her surprise, Rebekah placed him on the older woman's lap. Wanda pointed to the plate on the table beside her.

"I've never met a boy who didn't like chocolate chip cookies." Wanda smiled when Sammy reached past her to take a cookie. "What a *gut* boy you are! Only taking one."

"More?" he asked.

"Why don't you try this one?" the older woman asked. "Tell me if you like *Grossmammi* Wanda's cookies."

"*Grossmammi* Wanda," he repeated as he stared at the cast. "Boo-boo?"

"*Ja*, but it is getting better."

"Give kiss to make better?"

"Aren't you a sweet little boy?" She nodded and tapped her cheek. "Why don't you kiss me right here?"

Rebekah was surprised when Sammy did. After serving tea to her mother-in-law, Rebekah gave the *kinder* glasses of milk. She sat and joined the easy conversation about the end of the school year, two new babies in the district and Deborah's friend Mandy, who seemed to be a favorite of Wanda's, too, because the little girl was often at the house. Nothing strayed too close to the unusual circumstances of Rebekah's marriage. Like her son, Rebekah grew comfortable with the kind older woman.

As soon as he'd finished his first cookie, Sammy had another and downed his milk with a gulp. He nodded when Rebekah asked him if he wanted more, then he looked across the table.

"Debbie!" He pointed with his cookie. "Milk, too?"

"Ja." Deborah grinned. "*Danki*, Sammy."

Rebekah refilled both glasses. "It sounds as if you've got a new name."

"He has trouble saying my whole name. So now we're Sammy and Debbie."

Wanda nodded. "That sounds perfect for a sister and brother."

"I have lots of brothers now." The little girl leaned on the table. "Rebekah, please have a girl."

Though she secretly harbored the same hope, Rebekah replied, "We shall be blessed with the *boppli* God has chosen for us." Even at her darkest times while she had been pregnant with Sammy, she hadn't doubted God was sending her a *boppli* to help ease her heart.

Before anyone could reply, the back door opened, and Joshua walked in. He smiled as he hung his straw hat on the peg by the door.

Her heart quivered, missing a beat when his gaze met hers. A warmth she'd never felt before swirled within her like a welcome breeze on a hot day. His light blue shirt bore the stains from his work at the buggy shop, and more grease was ingrained across his hands, emphasizing his roughened skin. She had always considered him a *gut*-looking man, but as his eyes crinkled with his broadening smile, she could not keep from thinking that he was now her *gut*-looking husband.

But he wasn't. Theirs wasn't a true marriage. It was an arrangement to ensure Sammy and his *kinder* were taken care of. Her head knew that, but not her heart that continued to pound against her breastbone.

"I didn't realize you were here, *Mamm*," Joshua said after greeting them.

"Your sister is cleaning the house, and she made it clear I was in the way." She smiled to take any sting from her words. "She's so worried I'll slip and break something else."

"Because you try to do everything as you did before you broke your arm." He reached across the table and snagged a pair of cookies.

"One," Sammy scolded. "Only one."

Rebekah's heart faltered again, but for a very different reason. Lloyd never tolerated his son telling him what to do. How would Joshua react to being scolded by a toddler? She clenched her hands. If he raised his hand to strike Sammy, she would protect her son.

But Joshua chuckled. "You're right, Sammy. One cookie at a time. But *Grossmammi's* cookies are *gut*, aren't they?"

Sammy smiled and nodded. When he picked up his glass that was coated with crumbs, he offered it to Joshua.

After taking it, Joshua pretended to drink before saying, "*Danki*, Sammy. Just what I needed."

Her son's smile glowed. Rebekah looked from him to her husband. Was Sammy sensing, as he had with Wanda, that he had nothing to fear from Joshua?

"What are you doing home in the middle of the day?" Wanda asked. "Come to see your pretty new wife?"

"*Ja*, and my pretty daughter." He winked at Deborah, who giggled. "I told Levi I'd stop by on my way back from dropping off a repaired buggy. He's riding in with me so he can help Daniel at his shop."

"How is Daniel doing with him?" his *mamm* asked.

"Well. Having someone to teach has given my little brother a purpose."

"He is a *gut*, hardworking boy, but he's avoiding decisions he should make about joining the church and finding a wife." Wanda sighed. "I shouldn't feel *ho-*

chmut that four of my *kinder* so far have made the decision to be Amish."

"It isn't pride, *Mamm*." Joshua patted her right shoulder carefully. "You want what is best for each of us."

"True." Wanda smiled again. "And it sounds as if Daniel teaching Levi is *gut* for both of them."

"Levi is eager to learn. I wish I could say the same about his brother." He glanced at the two *kinder*. "Deborah, will you take Sammy outside and wash the cookie crumbs off his hands and face?"

"Ja," she replied, though her expression said she'd prefer to stay.

As soon as the *kinder* had closed the door after them, Joshua sighed. "I could use some advice, *Mamm*. Timothy is growing less and less interested in learning about buggies."

Rebekah went to get a dishrag to scrub off the cookie crumbles that would grow as hard as concrete if left on the table. She listened as Joshua and Wanda discussed Timothy's reluctance to do anything at the shop. Not even building wheels, a task he used to look forward to, engaged his attention now.

She should say nothing. Timothy wasn't her son, and, other than being enthusiastic about the food she put on the table, he hadn't said much to her. She seldom saw him other than at breakfast and dinner. He was with Joshua during the day, and he always seemed to be somewhere else once the evening meal was over. He came in for Joshua's nightly reading from the Bible or *Martyrs Mirror*, but vanished again after their prayers.

"I don't know what else I can tell you," Wanda said with a sigh. "You've tried everything I would have."

"Having every day be one long debate about what I

need him to do is getting old very fast." Joshua ran his fingers through his beard and looked at Rebekah. "Do you have any ideas?"

"Timothy does his share of chores here, doesn't he?" she asked, choosing her words carefully. Joshua might not like what she was about to say, but he'd asked her opinion.

"Ja."

"Without complaint?"

"Usually." His brows lowered with bafflement. "What does that have to do with his attitude at the buggy shop?"

"Maybe Timothy doesn't show any interest in your work because it isn't the work he wants to do."

Joshua stared as if she'd suggested he flap his arms and fly around the yard. "I plan to hand the business over to him when I am ready to retire."

"It's *your* plan. Not his." She met his gaze steadily.

Wanda stood and patted Rebekah's arm. "Now I'm even more glad you're a part of our family. You have put your finger on the crux of the problem." She looked at her son. "Have you asked Timothy if he wants to take over the shop?"

"No." He drew in a deep breath and let it out slowly. "I assumed because he used to be curious about what I was doing that he wanted to learn the work himself."

"He was a *kind*," his *mamm* said with a gentle smile. "As his *daed*, you were what he wanted to be when he grew up. Now he is nearly a man, and he sees the world and himself differently." She made a shooing motion with her fingers. "You need to talk with your son, and it's not going to get easier by putting it off."

"True." Joshua's tone was so dreary his *mamm*

laughed. When he began to chuckle along with her, Rebekah joined in.

She'd forgotten how *wunderbaar* shared laughter could be. She hoped she wouldn't have to forget again.

The rumble of a powerful engine surprised Rebekah. Turning from where she was folding the quilts she had aired, she stared at the bright red car slowing to a stop not far from the house. She grabbed Sammy's hand when he took a step toward it.

"Go! See!" he shouted.

She was about to reply when Timothy ran around the house and toward the car. She hadn't realized he was home yet.

The driver's window rolled down, and Timothy leaned forward to fold his arms on the open sill. She heard him laugh and wondered if it was the first time she'd ever heard him do so.

After dropping the quilt in the laundry basket, she began to cross the yard to where the teen was now squatting so his face was even with whoever was inside the car. She absently pushed loose wisps back under her *kapp*, because she wasn't sure who was behind the wheel.

Deborah skipped down the front porch steps. She'd been beating dust out of rag rugs. She waited for Rebekah and walked with her toward the vehicle.

Rebekah's eyes widened when she realized the driver was an *Englisch* girl, one close to Timothy's age. The girl's black hair was pulled back in a ponytail. Unlike many *Englisch* teenagers, she wasn't wearing layers of makeup. She didn't need any because her lightly tanned cheeks were a healthy pink. She wore a simple and modest black blouse.

"I'm Alexis Granger," said the girl. "Hey, Tim, move back so I can see your new mom." She laughed, and Timothy did, too. Leaning her elbow on the car's open window, she said, "You must be Joshua's new wife."

Startled by the *Englisch* girl's effusiveness, Rebekah smiled. "*Ja*, I am Rebekah." She looked at Sammy who was eyeing the girl and the car with the same interest Timothy was. "And this is my son Samuel."

"A big name for a cute, little boy."

"We call him Sammy."

The pretty brunette chuckled. "Much better. Hi, Sammy."

He gave her a shy grin but didn't say anything.

"He's a real cutie," Alexis said before holding out a stack of envelopes. "These were delivered to our mailbox by mistake, and Mom asked me to drop them off over here on my way to work."

"Where do you work?" Rebekah asked to be polite.

"At one of the diners in Bird-in-Hand where the tourists come to try Amish-style food." She hooked a thumb in Timothy's direction. "*He* thinks I got the job because my boss was impressed my neighbors are plain, but it was because I was willing to work on weekends." She rolled her eyes. "Saving for college, y'know. Anything I can pick up for you while I'm in town?"

"*Danki*, but we're fine."

"Okay. See ya, Tim!" She backed the car out onto the road. Small stones spurted from under the back tires.

Rebekah half turned to protect Sammy. Even though the tiny stones didn't come near them, a dust cloud billowed over them.

The glow that had brightened Timothy's face while Alexis was there faded. Without a word, he walked back to the house. As he did, he tucked his fingers into one side of his suspenders and tugged at them on each step, clearly deep in thought.

"Don't mind him," Deborah said, warning Rebekah she'd stared too long. "He's like that when Alexis stops by."

"She comes often?"

"*Ja*, but not as much as she used to. She's always got something going on at school or at work. Timothy misses having her around. He thinks she's hot."

Shocked, Rebekah began, "Deborah—"

"Will you call me Debbie as Sammy does?" the little girl asked with a grin.

"We'll talk about your name in a minute. You shouldn't make such comments about Alexis. It isn't nice."

The girl frowned. "Timothy said it was a compliment."

"I'm sure he did, but your brother hasn't learned yet that what's inside a person is more important than the outside."

"But *Daedi* said *you're* pretty when he told us he was going to marry you."

Rebekah ignored the delight that sprang through her, but it wasn't easy. "He and I have known each other for years. He didn't marry me for what I look like." She put her hands on her distended belly. "Certainly not now!"

That brought a laugh from the little girl, and Rebekah changed the subject to the chores they had left to do before Joshua and Levi got home.

As Deborah turned to head back to the front porch, she asked, "Will you call me Debbie?"

"As long as your *daed* agrees. He'll want you to have a *gut* reason."

The little girl considered her words for a long minute, then said, "I want to be called Debbie so Sammy feels part of our family."

Unbidden tears filled Rebekah's eyes. What a *wunderbaar* heart Debbie had been blessed with! As she assured Debbie she would speak with Joshua about the nickname after dinner, she had to keep blinking to keep those tears from falling. She hugged the *kind.*

Dearest God, danki *for bringing this little girl into my life.* Sweet Debbie was making Sammy a part of her family, and Rebekah, too. For the first time in longer than she could remember, Rebekah felt the burden she carried on her shoulders every day lift. It was an amazing feeling she wanted to experience again and again. Was it finally possible?

Joshua heard the screen door open after supper, but he kept reading the newspaper's sports section. The last light of the day was beginning to fade, and he wanted to finish the article on the new pitcher who had signed with the Phillies. He'd been following the Philadelphia baseball team since he wasn't much older than Sammy. His sons were baseball fans, too, and he'd expected Timothy or Levi to come out and ask for an update before now.

When a question wasn't fired in his direction, he looked up. His eyes widened when he saw Rebekah standing there.

Alone.

The last time she'd spent any time with him without one of the *kinder* nearby was the first evening when they'd tried to work out aspects of their marriage. How guilty he'd felt afterward! Though he knew his life was now entwined with Rebekah's, his heart belonged to Tildie. He wanted to be a *gut* husband, but how could he when he needed to hold on to his love for the first woman he had exchanged vows with?

My brother, do you take our sister to be your wife until such hour as when death parts you? Do you believe this is the Lord's will, and your prayers and faith have brought you to each other?

The words Reuben had asked him at the wedding ceremony rang through his head. They were identical to the vows he had taken with Tildie. Why hadn't anyone told him how he was supposed to act once death parted him from Tildie? The *Ordnung* outlined many other parts of their lives. Why not that?

Renewed guilt rushed through him when he saw Rebekah regarding him with uncertainty. She must be enduring the same feeling of being lost without Lloyd, though she never gave any sign. Perhaps she was trying to spare him.

"I'm sorry if I've disturbed your reading," she said. "The *kinder* are practicing their parts for the end-of-the-school-year program next week. Sammy is their rapt audience."

He chuckled. "The end-of-the-school-year program is important to them. It's hard to think how few more Levi will be in. At least there will be others with Deborah and Sammy."

"I thought you should know Deborah wants to be called Debbie now."

"Why?"

Her soft blue eyes glistened as she told him how his daughter longed to help Sammy feel more at home with his new family. Were those tears, or was it a trick of the light?

His own voice was a bit rough when he said, "Debor—Debbie has always been thoughtful. I wish I could say the same for her older brother."

"May I talk to you about Timothy?"

He lowered the newspaper to his lap and lifted off his reading glasses. "Has he been giving you trouble?"

"No," she said as she sat in the rocker. "He treats me politely."

"I'm glad to hear that." He didn't add he'd worried his older son would take out his frustrations with his *daed* on Rebekah. He was jolted when he realized that unlike his younger siblings, Timothy had perceived the distance between the newlyweds.

Was it obvious to everyone?

He didn't have a chance to answer the unanswerable because Rebekah said, "But I have noticed something about Timothy that concerns me."

"What?" He silenced his sigh. After trying to motivate his son to do something other than mope around the buggy shop, he didn't want to deal with Timothy again tonight.

Instantly he chided himself. A parent's job didn't end when the workday did. Because he was worried about his failure to reconnect with the boy who once dogged his footsteps was no reason to give up. His son was trying to find his place in the world, as every teenager did.

"Have you noticed," Rebekah asked, drawing his attention back to her, "how Timothy stops whatever he's doing whenever Alexis Granger and her snazzy car goes by?"

"Snazzy?"

"It's a word, right?"

He smiled. "It is, and it's the perfect description for the car. I know Brad wishes he'd gotten a less powerful one. Letting a new driver like Alexis get behind the wheel is like giving Sammy the reins to our family buggy."

"I'm not as worried about the car as I am about Timothy's interest in it…and the girl who drives it."

"They've been friends since they were little more than babies."

"But they aren't babies any longer." She sighed. "I don't want to cause trouble, Joshua, but Timothy lit up like a falling star when she was here, and I noticed him watching her go the whole way up the Grangers' driveway tonight. As soon as supper was over, he was gone."

"Saturday nights are for him to be with his friends."

"I realize that, but Alexis fascinates him. If you want my opinion…"

"I do."

She met his eyes evenly. "He'd like more than a friendship with her."

Joshua folded his glasses and put them on the windowsill by his chair. He did the same with the newspaper as he considered her words. Maybe he had been turning too blind an eye toward his oldest's friendship with the neighbor girl. He didn't want to do anything to cause his son to retreat further from the family. To confront Timothy about the matter could create more problems.

When Rebekah didn't say more, he was grateful. She

wasn't going to nag him about his son as his older sister Ruth did. Ruth's *kinder* didn't seem to have a rebellious bone in their bodies, so she couldn't understand what it was like to have a son like Timothy. But he'd think about what Rebekah had said.

"*Danki* for caring enough for my son to be worried about him," he said, reaching out to put his hand on hers.

She moved her fingers so smoothly he wouldn't have noticed if he hadn't seen her flinch away too many times. As she came to her feet, unable to hide that she wanted to put more space between them, she said, "I'm not Timothy's *mamm*, but I care about him."

Do you care about me, too? The question went unasked, and it would remain unasked, because he realized how much he wanted the answer to be *ja* and how much he feared it would be no.

Chapter Seven

The yard of the simple, white schoolhouse at the intersection of two country roads was filled with buggies, and more were pulling in as Rebekah climbed the steps after Joshua. She was glad Sammy could manage the steps on his own, because it was more difficult each day to pick him up and carry him. Inside, the schoolroom looked almost identical to the one she had attended. The same textbooks were on the shelves at the back of the room, and the scholars' desks were set in neat rows with the teacher's desk at the front of the blackboard.

An air of anticipation buzzed through the room. The scholars were eager to begin their program as well as their summer break. Younger *kinder* looked around, excited to get a glimpse of where they would be attending school. Parents used the gathering as a chance to catch up on news.

Most of the *mamms* sat at the scholars' desks, but Rebekah decided to remain at the back with the *daeds* and grandparents and other relatives. She was unsure if her ever-widening belly would fit behind one of the small desks.

The room was filled with sunshine, but its glow wasn't as bright as the smiles on the scholars' faces while they stood near their teacher's desk. On the blackboard behind them, someone—probably Esther Stoltzfus, their teacher—had written in big block letters: HAVE A FUN AND SAFE SUMMER!

Joshua's younger sister looked happy and harried at the same time. Levi and Debbie talked with fondness and respect for their teacher who was also their *aenti*. Now Esther was trying to get each of the scholars in the proper place for the beginning of the program. The youngest ones complied quickly, but the oldest ones, knowing this was their final day of school, seemed unable to stand still or stop talking and giggling.

But Esther treated each *kind* with patience and a smile. When two of the younger scholars went to her and whispered below the buzz of conversation in the room, she nodded. They ran out the side door and toward the outhouses at the back corner of the schoolyard.

After she turned to scan the room, Esther smiled warmly when her eyes met Rebekah's. She went to her desk and pulled out her chair. She rolled it to the back of the room and stopped by Rebekah.

Esther motioned at the chair. "Would you like to sit down?"

"I don't want to take your chair."

"I won't have a chance to sit." Her dimples rearranged the freckles scattered across her cheeks and nose. "Please use it."

"Danki." She wasn't going to turn down the *gut*-hearted offer a second time.

Joshua took the back of the chair from his sister and

shifted it closer to the last row of desks. "You should be able to see better from here, Rebekah."

"Danki," she repeated as she sat with a relieved sigh. She settled Sammy on her knees. While the men talked about farming and the weather and the latest news on their favorite baseball teams, she pointed out the posters and hand-drawn pictures tacked on cork strips that hung about a foot below the ceiling. He was delighted with each one and asked when he could come to school with the older *kinder.* With a smile, she assured him it would be soon.

When the two young scholars returned, they took their places. Rebekah smiled when she saw Debbie at the far right in the front row of girls while Levi peered over the head of the scholar in front of him from the other end of the back row.

"Debbie! Levi!" called Sammy as the room became silent.

Everyone laughed, and Rebekah whispered to him that he needed to be quiet so he could hear the songs.

Sammy bounced on Rebekah's knees as the *kinder* began to sing. He clapped along with the adults at the end of each song. The recitations made him squirm with impatience, but each time another song began, he tried to join in with a tuneless, "La, la, la."

Rebekah enjoyed the program and was pleased when Debbie and Levi performed their poems without a single hesitation or mistake. She glanced up to see Joshua smiling. Though pride wasn't considered a *gut* thing among the Amish, she could tell he enjoyed seeing his *kinder* do well after their hard work to memorize each word.

Sammy grew bored during a short play performed

by the oldest scholars. Other toddlers were wiggling and looking around, as well. Even a cookie couldn't convince him to sit still.

"Down," he said. When she didn't react, he repeated it more loudly.

Not wanting him to disrupt the program, she let him slide off her knees. She whispered for him to stay by her side.

"Hold hand?" he asked.

She nodded and held out her hand. She was astonished when he took Joshua's fingers. Leaning his head against Joshua's leg, he smiled when her husband tousled his hair without taking his eyes off the program.

Sammy obviously had changed his mind about Joshua. A warm glow filled her. She'd seen signs of the change in recent days, but her son had remained tentative around Joshua in public. For the first time, he wasn't clinging to her.

Her joy disappeared when Sammy suddenly darted past her as the *kinder* began to sing again. She jumped to her feet, but he grasped Debbie's hand and announced, "Sammy sing, too."

Rebekah's face burned as she started toward the *kinder* who were giggling at her son's antics. Her sneaker caught, and a broad hand grasped her shoulder, halting her. Time telescoped into the past to the night Lloyd had kept her from leaving the house by seizing her from behind and shoving her against a wall. Her reaction was instinctive.

Her arm came up to knock her captor's hand away. "No! Don't!" she gasped and whirled away so fast she bumped into a desk and almost tumbled off her feet.

Hands from the people around her steadied her. She

was grateful, but as panic drained away, she saw startled and alarmed expressions on all the faces around her.

No, not *all* the faces. Joshua's was as blank as the wall behind him. He stood with his arm still outstretched. To keep her from falling, she realized. His eyes contained a myriad of emotions. Mixed in with confusion and annoyance was…hurt. A new wife shouldn't shy away from her husband's touch. She had embarrassed him in front of his family and neighbors. If she could explain without risking Sammy's future…

Esther's cheerful voice sounded forced. "Let's start over with our final song of this year's program. Sammy and any of the other younger *kinder* are welcome to join us."

While more little brothers and sisters rushed up to stand beside their siblings, Rebekah groped for her chair. Joshua steadied it as she sat, but she couldn't speak, not even to thank him. She lowered herself to sit and stared straight ahead.

Sammy now stood beside Levi in the back row with the other boys. As the *kinder* enthusiastically sang their friendship song, he looked up at Levi with admiration and tried to sing along, though he didn't know the words.

It was endearing, but she couldn't enjoy it. Adrenaline rushed through her, making her gasp as if she had run a marathon. Her pulse thudded in her ears so loudly she had to strain to hear the *kinder*'s voices. She clapped along with everyone else when the song came to an end.

The *kinder* scattered, seeking their parents. Hugs and excited voices filled the schoolroom.

Rebekah pushed herself to her feet again when Levi, Debbie and Sammy eased along an aisle to where she and Joshua waited. She hoped her smile didn't look hideous while she thanked the *kinder* for a *wunder-*

baar program. If her voice was strained, the youngsters didn't seem to notice.

However, the adults around her must have. More than one gave her a smile. Not pitying, but sympathetic, especially the women who carried small babies. Their kindness and concern was almost too great a gift to accept.

And, she realized, nobody looked toward Joshua with censure. None of them could imagine him hurting her on purpose. That thought should have been comforting, but who would have guessed Lloyd could be a beast when he drank? She certainly hadn't.

She'd made one mistake. Now she wanted to avert another, but would the mistake be trusting Joshua or not trusting him?

The schoolyard was filled with happy shouts and lighthearted conversation. Everywhere, including where Joshua stood with his family. The noise came from the *kinder*, who were as agitated as if they'd eaten a whole batch of their *grossmammi's* cookies. But he was glad no one paid attention to the fact neither he nor Rebekah said anything as they walked with their *kinder* to the buggy. Everyone was too wound up in happiness to notice his misery.

And Rebekah's?

He wasn't sure what she was thinking or feeling. She hid it behind a strained smile.

What happened? he wanted to shout, though he seldom raised his voice. Nothing could be gained by yelling and things could be lost, but his frustration was reaching the boiling point.

He hesitated as he was about to assist Rebekah into the buggy. Would she pull away as she had in the schoolhouse? Humiliation burned in his gut as he recalled the curious glances aimed in his direction, glances quickly averted.

But stronger than his chagrin was his need to know why she'd acted as she had. Until she'd pulled away from him, he'd thought they were becoming accustomed to each other and had found a compromise that allowed them to make a *gut* and comfortable home for the *kinder*. He had dared to believe, even though theirs was far from a perfect marriage, it had the potential to become a comfortable one.

Now he wasn't sure about anything.

God, help me. Help us! Something is wrong, and I don't know what it is.

Wondering if he really had anything to lose, Joshua offered his hand to Rebekah, and she accepted it as if nothing unusual had happened. As the *kinder*, including Sammy, scrambled into the back, he stepped in, as well. He picked up the reins and slapped them against the horse.

Rebekah remained silent, but he doubted she would have had a chance to speak when the *kinder* chattered like a flock of jays rising from a field. Sammy was eager to learn the words to the final song they had sung, and Debbie was trying to teach him while Levi described every bit of the program as if none of them had been there. They kept interrupting each other to ask him and Rebekah if they'd liked one part of it or another.

He answered automatically. Every inch of him was focused on the woman sitting beside him. Her fingers quivered, and he was tempted to put his own hand over them to remind her, whatever was distressing her, she wasn't alone in facing it. He resisted.

The *kinder* rushed out of the buggy as soon as it stopped beside the house. When Rebekah slid away and got out on her side, he jumped out and called her name. She turned as he unhooked the horse from the buggy.

"Come with me and Benny," Joshua said simply.

"I should…" She met his gaze and then nodded. "All right."

She walked on the other side of the horse as they went to the barn. She waited while he put Benny in a stall and gave him some oats.

He stepped out of the stall. "Rebekah—"

"Joshua—" she said at the same time.

"Go ahead," he urged.

"Danki." She paused so long he wondered if she'd changed her mind about speaking. He realized she'd been composing her thoughts when she said, "I don't know any other way to say this but I'm sorry I embarrassed you at school. I will apologize to Esther the next time I see her."

"Rebekah, if I was embarrassed or not isn't important. What's important is why you said what you did. Tell me the truth. Why did you pull away like you did?"

"Haven't you heard pregnant women often act strangely?" Her smile wobbled, and he guessed she was exerting her flagging strength to keep it in place.

"*Ja*, but…" He didn't want to accuse her of lying. Not that she was, but she was avoiding the truth. Why? "I was trying to prevent you from falling."

"I know." Her voice had a soft breathlessness that urged him closer, but her face was stiff with the fear he'd seen at school. "I need to be careful I avoid doing anything that might injure my *boppli*."

Maybe he'd misread her reaction, and her anxiety about the *boppli* had made her words sound wrong. He hadn't always been correct in his assumptions about Tildie's reactions, either.

The thought startled him. Since Tildie's death he hadn't let such memories into his mind. At first he'd felt ungrateful if he recalled anything but the *gut* times they'd shared. Even a jest from his brothers about married life had fallen flat for him. He didn't want to admit, even to himself, his marriage to Tildie had been anything less than perfect.

But that was the past. He had to focus on keeping his current marriage from falling apart before it even had a chance to thrive. He refused to believe it was already too late.

"One of the reasons I asked you to be my wife is to make sure you and your *kinder* are taken care of," he said as he walked with her out of the barn. "I told you that right from the beginning."

"I know you did."

"Do you believe I was being honest?"

When she paused and faced him, he was surprised. He'd expected her to try to keep distance between them. Now they stood a hand's breadth from each other. She tilted her head enough so he could see her face beneath her bonnet's brim. Even as she drew in a breath to speak, he wondered if he could remember how to breathe as he gazed into her beautiful blue eyes.

"I believe you aspire to being as honest as any man can be, Joshua Stoltzfus," she whispered.

"Then believe I don't want you to worry about you and your *kinder*. I take my vows seriously to face every challenge with you, Rebekah. God has brought us together, and I believe His plans are always for *gut*."

"I do, too."

"It pleases me to hear you say that." He admired the scattering of freckles that drew his gaze to the curve of her cheekbones and then to her full lips. His imagination sped faster than a runaway horse as he speculated how her red hair would brush her face and his fingertips if it fell, loose and untamed, down her back. She was his wife, and he'd thought often during the long nights since their wedding of her sitting in their bedroom and brushing out those long strands.

She was his wife, and he was her husband.

He framed her face with his hands before another thought could form. Her skin was soft and warm…and alive. How many times had he reached out in the past few years and found nothing but the chill of an old memory?

Her blue eyes beckoned but he hesitated. A man could lose himself within their depths. Was he ready to take the step from which there would be no turning back? The memory of Tildie and their love remained strong, and Rebekah's loss was still fresh and painful.

But didn't God want them to put others aside and cleave to one another, heart to heart, now that they were wed? The thought shook him. He wanted to live the life God had set out for him, but he hadn't been when he let the past overwhelm the present.

He saw her lips forming his name, but the sound never reached his ears as he bent toward her…toward his wife…his lovely Rebekah…

The squeal of tires on the road jerked him back to reality, and he released her as Timothy strolled up the driveway whistling. His son grinned as he waved at Alexis who tooted the car's horn to him.

Joshua heard the kitchen door shut, and Rebekah was gone. He stood there with his hands empty. He had let his opportunity to hold her slip away. He prayed it wouldn't be his only chance.

Chapter Eight

A dozen contrasting emotions flooded Rebekah as the buggy entered the lane leading to the house where she used to live with Lloyd. It had been her home for more than five years, but the site of her greatest nightmare. Sammy had been born there and taken his first steps in the kitchen. It was also the place where Lloyd had first struck her in a drunken rage.

She hadn't expected Joshua to suggest a drive on the Saturday morning a week and a half after the school program. Previously on Saturdays he'd tended to chores in the barn or gone through catalogs to plan for what he needed to order for the buggy shop. Her heart had leaped with excitement because she'd hoped he was going to give her a tour of his shop. She wasn't sure why he hadn't asked her and Sammy to visit, but as each day passed, asking him seemed more difficult.

At first she'd needed to concentrate on getting the house back into acceptable shape. A stomach bug had made the three younger *kinder* sick and claimed her time and attention last week. As soon as they were well, Timothy had gotten sick. Yesterday was the first day he'd joined them for a meal, and he'd eaten no more than a few bites before he'd excused himself and returned to bed.

Keeping herself busy allowed her not to spend time alone with her husband. He hadn't said anything, but she knew he was curious why she continued to avoid him. If his son hadn't arrived when Joshua had clasped her face in his broad hands, he would have kissed her. What she didn't know was what would have happened if she'd kissed him back. The precarious balance of caring for the *kinder* at the same time she struggled not to care too much for her husband was a seesaw. A single step in the wrong direction could destroy that fragile equilibrium.

Now he had asked for her to go for a drive with him, and she'd accepted because she didn't have a *gut* excuse not to, especially because she liked spending time with him as long as they kept everything casual. She had been astonished when she learned their destination wasn't Joshua's buggy shop but Bird-in-Hand and Lloyd's farm. She'd agreed it was a *gut* idea to check on the house. When Joshua had told her that Timothy would bring the other *kinder* over in the open wagon after they finished their Saturday chores, she was grateful for her husband's thoughtfulness. She couldn't put any of the larger items she wanted to bring back to Paradise Springs in the family buggy, but they would fit easily in the wagon.

While they drove on Newport Road to bypass most of the busy tourist areas, she'd pointed out various landmarks. Joshua nodded as they passed the butcher's shop and suggested they stop on the way back to Paradise Springs, because his brother's store had a very small meat section with not a lot of items. She'd showed him the white schoolhouse Sammy would have attended and the medical clinic between a florist shop and a store selling quilts and Amish-built furniture.

"They've contacted my brother Jeremiah about selling some of his pieces there," he had said. "He's done well enough at our family's shops, but he's wavering. He likes the work, but not the paperwork that selling directly to customers requires." He looked at the medical clinic. "Shouldn't you be seeing a doctor for regular checkups?"

"I went before the wedding, and the midwife suggested I find another clinic in Paradise Springs. Is there one?"

"Ja," he had replied. "Do you want me to make an appointment for you?"

"That might be a *gut* idea."

He had changed the subject, but now neither she nor Joshua said anything as he brought the buggy to a stop near the kitchen door. He stepped out, and she did the same. She looked around.

Each inch of the house and the barns and the fields held a memory for her, *gut* and oh-so-bad. It was as if those memories were layered one atop another on the scene in front of her. The most recent ones of her and Sammy were the easiest, because they weren't laced with fright.

The farm had been her prison, but it had become a symbol for her freedom from fear since Lloyd's death. It still was, she realized in amazement. The farm was her sanctuary if she needed it. She didn't know if she would, but she wasn't going to be unprepared ever again.

Joshua crossed his arms over his light blue shirt. "What do you think?"

"About what?" She wasn't going to share the true course of her thoughts.

"The appearance of the farm. From what I can see, most of the buildings don't need much more than a coat or two of paint to make them look *gut*."

"I agree, except the roof on the field equipment barn is sagging. It should be shored up."

He gave her a warm smile. "True, and I know just the man for the job."

"Your brother Daniel?"

"*Ja*. He has repaired buildings in worse condition. I asked him to meet us here, so he can see what needs to be done. We want the buildings to look their best, so someone will offer a *gut* amount of money for the farm."

"Money for the farm?" she repeated, shocked at how easily he spoke of selling the farm. *Her farm!*

"*Ja*. Once it is fixed up, I thought we'd hold an auction for the land and buildings, as well as for anything else you want to sell—furniture, household goods and any farm equipment. Several neighbors have stopped by the buggy shop in the past couple of weeks to ask me when I plan to put it on the auction block, so the bidding should go well."

He was going to sell her farm. Just like that. Lloyd had insisted on making the big decisions, too, and she'd learned not to gainsay him. Why had she thought Joshua might be different?

Or maybe he wasn't the same as Lloyd. After all, Joshua had invited her to the farm to consider what needed to be done in order to sell it. He hadn't sold it without allowing her to see her home one more time.

The thought gave her the courage to say, "Joshua, I don't know if I'm ready to sell the farm yet."

"Why do you want to hold on to it?" He glanced from her to the weatherworn buildings. "If you're thinking you shouldn't sell it because it's Lloyd's legacy to Sammy, you need to consider how much upkeep it's going to need until he's old enough to farm. You could rent out the fields and the house, but buildings require regular upkeep, and it might cost as much or more than what you'd get from the rent. Selling the farm will provide money for Sammy when he's ready to decide what he wants to do as a man."

She knew he was right…about Sammy. But he had no idea about the true reason she couldn't bear to let the farm go. How she'd longed for a refuge when Lloyd had been looking for someone to blame for his ills! Nothing Joshua had done suggested he would be as abusive as her first husband, but she needed a place to go with Sammy if that changed.

Not just Sammy, but the other *kinder* if they needed shelter, too.

Rebekah hoped her shrug appeared nonchalant. "I hadn't thought about what would happen with the farm." That much was the truth. "I need time to think about selling it." Walking to where hostas were growing lush near the porch, she took the time to pray for the right words to persuade Joshua to listen.

From where he hadn't moved, he said, "It'll take time to repair the buildings, especially as Daniel will need to do the work around his other jobs. At this time of the summer we can't ask for others to help." He paused, then asked, "Rebekah?"

She faced him. *"Ja?"*

"You'll have plenty of time to make up your mind. You don't need to decide today." He gave her a cockeyed smile that made something uncurl delightfully in her center.

Something drew her toward him, something that urged her to think of his arms around her. She halted because she'd learned not to trust those feelings after they'd led her to Lloyd.

The rattle of the open wagon came from the end of the lane, and Rebekah saw Timothy driving the other *kinder* toward the house. As they neared, the older ones looked around, their eyes wide with astonishment. She guessed they were comparing their *onkel* Ezra's neat and well-maintained farm to this one.

But her gaze went to her son. She'd protected him from much of what had happened between her and his *daed*, and his young age would wash away other memories. Still, she didn't want this visit to upset him. She realized she didn't have anything to worry about when she heard his giggles as he played in the back of the wagon with Debbie.

Joshua lifted the younger *kinder* out while the boys jumped down. At the same time, he asked Rebekah where the lawnmower was. He sent Levi to get it from the shed. Timothy was given the task of collecting any canned food and other supplies from the kitchen and the cellar, while Debbie volunteered to look for any vegetables in the neglected garden.

"Sammy help?" her son asked.

"Help me," Timothy said, picking him up and hanging him upside down over his shoulder. While Sammy kicked his feet and chortled in delight, he added, "I'll keep a close eye on him in the kitchen, Rebekah. Before I go down to the cellar, I'll take him out to help Debbie."

"Danki." She didn't add how pleased she was Timothy had volunteered to spend time with her son. It would be *gut* for both boys.

If Joshua was surprised by his oldest's actions, he didn't show it as he walked into the backyard. He went to the chicken coop, which she'd kept in excellent shape. It was the only building that had been painted in the past three years.

"Where are the chickens?" he asked as he looked over his shoulder.

"I gave the leftover chickens to my *mamm* so she can have fresh eggs." As she crossed the yard to where he stood, she rubbed her hands together, then stopped when she realized the motion showed her nervousness at being on the farm again. Maybe it wouldn't be the best haven.

But it was her only one.

She shivered and hastily added, "Most of the chickens were used for the wedding."

"I remember." He gave her a wry grin. "Though I don't remember much about what else we ate."

"I don't, either."

He paused and faced her. She took a half step back before she bumped into him. His mouth tightened. She'd given him every reason to believe a commonplace motion like trying not to run into someone had a great significance.

Before she could think of a way to explain, his expression eased again. He took her right hand between his and gazed into her eyes with a gentle honesty that threatened to demolish her resolve to keep her secrets to herself.

"What I do remember vividly," he said in little more than a whisper, "is how when you came down the stairs I forgot everyone else in the room. I remember how you made sure my *kinder* didn't feel left out and how you welcomed them to participate in each tradition. Not many brides would have insisted on the *kinder* sharing our special corner during the wedding meal."

"Sammy was fussy, so I wanted to keep him nearby. How could I have had him there with us and not the others?"

"You don't need to explain, Rebekah. I'm simply saying I know our marriage isn't what either of us planned on, but—"

"It could be worse?"

When he laughed hard, she released a soft breath of relief. His words had become too serious, too sincere, too…everything. She couldn't let herself be swayed by pretty words as she had with Lloyd. Hadn't she learned her lesson? Even if Joshua wasn't like Lloyd, and she prayed every day he wasn't, she couldn't forget how he still loved his late wife.

"I don't want to farm this land or any other, Rebekah." He gave her a lopsided grin. "I know every Amish man is supposed to want to be a farmer, but I don't. God didn't give me the gifts he gave my brother. Ezra seems to know exactly when to plant and when to harvest. He can communicate with his herd of cows like he's one of them. That's why we agreed, rather than having the farm go to Daniel as the youngest son, Ezra should take over after *Daed* died. To be honest,

Daniel was relieved, because he likes building things. It worked out well for each of us."

"It did."

He became serious again. "Rebekah, if you hoped I'd farm here, I'm sorry. We probably should have discussed this before our wedding."

As well as so many other things, she wanted to say. But the most important truths must remain unspoken.

"*Danki* for being honest with me," she said. "No, I didn't expect you to take over the farm, especially when it's so far from your home and your shop." She didn't hesitate before she added, "I hope you'll invite me and Sammy to visit the shop one of these days."

His eyes grew wide. "You want to visit the buggy shop? I thought you weren't interested, because you haven't said anything about going there."

"Joshua, you love your work, and as your wife I want to understand what is important to you."

He smiled as broadly as Sammy did when offered a sweet. "Whenever you want to visit, drop in. I'll show you around so you can see how we make and repair buggies. Come as often as you wish."

When she saw how thrilled he was, happiness bubbled up within her from a hidden spring she thought had long ago gone dry. She felt closer to her husband than she ever had.

Had he sensed that, too? She couldn't think why else he would rapidly change the subject back to the condition of the farm buildings.

"Daniel should be here soon," he said. "The project he's been working on isn't far from here. If you see him, will you send him to the main barn? I'll start there."

"All right." She felt as if she'd been dismissed like a *kind* caught eavesdropping on her elders.

As she turned to go to the house, he added, "It's going to take time to get the buildings fixed up. Once everything is in decent shape, we'll talk about the future of the farm. Okay?"

"Ja," she said, though they were postponing the inevitable clash of wills. There must be some way to explain why she needed to keep the farm without revealing the truth about Lloyd.

But how?

Joshua watched as his youngest brother poked at a beam with a nail, and he tried not to sneeze as bits of hay and dust and spiderwebs drifted down onto his upturned face. Daniel was trying to determine if any insects or dry rot had weakened the wood. If the nail slid in easily, it was a bad sign. A board along the side of the barn could easily be replaced, but if one of the beams failed, the whole building could collapse. From where Joshua stood at the foot of the ladder, he couldn't see what his brother was discovering at the top.

"Looks *gut*," Daniel said as he came down the ladder at the same speed he would have walked up the lane.

His younger brother was finally filling out after spending the past five or six years looking like a black-haired scarecrow, disconnected joints sticking out in every direction. His shoulders were no longer too wide, and his feet and hands seemed the right size. The gaze from his bright blue eyes was steady. He and his twin Micah looked identical except for the cleft in Daniel's chin, something Daniel hated and was looking forward to hiding when he grew a beard after he married.

"No dry rot?" Joshua asked.

He shook his head. "In spite of how it looks, the barn was kept up well for many years. Any damage is recent, say the past five years or so, and it's only on the surface." He dropped the nail into a pocket of his well-worn tool belt. "But if the barn doesn't get some maintenance soon, it'll tumble in on itself."

"I know at least that much about construction, brother *boppli*." Joshua smiled, knowing how the term annoyed Daniel, who had been born more than a half hour after his twin.

"Are you sure your ancient mind can hold so much information?" his brother shot back.

Laughing with Daniel erased the rest of the tension he'd been feeling since he decided to bring Rebekah and the *kinder* to Lloyd's farm. Much of it had eased when she'd told him she would like to visit the buggy shop. Her effort to learn more about his life showed she wanted their marriage to have a chance, too.

His relief at hearing that revealed how uncertain he'd been about her expectations from their marriage. *Maybe you haven't given her a chance before today to tell you that she wanted to visit*, scolded the little voice from his conscience. He couldn't expect her to be candid when he withheld himself from her. At first he hadn't wanted to mention Tildie, because he hadn't wanted Rebekah to think he was comparing her housekeeping and interactions with the *kinder* to how his first wife would have handled them. Again he regretted not taking more time to talk before they spoke their vows. If they'd had more discussions then, the situation might be easier now.

"So how long to fix up the place?" Joshua asked.

"At least a month to do the basics, including the painting. That's assuming I can get *gut* helpers. It's not easy this time of year when everyone's so busy." He rubbed the cleft in his chin and arched his brows. "If the barn burned, everyone would be here even sooner."

"I'm hoping you aren't suggesting burning it down so we can have a barn raising."

Daniel laughed. "I never thought I'd hear my big brother, the volunteer fireman, make such a comment."

"I wanted to make sure *you* didn't." He clapped his brother on the shoulder, then looked around again. "Just a month to repair and paint? That's faster than I'd guessed."

"That's assuming I can get plenty of help. I may be able to get it done even more quickly if you're willing to hire a few of my *Englisch* coworkers."

Now Joshua was surprised. "Why wouldn't I?"

"*Englischers* think we Amish are the most skilled construction workers. I wasn't sure what you thought."

"I think I want this job done quickly and well."

"*Gut*. There are a couple of *Englisch* guys I work with who can run circles around me with a hammer and nails. I can ask them if they'd like some extra work."

He knew his brother was being modest, because Daniel's skills had an excellent reputation. "Sounds like a plan."

"I'm pretty sure one will, because he's been talking about his wife wanting him to take the family on a trip to Florida."

"How much are you planning to charge me?" Joshua asked with mock horror.

"Don't worry. It'll be fair. Let me talk to the guys I have in mind, and I'll get back to you soon. Okay?"

"Ja."

After Daniel left, Joshua wiped his brow with a soiled handkerchief and walked across the freshly mown backyard. He waved to Levi, who was now cutting the front yard. A glance at the garden told him Debbie and Sammy had finished there. The back door was open, so he headed toward it to find out how much longer Rebekah needed at the house.

He jumped back as a large box was carried out of the kitchen. Only when it had passed did he realize his oldest was toting it. He watched, puzzled, as Timothy set it in the wagon beside a pair of ladder-back chairs.

"What's in the box?" Joshua asked.

"Some stuff Rebekah wants to take home with us."

He nodded, even though he was curious what was in the box. Her clothing and the boy's as well as the clothing she'd prepared for the *boppli* were already at his house. He'd brought Sammy's toys and several of her quilts the first week after they were married.

"I hope the rest will fit," his son said.

"Depends on how much else there is," Joshua replied as his mind whirled.

Rebekah hadn't said anything to him about bringing any of her furniture to his house. Tildie had remarked often what a comfortable home it was. Didn't Rebekah have everything she needed?

What if their situations were reversed? There were some items he'd want to bring with him into her house. His buggy supply catalogues, the lamp that was the perfect height when he was reading, his favorite pillow and the quilt *Grossmammi* Stoltzfus had made for him, some of Tildie's rag rugs…and, most important, the family Bible.

"I don't know what else she's planning to bring," Timothy said. "She's in the house. You can ask her while I pack the rest of the canned food."

"I will."

As his son headed toward a bulkhead door and vanished down the stairs to the cellar, Joshua went to the kitchen door. The last time he'd come this way was to ask Rebekah to marry him.

He entered the kitchen. "Do you intend on bringing much more...?" His voice faded as he glanced around in disbelief. The kitchen cabinets looked abandoned because the stove and refrigerator were gone. The table where he'd sat while he discussed marriage with Rebekah had vanished, too. He looked through to the living room. Except for the sewing machine, the other room was empty, too. He frowned. Timothy had brought out only a box and the two chairs. Where was everything else?

He heard footfalls upstairs. He climbed the steps two at a time and followed the sound of muffled voices past a bathroom. Glancing into a room on the other side of the hall, he guessed it'd been a bedroom. It was empty except for a carved blanket chest. The top was open, and a tumbling-blocks quilt in shades of green, black and white was draped over the edge.

He kept going and looked into the other bedroom. Rebekah stood in the middle of it, her hands pressed to her mouth as if trying to hold in a cry. Debbie and Sammy stood on either side of her, for once silent.

Catching his daughter's eyes, Joshua motioned with his head for Debbie to leave. She obeyed, bringing Sammy with her. He smiled at her and patted her shoulder.

"Rebekah's sad," she whispered before she led the little boy down the stairs.

No, he thought as he walked into the room. Rebekah wasn't sad. She was furious. Every inch of her bristled with anger.

"Where is your furniture?" he asked when she didn't acknowledge him.

"Gone," she said, slowly lowering her hands.

"Gone?" He knew he sounded silly repeating what she'd said, but he was stunned to find another room stripped of everything including the dark green shades. "We need to let the bishop know you've been robbed. He can inform your neighbors and the police."

She put a hand on his arm, halting him. His astonishment that she'd purposely touched him instead of shying away eclipsed his shock with the stripped house.

"There's no need to alert the bishop. The day of our wedding I told my *mamm* to let Lloyd's family know they were welcome to take anything they could use." She drew in a deep breath and gave him a weak smile. "I guess they needed a lot."

"They took all the furniture?"

"Except my sewing machine, a pair of wooden chairs that belonged to my *aenti* and the blanket chest my *grossdawdi* built for me when I was twelve." She struggled to hold back the tears shining in her eyes. "I put the linens they left in the box Timothy's already taken out."

He thought about the box in the wagon. It wasn't very large. "What about your cradle? Where is it?"

"I don't have a cradle. Sammy slept in a drawer for a few months after he was born, and then I devised a pallet for him until he was big enough to sleep in a regular bed."

Joshua frowned. He recalled very clearly Lloyd bragging about the beautiful, handmade cradle he had ordered from a woodworker in Ephrata. His friend apologized for his boasting, saying he was excited to be able to give such a fine gift to his wife. He'd even stopped by to show it off. Joshua remembered it well because it'd been his and Tildie's wedding anniversary, and Joshua had had to push aside his grief to try to share his friend's excitement. Lloyd had said he planned to present it to Rebekah the following week.

But he hadn't. What had happened to the beautiful cradle? Uneasiness was an icy river running through him. For some reason, Lloyd must have needed to sell the cradle before he gave it to Rebekah. Joshua tried to guess what would have been more important to his friend than providing for his wife and *kind*.

Chapter Nine

Rebekah drew back on Dolly's reins to slow the buggy as it neared the parking lot where a sign painted with Stoltzfus Family Shops was set prominently to one side. The long, low red clapboard building held the local grocery store, which was owned by her brother-in-law, Amos, as well as the other shops where the brothers worked. The scent of hot metal came from Isaiah's smithy behind the main building, a *gut* sign because Isaiah was again working after taking time off in the wake of his wife's death.

Joshua's brother was moving forward with his life, and she must do the same. The sight of the empty rooms at the house in Bird-in-Hand had been shocking, but also felt like closing the pages of a book. An ending. She was beginning a new story with Joshua's family in Paradise Springs. Everything that had been part of that life was gone, except for the farm. She was grateful she wouldn't have to make a decision about it now.

A few cars and a trio of buggies were parked in front of the grocery store. When she halted her buggy, she heard the clip-clop of several horses. An *Englisch* man came around the end of the building leading four horses. He nodded toward her as he walked toward a horse trailer at the far end of the parking lot.

She watched him load the horses in with the ease of practice. It was amusing to think of horses riding.

"Sit here? No go?" Sammy asked when she didn't move to get out of the buggy.

Rebekah looked at her son, who held a bag of cookies he'd brought from the house. He wanted to see the buggy shop, too. The other *kinder*, who'd been to the shop often, were helping *Grossmammi* Wanda and *Aenti* Esther prepare pots of flowering plants to sell at the end of the farm lane. Passersby stopped and bought them along with the cheeses Joshua's brother Ezra made.

"Let's go." She smiled at his excitement. It was infectious. She was eager to see where Joshua spent so many hours each day.

Still holding the bag, Sammy grabbed her hand as soon as she came around the buggy and swung him down. She winced when the motion she'd done so often sent a streak of pain across her back. A warning, she knew, to be careful. The ache subsided into a dull throbbing that matched her steps across the asphalt parking lot and up onto the concrete sidewalk in front of Joshua's shop.

Stoltzfus Buggy Shop.

The small sign was in one corner of the window beside the door next to another one announcing the shop was open. The hours were listed on the door, but Joshua was willing to come in early or stay late to help a customer.

As she opened the door, a bell chimed overhead and a buzzer echoed beyond an arch at the far end of the large room. It must lead into another space, but a partially closed door kept her from seeing. A half wall was a few paces from the doorway. On the other side were partially built buggies, spare parts and several hulking machines. The only one she recognized was a sewing machine with a table wider and longer than her own. She guessed it was for sewing upholstery for the buggies.

"What are you doing here?"

Rebekah recoiled from the deep voice coming out of a small room to the right, then realized it belonged to Timothy. She hadn't realized before how much he sounded like a grown man. There wasn't any anger on his face, even though his voice had been sharp. Maybe it was as simple as he always sounded annoyed.

"Cookies!" Sammy announced, oblivious to the teenager's tone. Running to the half wall, he held up the bag. "Yummy cookies."

"*Danki*, little man." Timothy gave a gentle tug on Sammy's hair.

Her son smiled as if Timothy was the greatest person in the world. He offered the bag again to the teenager. Timothy took it, unrolled the top and held it out so Sammy could select a cookie.

Biting her lower lip, Rebekah stayed silent. It was such a sweet moment, and she didn't want to do anything to shatter it.

The older boy looked over Sammy's head. "*Danki*, Rebekah."

"The cookies are—"

"No, I mean *danki* for telling *Daed* I don't want to build buggies. We had a long talk about it this morning."

"You did?"

"*Ja.* He suggested I try working a while with each of my *onkels* and see if I want to learn a craft from one of them." He grinned. "So, starting next week, I'll work here half the day and with *Onkel* Jeremiah the other half. If making furniture doesn't interest me, and I'm not sure it will, I can apprentice with a different *onkel.* I think I'll like working at *Onkel* Isaiah's smithy or at the grocery store best."

"What a *gut* idea!"

"It was mine. *Daed* actually listened when I suggested it."

"Your *daed* is always willing to listen to a well-thought-out idea shared with him in a calm tone."

He rolled his eyes, making Sammy giggle. "Okay, Rebekah. I get the message. Lower volume, more thought."

She laughed and patted his shoulder, pleased he allowed it. "Timothy Stoltzfus, that sounds like something a grown man would say."

He started to roll his eyes again, but halted when Joshua came around the door in the arch. "Who's at the door, Timothy?" He wiped his hands on an oily cloth as he walked toward the half wall. A smile brightened his face. "Rebekah, you should have told me you were planning to come this afternoon. I would have cleaned up some of this mess."

"It looks fine," she replied. "We decided you needed some cookies."

"Cookies!" Sammy pointed to the bag Timothy held.

"More like crumbs." Timothy shook the bag so they could hear the broken cookie pieces in it. "But they taste *gut*, don't they, Sammy?"

"Gut! Gut! Gut!" The toddler danced around in a circle.

Joshua chuckled. "Why don't you take Sammy over to *Onkel* Amos's store, Timothy, and buy each of you something cool to enjoy with your cookie bits? Tell him I'll stop by later to pay for it."

"I've got money." Timothy squared his shoulders, trying to look taller. "Brad Granger paid me for helping him clean out his garage a couple of weeks ago. C'mon, little man. Let's see what *Onkel* Amos has that's yummy."

Sammy gave him his hand and went out the door. He waved back through the glass.

"What a surprise!" Joshua ran his fingers through his beard as he stared after the boys until they walked out of view. "I didn't expect him to spend his hard-earned money. He's been saving up for something, though he hasn't said what."

"Timothy has a *gut* heart," she said.

"Which he hides most of the time."

"All the more reason to be appreciative when he reveals it."

"True." He opened the swinging door in the half wall and motioned for her to come in. "What would you like to see first?"

"Everything!" She laughed as she lifted off her bonnet and put it on a nearby table. Smoothing her hair back toward her *kapp*, she said, "Now I sound like Sammy when he's excited. Can you show me what you're working on?"

He led the way past the machines, identifying each one by what it did. All were powered by air compression. Most were for working with metal when he built buggy wheels or put together the structure for the main part of the buggy. As she'd guessed, the sewing machine was used for making the seat upholstery. Tools hung from pegboard along one long wall. Hammers of every size as well as screwdrivers and wrenches. Those were the tools she recognized. Others she'd never seen before. She wanted to ask what they were used for, but her attention was caught by the fancy vehicle on the other side of the arch.

The grand carriage was parked in front of wide double doors. It was much larger than their family buggy and painted a pristine white. Open, with its top folded down at the back, it had two sets of seats that faced each other behind a raised seat, which had been painted a lustrous black at the front. The curved side wall dipped down toward a single step so someone could enter the carriage. The tufted seats were upholstered in bright red velvet. Large white wheels were topped by a curved piece of metal so no mud or stones from the road could strike the occupants. Narrow rubber tires edged the wheels.

"This is my current project," Joshua said as he placed one hand on the side of the carriage.

"What is it?"

"Mr. Carpenter, the *Englischer* who asked me to restore it, told me it's called a vis-à-vis. It's a French phrase that means the passengers face each other."

"It's really fancy and really fanciful, like something a princess would ride in." She stroked the red velvet. "Does he drive it?"

"Apparently he intends to use it on his daughter's wedding day. He tells me he has two matched bay horses to pull it to the church."

She arched her brows, and he chuckled. After walking to the body of a plain gray buggy, she bent to look inside it. "Are you repairing this, too?"

"No. I'm building it for a family near New Holland. I start with a wood base, then make the frame out of metal. Once it's secure, boards enclose it and the body is painted. Next I need to add wiring for lights and put in the dashboard Jeremiah is making." He glanced at a wall calendar from the bank in Paradise Springs. The squares were filled with notations in a multitude of colored inks. She guessed it was Joshua's schedule for each vehicle he was working on when he added, "He's supposed to have the dash to me soon."

She listened, fascinated, while he described making and fitting the wheels to a vehicle, as well as building the shafts to harness the horse to it. The interior would be completed to the new owner's specifications. He pointed to a list of options tacked on the wall. She was amazed to see almost two dozen items until she realized it was for many different kinds of vehicles. A young man wanted a certain style of seat in his courting buggy, while a family might need an extra bench seat or choose to have a pickup-style bed for moving bulky items.

"I never guessed it took so many different steps to make a buggy," she said when he finished the tour. "They're far more complicated than I'd guessed."

"It's our goal to let our customers think their buggies are simple so they won't need much maintenance to keep them going. That's why I want each buggy we make to be the best we can do."

"That sounds like pride, Joshua Stoltzfus," she teased.

"It does." He patted the unfinished buggy. "But what if I say I'm glad God gave me the skill to put a *gut* buggy together?"

"Better."

"*Gut*. Let me show you the sewing machine. I think you'll find it interesting."

Rebekah took a single step to follow him, then paused as she pressed her hands to her lower back. The faint throb had erupted into an agonizing ache when she moved.

Did she groan? She wasn't sure, but Joshua rushed to her. He put his arm around her shoulders, urging her to lean on him. Her cheek rested on his chest while he guided her to a chair by the half wall, and she felt the smooth, strong motion of his muscles.

"Are you okay?" His warm breath sifted along her neck, making her *kapp* strings flutter…and her heart, as well.

"*Ja*. I strained my back while lifting Sammy out of the carriage. He's getting bigger, and so am I." She tried to laugh, but halted when another pang ricocheted up her spine. "I won't make that mistake again."

"Take Debbie with you when you're going out with Sammy. She'll be glad to help."

"I know." She glanced up at him. "She's helping your *mamm* and Esther today. She was hoping her friend, Mandy, would come over, too."

"But she would be happy to help you."

"I know. You have raised a very sweet daughter."

Her words touched him, she saw. *Hochmut* wasn't a part of the Amish way, but he knew how blessed he was that his *kinder* had stayed strong after the death of their *mamm*.

With his hand at the center of her back, he steered her toward the half wall, where she could sit while they waited for Timothy and Sammy to return. It was a simple motion she'd seen him use with the *kinder*, but his light caress sent a powerful quiver along her. Even when he didn't touch her, she was deeply aware of him. To have his fingers brushing her waist threatened to demolish the wall she had built around her heart to keep any man from ever touching it.

When she lowered herself to the chair, he knelt beside her. He took her hand between his much broader ones. Worry etched deep threads in his brow. Before she could halt them, her fingers stroked his forehead to ease those lines. They slipped down his smooth cheek, edging his soft but wiry beard.

His brown eyes, as liquid and warm as melted chocolate, were filled with pleasure at her caress and questions about what she intended it to mean. How could she explain when she didn't know herself?

Drawing her hands away, she clasped them atop her full belly. The motion seemed to free them from the powerful connection between them. Or so she thought until he put his hand over hers, and the *boppli* kicked hard enough that he must have felt it, too. A loving glow filled his eyes exactly like when he looked at his own *kinder*.

"A strong one," he murmured.

"The *boppli* doesn't like to be ignored."

A slow smile curved his lips and sparkled in his eyes. "Maybe it's giving us fair warning to be prepared for when it's born."

She laughed. "I would prefer to think it's getting its antics out of the way so it'll be a *gut boppli*."

"You sound as if you're feeling better." His voice remained low and tender.

"I am. Sitting helps."

"*Gut*. Tomorrow I'll stop at the clinic and make an appointment for you. I'll ask them to see you as soon as possible."

"I told you, Joshua, the back pain was nothing but me being foolish."

He shook his head. "That may be so, but you need to see a midwife. You've been here more than a month, and if I remember right, you should be having appointments with her frequently at this point."

"I should." She resisted stroking his face again. "*Danki*, Joshua. I appreciate your kindness more than words can express."

He opened his mouth to reply, but whatever he intended to say went unspoken because the door opened and the boys rushed in. As Timothy launched into an explanation of how long Sammy had taken to select something to drink and how the little boy had delighted the other customers with his comments, Joshua stood and pretended to admire the sweet cider Sammy had chosen.

She watched and smiled and complimented her son on his choice, but her eyes kept shifting toward Joshua. He was watching her, too. Something huge had changed between them. Something that could not go back to the way it had been.

Joshua greeted his family as he came into the kitchen the next evening. He glanced first at Rebekah, but she was, as she'd assured him at breakfast, recovered from the muscle strain that had sent waves of pain across her face at the buggy shop.

Walking to the stove where Rebekah was adding butter to peas fresh from the garden, he asked, "How are you doing today?"

"Fine." She smiled at him, and his insides bounced like a *kind* on a trampoline.

"I made an appointment for you at the clinic." He held out the card he'd been given.

"Danki." She took the card and slipped it into a pocket in her black apron. "Why don't you sit? Dinner is almost ready."

"And I'm in your way?"

He heard Debbie giggle by the sink as Rebekah nodded. Walking back to the table, he lifted Sammy into the high chair set between his chair and Rebekah's. His gaze slipped to the far end of the table where the chairs Rebekah had brought from Bird-in-Hand awaited guests. It was odd to have the extra chairs by the table, but he knew they would be useful when company came.

He still wasn't accustomed to seeing her sewing machine by the largest window in the living room or having Tildie's blanket chest at the foot of Debbie's bed. Tildie's old sewing machine was stored in the attic, waiting for someone who could use it. He'd planned on giving his daughter the chest when she married, not so soon.

His sons came in freshly washed and making no secret of how hungry they were. Rebekah put the peas and thick, smoky slices of ham in the middle of the table. Debbie filled their glasses from a pitcher of ice water before getting warm biscuits from the oven.

Another feast! Joshua patted his stomach when it growled and everyone laughed. As soon as Rebekah was sitting beside the high chair and Debbie across from her brothers, he bowed his head for grace. He had so much to be thankful for: his family, the food and how God had brought Rebekah into his life. Grateful his prayer was silent because he could speak directly from his heart, he cleared his throat and looked up when Sammy moved impatiently beside him.

The conversation was easy and as plentiful as the food. When Joshua reached for another biscuit, a strange sound erupted from beneath the table. A dull thud. He looked at his glass. The water inside was fluttering.

"What was that?" Debbie asked, her eyes round and wide.

The *kinder* as well as Rebekah looked at him in bafflement. He wished he had an answer, but he didn't.

"Maybe it was an earthquake." Levi nearly bounced off his chair with excitement. "*Aenti* Esther taught us about them last year, and I read a book from the school library about the big ones in California. Maybe we're having one, too."

"Unlikely," Joshua said. "There aren't many earthquakes in Pennsylvania."

"Oh." His son looked disappointed.

"Then what was that sound?" asked Timothy. "Why did the table shake?"

"I don't know."

Rebekah shrugged her shoulders when Joshua glanced at her again. "I don't have any idea, either."

"Whatever it was is over," he said. "Eat up. If—"

A louder thump sounded. The table vibrated hard enough so the silverware bounced. Faces around the table paled.

Joshua looked down. This time, he'd felt whatever it was hitting the floor under his feet. No, not the floor.

Something had struck the cellar's ceiling…right below the kitchen table. Right where the fuel lines came into the house from the propane tank in the backyard.

He jumped to his feet. "Rebekah, take the *kinder* outside. Now!"

"You should come, too." Her face had lost all color. "Timothy, go next door and call 911."

"Let me do a quick check before you make that call." He locked eyes with his oldest. "Be ready to run to the Grangers." He crossed the kitchen in a trio of quick steps.

"Joshua?"

He looked back to see Rebekah picking up Sammy who held a piece of bread in one hand and a slice of ham in the other. "What?"

"Be careful." Her intense gaze seconded her soft words. She'd lost one husband, and she didn't want to lose another.

For a second he was warmed by that thought and considered heading out with the rest of the family, because he didn't want to be separated from a single one of them. It would mean another of the volunteer firemen having to go into the cellar to find out what was happening. He couldn't ask another man to do what he wouldn't.

Throwing open the cellar door while his family hurried out of the kitchen, he instinctively ducked when something exploded not far from the bottom of the steps. He sniffed, but didn't smell any gas. If it wasn't a fuel leak, what was blowing up?

He took one cautious step, then another. Groping along a shelf, he pulled out the flashlight he left there for emergencies. He took another deep breath to assure himself there wasn't a gas leak. Even the small spark created by the switch on the flashlight could set off a huge explosion if the cellar was filled with propane.

The air smelled sweet. No hint of the rotten odor added to propane to alert them to danger.

Even so, he held his breath as he turned on the flashlight. Nothing erupted. He swept the cellar with light. Everything looked as it should. He took a step. When something cracked beneath his boot, he aimed the light at the floor. Shards of glass were scattered across it.

He whirled when he heard footsteps overhead. Who was in the house? He saw Rebekah at the top of the stairs. "What are you doing? I told you to get out."

"Timothy opened some of the cellar windows from the outside, and he didn't smell any gas."

"I don't, either. I don't know what exploded. I—"

He put his arms over his head as a detonation came from his left. Something wet struck him. His skin was sliced by shattered glass.

"Joshua!" Rebekah shouted.

"Daed!" That was Timothy.

"Daedi!" The younger *kinder* yelled at the same time.

Raising his head and lowering his arms, he grimaced as liquid dripped from him. Some of it was blood, he realized when a drop splattered on his boot. Above him on the stairs, Rebekah and the *kinder* wore identical expressions of dismay.

He shook the fluid off him. Or tried to. It was sticky. He sniffed his lacerated forearm. "Root beer."

Glancing at the shelves where the canned food was stacked, he saw four more bottles of root beer. He grabbed them and stuffed them beneath a wooden crate. Just in time because another exploded, making the crate rise an inch from the floor.

"No," he heard Rebekah say. "You can't go down there until you put on shoes."

Within minutes, his sons had joined him and Rebekah in the cellar. Sammy stayed with Debbie at the top of the stairs, because the little boy was too young to help clean up glass. After he reassured them he was fine other than being covered with root beer from head to foot, Joshua asked Timothy to bring water from the spring at the back corner of the cellar. They needed to wash the concrete floor before ants discovered the spilled soda. When another bottle erupted beneath the crate, everyone jumped even though they'd known it could happen.

"I didn't realize there was any root beer left," Joshua said as he swept water and glass toward the center of the floor where Timothy scooped it up and put it in the bag Levi held. "I wonder why it exploded tonight."

"It's my fault, *Daedi*." Levi stared down at his sneakers.

"Your fault? How?"

"I moved the bottles." He looked up quickly, then at his feet again. "Rebekah asked Debbie and me to help sort out what was down here. I found the bottles and hid them behind the canned peaches."

"So you didn't have to share them? Levi, that isn't like you."

Rebekah put a hand on Joshua's arm, startling him. When he turned to her, she shook her head and gave him a gentle smile. He realized her thoughts were on his son, not on him. As he replayed his words in his mind, he knew he had spoken too harshly.

Levi was a *gut* boy, but no boy was perfect. If one who loved root beer tried to hide a few old bottles to enjoy later by himself, he should be reminded sharing something special was the best way.

"I won't do it again, *Daed.*" Levi was near tears.

He clasped his younger son's shoulder. "I know you won't. Are there any more bottles back there?"

"Let me check." Timothy stepped toward the shelves. "You need to get those cuts looked at, *Daed.*"

"He's right," Rebekah said gently. "Levi can finish cleaning up this mess while I tend to your injuries."

He nodded when he realized this was her way of ensuring his son wouldn't forget the bad decision he had made. Handing the broom to Levi, he said, "I know you will do a *gut* job, son."

The boy sniffed back tears, but said, "I will, *Daed.*"

Joshua walked up the stairs after Rebekah. When she wobbled, he put his hand at her back to steady her. She didn't pull away. His steps were light as he went into the kitchen. Timothy being helpful, Levi admitting to the truth right away…and Rebekah not shrinking from his touch. Maybe they'd reached a turning point and their lives would get better. As he sat at the kitchen table so Rebekah could put salve on the many small cuts on his arms, he prayed that would be so.

Help me find a way to bring happiness into our lives. He hoped the prayer would be answered soon.

Chapter Ten

When Levi brought the buggy and Dolly out of the barn, Rebekah smiled. The boy had made every effort to be on his best behavior since the episode with the exploding root beer bottles three nights ago. Even on Sunday during the church service, he hadn't squirmed once or poked the boy beside him.

Now she thanked him for hooking up the horse. He gave her a shy smile beforc jogging toward the house where Debbie was washing the breakfast dishes and keeping an eye on Sammy.

The road was empty while Rebekah headed toward the village. The sunlight shimmered on the road in front of her, warning the day was going to be a hot one. Usually she looked forward to summer heat, but not while she was pregnant. Every degree higher on the thermometer added to her discomfort.

She went past the Stoltzfus Family Shops sign. The parking lot was filled as usual with cars and buggies. When the door of Joshua's shop opened and he bounded out, waving his hands, she drew back on the reins in astonishment.

"What's wrong?" she asked.

He didn't answer her question. He asked one of his own. "Where are you bound?"

"To my appointment with the midwife."

He grimaced, then looked down at his grease-stained shirt and trousers. "I forgot your appointment was today. Let's go." He put his foot on the step, then halted because she didn't slide across the seat.

"You don't need to come with me, Joshua. I know you're concerned about getting Mr. Carpenter's carriage done on time."

He shook his head, his most stubborn expression tightening his lips as he dropped back on to the ground. "I need to come with you. You are my wife. We will, God willing, be raising this *kind* together for many years to come." He put his foot on the step again and held out his hands.

She gave him the reins and moved to the left side of the buggy. She was glad her bonnet hid her face, because she wasn't sure what his reaction would be to the tears filling her eyes. She thought of the days since she'd visited the buggy shop and how solicitous he had been, making sure the *kinder* helped in the house and with Sammy so she could rest a short while each afternoon. Each kindness was a *wunderbaar* surprise she treasured, knowing how fleeting such benevolence could be. He'd welcomed her concerns about Timothy and accepted her silent chiding to be more gentle with his son after Levi had stashed the bottles of root beer in the cellar.

Am I being foolish to consider trusting again, God? The question came from the depths of her heart, bursting out of her unbidden. Only now did she recognize how desperately she longed for a real marriage.

As Joshua steered the buggy on to the road, a white van pulled up in front of Amos's store. An elderly man and woman were waiting with their bags of groceries, each of them holding an ice cream cone. The driver parked, jumped out and opened the door to let them in while he put their purchases in the back.

It was a scene Rebekah had witnessed often at the grocery store in Bird-in-Hand, but her breath caught when she noticed how the elderly man helped his wife into the van as if she were as precious and essential to him as his next breath. Every motion spoke of the love they shared, a love that required no words because it was part of them. She felt a pinch of envy as she imagined having a love like that to share.

When Joshua spoke, it unsettled her to realize his thoughts closely mirrored hers. "The Riehls were married before I was born. Even though Amos has offered to deliver groceries to their house, they insist on coming to the store. He suspects the real reason is the soft ice cream machine he put in last year."

"Ice cream *is* a *gut* reason." She smiled, letting her uncomfortable thoughts drain away. "Do you ever make ice cream with the *kinder*?"

"Our ice cream maker broke a few years ago."

"I brought one from the farm."

He flashed her a grin. "I'm surprised Levi hasn't been begging to make ice cream. The boy has a real sweet tooth."

"He's mentioned it several times, but..." She sighed. "There are only so many hours in each day."

"I was wondering, Rebekah, if it is wise for you to be doing so much of the housework."

She looked at him, baffled. Why wouldn't she do the house chores? It was what a wife did. Dismay twisted in her middle. Had she failed to keep the house or make his meals or clean the laundry as well as Matilda had?

"Why?" It seemed the safest question to ask.

"I see how exhausted you are. You cook and clean for four *kinder* as well as you and me. In addition, you work in the garden every day and spend hours making and keeping our clothes in *gut* repair."

"You work as hard at the buggy shop."

"But I'm not going to have a *boppli* soon." He shot her a grin. "What do you say to getting a girl in to help before the *boppli* is born? She could do the heavier chores so you can rest?" His smile broadened. "And have time to supervise making ice cream for Levi."

"That would be *wunderbaar*." Again she had to blink back tears. They seemed to be her constant companion recently. His concern touched her heart, piercing the barriers she'd raised to protect it from being hurt over and over.

"I asked around and Sadie Gingerich may be available." He drew in the reins when they reached the main highway.

Route 30 was always busy. The buggy rocked when eighteen-wheelers roared past, but Dolly acted as if she encountered them every day. The horse stood still until given the command to go. The buggy sped across, and Rebekah grasped the seat with both hands to keep from being rocked off.

When they were driving along a quiet residential street, Joshua added, "Sadie helped my sister Ruth during her last pregnancy, and Ruth was very satisfied. You haven't spent much time with my sister, but I can tell you she's not easy to please."

"Ruth knows what her family needs, and she isn't afraid to voice her opinions."

He smiled. "That's a nice way of saying she's bossy, but she's the oldest, so she's used to looking out for us. If you want, I can contact Sadie's family. They live south of Paradise Springs, closer to Strasburg. If she can't help, she might know someone she can recommend." He glanced across the buggy. "Do you want me to check if she can come?"

"Ja." She couldn't say more. The tears that had filled her eyes were now clogging her throat until she felt as if she'd swallowed a lump of uncooked bread dough.

"Are you sure?"

She realized he'd taken her terse answer as dismay instead of overwhelming relief and gratitude that he cared enough about her to hire Sadie Gingerich to help. Blinking the tears hanging on her lashes, she said, "*Ja*, I'm sure. *Danki*, Joshua."

"I'll see if she can stop by soon. If you like her—and I think you will because she's a nice girl—she can start right away." He tapped her nose. When she stared at him as if he'd lost his mind, he laughed. "Then maybe my pretty wife won't have dark circles under her eyes because she's doing too much and not getting enough sleep."

"Nice way to give your wife a compliment."

"I don't want you to grow prideful." His gaze cut into her as he added, "And that can't be easy for someone as beautiful as you."

She knew she was blushing, but she didn't care.

Lloyd had never given her a compliment. Not even when they were courting. She should pay no attention to fancy words. Yet when Joshua said something nice to her, happiness filled her, making her feel as if the sun glowed inside her.

He didn't add more as he slowed the buggy again and hit the toggle that activated the right turn signal. He pulled into an extrawide driveway and stopped by a hitching post. After jumping out, he lashed the reins to it, though Dolly would wait for them to return.

Rebekah was glad when he assisted her out of the buggy. It wasn't easy to see her feet now, especially on the narrow step. Gravel crunched beneath her feet as she walked with him toward the single-story white building that looked as if it had been a home. Dark green shutters edged the windows. A bright wreath with purple and white blossoms hung on the yellow door, and a small plaque to one side announced: Paradise Springs Birthing Clinic.

Joshua reached past her to open the door. It wasn't until she was inside that she realized she hadn't cringed away from his arm when it had edged around her. She was torn between joy and praying that she wasn't making another huge mistake. She wasn't going to think about the dark times. They had shadowed her life for too long. She was going to focus on the here and now. And the *boppli* who would be born soon.

The clinic was as cheerful and bright inside as it was on the exterior. A half dozen plastic chairs in a variety of colors edged each side of the room. Three were occupied, and none of the women were dressed plainly. They looked up and smiled as she walked past. She returned their smiles and told herself to relax.

After going to the registration desk near a closed door at the far end of the narrow room, Rebekah gave her name to the receptionist who wore large, red-rimmed glasses. The receptionist welcomed her and handed her a clipboard with forms to fill out.

Rebekah sat and concentrated on answering each question. Joshua took the chair beside her.

"Measles?" he asked when she checked a box on the long list of common diseases. "Didn't you have the shot when you were a *kind*?"

"I did, but I caught them anyhow." She chuckled. "The doctor told *Mamm* it sometimes happens that way and that I would have been much sicker if I hadn't had the shot. I couldn't imagine how, because I was pretty sick with them."

Turning the page over, she was glad the portion on health insurance had already been crossed out. That showed the clinic was accustomed to dealing with the Amish, who weren't required to purchase health insurance because their community took care of any medical bills a family couldn't pay on their own.

But how was she going to pay for the *boppli*'s birth? She couldn't expect Joshua to pay the costs. The *boppli* wasn't his. The answer came instantly: she'd have to sell the farm in Bird-in-Hand. Once the farm was gone, her haven would be, too, but what choice did she have?

Finishing the rest of the pages, she started to rise to take the completed forms to the desk.

Joshua stood and held out his hand. "Let me do that. You should sit while you can."

As she thanked him, a woman sitting on her other side leaned toward her. "You have a very considerate husband," she whispered. "I wish my husband understood like yours does how tough it is to get up and down." She laughed. "My ankles are getting as big as a house."

Taken aback, Rebekah wasn't sure how to reply. She gave the woman a smile, which seemed the perfect answer because the other woman laughed and went back to reading her book.

Joshua sat beside her again. "The receptionist said it shouldn't be long before you're called in."

"Gut." The plastic chair was uncomfortable.

A few minutes later the inner door opened. A tall woman stepped out. Her dark brown hair was swept back beneath a *kapp* that identified her as a Mennonite. The back was pleated and square rather than heart-shaped like Rebekah's. Her plain gown was worn beneath a doctor's white coat, and a stethoscope hung around her neck. She called out Rebekah's name. When Joshua stood, too, the woman asked him to wait, saying he'd be called back in a few minutes.

He nodded and took his seat. He gave Rebekah a bolstering smile as she went to the door and stepped through into a hallway that branched off past two open doors on either side.

"This way, Rebekah," the woman in the white coat said.

In spite of knowing she shouldn't, Rebekah stared at the woman who limped as she walked. A plastic brace ran from below her right knee into her black sneaker. It was held in place atop her black stockings by a wide strip of what looked like Velcro.

She recovered herself and followed the woman into a room. The midwife's warm smile was so genuine that she was instantly at ease.

"I am Elizabeth Overholt, but everyone calls me Beth Ann," said the woman before she asked Rebekah to get on the scale. She then checked Rebekah's blood pressure. Rebekah was pleased with both, and so was Beth Ann.

"Excellent," Beth Ann said and led her to a room across the hall. She motioned for Rebekah to come in. "Do you need help getting on the table?"

"I think I can manage still."

"Don't be brave. Ask for help when you need it." She kept her hand near Rebekah's elbow until Rebekah was sitting on the examination table. "Okay, I have your file from your midwife in Bird-in-Hand, so let's see what it says."

Looking around the pleasant room while Beth Ann read the file, Rebekah smiled. Childish drawings hung on the wall. She guessed one of them depicted a kitten or maybe a lamb. Something with curly, fuzzy hair. The other was of a *kind* holding a woman's hand. A small house and a huge tree were behind them, and the sun was bright yellow while a rainbow arched over the whole scene.

Booklets she recognized from when she'd been pregnant with Sammy were stacked neatly by the window. Then she had read every word, hungry for information to make sure her *boppli* was born healthy. Not one had contained any advice on how to keep her husband from damaging their *kind*.

She pushed the dreary cloud of memory away. Lloyd was gone, and Joshua hadn't raised his hand to her. Not yet.

Oh, Lord, help me to trust he's not the man Lloyd

was. I want to be able to believe he won't hurt me or the kinder.

Beth Ann looked up, and her smile vanished. "Is everything okay, Rebekah?"

"Ja." She forced a laugh that sounded brittle in her ears. "It's impossible to get comfortable at this point."

"Are you having contractions?"

She shook her head, sorry she was causing the midwife worry. But how could she be honest? She could not let Lloyd's sins become a shadow over his son as people watched to see if he had inherited his *daed's* violent outbursts.

As she began to answer Beth Ann's questions, she told herself again, *Think about now.* Maybe if she reminded herself of that enough times, she'd make it a habit and would finally be able to leave the darkness behind her once and for all.

Joshua had been in places, but not many, where he felt less comfortable than in the waiting room with a group of *Englisch* women who looked ready to give birth at any moment. None of the magazines stacked on the tables interested him enough to page through one until he noticed a sports magazine tucked at the bottom of one pile. He drew it out and almost laughed out loud when he saw it was a year old. The cover story was on baseball, so he began to read. He glanced toward the inner door when it opened, but it was a different woman calling out the name of one of the pregnant women.

"Mr. Stoltzfus?"

At his name, he looked up and saw the midwife who wore the brace and who'd come to get Rebekah was holding the door open again.

"Will you come with me?" she asked with a smile that suggested she knew exactly how eager he was to escape the waiting room.

Joshua had a smile of his own when he entered the room where Rebekah sat on a paper-topped examination table, her feet swinging as if she were no older than Sammy. He went to stand beside her.

After the midwife introduced herself, Beth Ann pulled out a low stool and sat. She handed him a sheet of paper. Scanning it, he saw it was a to-do list for when Rebekah's contractions started, including when to call Beth Ann.

"At that point, I will contact the doctor so he'll be there if we need him," the midwife said. "As Rebekah didn't have any complications with her first pregnancy, I don't see any reason to expect any this time. God willing, of course."

He nodded. "We have been praying for God's blessing on this birth."

"Do you have any questions?" Beth Ann asked.

"Not after having been present at the birth of my three *kinder*."

"All right, *Daedi*," she said with a laugh. "You are clearly an expert."

"I know enough to call for you to come."

That Rebekah didn't correct Beth Ann's assumption he was the *boppli*'s *daed* pleased him for a reason he couldn't decipher. He didn't want to. He wanted to enjoy the *gut* news that Rebekah and the *boppli* were doing well.

He assisted Rebekah from the table, thanked the midwife and nodded when she instructed them to make another appointment for two weeks from today. He took the small bag Rebekah held. She told him it contained vitamins. While she made an appointment, he went to get his straw hat and her bonnet from the rack by the door.

Cautiously he put his hand on her elbow to guide her on the steps and across the driveway to the buggy. Again he was relieved when she didn't tug away or flinch.

She was quiet as he started the drive toward home. He guessed she was exhausted. Crossing the highway took more than twice as long this time because the traffic was even heavier. When a tourist pointed a camera at the buggy, he leaned into the shadows so his face wouldn't be visible in the photograph. Most visitors understood the Amish didn't want to have their picture taken, but a few didn't care.

Once they crossed Route 30 and drove out of the village, no more cars zipped past them. He waved to an *Englischer* who was driving a tractor. He recognized the man from the charity mud sale at his *mamm*'s house in the spring. From what he'd heard, the *Englischer* was planning to run an organic vegetable farm. Joshua appreciated the man's determination to practice *gut* husbandry.

After stopping to collect the mail, Joshua drove up the driveway. He glanced at Rebekah when she stirred. Had she fallen asleep? He didn't want to embarrass her by asking.

"*Danki* for taking me to my appointment today," she said.

"You are my wife, and that *boppli* will be growing up in my house." He felt her tense, but her shoulders became softer next to his as he added, "In our house. I'm sorry I didn't say that first."

"You don't have to apologize. That house has been yours for years. You can't expect to change old habits overnight." She flashed him a smile. "I know I haven't been able to change mine, though I'm trying to."

Was she talking about how she flinched from him? If so, he hoped her words meant she was making an effort to accept him being close to her. Because, he realized, he wanted to be close to her. The sound of her laughter, the twinkle in her eyes when she looked as mischievous as Sammy, the gentleness she used with the *kinder*, the ruddy warmth of her hair…each of these and more drew him to her.

He assisted her out of the buggy, teasing her because she was getting almost too wide for the narrow door. He started to suggest that he grill some hamburgers for their supper tonight so she could rest, but halted when he saw Sammy running toward them with Debbie on his heels. The *kinder* were barefoot, and their clothes were spotted with water above the wet hems.

"*Daedi*, come see!" yelled Sammy. "Froggie!"

Joshua couldn't move as Lloyd's son called him *Daedi* again as he tugged on Joshua's hand. This was a complication he hadn't seen coming. What should he do?

He didn't look in Rebekah's direction, fearing he would see pain and grief on her face when her late husband's son called another man *Daedi*. An apology burned on his tongue, but what could he say even if he let the words out? He wouldn't apologize for loving the *kind*, especially when Sammy reminded him of his own boys at that age. Curious and excited over the most mundane things, filled with joy and eager to share his happiness with everyone around him. Even something as commonplace as a frog was a reason for celebrating.

"Daedi!" Sammy's voice tore him away from his musing. "Quick! Froggie jumping."

"We're coming," Joshua said. "Go ahead. We'll be right behind you." As the *kinder* raced toward the stream beyond the barn, he began, "Rebekah…" Again words failed him.

She gave him the same gentle smile he'd seen her offer the *kinder* when they were distressed. It eased the tightness in his gut.

"It's all right, Joshua. He needs a *daed*, and if you're willing to be his, that's *wunderbaar*."

"Are you sure?"

"*Ja*. I think you'll be the very best *daed* he could have."

"Now, you mean." He didn't want to be compared to his best friend when Lloyd had no chance to prove he would be a *gut daed* for Sammy.

She nodded, but her gaze edged away. She was hiding something, but what? He was certain if he could answer that question, so many other puzzles would be solved, too.

Chapter Eleven

The day was beautiful, and that morning before going to the shop, Joshua and Timothy had finished stringing the new clothesline out to the maple tree. Rebekah gazed at the puffy clouds as she hung a wet sheet that flapped against her in the breeze. She saw no sign of a storm, which meant she could do another load of laundry and have it dried and folded before she needed to leave for her scheduled appointment with the midwife. She'd persuaded Joshua that she was fine to go on her own. He relented only when she reminded him how his *Englisch* client would be stopping by tomorrow to collect his fancy carriage, and Joshua wanted to check it from front to back one last time to make sure he hadn't overlooked something.

"Are you Rebekah?" A cheery voice broke into her thoughts.

She looked around the sheet and saw a woman close to her own age walking toward her. Glancing past her, she didn't see a buggy. Had the woman walked to the house?

The woman's dark brown eyes sparkled in her round

face. Rather short, she was what Rebekah's *mamm* might have described as pleasingly plump. Not overweight, but her plain clothes didn't hide that she had softer curves than what the *Englischers* deemed ideal.

"Ja," Rebekah replied. "I'm Rebekah."

"I'm Sadie Gingerich. Your husband asked me to stop by to talk about working for you." Her gaze slipped along Rebekah. "That *boppli* is coming soon, ain't so?"

She laced her fingers over her belly. "No secret about that. Let's go inside and sit while we talk."

"Sounds *gut*," Sadie agreed, but Rebekah quickly discovered that Sadie's idea of a conversation was doing most of the talking herself.

They'd no sooner sat at the kitchen table than Debbie and Sammy came from the living room where they'd been playing a game. Rebekah was pleased to see how quickly Sammy hoisted himself into Sadie's lap while she explained what work she did for a family before and after a *boppli* arrived.

Even though she didn't get a chance to ask many questions, Rebekah decided Sadie would be a great temporary addition to their household. Sadie, though she was unmarried and had no *kinder* of her own, had helped raise her eleven younger siblings. She'd started hiring out after her *daed* died and clearly loved the work she did. Whenever she spoke with Debbie or Sammy, her smile broadened, and she soon had them giggling.

"When can you start?" Rebekah asked.

"I have another week at the Millers' in the village, but I can begin after that if that works for you." She bounced a delighted Sammy on her leg as if he were riding a horse.

"That would be *wunderbaar.* Oh..." She abruptly realized they didn't have an extra bedroom for Sadie.

When she explained that, Sadie waved aside her concerns. "If Debbie doesn't mind, I'll share with her. I have almost a dozen sisters and brothers. Sharing with one other person will seem like luxury."

"Say *ja*, Rebekah," the little girl pleaded before turning to Sadie. "I've been praying the *boppli* is a girl because I want a sister."

"I'll be your practice sister." Sadie looked at Rebekah. "If that's okay with you."

"It sounds like a *gut* solution." She'd have to explain to Sadie eventually that Joshua had his own room upstairs, but that was a conversation she wanted to delay as long as possible. It wasn't that she was ashamed of the situation. She felt... She wasn't sure what she felt about it. She simply knew she didn't want to discuss it.

They spoke a while longer, then Sadie said she needed to return to the Millers' house. She left on a scooter like the ones the *kinder* rode to school, which explained why Rebekah hadn't heard a buggy approach.

Rebekah couldn't wait to tell Joshua that Sadie Gingerich had agreed to help. That made her smile even more as she went back outside to the clothesline. Lately, the idea of sharing events of the day and telling him funny stories about the *kinder* seemed natural. And she liked that they were becoming more and more a part of each other's lives. Their marriage wasn't a perfect love story, but it was getting better each day.

Once she'd finished hanging the rest of the laundry, Rebekah picked up the basket and went into the laundry area off the kitchen. She started the washer and dumped in detergent. Of all the conveniences they enjoyed from the solar panels on the roof, having a washer that wasn't run by a gasoline motor was her favorite. She'd despised the raucous noise and the fumes, even with an exhaust pipe stuck out a window, from the washer in Bird-in-Hand.

She went to the pile of light-colored clothes waiting to be washed. The *kinder* brought their dirty clothes to the laundry room, saving her extra trips up and down the stairs. They tried to sort them properly, but she occasionally found a dark sock in with the whites. She picked up each garment and shook it to make sure nothing hid within it.

When she lifted one of Joshua's light blue shirts to put it in the washer, a familiar odor, one she'd hoped never to smell again, swirled through her senses, stripping her happiness away as if it'd never existed. Her nose wrinkled. She knew that odor…and she hated it. The scent of alcohol. She'd smelled it too many times on Lloyd's breath and on his clothes.

Where was it coming from?

She sniffed the shirt. No, not from that. Dropping it into the water filling the tub, she held another piece of clothing to her nose, then another and another, and drew in a deep breath with each one. She identified the musty scent of sweat and the tangy sauce from the casserole she'd made two nights ago. The unmistakable scent of horse and another of the grease Joshua used at the buggy shop. Green and earthy aromas from the knees of the pants Levi had been wearing when he helped her weed the garden and harvest the cabbage and green beans.

But the scent of liquor was gone. Had she actually smelled it? Maybe the combination of laundry detergent and heat in the laundry room had created the odor she dreaded. After all, though she'd watched carefully, she'd never heard Joshua slur his words or seen him unsteady on his feet. He never struck her or the *kinder.*

Was the smell only her imagination? It must have been.

But what if it wasn't?

She leaned forward against the washer and whispered, "Help me, God! Help us all."

The rest of the day passed in a blur. Rebekah couldn't help taking a deep breath every few minutes. The odor of alcohol, if it'd existed at all, had vanished. It was impossible to forget the stab of fear in the laundry room. Even at her appointment with Beth Ann, she'd struggled to focus on the midwife's questions and suggestions. She'd managed little more than a faint smile when Beth Ann had congratulated her on hiring Sadie Gingerich.

The comment reminded her that Joshua was paying the expenses for Lloyd's *kind.* She shied away from the idea of selling the farm. Even after the house had been stripped clean by Lloyd's relatives, there was enough farm machinery to sell to cover the costs of the delivery and Sadie's help. How could she hold on to the farm when Joshua worked so hard to provide for the family?

By the time she returned home, her head was pounding. She must have looked as bad as she felt, because Debbie urged her to rest. She hesitated until the little girl reminded her that Joshua had volunteered to bring home pizza to celebrate finishing the work on the carriage.

Sleep eluded her. The *boppli* seemed to have acquired a love for step dancing, and her thoughts were strident. Each time she tried to divert them by praying or thinking of something else, she was drawn right back into the morass.

Usually she loved having store-bought pizza with its multitude of toppings, but she could barely tolerate the smell. She picked at a single piece while the rest of the family enjoyed the treat and the celebration. Somehow she managed to put on a *gut* front, because neither the *kinder* nor Joshua asked if something was bothering her. In fact, the whole family seemed giddy with happiness.

She wanted to feel that way, too. Was she going to allow a single scent, which might not even have been there, ruin her whole day? Again she prayed for God's help, adding a silent apology for spiraling into the terror that had stalked her during her first marriage.

The feeling of a worthless weight being lifted from her shoulders brought back her smile…and her appetite. Rebekah finished the slice of pizza and then had two more. She smiled when Timothy and Debbie began to tease Levi about a girl he'd been seen talking to several times during the past week while working with *Onkel* Daniel. As he turned the tables and jested with his sister about fleeing from the chicken coop and a particularly mean hen that had chased her halfway to the house, Rebekah joined in with the laughter.

After they finished their treat, Joshua volunteered his and the boys' help to clean up the kitchen. She started to protest, but he insisted. Grateful, she went with the younger *kinder* into the living room and sat next to the sewing basket where her hand mending was piled. No matter how often she worked on it, the stack never seemed to get smaller. She took the topmost item, a pair of Levi's trousers that needed to have the hems lowered…again! The boy was sprouting up faster than the corn in the fields.

It didn't take Joshua and his sons long to redd up the kitchen and join them. The boys sat on the floor, and she assumed Joshua would read to them as he did each evening.

"I have something else for our celebration tonight." He smiled at Rebekah. "A birthday gift."

"Joshua, it's not my birthday," she replied.

"Who said it was for you?"

She stared after him as he walked out the door. Hearing a muffled giggle from Debbie, she saw the little girl had her hands clamped over her mouth. Her eyes twinkled with merriment. Levi wouldn't meet Rebekah's gaze and Timothy, for once, was grinning broadly. Only Sammy, playing with his blocks on the braided rug, seemed oblivious.

What were they up to?

Her answer came when Joshua returned to the living room. He placed a cradle by her chair.

She gasped when she ran her fingers along the cradle's hood. The wood was as smooth as a rose petal, and it had been polished to highlight the grain. Maple, she guessed, because it had been finished to a soft honey shade. Not a single nail head was visible, and she saw dovetail joints at the corners. Her eyes widened when she realized it had been built with pegs. Only an extremely skilled woodworker could have finished the cradle using such old-fashioned techniques.

"What do you think?" Joshua asked, squatting on the other side of the cradle. "As a birthday gift for the *boppli*? Like I said, it isn't for *your* birthday." He chuckled and the *kinder* joined in.

Rebekah was speechless at the magnificent gift and even more so that Joshua had gotten it for her. A warmth built within her, melting the ice clamped on to her heart.

She whispered the only word she could manage, *"Danki."*

"I hope you like it. Jeremiah built it."

"It's beautiful."

"He does *gut* work."

She stared at the cradle and knew that *gut* was a feeble description of the lovely piece. Jeremiah must have spent hours sanding the wood and staining it and polishing it until the grain was gloriously displayed. She couldn't imagine the amount of time it had taken to cut the corners to fit together so smoothly.

"Do you like it?" Debbie asked, inching across the floor to run her fingers along the wood.

Before she could answer, Levi began a story about how Joshua had asked them to keep the secret until the cradle was finished. Even Timothy added to the tale.

Looking at their animated faces, she smiled at her family.

Her family.

Sometime in the past weeks, this house had become home and these *kinder* as much a part of her life as Sammy. And Joshua? She couldn't imagine her days without him being a part of them. His gentle teasing, his solicitude, his joy when Sammy called him *Daedi.*

Because Sammy loved him.

And, she realized with a start, she wanted to let herself fall in love with him, too. Really in love, not this make-believe marriage. She wished they could share a love not overshadowed by fear and uncertainty.

"It's lovely," Rebekah said to Debbie, giving the girl a hug. "*Danki* for letting this be a surprise."

"*Daedi* said you didn't have a cradle for Sammy, and we wanted you to have one for my little sister." She winked as Levi insisted, as Debbie had hoped he would in response to her teasing, that the *boppli* was a boy.

Joshua glanced at his *kinder*, then said, "I'm glad you like it, Rebekah. I was surprised you didn't have one for Sammy." His gaze slid away from hers, and she wondered if he thought she wouldn't want him speaking poorly of Lloyd.

Hoping to ease his abrupt discomfort, she said, "Lloyd told me that he intended to get Sammy a cradle, but then I guess he didn't have the money for it." She ran her fingers over her belly. "This little one won't have to sleep in a drawer. *Danki*, Joshua."

Before she could think about what she was doing and halt herself, she leaned forward and kissed his cheek.

Joshua wasn't sure who was more surprised at Rebekah's kiss, him or her. She pulled back so quickly and turned away to say something to the *kinder* that he couldn't guess what she was thinking.

But he'd heard what she said. Lloyd had promised to get a cradle for their firstborn, but then hadn't given her the extraordinary one he'd purchased. Where had that cradle gone? Joshua knew it was unlikely that he'd ever get an answer. That bothered him less than the grief he'd heard in Rebekah's voice when she spoke of her late husband.

How could he hope to win her heart when it belonged to the *daed* of her two *kinder*? He hadn't relinquished his love for his late wife. Astonishment ran through him. Tildie! When was the last time he'd thought of her? He was shocked that he couldn't recall.

He went through his normal evening routine, but his gaze kept wandering to Rebekah. She worked on lengthening Levi's church pants until it was time for prayers and for the younger *kinder* to go to bed. Before she took Sammy into the downstairs bedroom, she gave Debbie and Levi each a kiss on the cheek, and his own skin sizzled with the memory of her lips against it.

Soon the footsteps upstairs disappeared as the *kinder* found their beds. Timothy had gone outside without any explanation, but Joshua was used to his son's changing moods. Not that he appreciated them, but he expected them.

When Rebekah returned, she continued her sewing while he perused a new buggy parts catalogue that had come in today's mail. Neither of them spoke as they sat facing each other across the cradle.

"Joshua, it's time," she said suddenly.

He leaped to his feet and stared at her, dropping the catalogue on the floor. "Already? I thought the *boppli* isn't due for a few more weeks. Will you be okay here while I call Beth Ann?"

She put her fingers lightly on his arm. "Joshua, it isn't time for the *boppli*. It's time to talk about selling Lloyd's farm."

Glad that the *kinder* were elsewhere so they hadn't seen him jump to conclusions, he lowered himself into his chair. He didn't wait for his heart to slow from its panicked pace as he asked, "What has changed your mind?"

"I told you I needed time to think over the decision, and I have," she said.

Joshua's teeth clenched so hard his jaw hurt. She was shutting him out again. He glared at the cradle, which had reminded her of the husband she'd chosen with love instead of the one she'd agreed to wed for convenience's sake. He'd never imagined he'd be jealous of a dead man, but he couldn't restrain the horrible emotion.

Lord, help me walk the path You have chosen for me and forget about other men's. You brought Rebekah and her family into my life for a reason. Let me be Your instrument in helping them live as You would wish for them.

"All right," he said, hoping hurt hadn't seeped into his voice. "I'll make the arrangements with Jim Zimmermann to set an auction date. It'll take some time to prepare the auction and advertise it. He'll want the most bidders there possible so you can get plenty of bids for the farm and the equipment."

"It's been this long. A little longer won't make any difference." She didn't look up from her sewing. "I'd rather not go."

"I understand," he said, even though he didn't. Actually, he comprehended why she didn't want to watch the farm as well as her house go on the block. What he didn't understand was why she'd come to the decision to sell now.

"*Gut*. Lloyd asked you to take care of us as you think best. He'd have trusted you to oversee what needs to be done, Joshua."

"Do you trust me, too?"

She finally met his eyes. *"Ja."*

His heart seemed to bounce in his chest, beating madly as if it hadn't made a sound since Tildie had drawn her last breath and it was finally coming to life again. Rebekah trusted him. As he held her steady gaze, he knew her faith in him wasn't because he'd given her the cradle and a home for her family. He saw something more in her eyes, something that spoke of respect and camaraderie. He didn't dare look for more. How could he ask for her love when he withheld his own heart? The thought of loving any woman other than Tildie seemed a betrayal.

Or was he seeing what he hoped to in Rebekah's gaze?

He would know, one way or the other, with his next words. "I'd like to talk to you about one very important matter."

"I told you. I trust you to handle the farm auction."

He shook his head. "This doesn't have anything to do with the farm. It's about Sammy and the little one."

She curved her hand over her stomach. "What about them?"

"What do you think of me adopting them?"

Her breath came out in a gasp, and she stared at him without speaking. For the second time that evening, he had shocked her into silence.

"Rebekah, I should have phrased that better. I've been thinking about this since Jeremiah dropped off the cradle. He asked if I intended to become the *kinder*'s legal *daed*."

She started to speak, then stuttered into silence again.

"Take all the time you need to consider it and pray about it, Rebekah," he said. "I'm not asking you to take this step because I want you and the *kinder* to forget Lloyd is their true *daed*, but if Jeremiah is asking, others may be, too. I think we should have an answer to give those who ask."

Finally she spoke in a whisper, "*Ja*, we should have an answer." She put the garment she'd been working on back into the mending basket and slowly stood. "I need to pray about this, Joshua."

"I will, too."

She nodded and again started to speak, but said nothing as she walked out of the room.

He heard the bedroom door softly close behind her, shutting him out as she did each night.

With a sigh, he rose. He glanced at the stairs, but how could he sleep after the evening's events? Rebekah had kissed his cheek, albeit as chastely as she did the *kinder's*. She'd expressed her faith in him. She hadn't turned him down when he spoke of adopting her and Lloyd's *kinder*, even though he'd failed to mention the true reason why he asked. Not his brother's curiosity or anyone else's mattered as much as how much he had come to consider Sammy his own and the *boppli*, as well.

He walked into the kitchen and noticed light flowing across the floor. He looked out the window and saw two figures silhouetted against the faint light from the lantern in the barn. One was Timothy. Joshua frowned when he realized the other person was Alexis Granger. She held the handles of a large tote bag with both hands, and she was talking earnestly. He couldn't hear what they were saying, but their posture suggested they were discussing something important.

What was the *Englisch* girl doing over here at this time of night? Brad had mentioned more than once that he insisted his daughter be home by dark, except on weekend nights when she could be out until midnight with her friends.

He took a step toward the door, then heard a soft voice say, "Don't."

Turning, he discovered Rebekah coming around the kitchen table. "I thought you'd gone to bed," he said.

"Sammy wanted a drink of water, so I came to get it." She looked out the window. "If you confront Timothy in front of his friend, he won't heed anything you say. You have to talk to him as you did about working with his *onkels*. He listened to you then."

"He needs to listen to me now."

"I agree, but he won't hear you if he feels he has to defend himself. Talk to him tomorrow when you can be calm and present a reasonable argument about how he could hurt his friend's reputation if it's discovered he's meeting her after dark in the barn."

"Do you think they—"

"I think they are *gut* people who care about each other, but I don't think she sees him as anyone other than a friend. He might have a different opinion of their relationship. Even so, you've taught him well. Trust him to know the right thing to do."

He glanced once more at the teenagers, then nodded. "How do you know so much about teenagers when Sammy is only a toddler?"

"I don't know. I'm going with what my instincts tell me."

"I hope your instincts are right." He looked out to see Alexis sprinting across the yard in the direction of the Grangers' house. The large bag flapped against her legs on each step.

"So do I." He heard the fervor in her voice. "So do I."

Chapter Twelve

On the day the farm was to be auctioned, the *kinder* pleaded to attend with Joshua. Rebekah agreed because she had always enjoyed auctions. She warned them that, other than Timothy, none of them must join the crowd that was bidding unless they were with Joshua or one of their *grossmammis*. Buyers would be annoyed if they were distracted by *kinder* running about.

Grossmammi Wanda handed covered dishes to the *kinder* in the family buggy. Now that her cast was off, she seemed to be trying to make up for lost time. Each *kind*, including Sammy, was given a plate or a pot to watch over. Wanda had insisted on bringing food, even though the members of Rebekah's old district would be offering food for sale. It was a fund-raiser for a husband and wife in the district who each needed surgery.

When Joshua stepped up into the buggy, he said to his *mamm*, "We'll see you at the auction later."

"We'll be there as soon as Esther finishes frosting the cupcakes she's making." After offering a wave, Wanda climbed into her own buggy, turned it and drove down the driveway.

"I get tired trying to keep up with her," Joshua said, shaking his head. "She has more energy than a dozen people."

"True." She looked from Wanda's buggy to the one holding her family.

Sammy was giggling and trying to peek into the plastic bowl on his lap. Debbie steadied it and whispered in his ear. That set him to chortling even more. Beside them, Levi was squirming as he always did when he was excited. Timothy sat in the front with his *daed*, trying to wear an expression of world-weary boredom, though she suspected he was as eager to go to the auction as his siblings were.

They were going away for the day, and she'd be alone in the house. Sadie had gone home for the weekend, leaving food for their meals in the refrigerator. Mending waited, as always, but she didn't want to spend the day doing that or trying to work in the garden. Bending over was getting harder every day.

She wanted to spend the day with her family.

Instantly she made up her mind. "Joshua, can you wait a minute while I get my bonnet and shoes?" She smiled. "It may take more than a minute for me to find my feet and get my shoes tied, but not so long that we'll be late for the auction."

"You want to go, too?" Joshua asked.

She understood his surprise. She'd been adamant about not being there. Joshua believed it would make her sad because of memories of Lloyd. In a way, he was right, but her sorrow focused on how her dreams for a life with Lloyd had faded away into a desperate struggle to survive and protect Sammy from his *daed*.

When Joshua had asked her about adopting Sammy

and the *boppli*, he hadn't had any idea how difficult it had been not to shout out *ja* immediately. Once the *kinder* had the Stoltzfus name, they could grow up without anyone watching for Lloyd's weaknesses. Best of all, she wouldn't have to disillusion Joshua about his friend. The secret of Lloyd's abuse could truly and completely be buried along with him.

She needed to find the right time to tell him that she wanted him to be the *kinder*'s legal *daed*. A time when they were alone so the *kinder* didn't hear, and a time long enough after he first asked so he wouldn't ask the questions she didn't want to answer.

"Ja," she said. "I've changed my mind. Women do that, you know."

"So I've heard. More than once." He motioned for Timothy to move to the back with his siblings. Joshua walked with her to the house, offering to help her with her shoes, and gave her the tender smile that made her heart do jumping jacks. "I'm glad you're coming with us."

"Me, too." In fact, she couldn't remember the last time she'd been this happy. She held that close to her heart, intending to savor it through the whole day.

The sale was going well. The farm that had been quiet for so long had come alive as if a county fair had set up its midway between the house and the barns. A crowd of nearly a hundred people stood beside the recently painted barn that shone in the bright sunlight. More mingled and chatted among the buggies, wagons and cars parked in the yard and down the farm lane and out on the road. The auctioneer was making the bidders laugh with his antics as he tried to cajole a few more dollars out of them for each item.

Smoke from grills brought by the members of Rebekah's old district was laced with delicious scents of meat, peppers and onions. Rows of baked goods awaited buyers with a sweet tooth. Cans of soda and iced tea were encased in galvanized buckets of quickly melting ice.

Joshua stood to the side and watched the enthusiastic bidding for a plow that looked as if it had hardly been used. The work his brother had done to fix the buildings was going to pay dividends, he was certain, because he'd heard several groups of men discussing the value of the acreage and buildings. Their numbers were higher than his estimates. His work to arrange the machinery to its best advantage was helping each piece sell for more than he'd dared to hope. The *gut* Lord had brought generous hearts to the auction today.

He smiled as his favorite verse filled his head: *This is the day which the Lord hath made; we will rejoice and be glad in it.*

The *gut* Lord had also brought several young Amish men who were eager to set up their own farms. He recognized a few from Paradise Springs and guessed the others were from the surrounding area. Most of them worked at jobs beyond their families' farmsteads, and they longed to return to the life beloved by most plain men: husbanding God's beautiful creation. By day's end, he hoped one of them would be the new owner of Lloyd's farm, because there were a handful of *Englischers* talking about bidding on it, as well, and it was always disappointing when *gut* farmland was subdivided for another neighborhood. But, either way, the farm should sell well.

Lloyd's legacy to his wife and son and unborn *kind.*

Joshua scanned the crowd, which was intent on what the auctioneer was listing as the next lot. Where was Rebekah? He saw Levi and Debbie playing volleyball with others their age. Timothy had worked with other teens to set up a makeshift baseball diamond where abandoned hubcaps, salvaged along the road, served as bases. Home plate was simply an area scratched out in the dirt.

When the house's front door opened, Rebekah emerged with a pitcher of some fruity drink and paper cups. She went with care down the steps, and he held his breath until her feet were securely on the ground. For her to fall now could turn the *boppli* and make the delivery much more difficult and dangerous.

"Now there's a man who's in love with his wife," teased Ezra. His brother nudged him with an elbow and chuckled. "Can't keep his eyes off her."

Joshua didn't want to admit that his younger brother was right. "Don't you have better things to do than lurk around spying on me?"

"Nope." He rested his shoulder against a nearby fence post. "I've been looking for a seeder, but that one went for more than I thought it was worth. *Gut* for Rebekah, not so *gut* for me. That was what I was mainly looking for, so I need to find something to do while *Mamm* enjoys time with our neighbors."

"And Leah Beiler is here." He eyed his brother with a grin. "Are you two going to be the first to publish your marriage this fall?"

"You know better than to ask that." He chuckled.

"And that's a clumsy way of trying to divert me from noticing how you're mooning over your pretty Rebekah."

Joshua changed the subject to the work Daniel had done on the farm. That seemed to distract his brother, or perhaps Ezra was so enthralled with anything to do with agriculture that he was eager to talk about it anytime. Giving his brother half of his attention, Joshua continued to watch Rebekah.

Like his *mamm*, she was unwilling to sit while others worked. She must not overdo when she had to think of her own health and the *boppli*'s.

Ezra's laugh intruded on his thoughts. Slapping him on the arm, his brother said, "Go ahead and moon, big brother. I'll talk to you later *if* you can think of anything other than your wife." He walked away still laughing.

Joshua considered retorting, not wanting to let his brother get the last word, but what could he say? Ezra was right.

He strode across the field in the opposite direction, away from the crowd and the noise. He needed some quiet to think. He paused by the farm pond where the only noise was the chirping birds and the breeze in the reeds along the water.

Why was he trying to deny the truth? Rebekah was always in his thoughts. When he considered staying another hour at the shop to finish work, he imagined her waiting at home with his meal ready and worrying that he hadn't arrived home at his usual time. He remembered how delicate her touch had been and how she'd fretted about causing him more pain when she cleaned his cuts in the wake of the exploding root beer. Even when his *kinder* came to mind, Rebekah was there, smiling, encouraging them, scolding when necessary, loving them with an open and joyous heart.

Exactly as he longed for her to love him.

Exactly as I love her.

That thought sent a deluge through him, washing away the last remnants of his resolve never to fall in love and put his heart in danger again. Whether he turned his back on her love or tried to win it, he couldn't guarantee that he was avoiding heartbreak. But he was if he ignored the truth.

He'd fallen in love with his sweet wife, the woman he'd promised to cherish. Overwhelmed by the gift of love that God had brought twice into his life, he dropped to his knees and bowed his head as he thanked his Heavenly Father.

To that prayer he added, "Give us your blessing, too, Tildie. I know now that if I'd gone first, I would have wanted you to find someone to bring you and the *kinder* love and happiness. Please want the same for me."

A sense of peace settled upon him as he stopped fighting himself. He almost chuckled at the thought. An Amish man was supposed to play no part in any sort of war, but he'd been fighting one within himself…a futile one, because the resolution was what he'd known all along. God came into their lives and hearts through love.

He needed to remember that.

The raised voice echoed oddly through the empty house. Joshua frowned. What was going on? His *mamm* had told him that Rebekah had gone inside to get out of the hot sun. He'd expected to hear the muffled sound of the auctioneer's voice, but he heard shouts.

He strode into the living room. The room silenced, and he looked from Rebekah who was backed into a corner, one arm protectively around Sammy and the other draping her stomach, to two men he recognized as Lloyd's brothers, Aden Ray and Milo. The latter stood too close to her, clearly trying to intimidate her. Both men stepped back and let Rebekah and Sammy rush to his side.

He urged her to take the *kind* and leave, but wasn't surprised when she shook her head. She didn't want to abandon him to deal with the two Burkholders. He took her hand and drew her closer, feeling her fingers tremble against his palm. Beside her, Sammy clung to her skirt.

"What is this?" Joshua asked in the calmest voice he could.

"Family business." Aden Ray glowered. "As Lloyd's brothers, we've got a right to a share of the profits from this farm."

"Rebekah has been generous with you already. She gave your family permission to take whatever you wanted out of the house. You did. However, the equipment and farm belong to Lloyd's son."

"Which means it goes into your pockets. How convenient for you! Marry the widow and collect the fruits of our brother's labors."

"I would have married her myself if I wasn't already married." Milo, Lloyd's older brother, sneered. "She's not bad to look at when she's not blown up like a balloon."

He stared at the man's crude, greedy smile, not dignifying the stupid comment with an answer. Tugging on Rebekah's hand and calling to Sammy, he turned on his heel to walk away.

They walked out the door. As they reached the bottom step on the front porch, his arm was seized, shocking him. He hadn't expected another Amish man to lay a hand on him in anger.

"Rebekah," he said as he drew his arm away from Milo Burkholder, "*Mamm* would like your opinion about which cakes to auction off first." That wasn't true, but he didn't want her to suffer any more of her brothers-in-law's comments. "Why don't you and Sammy find her now so they can be sold while the crowd is still large?"

She backed away, frustration and fear in her eyes that were as wide and dismayed as her son's. But anger, too, because her face had reddened, making her freckles vanish. He was astonished how much he missed them. As strong as she was in facing every challenge, the freckles softened her expressions while reminding him how gentle she was at heart. He gave her a wink, and her lips quivered before she turned and crossed the yard toward the refreshment area.

"Gut," Milo growled. "Now with her gone we can talk man-to-man."

"We don't have anything to talk about. *Englisch* law and our own traditions are clear on this. The widow and her *kinder* inherit her husband's estate. As I said, she has been very generous and offered your family everything in the house."

"It's not enough!"

"I'm sorry you feel that way, but I believe it is."

Aden Ray's hands curled into fists. As his voice rose in anger, his fists did, too. "We don't care what *you* believe! We want our share!"

Joshua couldn't believe that Lloyd's brother would actually try to strike him until the younger man swung at him. Fortunately the blow went wide. Moving out of range, he said, "We can ask our bishops to decide."

"I can make that decision on my own, and we want our share." He jabbed out with his other fist.

Again Joshua jumped away and bumped into someone. A glance over his shoulder shocked him. Timothy and several of his own brothers stood behind him. Nobody spoke, but Aden Ray lowered his fists.

This time when Joshua walked away along with his son and brothers, he wasn't stopped. He heard the Burkholders stamp in the opposite direction. Thanking his brothers, who nodded in response before they returned to the auction, he kept walking with Timothy until he had strode past most of the bidders who were so focused on the sale that, praise God, they hadn't noticed his unexpected encounter with Lloyd's brothers.

"Are you okay, *Daed*?" asked Timothy as soon as they stopped.

"I will be. This policy of always turning the other cheek is easier some days than others."

His son chuckled. "I know."

"Go and enjoy your game." As his son started to leave, Joshua called his name. He walked to Timothy and gave him a quick hug. He knew his son wouldn't allow more than that when his friends were watching. "*Danki*, son."

"Anytime, *Daed*."

"I hope not."

They laughed, and Joshua went to find Rebekah. He didn't intend to let the Burkholders—or anyone else—bully her again.

It was almost, Rebekah thought, like the night of their wedding day. The *kinder* were slumbering in the back of the buggy, including, this time, Timothy, who'd had as much fun as the younger ones at the auction. Their clothes were dotted with mustard and spots of ice cream, and she was astonished none of them had sickened from the amount of food they'd eaten.

Beside her, Joshua watched the road beyond Benny's nose. "I was glad to see the farm stay with an Amish farmer."

She smiled, recalling how one of the young women had been as giddy as a toddler with a new toy when one of the Tice boys was the highest bidder. "I hope the house and farm have many happy times for its new family."

"God willing, it will." He glanced at her as he said, "I didn't expect you'd want to stay for the sale of the farm equipment."

"Why?"

"Tildie and my sisters only watched when the lots were household items. I assumed women weren't interested in manure spreaders and plows." He grinned, his teeth shining in the streetlight they drove under. "You don't have to remind me that not all women are alike. Esther often tells me that."

"No, all women aren't alike, just as all men aren't." She relaxed against the seat and discovered his arm stretched along it. When his fingers curved down around her shoulder, she let him draw her closer.

All men were *not* alike, and she was more grateful for that truth than words could say.

His thoughts must have been the same because he said, "I didn't realize the Burkholders had such tempers."

"They do, and it doesn't take much for them to lose it." She didn't add more.

"I never saw Lloyd lose his temper."

"I know." This was the perfect opening to explain about what happened when Lloyd did fly into a rage, but she held her tongue.

Fortunately, his family had left. They discovered they couldn't gain sympathy from the crowd after word spread about how they'd stripped the house of almost everything, which was why there were no household goods for sale. She was glad to see them go.

Forgive me, Father, for not being able to forgive them for their avarice. I try to remind myself that they are a gut *lesson about the importance of being generous to others.* She smiled to herself, hoping God would understand her prayer was facetious. She wished the Burkholders could find the peace and happiness within themselves.

It was too nice a night to discuss Lloyd and his troublesome brothers. "Timothy seems very interested in that red-haired Yutzy girl. He was hanging on her every word when he talked to her after the ball game."

"Like *daed*, like son." He chuckled. "We find redheads catch our eyes."

She chuckled, then put her fingers to her lips, not wanting the sound to rouse the *kinder*. She glanced back to see Sammy curled up between Levi and Timothy, who had his arm protectively around the little boy.

"Thank you for a *wunderbaar* day," she whispered. "I can't remember when I've had so much fun."

"How about the time we went for a canoe ride on the pond and ended up tipping the canoe over?"

She held her breath as she did each time he mentioned a memory that contained Tildie and Lloyd. She had to choose her words with care. This time it wasn't so difficult because she had fond memories of that day, too. "Because you were being silly." She smiled. "It was a *gut* thing that we could get the mud out of our best dresses."

"*Ja*. I heard about that for a long time. Lloyd must have, too."

"That was a long time ago," she replied, not wanting to admit that she never would have dared to scold Lloyd. The next time he was drunk, he would have made her regret her words. "Joshua, I've been thinking about your adopting Sammy and the new *boppli* after it's born."

"And?" Anticipation filled his voice. "What's your answer?" He halted her from answering by saying, "Before you tell me, let me say what I should have the night I asked you. Even before your son called me *Daedi* for the first time, he'd found his way into my heart. I love to hear his laughter and watch him try to keep up with the older boys. I've dried his tears when he has fallen and scraped his knee, and I've taught him the best way I know to catch a frog down at the pond. Rebekah, even though he wasn't born as my son, in my heart it feels like he's always been my son."

She stretched to put a finger to his lips as she whispered, "I know. Don't you think I've seen how you two have grown together like two branches grafted onto the same tree?"

"So what's your answer?"

"*Ja*, I would like you to adopt my *kinder*."

He turned to look at her, his face visible in the light from the lantern on her side of the buggy. But its faint beam wasn't necessary. His smile was so broad and so bright that it seemed to glow with his happiness.

"That is *wunderbaar*," he said.

"How do we do this? I'm sure there's a lot of paperwork, but I don't know where to start."

"We'll start by asking Beth Ann."

"Why?"

His eyes twinkled like a pair of the stars glistening overhead. "Didn't you know? She has an adopted daughter."

"I didn't realize that." She thought back to the drawings that hung in Beth Ann's examination room. They obviously had been done by a *kind* because the bright colors had been created with crayons. "I'll ask her at my next appointment."

"When's that?"

"On Tuesday. If you have any questions, I'll be glad to ask her."

"I'll ask her myself. At this point, I don't think you should be driving into the village on your own."

She heard an undercurrent of anger lingering beneath his words. It halted her automatic response that she could handle matters on her own. When she thanked him, his arm drew her closer. It would be so easy to imagine them riding in a courting buggy he'd built himself, except Levi was softly snoring in the back. She shut out that sound and leaned her head against Joshua's strong shoulder.

His breath sifted through her bonnet and *kapp* as he said, "We'll keep Sammy's memories of Lloyd alive by telling him about his *daed*."

"We don't need to worry about that now." *Or ever*, she longed to add, but if she did, then she'd have to reveal how little Joshua comprehended of the man he'd called his friend.

"*Danki*, Rebekah, for agreeing. I should have said that before."

"There is no reason to thank me. It is what's for the best for the *kinder*." She didn't add that it was the best choice for her, as well.

God, am I being selfish? I don't want Sammy to suffer any longer for the sins of his daed. *Sammy deserves to be happy and secure. And so do I.*

That last thought startled her. For so long she had listened to Lloyd telling her how worthless she was. Only her determination to remain strong for her son and her faith that God would never stop loving her as Lloyd had, had kept her from believing his cruel words.

Not tonight. She wasn't going to let the memory of Lloyd intrude tonight when she sat beside Joshua while they followed the moonlight along the otherwise deserted road. The steady clip-clop from the horse provided a rhythmic undertone to the chirps of the peepers. Lightning bugs twinkled like earthbound stars, creating flashes of light in the darkness.

It seemed too soon when they entered their driveway and came to a stop by the dark house. Beyond the trees lights glowed in the Grangers' house, but in the buggy they were enveloped in soft shadows.

"Rebekah?"

At Joshua's whisper, she looked at him. His lips brushed hers, tentative and giving her a chance to pull back. She didn't want to. His lips were warm and tasted of the fudge some of the women had been selling at the auction. Or were his lips always so sweet? She pushed that silly thought from her mind as she put her arms around his shoulders and kissed him back.

He slanted her closer to him, holding her tenderly. He

kissed her cheeks, her eyelids, her nose before finding her lips again. Her fingers sifted up through his hair, discovering it was just as soft as she'd imagined. But she'd never imagined how *wunderbaar* his kisses would be while they lit the dark corners of her heart, banishing the fear and the contempt. Joy danced through her and she melted against him.

At the sound of the *kinder* stirring in the back, he lifted his mouth from hers. She curved her fingers along his face, savoring the variety of textures. She had so many things to say, but not when the youngsters were listening.

She couldn't wait until she had a chance to tell Joshua of the state of her heart and how she had come to trust him as she hadn't thought she ever could trust any man again.

Chapter Thirteen

"Do you want us to carry those bags?" asked Debbie when the buggy stopped under the tree at the edge of the yard early the following Friday.

"I'd appreciate that." Rebekah struggled to smile as the little girl handed a bag of groceries to her brother before picking up the other one.

Last night Rebekah had been awakened by a low, steady ache near the base of her spine. Whether she shifted to her side or her back, she hadn't been able to find a comfortable position. Sleeping had been impossible, so around midnight she'd gotten up and worked on mending more of the *kinder*'s clothing. It was something she could do quietly and without much light, because her fingers had guided her stitches around a hem or a patch.

Now she was so exhausted it felt as if she were wading through knee-deep mud with each step. The idea of getting out of the buggy seemed too much. All she wanted to do was crawl into bed and nap away the rest of the day and maybe tomorrow and the day after.

Nonsense! The best way to stay awake was to keep

busy. Otherwise she might not be able to sleep again tonight.

And maybe tonight there would be a chance for her and Joshua to talk. Every other evening since the auction, either he or she had been busy. Sammy had started resisting going to bed without her being there until he went to sleep. He was frightened after what he'd witnessed with Lloyd's brothers. She thanked God that her son wouldn't have to have much to do with that family from this point forward.

As she got out of the buggy, she motioned for Levi to follow his sister and Sammy into the house. "Go ahead. I'll take care of Benny and the buggy." She glanced at the clouds building up along the western horizon. "Will you ask Sadie to bring in the laundry? And please ask Debbie to cut up some of the fruit we bought and make us a salad with the berries you picked yesterday."

He nodded. She was grateful for Sadie's help because she was finding it more difficult with each passing week to hang out the wash and take it down. Last time she'd done laundry, three pieces of clothing had fallen on the grass, and she'd had to ask Sammy to collect them. It was impossible to find the basket by her feet.

Her feet? She almost laughed. She hadn't seen them in so long she doubted she'd recognize her own toes any longer.

She unhooked the horse and led Dolly toward the barn. She wasn't sure how bad the storm was going to be, and she knew Dolly didn't like getting wet. She'd put her in a stall until the rain passed. After that Levi could let the mare out into the pasture. The horse had taken a liking to the boy and vice versa.

The air in the barn was heavy. She made sure the

horse had plenty of water, and she thought about having a lovely cold glass of lemonade.

She shut the stall door and turned to leave. Sunlight glinted off something on the floor near a discarded horse blanket. She went to check, not wanting one of the horses to pick up a nail in a hoof.

She started to bend to check the shiny object, then laughed. Hadn't she been thinking that bending was impossible? Squatting was almost as difficult without something to assist her to her feet. She considered calling one of the *kinder* to help her, or she could wait until Joshua came home.

Her eyes were caught by the extra wheel leaning against the stall's wall. She could use it to help her. Checking that it would not tumble over when she grasped it, she chuckled.

"Lord, you keep me humble by reminding me that I can't do everything." She chuckled again and put her hand on the wheel. She hunkered and reached for the glistening piece of metal.

Her laughter disappeared as she realized it wasn't a piece of metal, but a metal can. Connected to five other metal cans. A six-pack of beer. A brand that must be popular among *Englischers* because she'd seen large trucks with the beer's name passing through Paradise Springs.

Her stomach heaved, and she feared she was going to throw up. Lloyd had hidden his stash of beer in the barn. Icy shudders thudded along her, battering away the happiness and contentment she had felt seconds ago.

Had Joshua hidden it here so she wouldn't suspect that he drank as Lloyd had? Her stomach twisted again. She'd thought she'd smelled liquor on Joshua's clothing while doing laundry. Since that day she'd convinced herself that she hadn't really smelled it, that it'd been her imagination or one of the lacquers Joshua used at the buggy shop.

Was this all the beer or was there more?

Rebekah shoved the six-pack under the blanket and then pushed herself to her feet. At the best speed she could manage, she went to the house, not even pausing to answer when Sadie called out a greeting. The *kinder* looked up when she came in. She rushed past where Debbie was slicing fruit and the boys were watching with eager anticipation.

"Are you looking for something?" asked Levi.

"Ja," she replied.

"Can we help?" the ever-helpful Debbie asked.

"Watch Sammy. Make sure he eats with a spoon, not his fingers. I'll be right back." She threw open the cellar door. "I need to get…" Her brain refused to work, stuck on the image of that beer in the barn. Shaking herself, she said, "I need to get a couple of bottles of your *grossmammi's* pickles for supper."

"Let me carry them up for you." Levi stuck out his thin chest. "*Daedi* asked us to help you when Sadie is busy doing something else."

Tears flooded her eyes. She longed to put her arms around these darling *kinder* and hug them so tightly while she kept the evils of the world away from them. To do so would create more questions. Questions she couldn't answer until she had more facts. Accusing their *daed* of being as weak as Lloyd would hurt them as deeply as it had her.

"*Danki*, but I think I can manage. I'll call if I need help." She hoped her smile didn't look as grotesque as it felt. *"Ja?"*

"Ja," he replied, but she didn't miss the anxious glance he shared with his sister.

Thankful that Sammy was too young to take notice of anything but his sandwich, Rebekah hurried down the stairs before one of the *kinder* could ask another question. She picked up the flashlight from the shelf by the steps and went to the shelves where fresh jars of fruit had been stored in neat precision along with the ones she's brought from Lloyd's farm. A gasp sent a pain through her. The only sanctuary she had from another alcoholic husband was that farm and now it was gone.

Why, God, did You let me discover this *after the farm was sold?* The pain burst out of her in a single, painful blast.

She couldn't blame God for a man's weaknesses. She did, however, blame herself for not seeing any signs that Joshua hid beer as Lloyd had. Even looking back over the past months, she couldn't recall a single clue that would have tipped her off. Other than that Joshua had been Lloyd's best friend, and they'd spent time together fishing and hunting. Had they been drinking together, too?

Spraying light over the shelves, she looked but didn't see anything that wasn't supposed to be there other than a few spiders. She lowered the flashlight, so the beam narrowed to a small circle on the concrete floor. There were other places where beer or a bottle of liquor could be hidden, but she couldn't squeeze past the shelves to reach them. At that thought, she aimed light through the shelves. She saw tools and what looked like cast-off furniture against the stone foundation, but everything was covered with a thick layer of dust. If it had been disturbed recently, she saw no sign.

Looking up at the ceiling, she wondered if there was a place in the attic where cans or bottles could be hidden. Lloyd had put his beer there once. A cold snap had frozen the beer and shattered the bottles, making a mess that he'd refused to clean up. She recalled the ignominy of washing the floorboards on her hands and knees while pregnant with Sammy. Rather than being grateful, Lloyd had walked out and hadn't come back for almost a week, lamenting how he'd run out of money.

Tears rolled down her cheeks. She wrapped her arms around herself and her unborn *kind.*

God, I thought Joshua was a gut *man. I dared to let him into my heart, believing that You wanted me to share his life. What do I do now?*

There was one more place to check. Lloyd often put his beer in the well house because the water stored in the tank kept it cold.

Her lower back ached more with each step she took up the stairs, but Rebekah didn't slow when she reached the kitchen. Again she was aware of the anxiety on the *kinder's* faces. She wished she could say something to comfort them, but she wouldn't lie to them.

Sadie was bringing in a basket of laundry and nearly collided with Rebekah. Waving aside the young woman's apology, Rebekah hurried around the side of the house to where the small well house contained the diesel pump and a holding tank for water. The walls were built with slats so fumes wouldn't build up inside.

After going in, she waited for her eyes to adjust. As soon as they did, she saw sunlight glinting off more metal. She leaned against the slatted walls and wrapped her arms around her belly as if she could protect her unborn *kind* from what was right in front of her eyes.

Five six-packs of beer.

She'd never seen such a collection. Lloyd seldom had had more than two or three six-packs on the farm at any one time. Or at least as far as she knew. Why would Joshua want enough beer for a dozen people?

Her eyes widened. What if the beer didn't belong to Joshua? Maybe she was jumping to conclusions about her husband. What if the cans belonged to Timothy? The teenager was so moody, leaping from cheerfulness to sullen scowls in a single breath. Lloyd had been like that, too, especially contentious when his head ached as he suffered yet another hangover.

She looked down at the six-packs. Timothy went out by himself in the family buggy on Saturday nights. How easy it would be for him to retrieve the beer and hide it beneath the backseat so even if his *daed* or another adult stopped to talk to him the beer would go unnoticed. She had no idea how many members were in his running-around gang, but she knew the gatherings often included a mix of Amish and *Englisch* teens.

So whose beer was it?

Rebekah waited impatiently for Joshua and Timothy to get home. As soon as they did, she went out into the shimmering heat to meet them. Her husband waved as he led Benny into the barn because the slow-moving storm seemed ready to pounce on them.

"Timothy," she said as the teenager started across the yard in the direction of the Grangers' house, "I need to talk with you."

"It'll have to wait. I'm already late."

"Late for what?"

He stopped and frowned. It was the expression he usually reserved for his *daed*, but she wouldn't let it halt her from saying what she must.

"Timothy, it'll take only a second."

"It'll have to wait." His voice got louder on each

word until she was sure their neighbors could hear. "I'm going out with friends. I told *Daed* last night. He said it was okay for me to go out on a Friday night as long as I get my chores done tomorrow. Why are you grilling me like I'm some sort of criminal?"

Rebekah hardly considered a single question an interrogation, but her voice had been forceful. All she could think of were those cans of beer. She needed to know the truth. She'd heard about boys racing their buggies when they were intoxicated and how they ended up paralyzed or worse.

"Timothy—"

"Leave me alone!" He stamped away.

Joshua came out of the barn and looked in the direction of his son's angry voice. What was distressing Timothy *now*? When he saw his son striding away with Rebekah trying to keep up with him, he was astonished. Timothy had never raised his voice to her before. Not like this.

They stopped and his son jabbed a finger in Rebekah's direction. His gut twisted when he noticed how she didn't flinch away as she did too often when he reached toward her.

Timothy stepped back when Joshua approached. Fury twisted his son's face, and Rebekah's was long with despair.

Joshua didn't get a chance to ask what was wrong because Timothy snapped, "She's your wife. Tell her to stop trying to run my life. She's not my *mamm*, and even if she was I'm sixteen and I don't need her poking her nose into my business." He stormed past Joshua and into the trees that divided the two houses.

Joshua started to call after him but halted when Rebekah said, "Let him go."

"Why? He owes you an apology for speaking like that."

"No, I owe him one."

Her words kept him from giving chase after his son. "Why?"

"I wanted to ask him something, and I pushed too hard. He's right. I'm not his *mamm*."

"But you are my wife. He should respect that."

"He's sixteen, Joshua."

"A *gut* reason for him to know he needs to respect his elders."

Her smile was sad, and she stared at the ground. "And there's the crux of the problem. He doesn't think of me as his elder. Oh, sometimes I'm sure he thinks I'm too old to recall what it's like to be sixteen. At other times, he thinks I'm too young to be his *mamm*. Either way, he doesn't believe I have the right to tell him what to do."

"I'll talk to him." He started to put his arm around her, but she flinched. As she had when she'd first come to live at his house. He watched in disbelief as she widened the distance between them. She hadn't acted like this since the auction. What had changed?

"I don't think it matters," she said with a sigh. "Timothy isn't going to tell me the time of day at this point. Let me see if I can mend fences with him before you get involved. I don't want him to think we're siding together against him."

He nodded reluctantly. His son needed to show Rebekah respect, but trying to talk sense to Timothy when they both were upset might make matters worse in the long run. But didn't Rebekah owe him the truth, too, about why she was again acting as skittish as a doe?

He couldn't ask. Not when her color was a strained gray beneath her summer tan. He urged her to come inside and allow him to get her something cool to drink.

Maybe later she would tell him why she suddenly found his touch abhorrent.

Please, God!

A crash reverberated through the house, and Joshua sat up in bed. Rain splattered on the window, but that hadn't been thunder. It had been louder and much closer.

He leaped out of his bed and banged his head on the slanted ceiling. He rubbed the aching spot but didn't slow as he raised the shade on the window.

At the end of the driveway a car was stopped. Its lights were at an odd angle, one aiming up into the trees and the other on the grass. It couldn't be on the road any longer.

He grabbed his boots and shoved his bare feet into them. He threw open his door. When Debbie peeked sleepily out of her room, he ordered her in a whisper to go back to bed and stay there. He didn't want her to wake her brothers who were heavier sleepers. Even more important, he didn't want her to follow him out to the car in case someone was badly hurt.

His boots clumped on the stairs and he realized he should have laced up their tops to hold them on more tightly. Too late now to worry about waking up Rebekah and Sammy.

"Joshua?" he heard as he reached the bottom step.

Rebekah stood in the bedroom doorway. She wore a sweater over her nightgown. It could not reach across her distended belly, but she tugged at it.

He reached for the door. "There's a car at the end of the drive. Its lights are shining all wrong."

"A crash?"

"That's what I'm going to find out."

By the time he reached the front door, the rain was coming down hard. He grabbed an umbrella from the crock by the door. After throwing the screen door aside, he went out on the porch. He opened the umbrella and handed it to Rebekah, who had, as he'd expected, followed him from the house.

"Stay here," he ordered over a rumble of thunder.

"I'll wake Timothy."

"He may not be home yet."

Even in the darkness, he saw her face grow ashen. Her voice shook as she said, "Then I'll wake Levi. If someone is hurt, he can run to the Beilers' barn and use their phone to call an ambulance." She glanced toward their *Englisch* neighbors' house. Light glowed in the windows. "The Grangers are up. He can go there. It's closer."

He nodded, relieved that she hadn't argued about coming with him. He turned up the collar on his coat before running down the steps. The grass was slick. Flashes of lightning illuminated the sky and blinded him as darkness dropped around him and thunder boomed above him. He almost lost his footing twice on the grass, so he went toward the driveway. The gravel would be easier to run on. He saw someone moving by the bright red car. He increased his speed, but skidded to a stop when he heard a familiar voice shout for him to stop.

Right in front of him, the mailbox was sheared off. He almost had run into the sharp spikes of wood.

And his older son was leaning on the hood of the battered car.

Chapter Fourteen

Someone must have called the police, or maybe a patrol had been driving by, because they were there before Levi could go next door and call 911. One police car soon became two and an ambulance, even though Timothy insisted he wasn't badly hurt.

Rebekah had joined Joshua when the first police car arrived. A short, stocky man who introduced himself as Steven McMurray, the chief of the Paradise Springs Police Department, insisted that Timothy be checked by the EMTs. The man and woman with the ambulance kept the younger *kinder* entertained while they examined Timothy.

Joshua wished the *kinder* had remained in the house, but the rain had eased so he allowed them to watch as Timothy's blood pressure was taken and a cut on his forehead cleaned and bandaged. He was glad when they took the extra gauze and tongue depressors back to the porch to play with them.

Chief McMurray finished talking with the other officers. Joshua heard them say it was *gut* that his son had been wearing a seat belt. Even though the airbag had gone off, Timothy could have been hurt far worse than a lacerated forehead and what would probably become a pair of black eyes.

The chief worked with easy efficiency as the storm ended, leaving hot and humid air in its wake. Joshua recalled how years ago Steven had been a troublemaker along with Johnny Beiler. Now Johnny had died, and Steven was in charge of the Paradise Springs police. The Lord truly did work in mysterious ways.

Another officer handed the chief a slip of paper and spoke quietly to him. Even though he strained his ears, Joshua couldn't hear what the officer was saying.

"Maybe you should go back to the house, Rebekah," he murmured. "You are shivering."

She shook her head. "No, I'm staying."

He recognized her tone and the futility of arguing with it.

Chief McMurray walked over to them. His expression in the flashing lights from the vehicles was grim. "I wanted you to know that we ran the plates, and the car is registered to Brad Granger." He glanced along the road to their neighbor's house, then frowned at Timothy who still sat on the back bumper of the ambulance. "How did you come to have it, son?"

Timothy held an ice pack to his forehead and shrugged. "It's my friend's car, and she wouldn't care if I used it."

"Her father will care when he realizes the front end is smashed up. Taking someone else's car for a joyride with your friends is a felony."

Beside him, Rebekah gasped, knowing as Joshua did that a felony could mean time in jail.

"Who was with you?" asked Chief McMurray.

"I told you before. I was driving by myself."

The chief shook his head and frowned. "I know you teenagers think adults are stupid, but both airbags went off. The passenger side one doesn't go off unless someone is sitting there."

"Maybe it was broken."

"There's no maybe about it being a really bad idea to lie to the police. Someone most likely saw you and this car tonight. If you had someone with you, they probably saw that person, too."

Timothy blanched even paler.

"It's better for you to be honest now than later." Chief McMurray gave Timothy a chance to answer. When he didn't, the police chief looked at Joshua and Rebekah. "You also need to know that we found half a dozen empty beer cans in the car. We'd like to run a Breathalyzer on your son with your permission."

Joshua nodded, unsure if he could speak. Why hadn't Timothy heeded his warnings about the dangers of drinking and driving a buggy? His son was smart, and he should have realized that those hazards were compounded if he was behind the wheel of a car.

Beside him, Rebekah gave a sob. He started to explain the test wouldn't hurt in any way. She turned away. That surprised him. She wasn't usually squeamish.

The police administered the test, and Timothy seemed to shrink before his eyes. The cocky teenager was becoming a frightened *kind*. Every inch of Joshua wanted to comfort him, but his son had demanded the rights of an adult and now he would have to face the consequences of making stupid choices. Even knowing that, Joshua had to swallow his cheer when the test came back negative.

But if his son hadn't drank the beers, who had?

As a tow truck backed up to take the damaged car away, Chief McMurray came to where Joshua and Rebekah stood beside his son. He handed Timothy a piece of paper.

"This is a ticket for driving without a license," the police chief said. "Don't assume it's the only ticket you're going to get. Joshua, as your son is a minor, I'd like to leave him in your custody while we investigate what happened here." He ran his hand backward through his thinning hair, making it stand on end, before he put his hat on again. "I don't like to see any kid sitting in a jail cell, but I won't hesitate to put him there if I find out he took the car without permission. Do you understand?"

"*Ja*, I understand." He looked at his son, but Timothy wouldn't meet his eyes. "What happens now?"

"As he has been put in your custody, you or your wife must be with him every minute. Don't let him out of your sight. If he does something foolish like trying to sneak out, it won't look good for him when he goes before a judge. Judges, especially juvenile court judges, don't take kindly to such things. He's already in a ton of trouble. Making it worse would be foolish."

"We'll do as you ask. Is there anything else we should do?"

The chief smiled swiftly. "Pray. I know you folks are good at that."

Joshua nodded, but didn't say that he'd been praying since he'd looked out the window and seen the car lights shining at odd angles.

"Danki," Rebekah said softly. "Thank you, Chief McMurray."

"You're welcome." The police chief's gaze shifted to Timothy. "I hope you're being honest when you say you had permission to drive the car." He looked back at Joshua. "We're going to be talking to the Grangers next. If they corroborate his story, I'd still like to send one of my officers over to speak with Timothy about the importance of taking driving lessons and getting his license if he intends to drive again."

"And if the Grangers disagree with what Timothy says?" Rebekah clearly was too worried to wait for Joshua to ask the same question.

"You'll have to bring him to the police station where he'll be booked for stealing a car." The chief looked from her to Joshua. "I hope we don't have to do that, but if he's lying..."

"We understand, Chief McMurray." He motioned for Rebekah to return to the house.

He thanked the policemen and the tow truck driver before he led Timothy toward the house. His son was silent. Why wasn't he apologizing and asking to be forgiven? On every step, Joshua's frustration grew.

As soon as they were inside, he ordered the younger *kinder* to their rooms. They stared at him as if they feared he'd lost his mind, because he seldom raised his voice to them.

For some reason that infuriated him more. As Levi and Debbie hurried up the stairs and Sammy grasped a handful of his *mamm*'s nightgown, Joshua spun to face his oldest and demanded, "Have you lost your mind?"

"Daed—"

"No!" he snapped. "I'll talk and you'll listen. After all, you didn't want to talk to the police. You took your friend's car and smashed it into our mailbox. You were driving a car filled with empty beer cans. Where did those come from?" He didn't give his son a chance to answer. "You act as if everyone else is to blame except you. You spin tales nobody would swallow. On one hand you expect to be treated like an adult, but then you make decisions Sammy knows better than to make."

"You don't understand, *Daed*!"

"Then help me understand. Why don't you start with why you had Alexis's car? If you don't want to start there, start with how the beer cans got into the car and who drank the beer. Don't think that I didn't understand what the police were saying. They didn't say you hadn't been drinking. Only that you hadn't drunk enough to be legally intoxicated." When he saw the tears in his son's eyes and saw bruises already forming around the bandage on his forehead, he wanted to relent. He couldn't.

He reached out to grasp his son's shoulder, hoping a physical connection would help Timothy see that Joshua truly wanted to help him. His hand never reached Timothy.

"No!" Rebekah stepped between them, batting his hand away. "Calm down, Joshua, before you do something you'll regret."

"I am not the one who needs to worry about that." He scowled at his oldest and at Rebekah. Didn't she realize what an appalling situation his son was in? Timothy could be arrested.

He took her by the arm and drew her aside. She stared at him, hurt and betrayal in her eyes. When he reached toward her again, she skittered away, wrapping her arms around herself as she had when the Burkholder brothers threatened her. Did she think he was doing *that*? He wasn't angry as much as he was frustrated.

With her, with his son, with himself for not being able to handle the rapidly deteriorating situation.

"Rebekah," he said, trying to keep his voice even. "The boy needs to realize the consequences of what he's done. Drinking and driving—"

"I didn't drink and drive!" Timothy shouted.

"Listen to him," she urged.

Looking from one to the other, he said, "Be sensible, Rebekah. Even if he wasn't drinking, he was with kids his own age who were. Kids who think they can make the rules because they know more than anyone else. I know how it goes. They start drinking together occasionally, then more often. A couple of times a week become every day. By that time, they need more and more to get the buzz they're looking for. Who knows where it'll lead?"

"I know." Her voice, though barely more than a whisper, cut through the room like the snap of a whip. More loudly, she ordered, "Don't lecture me about the dangers of alcohol, Joshua Stoltzfus! I know them too well." She held up her right hand and tapped her smallest finger. "I know how it feels when my bones are broken in a drunken rage. I know too well how a fist can shake my teeth loose and how to look through one eye when the other has swollen shut. I know what it's like to pray every night that tonight is the night my husband doesn't turn to alcohol, that tonight isn't the night his fists will harm our unborn *kind*. I know what it's like to keep all of it a secret so the shame that is my life won't ruin my son's."

"Lloyd?" he gasped. "Lloyd struck you?"

"Ja." Tears edged along her lashes, then rained down her cheeks as she said, "He loved drinking more than he

loved me. I learned that when I found out he was selling our wedding gifts to pay for his beer."

"And selling your cradle for it." Joshua wished he could take back those words as soon as he said them because he saw devastating pain flash across her face.

Her voice broke as she whispered, "My cradle? He sold the cradle he promised me for our son in order to buy himself beer?" She pressed her hands over her mouth, but a sob slipped past her fingers. Closing her eyes, she wept.

No one spoke. Even Sammy was silent as he stared at her. How much of what she'd recounted had the little boy witnessed? How much did he remember? No wonder Sammy had shied away from him at first. If the one man he should have been able to trust—his own *daedi*—had treated his *mamm* so viciously, then how could the *kind* trust any man?

How could Rebekah trust any man, either?

He watched Timothy cross the room and embrace Rebekah. She hid her face against his shoulder as sobs swept through her. Over her head, his son's eyes shot daggers at him.

None of them could pierce Joshua's heart as deeply as his own self-recriminations. How could he have failed to see the truth? He'd seen her bruises, but accepted Lloyd's excuses that she was clumsy. She wasn't clumsy. Even pregnant, she was as graceful as the swans on the pond near the shop.

He thought of the many times she'd avoided his hand when it came close to her, though he never would have raised it toward her in anger. She'd begun to trust him enough not to flinch…until today. What had changed today? He needed to ask, but how could he when he had failed her completely?

Where did he start to ask for her forgiveness?

Why didn't Joshua say something? He stood there, staring at her as Rebekah thanked Timothy for the hug. The teenager murmured that he was sorry.

"For what?" she asked. "You didn't even know Lloyd."

"I'm sorry for everything." He shuffled his foot against the rag rug, then looked at his *daed*. "I really am."

Joshua nodded and put his hand on Timothy's shoulder and gave it a squeeze, but his gaze met hers. "All I can say, Rebekah, is that I am sorry, too. I had no idea what was going on."

"I know. Nobody did."

"Why didn't you go to your bishop for help?"

She hung her head and sighed. "I tried. Once. But I didn't tell him the whole story because I knew Lloyd would be furious if he discovered what I'd done. The bishop told me to try to be a better wife. I tried, but I kept making mistakes. Lloyd would yell at me at first and then…" She glanced at Sammy. She'd already said too much in his hearing.

"You did nothing wrong. None of this was your fault."

Tears streamed down her cheeks, and she didn't bother to wipe them away. "I believed that. At the beginning. Then I began to wonder if I'd failed him in some way that caused Lloyd to drink." Her shoulders shook so hard, she wobbled.

He rushed to her side. "Rebekah, you need to sit down."

"Help me?"

"Gladly." He put his arm around her, and she leaned against him as he guided her to a chair. She wished she could always depend on his steady strength.

As Timothy took Sammy's hand, Joshua knelt beside her and put his fingers lightly over hers, which were protectively pressed to her belly. "Listen to me, Rebekah. I'm going to tell you two things that are true. If you don't believe me, ask God."

"You've never lied to me."

"And I won't. Look deep in your heart, and you'll know what I'm about to say is the truth. First, any choices Lloyd made were *his* choices. Nothing he chose to do or not do is your fault. God gives us free will, even though it must pain Him when we make bad choices." When Timothy shifted uncomfortably behind them, he didn't look at his son. His gaze remained on her. "Second, Rebekah, with our *kinder* here to witness my words, I vow to you that I will never intentionally hurt you in word or deed."

A hint of a smile touched her trembling lips as she spoke the words she had the day he asked her to marry him. "You know it isn't our way to make vows."

"Other than vows of love. Those we proclaim in front of everyone we can gather together. Before our *kinder*, I vow that I love you."

"You love me?"

"Ja, ich liebe dich." The words sounded so much sweeter in *Deitsch*, and her heart soared like a bird on a summer wind.

A loud knock sounded on the back door. Joshua rose

as Timothy tensed, fear on his face. Rebekah reached out and took the boy's hand. When he looked at her, she gave him a loving smile. If the police had returned, Timothy wouldn't have to face them alone.

When Joshua opened the door, Brad Granger stood on the other side. He was a balding man, who was wearing a plaid robe over a pair of gray flannel pants. He had on white sneakers but no socks. "May I come in?"

"*Ja*. Of course." Joshua glanced at her, but she had no more idea than he did what to expect from their neighbor.

Brad had every right to be furious if Timothy had taken the car without his permission. Their neighbor entered and called over his shoulder, "C'mon in. Lurking out there won't resolve any of this." His voice was raspy with the emotion he clearly was trying to control.

A slender form edged into the kitchen. Alexis's hair covered most of her face, but when she looked up, Rebekah could see that the girl's eye was deeply bruised, and a purplish black line followed the curve of her left cheekbone. She stared at the young girl whose face looked like reflections Rebekah had seen in her own mirror. Pain lashed her anew as she glanced at Timothy who quickly looked away. No! She didn't want to believe that the young man who had comforted her so gently had struck his friend. *Oh, please, God, don't let it be true!*

"How are you?" Timothy asked, stepping forward. She couldn't miss the concern in his words or his posture.

"It'll look worse before it looks better," Brad said with a sigh. "The EMTs who stopped by warned her that she's going to have two reasons for a headache in the morning. The bruises and a hangover." He looked at his daughter. "Go ahead. This won't get any easier if you put off doing what you should have done in the first place."

Rebekah was surprised when Alexis turned to her. "Tim thinks you found the beer in the barn."

"And the well house," she said, putting her hand on Joshua's arm when he opened his mouth to ask a question. He remained silent as she added, "I did find it. I was afraid it might belong to someone in this family, but it didn't, did it?"

"No. The beer in the barn was mine."

"Alexis—"

She interrupted Timothy with a sad smile. "You don't need to cover for me any longer, Tim. I've told my parents everything. Now I need to be honest with your folks so they know the truth."

He nodded, his shoulders sagging in obvious relief.

"I didn't think it was any big deal," the girl said, then shivered. "That is, until the police came to the house. They told me that Tim might get arrested because he took my car and crashed it. That's when I knew I had to be honest. I can't let Tim pay for my mistakes when he was simply trying to be a good friend." She took a deep breath and squared her shoulders. "I asked Tim to hide the beer so my parents wouldn't find it. I brought it over the other night and he agreed, though I could tell he didn't like the idea of deceiving our parents. Tonight I picked him and the beer up, and we went to a party out by the Conestoga River with some of my friends."

"Where you drank the beer?" Joshua asked.

"Yes. You must have seen the beer cans in the car."

She grimaced. "Chief McMurray sure did! But Tim didn't have any beer."

"I don't like it." Timothy shrugged and smiled weakly. "Tastes worse than it smells."

"I did drink some of the beer." Alexis sighed when her *daed* glared at her. "Okay, I drank a lot of the beer. Too much to drive home. Tim suggested I call my folks, but I didn't want them finding out that I'd had so much to drink. I insisted I was okay to drive home. He took my keys and wouldn't let me."

Rebekah patted Timothy's arm and said, "You did listen to your *daed* about drinking and driving."

"Hey, sometimes he's right."

Even Sammy laughed at that, though he couldn't have understood why. When he yawned, Joshua picked him up and cradled him in his arms. Rebekah's heart almost overflowed with joy at the sight of the strong man holding the little boy so gently.

Her attention was pulled back to Alexis, who was saying, "So it's true that Tim drove without a license, but he did it to keep me from driving drunk."

"And you told the police that nobody else was in the car, Timothy, because you didn't want Alexis to get into trouble," Joshua said as if he were thinking aloud. "You shouldn't have lied to the police."

"I was honest with them. I didn't say I was alone, *Daed*. I said I was driving by myself. I was because Alexis was asleep in the passenger seat, so she wasn't helping me."

"Timothy, a half truth is also a half lie."

"I know."

Alexis interjected, "If that deer hadn't jumped in

front of us, he would have gotten us home without anyone knowing the truth."

"But God had other ideas," Brad said quietly. "He was tired of Alexis's behavior and brought it out of the shadows." He turned to Timothy. "I'm sorry you were caught up in this mess, son, but thank you for being such a good friend to Alexis."

Timothy took the hand Brad held out to him and shook it. "I didn't want Alexis to risk getting kicked out of school. She has her heart set on attending the University of Pennsylvania."

Looking to where Joshua had come to stand beside Rebekah, Brad added, "You've raised a fine son, Joshua. I hate to think what might have happened if he hadn't been there tonight."

"Then don't think of it," Joshua said quietly.

Brad turned to Timothy. "The police will still want to talk with you, son, but now to confirm what Alexis has already told them."

"We will cooperate with the police." Joshua gave his son a look that said he would tolerate no more half truths.

"I know you find that uncomfortable, so I'm doubly thankful to you." Brad smiled. "Chief McMurray has assured me, Timothy, that any pending charges against you, other than the driving without a license, will be dropped. Even extenuating circumstances won't wipe out that ticket, but Alexis will be paying the fine for you."

"Danki," he said.

"No, son, thank *you* for making sure my daughter got home alive tonight."

"I'm sorry," Alexis whispered. "I hope we can still be friends, Tim."

"We'll always be friends." He glanced at his *daed.* "Just friends."

Brad and his daughter urged them to sleep well and left. As soon as the door closed, Timothy turned to Joshua.

"I am sorry about the half truths," the boy said. "Even though I thought I had a *gut* reason, I know there's never any *gut* reason to lie. I hope you can forgive me."

"I already have." He handed Sammy to Rebekah.

She took him and almost cried out as a pain cut through her back and around across her stomach. It faded as quickly as it had started, so she carried Sammy in and set him on the sofa. He curled into a ball, never waking.

Turning around, she watched Joshua put his hand on his son's shoulder. "If we expect to be forgiven, we must be forgiving. Now I must ask you to forgive me."

"For what?" Timothy asked.

"I should have given you a chance to explain. I shouldn't have jumped to conclusions."

"You didn't have far to jump. I *was* driving the car, and it's my fault it crashed."

"But it's a *daed's* job to listen and learn if he expects his *kinder* to do the same. I'll try to do better next time, if you'll forgive me for this mistake."

"I heard a wise man once say that if we expect to be forgiven, we must be forgiving."

Joshua glanced at Rebekah, and she smiled. There were many challenges before them with their *kinder*, but she and Joshua would weather each storm as it came.

Together.

"We have to stop hiding secrets from each other," Joshua said. "Secrets don't have any place among the loving members of a family. They ended up causing us even more pain."

"I know that now, *Daed*."

Joshua looked at her.

"I know it, too." She blinked back tears. "But I couldn't bear the thought of people looking at Sammy and judging everything he does to decide if he's starting to take after his *daed*."

"No one will. They'll see that he is like his *mamm*. Generous and loving. I've said it before, but I need to say it again, because I can't keep it a secret any longer. *Ich liebe dich*."

Happiness welled up in her at his words and his loving gaze. As she reached out to take his hands, she stiffened. Pain scored her again. Harder this time. When she bent, holding her hands over her belly, she heard Joshua and Timothy ask what was wrong.

She had to wait for the pain to diminish before she could gasp, "It's the *boppli*. It's coming."

Joshua kept one arm around her as he ordered, "Timothy, go to the Grangers and use their phone." He fished a piece of paper out of his trousers. "Here is Beth Ann's number. Call her and tell her to come *now*!"

Timothy grabbed the page and ran out.

With Joshua's arm guiding her, Rebekah went to the bedroom. She reached it as another contraction began. They were coming close together. Why hadn't she had more warning? Then she realized she had. Her aching back could have been mild contractions. She'd ignored them.

After he helped her lie down on the wide bed, he said, "And I thought we'd had enough excitement tonight."

She tried to smile, but another contraction bore down on her, and she couldn't think of anything but riding its crest until it receded. She opened her eyes and saw Joshua's worried face.

"Do you think Beth Ann will get here in time?" he asked.

"I hope so." She clutched his hand. Looking up at him, she said, "I'm glad you're here, Joshua."

"I wouldn't be anywhere else."

There was so much she longed to say, to tell him how she loved him and how sorry she was to have ever believed he would treat her as Lloyd had. Gripping his hand, she focused on the *boppli*, who was coming whether the midwife was there or not.

Chapter Fifteen

The bedroom was quiet. The *kinder* were upstairs, tucked in their beds for the night. Beth Ann had finished up and left along with the doctor. Sadie would be returning in a few hours to help with the new *boppli* and take care of the household until Rebekah could manage on her own again.

Joshua put the dish towel on the rack where it could dry. Taking a deep breath, he yawned as he gazed out the window. The moon had set, and the stars were a glittering tapestry of God's glory. To the east, a thin, gray line announced the coming of a new day.

The day another *kind* had joined their family.

This is the day which the Lord hath made; we will rejoice and be glad in it. His favorite verse echoed in his mind, this time a praise instead of an urging to get through yet another day while weighed down with grief.

Wanting to see the little one again, because it had been so long since there had been a *boppli* in the house, Joshua tiptoed into the downstairs bedroom to make sure *mamm* and *boppli* were doing well.

Despite his efforts to be quiet as he edged around the

bed, Rebekah's eyes blinked open. With her magnificent red hair scattered across the pillows and a joyful smile warming her lips, she was more beautiful than he'd imagined. She held out a hand to him.

Sitting on the very edge of the bed, he asked, "How are you doing?"

"Happy."

"*Ja*, I know." He didn't say any more. There wasn't any need.

The night had begun as a nightmare. One that left his hands shaking whenever he thought of what could have happened when his inexperienced son had driven that powerful car along the twisting, hilly road. It had ended with healing between him and his oldest, as well as the appearance of his youngest.

At that thought, he reached down into the cradle Jeremiah had made and lifted out a swaddled bundle.

"She is sweet," he said. "Debbie is going to be so pleased to have a sister."

"Wanda Almina Stoltzfus," Rebekah murmured. "Welcome to the world."

He handed the *boppli* to her. "*Mamm* will be pleased that you want to name this little one in her honor."

"I was named for my *grossmammi*, and I loved having that connection. Little Wanda will have that same connection with your *mamm* and mine."

"A very special gift for her very first birthday."

"I'm glad you think so." She looked from the beautiful *boppli* to him. "*Danki* for being here, Joshua."

"Where else would I be when our *boppli* was being born?"

"Our *boppli*," she whispered.

"I cannot think of her any other way. I am blessed to

have three sons and two daughters." He chuckled. "They make me *ab in kopp* way too often, but I am even crazier in love with you." He became serious. "I told you that earlier tonight how I love you. Do you love me?"

"*Ja*. Looking back, I think I started falling in love with you the day you came with your nervous proposal." She laced her fingers through his much wider ones. "At first I tried to stop myself because I knew you still loved Tildie."

"But—"

"Let me say this, Joshua." When he nodded, she continued. "I knew that you still love Tildie, and I thought there was no place in your heart for me. It took me far too long to realize that our hearts can expand to love many people. Timothy, Levi and Debbie hold a place in my heart as surely as if I had given birth to them. I see you with Sammy and Wanda, and I know you'll be a devoted and loving *daed* for them." She laughed. "Look how far my heart has expanded to welcome your *mamm*, your six brothers, your two sisters and the rest of your family. I'm blessed that there's no limit to the number of people a heart will hold."

"As long as there's always a place for me."

"There always will be."

He gently kissed her lips, knowing she was spent after the night's events. There would be plenty of opportunities in the future to kiss her more deeply, and, as Rebekah Mast Burkholder Stoltzfus's husband, he didn't intend to let a single one pass them by.

* * * * *

SPECIAL EXCERPT FROM

Love Inspired®

All Miranda Morgan wants for Christmas is to be a good mom to the twins she's been named guardian of—but their brooding cowboy godfather, Simon West, isn't sure she's ready. Can they learn to trust in each other and become a real family for the holidays?

Read on for a sneak peek of
TEXAS CHRISTMAS TWINS
by Deb Kastner,
part of the ***CHRISTMAS TWINS*** *miniseries.*

"I brought you up here because I have a couple of dogs I'd especially like to introduce to Harper and Hudson," he said.

She flashed him a surprised look. He couldn't possibly think that with all she had going on, she'd want to adopt a couple of dogs, or even one.

"I appreciate what you do here," she said, trying to buffer her next words. "But I want to make it clear up front that I have no intention of adopting a dog. They're cute and all, but I've already got my hands full with the twins as it is."

"Oh, no," Simon said, raising his free hand, palm out. "You misunderstand me. I'm not pulling some sneaky stunt on you to try to get you to adopt a dog. It's just that—well, maybe it would be easier to show you than to try to explain."

"Zig! Zag! Come here, boys." Two identical small white dogs dashed to Simon's side, their full attention on him.

Miranda looked from one dog to the other and a light bulb went off in her head.

"Twins!" she exclaimed.

LIEXP1117

Simon laughed.

"Not exactly. They're littermates."

He helped an overexcited Harper pet one of the dogs and, taking Simon's lead, Miranda helped Hudson scratch the ears of the other.

"Soft fur, see, Harper?" Simon said. "This is a doggy."

"Gentle, gentle," Miranda added when Hudson tried to grab a handful of the white dog's fur.

"Zig and Zag are Westies—West Highland white terriers."

Zig licked Hudson's fist and he giggled. Both dogs seemed to like the babies, and the twins were clearly taken with the dogs.

But she'd meant what she'd said earlier—no dogs allowed. At the moment, suffering cuteness overload, she even had to give herself a stern mental reminder.

She cast her eyes up to make sure Simon understood her very emphatic message, but he was busy helping Harper interact with Zag.

When he finally looked up, their eyes met and locked. A slow smile spread across his lips and appreciation filled his gaze. For a moment, Miranda experienced something she hadn't felt this strongly since, well, since high school—the reel of her stomach in time with a quickened pulse and a shortness of breath.

Either she was having an asthma attack, or else—

She was absolutely not going to go there.